The God of Smoke and Mirrors

A Novel by Sam Buntz

"Simon, Simon, behold: Satan hath desired to have you, that he may sift you as wheat." - Luke 22:31

Note: Wilbur College, along with its students and faculty, is entirely fictitious.

For Ken and Shelley Buntz

1. Squalor

I wasn't paying attention.

My consciousness had been caught up, toyed with, infiltrated. Naturally, I wanted to blame my circumstances for this (we're always loathe to pick on any internal weaknesses) beginning with the physical space in which I found myself.

It was not a nice place.

Living in that zone was like being trapped, permanently, in a mirror maze. Your attention bounced light-like off all surfaces, never settling on one object in any given moment. You weren't here and you weren't there, and you stumbled into everything crucial and shuffled wearily through everything trivial.

Of course, this state of affairs was probably pretty normal, considering that the place in question was a collegiate pad, or, really, four separate pads clustered together in one off-campus residence.

The house we shared at 185 Barnum Street reminded me of my grandmother's old home, but with a wide range of consistently depressing differences. Architecturally, the interior felt timelessly American, and you could picture a series of large, early 20th Century immigrant families celebrating Thanksgiving in it. But that warm, old-fashioned vibration quivered only in the shell.

All the antique charm was long gone, and you felt as if grandmotherly, devotional paintings of Jesus and The Sacred Heart had been ripped off the walls, leaving them bare where not replaced by the same Bob Marley poster featured in all undergraduate dorm rooms and apartments since time immemorial.

The detritus of masculine late-adolescence was everywhere and the living room perpetually smelled like an oft-used towel. Grandma's knick-knacks and turquoise ceramic hippos were nowhere to be found. A jockstrap hung from the headrest of an armchair. Dried remnants of exploded chili coated the inside of the microwave. The frenzied sounds of a porn video crept out of the crack beneath the door to someone's bedroom. The squalor was not precisely Dickensian…

2. Curds and Whey

Curtis Himmelman, one of the three other guys who were renting this small house with me, was lying on the hardwood floor of the living room with a large, open container of whey protein next to him. (This container, made of bright red plastic, was about the same size and shape as a small propane tank, the kind you use for a gas grill.) He would do twenty crunches and pause, before taking a handful of whey concentrate and shoveling it into his mouth. He would swish it around in his cheeks, saturating it with saliva, transforming it into a paste that could be swallowed more easily than dry powder.

At the same time, I was seated on the stained, rickety futon, playing *Halo 3* with another renter, Oscar Olazábal. But I remained so distracted by what Curt was doing that I found it hard to keep my mind on the screen. As I said, your attention was always being pulled in about five different directions in that house. Consequently, you felt like you were never really *present*, but rather inhabited a state somewhere between existence and non-being.

Finally, I said something: "I think you're supposed to make that into a shake…" I tried to keep all snottiness out of my tone and say this helpfully, like I was offering a piece of kindly, proverbial wisdom.

Curtis didn't hear me, or pretended not to. He kept doing crunches.

I shrugged, but remained inwardly concerned. After another thirty seconds of ruptured attention, I hit pause on the controller, while Oscar glowered at me and said, "What are you doing? I was just about to cap that squid thing in the nutsack…"

I ignored him and spoke to Curt.

"*Curt*."

I waited to see if I had his attention… After a couple crunches, he glanced at me.

"You're supposed to make that into a shake."

Again, I tried to state this casually, not like a know-it-all. It was friendly advice, though my inner tension palpably carried through.

"Yeah?" He said.

"Yeah. You're not supposed to just eat handfuls of it like an animal."

"Why not? What's the difference?"

"I don't know… You might overdose or something."

I knew this sounded stupid right after I said it… It was more that I didn't like the way it *looked*—him cramming whey down his throat. Bits of whey-rich foam would appear at the corners of his mouth as he gobbled. Then, he'd lick it up, sliding his tongue wildly about his lips, like a frantic dog trying to ensure it had ingested every last bit of peanut butter. The spectacle made me feel queasy, in addition to contributing to the generally bleak atmosphere.

"Dude, it's *whey*," Curt responded. "Like, *curds* and whey—from that Little Bo Peep song? I'm pretty sure it's safe. It's a safe way to put on mass."

"Alright," I said. "Fine… I don't know what I'm talking about. Fine."

Oscar and I went back to playing *Halo 3*.

I don't really like videogames, but I wanted to participate in the cultural life of the house, which focused on the drearily modern rite of collective masculine gameplay. It would've been all too easy to slink off to my room and listen to *Pet Sounds* on an endless loop of beautiful sadness. Instead, I played with intensity, acting like I really *wanted* to play videogames, when what I really wanted was to *like* playing videogames in the first place, to have some point of human contact, a shared interest.

I wasn't feeling it.

Finally, Oscar put down his controller. "Stuck on the same level for an hour, " he said. "We're done here." He stomped off to his room.

He always exited like that—promptly and without much forewarning. It was kind of irritating.

I sat on the futon with hooded, weary eyes and a jaw that wanted to hang open. I still had to write a short paper, and looked at my closed laptop the way Sisyphus looked at that hill once his bolder had rolled back to the bottom. This house wasn't the right place for work. It felt like an energy drain, as if gravity pulled down harder once you stepped inside. The Feng Shui was all wrong.

Curt groaned on the floor. "I think you were right about the whey, dude," he said. "I feel kind of funny. My heart's beating way too fast."

"Yeah?" I said. I couldn't summon up much concern, but added, "There's probably all sorts of additives in it."

"I think I'm just gonna lay here… I think I'm just gonna lay down for awhile."

"Sounds like a plan," I said. "I'm going to the student center."

"But…but shouldn't there be someone around to call the ambulance in case I have, like, a heart attack or whatever?"

"Oscar's still here," I said. "Just yell for him."

3. Wieners in Top Hats

With my laptop and a few books in my backpack, I shuffled out the front door and stared at the long and partially ice covered sidewalk ahead of me. At Wilbur College, it was always startling to walk outside in winter—buffeted by northern gales that immediately reddened your nose and set it running. The chill penetrated through all layers of clothing, entering even the navel.

Campus wasn't so far off, but it *felt* distant. Our little house sometimes seemed like the last outpost of a poorly supervised government department, an Antarctic substation where the scientists had long ago abandoned their research and taken to mindless forms of recreation.

It had been a rough winter, and we'd received over four feet of snow by mid-January. Your eyes continually turned down to the sidewalk, making sure you didn't slip. The walk into campus was straight and short, but my tail-chasing thoughts pursued a more circuitous route. This kind of unproductive, anxious mental activity was wearying, but I couldn't stop it. I kept thinking about the squalor and the malign gravity that tugged at me whenever I set foot in our house, insistently pulling me into a state of listlessness.

Outdoors, the generally cheerless atmosphere didn't bother me. I'm from the rust belt (Northeastern Pennsylvania, the town of Carlin to be specific) so I feel especially at home in New Hamelin, NH, when it's cold and depressing and seems less like the affluent burg it truly is.

If I'm standing outside, say, an abandoned brick factory on a bleak January evening, leaning against a rusting chain-link fence, it feels comfortingly familiar. This isn't to imply that I prefer winter to spring—that would be a perverse lie, trying to convert my honest displeasure into the enjoyments of masochism. I simply mean to say that I felt that my natural state was in a bleak, empty, limbo-zone, a muddy field in which all action seemed doomed to mire. It was in this atmosphere of futility that I would be trained in life.

Moving out of Barnum Street didn't seem like a bad idea, and frat rush was coming up. Albeit, they didn't actually let you move in during your first term as a frat bro, but it gave you a base of operations at least—somewhere else to be. Wilbur College only allowed you to pledge a frat after freshman year had ended, and, being a sophomore, I was now free to do it, if I really wanted to.

I didn't, particularly. The idea of being a stereotypical "bro" didn't suit my self-image, and I didn't want to get hazed in any bizarre ways. We'd all heard the rumors: stuffing pinecones up your asshole, wading in kiddie pools full of piss, dressing up in white robes and drinking food-coloring-dyed vodka before vomiting on each other in Technicolor, putting on puppet shows where you made your wiener wear a little top hat. The gamut. Some of it needed to be true.

But still… I wanted to get out of that house, escape the spell of its dark inertia. A frat didn't seem like the most appealing place to transfer one's headquarters, but maybe it could, if just barely, suffice. If it was even slightly better, I'd take it. I wasn't entirely sold on the idea, but my friend Peter Surface—the fourth renter at our house—had been chiseling at my defenses.

4. Black Northface Jackets

When I finally reached campus, I headed towards the student center, where there was always late-night food on sale—mozzarella sticks, fries, and bowls of Vietnamese Pho soup, along with coffee and hot chocolate—and tons of people studying in the common room. Students clogged the door, exiting and entering. The new arrivals stamped and wiped their boots on the rubber mats. Everyone was clad in the same black Northface brand jacket.

After each weekend, a few unlucky students invariably sent out campus-wide emails asking if anyone had happened to pick up one of these black Northface jackets by mistake at any frat parties. Such jackets were often stolen, or borrowed without permission, from the couches in the living rooms of fraternities, where they were typically strewn as students ventured down to the scene of the real party—the basement.
Hence, it was easy for a drunk person, intentionally or unintentionally, to take someone else's coat on the way out.

This phenomenon and the predictable regularity of these worried emails were the subject of numerous, rather tired jokes. However, my jacket was a black Patagonia—oddly rare on campus, though, aside from the logo, virtually identical to the Northface. (Not that I care about any of this commodity fetishism, but it's worth mentioning for reasons I prefer to leave vague and mysterious for the present).

Inside, the clomping boots had left a slushy mess on the hardwood halls of the student center. Transitioning from the frigid outdoors to the center's interior was like entering a warm, marsupial pouch. My glasses fogged up… I imagined a lonely janitor dipping a mop into a bucket later on, in the thickest hour of the night, once all the students had gone back to their dorms and apartments. He would leave one TV in the lounge tuned to SportsCenter with the volume loud enough to be audible in all the hallways, wherever the mop needed to roam…

As I stood in line with a cup of hot chocolate, I felt dazed, still shaking off that malign hypnosis. Around me there was convivial chatter, but I felt isolated in my own bubble of silence: little, crawling anxieties made me oblivious to the warm hum of life.

I sat down at one of the small tables in the main common room, and drank my hot chocolate. Then, I took out my laptop and tried to write a short paper on T.S. Eliot's "Burnt Norton" and listen to a podcast about an unsolved murder mystery at the same time. This made slow going—although I can normally write pretty fast. Eventually, I took off my headphones and buckled down.

5. "At the Still Point of the Turning World"

The paper developed, and I managed to finish more than half of it in an hour or so (it only needed to be 5 double-spaced pages—although the professor confusingly suggested a word count of 2500-3000 words, which is significantly more than five pages). After copying a particularly striking quote from the poem, I paused.

Eliot writes, "Except for the point, the still point, / There would be no dance, and there is only the dance."

I had to think about this. I liked Eliot, while the professor teaching my Major 20th Century Poets Class, Anne Moriarty, hated him. Actually, she seemed to hate all writers, preoccupied with details about their personal lives: Edgar Allan Poe was a drunk who married a thirteen year old and Wallace Stevens voted Republican. It was odd that she even became a professor.

I'd pursued my argument up to a point but stalled on what I was going to say next. The still point was so far away from the haphazard life of the house on 185 Barnum Street, and Professor Moriarty sure as hell had no idea what it was. She seemed positively bored with Eliot, teaching him only because it was a required part of Major 20th Century Poets. She said that Eliot was undoubtedly a "leather daddy," much like Shakespeare, who—she claimed—was also a foot fetishist and unexpectedly tall (7'2"). She deduced all this from a close reading of *Cymbeline*.

Yet, despite this apparent inability or unwillingness to say anything illuminating, and a passion for trafficking in speculative and sinister nonsense, Moriarty still managed to be intimidating. During our discussion sections she would pose questions and glare at whomever happened to answer, while utterly emptying her face of all expression, leveling a Gorgon stare determined to freeze you into stone. Even if the student was saying something clever or insightful, she managed to transfix her eyes into the same shade of marble. It was horrible... I think she lived alone with about eighteen cats.

Of course, in the final analysis, you have to feel bad for anyone who's that miserable and who can't even appreciate beauty when it comes tip-toeing up the bridge of his or her nose. Poor Moriarty... Her head was lodged firmly up her ass, in a fatal and final manner.

And Eliot was worth appreciating. His sense that there was both stillness, and a dance emanating from and reliant upon that stillness, resonated with me. I was badly in need of stillness. You stood at the center of your own life, alone and quiet on the inside, and the world leapt and shifted to variety around you. You could get caught up in that dance, that barbaric rite, but something always swept you back to the coolness and blessed emptiness within, the harborage of the soul.

I decided to compare Eliot's notion of "the dance" to the Hindu concept of the "Dance of Shiva"—the idea that the universe is itself a dance, or a form of God's cosmic play called *lila*. I'd learned a decent amount about this subject, and the fact that Eliot had studied Hinduism and Buddhism as a student at Harvard leant the idea credibility. Of course, Moriarty gave me a B- with only one note in the margins: "Failed to interrogate the capitalist underpinnings of Eliot's sexual fetishes."

6. Looks of Longing

Under the pretense of contemplation, I started slacking off again. At this point, the student center wasn't as busy as earlier, so I surveyed the winnowed stragglers to see if anyone I knew happened to be around. There was a scrawny kid with extremely thick lenses in his glasses who always wore a bandanna on his head and a hoop earring (I guess he was imitating David Foster Wallace). He was digging into a large-size bag of "Last Call Jalapeno Popper" Doritos and wiping the orange powder on the legs of his jeans as he stared with genuine interest at a sociology textbook.

Then, there was a pretty girl wearing clunky, plastic hipster glasses—just the frames, no lenses—studying at the same table as a muscle-bound Asian guy who was always doing squat thrusts at the gym. He sipped a bottle of protein shake almost gingerly, as though he were slowly savoring it. Maybe he was...

Aside from these three, there was virtually no one else—except for way over in the corner, where Emma Kaufman was typing at her laptop. You could hear her concentration clatter loudly in the keys.

She didn't type mechanically, but seemed immersed in a fit of inspiration, grasped and controlled utterly by one overriding thought after another. Then, suddenly, she would stop and gaze off into space, her lips parting very slightly. Her expression would become totally absorbed or totally vacant. It was hard to tell which. Whatever it indicated, I liked the way it looked on her. I always find it refreshing to see someone absorbed by an apparently genuine interest, and, in her case, it was especially attractive.

During one of these extended pauses, I realized how long I'd been looking at her, and felt embarrassed—like maybe someone had noticed. At almost exactly that moment, she turned her head and looked back at me. My eyes darted to the computer screen, and I started typing again. But I'd been caught…

7. Lab Partners

In my student years, I was almost never assigned a female lab partner. In high school, I was always paired with the same guy, Loren Perse, who carried a stuffed Pikachu doll in his backpack. (In case you're living in a future era, Pikachu was this Japanese lightning mouse monster thing from a cartoon). He didn't want anyone to see it, but sometimes he would take it out, and surreptitiously pet it while riding the bus home.

I don't know if I ever had a real conversation with him, despite all the titrations we did together. It may not have been possible: I recall him giving monosyllabic answers to all casual queries. And he really clammed up when I asked him (in, I think, an amiable fashion) about the Pikachu doll.

In an introductory chemistry class I took as a freshman at Wilbur, my lab partner was a dude named Randall Swope who wore a "Wilbur College Quidditch Team" T-Shirt and had a condition that prevented him from breathing through his nose. He was a little easier to talk to, as long as you restricted the conversation to comic books or superhero movies.

Emma was the one blessedly female exception in this state of affairs.

I met her in Astronomy 001, back in the spring of freshman year. We had to go out on the college green and locate and observe different objects in the night sky through a telescope. We were supposed to compare the magnitude of Sirius with that of Betelgeuse—or something… I tend to fall into the background when

15

doing any science project in which I'm working with someone else or with a group of people. But I felt mildly guilty letting her do all the work. It couldn't be helped, I suppose... I liked chatting with her too much to do my share, and reveled inwardly at the conscious waste of time. We stayed until everyone else had already noted whatever it was we were supposed to note. Our telescope was the last one out on the Green.

8. Emma

I'm very immature, yet not romantically inexperienced—at least, not in the strictest sense. I had a nerdy, mathlete girlfriend throughout my junior and senior years of high school. She was also an ardent Mormon. Actually, that's why we split up—I made some mildly sarcastic comments about the golden plates that Joseph Smith dug up, along with a few light barbs about receiving one's own planet after death. I liked her, though—I'm not excusing my behavior. I was intolerant and am duly ashamed.

Despite this previous romance, I still felt like a novice when it came to women—an absolute beginner, in all earnestness. That's what made my ongoing fantasies about Emma so pathetic. If only we could set another telescope upon that now snow-muffled green...

Emma had shoulder-length red-hair and hazel eyes that seemed wonderfully capable of expressing any emotion (a rarer trait than you'd expect). Sitting in the student center, I was witnessing her winter version: she was wearing a black sweater with a silver necklace hanging down over the collar. It had a nice effect, as if to say, "This is a Serious Person." But she wasn't all that serious... I mean, not *too* serious; only about as serious as a girl writing a paper late at night in the student center should be. She was admirably self-contained—wholly *there*.

16

She was from Brooklyn, and her parents were both professors—her mother taught sculpture at Pratt and her father taught chemistry at Brooklyn College. Yet, she didn't have the hyper-allergic, indoor-dwelling look of professoriat spawn: she played field hockey. I like New Yorkers, though I will say that some of the distinctly moneyed New Yorkers at Wilbur were a little hard to take… consciously jaded and posturing. Emma wasn't like that. New York can breed unreflective monsters, but it also produces a decent amount of fine people, with real inwardness, a sense for other minds and emotions. I suppose you either meld with the eternal blaring static of city life, or you carve out your own separate space.

She was a Jewess—is that considered offensive terminology? Obviously, "Negress" is offensive, but Jewess? It's unclear—to me, at least. If it isn't the accepted nomenclature, is that merely because it sounds antique? Yet, isn't that antiquated sound somewhat charming—isn't there a kind of regality to it? I don't know, but "Jewess" sounds regal to me.

At any rate, she wasn't a "wacky" redhead, like you see on TV sitcoms and nowhere else. Also, I suppose her parents were secular enough to give her a not-really-Jewish name like Emma. They weren't insisting on Rachel or Leah (despite the historical nobility of those names).

I kept typing, until a voice said, "Hey," and I looked up to find Emma standing next to my table. She was smiling, so I smiled back. I wanted to show that I was glad to see her, and may have distended my face into a creepy, Joker-ish grin in the process.

"How are things?" I said.

"Oh, not so bad, really," she said.

"What was, uh, engaging your attention over there?" I said, and nodded to a corner table where she'd been working. "You looked pretty absorbed."

"Well, it's this paper I'm writing for Professor Canzoni's class. It's on quantum mechanics—the class, I mean. String theory, all that stuff. It's really interesting—'Advanced Topics in Theoretical Physics.' I'm writing this thing about parallel universes, this whole idea of the multiverse… It's intense."

"Over my head, but sounds cool," I said. Should I have played down my intellect in that casual cool-dumb way? I didn't actually think the multiverse *was* over my head, however uninformed I may have been on these "advanced topics."

I asked, "What do you think of Professor Canzoni?"

"Oh, he's amazing, honestly… Really, the only professor I've had who might be an actual, certifiable genius. It's like being in class with Kepler or Einstein or Pythagoras or something. It has the actual feeling, you know, of being in Plato's Academy." She blushed at this display of nerdy over-reference.

But her tribute to Canzoni may not have been all that far off the mark. Everyone was amazed that he had come to Wilbur, instead of gracing the corridors of Harvard and Yale with his mustachioed presence. The Nobel Winner must have felt he needed the isolation of small town New England to get his work done.

9. The Next Tesla

Canzoni had recently been on the cover of *Time*—not in the actual picture, but his name was used in the smaller headline that they put in the upper right hand corner. Of course, no one reads print magazines anymore, except in dentist's offices. But it was still an honor. The headline read, "Carlo Canzoni: The Next Edison?" That's the greatest degree of popular recognition you can garner after winning the Nobel Prize in Physics. "The Next Tesla?" probably would've been a more appropriate headline, however: Canzoni and Nicola Tesla were both solitary eccentrics, men of secretive habits, yet, somewhat paradoxically, public figures.

Tesla was a pioneer of electrical engineering, while Canzoni was obsessed with sound and light. His interests were oddly fundamental—the most basic elements of our world and experience. He'd pioneered non-lethal riot control technology that could daze a crowd without causing any pain, all through his mastery of the science of vibrations. Yet, supposedly, he was reluctant to reveal his findings in full, lest they be abused. Rumor had it that his famous riot-control invention only became public knowledge after the plans were stolen by an operative working for a weapons manufacturer. Canzoni's ultimate goal was to use his innovations to end war, but he said that he hesitated to put all this non-lethal technology in the hands of powerful people who might use them purely as instruments of control. The powerful naturally took an intense interest in him.

Now, just as Tesla had once freaked out residents in Colorado and Long Island with his attempts to transmit energy wirelessly, Canzoni was conducting strange experiments in the backwoods of Vermont and New Hampshire—with Wilbur College's money of course, and perhaps a government grant or two (despite Canzoni's distaste).

In Lake Panoosacut Village, on the VT side of the Connecticut River, residents reported hearing an odd buzzing one Friday evening last year in October. The low vibration (which as one witness put it, was "not exactly a sound," since it seemed to tingle over the whole body, rather than localizing in the ears) went on for about a minute before the villagers—whether sitting at home, or hanging out in the local dive—burst into uncontrollable laughter. They had no idea why.

They roared for roughly another two minutes, as if each one had been given a gulp of nitrous oxide. And then, as soon as they had started mindlessly guffawing, they stopped, and stared at each other in confusion—confusion undergirded by a very fine terror.

Suspicions naturally gravitated to Canzoni. After all, Lake Panoosacut Village was not so far from the place on the Connecticut where a giant steel tower topped with a metallic sphere had recently appeared. It was rumored that this was Canzoni's big project… or else some sort of water tower.

Three local teenagers from New Hamelin—where Wilbur College is situated—tried to approach the tower in the middle of the night, scaling the barbed-wire-topped fence. Yet, they returned to town saying that they couldn't remember where they'd been or why they'd come back; they seemed to recall making it beyond the perimeter of Canzoni's property, but then… Each one drew a total blank. The teens could only recollect the last leg of the walk back.

Of course, the period of gestation for an urban—or, in this case, rural—legend is very short, I'd imagine. At any rate, I didn't know what to make of Canzoni. But Emma seemed enthralled.

10. Fringe Science

As we continued talking, it became clear that Emma had eccentric yet fundamental interests of her own. She was focusing her psychology studies on meditation, trying to determine the true nature of human attention—of consciousness. Just as Canzoni was looking at light and sound in the outer world, Emma was considering the subtle vibrations and illuminations of the inner realm.

Certain scientists, like Francis Crick, argued that consciousness had to be the result of some peculiar formation of neurons, but Emma was opposed to this hypothesis (putting her at odds with most of the neuroscientists at Wilbur, despite her undergraduate status). "No… It's something else…" she said, and frowned contemplatively at the wall behind me.

What was that power in humans—the very essence, the very self-ness—which we rather dully label "attention"?

She wanted to know… and so did I. It was intriguing, and also seemed related to the Eliot poetry I'd been wrestling with. The stillness at the center of the dance might've been nothing more (or, nothing less) than calmly awakened attention, surrounded by the swirling glitter and tinsel of the earthly pageant.

At the far reaches of her project—the "fringe," she said—she was dealing with some freaky stuff: supernatural powers, mind-over-matter. It had already been scientifically verified that certain Tibetan Buddhist monks had the ability to take control of certain involuntary functions—like the heart-rate and body temperature. But levitation? It was automatically suspect as pseudo-science. Yet Emma insisted she maintained an open mind.

This was more of a personal interest on her part, since none of the professors at Wilbur were intrigued by these questions—with the exception of Canzoni. And he was in the physics department, not psychology. Nonetheless, Canzoni had offered real support for Emma's research, putting her in touch with like-minded colleagues at other universities.

For whatever reason, I found this suspicious: the older man mentoring the young woman in matters mystical… It seemed an all-too-easy ploy. Such was my cynicism, even if I thought it well-placed. At the time, I believed that old piece of folk wisdom, "Where there's smoke, there's fire," and hadn't yet read Salinger's apothegm, "Where there's smoke, there's probably strawberry Jell-O."

11. Silly Squirrels

We chatted a bit more about the class—two nerds nerding out—before she realized how late it was.

"Nice seeing you, Simon," she said, with a smile.

"Nice seeing you too," I said.

Emma walked off.

After a few more minutes of work, I was finished with the paper. Making my way out, an unexpected noise prompted me to turn. It was emanating from the cell phones of the Asian bodybuilder and the girl with the lens-less glasses, simultaneously. It was apparently the theme song to a game they were playing, possibly against each other or in a companionable solitude, and it consisted entirely of the words—

"Silly squirrels
Pickin' up acorns!

"Silly squirrels
Pickin' up acorns!"

The tone of the voice was high-pitched and squeaky, blaring in rapid-fire mindlessness. Out of the corner of my eye, I saw two cartoon squirrels scurrying around under some trees on the girl's smart-phone.

12. Grave Glitter

I stopped on the student center's wide brick porch, and surveyed the empty scene. Most of the buildings on campus were very 19th Century New England—made of red brick or white-painted stone, with a decidedly pastoral feel. You could easily picture cows grazing on the college Green, as they had until somewhat recently. The word often bandied about in describing it was "quintessential"—as in "this is the quintessential small New England college town." But modernity made itself known through the jutting irregularity of the new library extension, which attached itself to the older library like a futurist parasite feeding off the life-energy of its host. However, the original building still had its tall clock tower, which remained the image that most defined the campus's look and overall vibe. It asserted itself against the inorganic menace, making a last stand of sorts.

I was glad to be finished with the paper and to have communed with Emma, however briefly. It eliminated the last depressive traces of the gloomy, spaced-out feeling that had been dogging me—never mind that I was about to walk back to the place that incubated those feelings. It was nice out. Sometimes something simple, like the sight of snowflakes slowly falling through the halo of a midnight lamppost is enough to transfigure your loneliness into an enchanted solitude. The elements conspire to alter your mood and make you receptive to certain benign influences.

Caught in this reverie, I didn't notice that someone else was standing not so far away, a lone figure on the sidewalk that wrapped around the Green. I squinted at him—the figure was male—before noting the telltale beard and eyes capable of communicating their grave glitter over the forty feet that separated us.

Professor Canzoni stood still, looking like an exorcist in the light from a single lamppost.

Although by day he always seemed inwardly absorbed and harmless, in the present instant he gave an impression of coiled power, which was not precisely physical but was equally immediate. He was lost in thought, and I stared at him, wondering what was going on in that Nobel Prize-winning cranium. And for the second time in the last hour, I got caught gawking. Canzoni looked up at me and nodded. The nod seemed to connote recognition, somehow, even though I'd never actually met him… Immediately thereafter, he went on his way, wandering off to bed or to whatever bizarre late-night experiments might await.

I could swear that when he walked past the lamppost its light glowed momentarily brighter, before shuddering back to its former state.

13. The Pyramid

Proceeding onwards to the house, I no longer kept my eyes glued to the sidewalk, and dodged the ice and deep puddles of slush purely by intuition. I felt unusually good. The winter months in New Hamelin can really grind you down. You feel trapped under the starry mill, continually reduced by one wintry trudge after another, pounded into miserable little fragments of yourself, each one full of complaint. Students who spent most of their evenings in frat basements drinking and most of their class-free mornings sleeping until noon, invariably developed a pale, living-dead flesh tone, with sad eyes, dark and small and watery, staring out of their gray putty faces. But, for no reason at all, as far as I could tell—aside from chatting with Emma—my dark mood had lifted and I felt like it was mid-May.

At the edge of campus, I passed The Pyramid, home to the college's oldest secret society—Wilbur's lesser version of Skull and Bones. I've always thought that the Egyptian Pyramids, while giving one an undeniable impression of sacred mystery and power, had a somewhat sinister feel to them, considering that they were constructed by slaves and served no real purpose beyond flattering the vanity of the dead. Also, the very shape of a pyramid suggests hierarchy and privilege, which—aside from the generally esoteric atmosphere of ancient Egyptian architecture—must have been why they picked it for this particular building. There were many tiers of servants and, at the top, a dark mystery. (I think I'm paraphrasing something William Blake once said about the symbolism of pyramids).

No one knew who belonged to The Pyramid. It squatted on a small hill with no apparent windows or doors. There was a widespread campus rumor that it had an insanely high water-bill, due to a private, Olympic-sized swimming pool hidden underneath it. Supposedly, only a secret passage led in, as is true of any ignorant and unapproachable heart.

Nevertheless, The Pyramid seemed to *see* you. Of course, it's possible that someone really *was* watching me, at the time, peering through an unknown, invisible aperture. The building itself was unnerving, as though it possessed intelligence; at least, at that hour of the night, it felt like an idling beast, about to bed down, still cocking a wary eye before it fell asleep.

14. Pee Bottle

When I got back to the house, Oscar was sitting on the futon playing the same game as the two kids from the student center. I heard that theme song start up again, annoying yet insistent—an eerie earworm.

"Silly squirrels
Pickin' up acorns!

"Silly squirrels
Pickin' up acorns!"

"What's that?" I asked.

Oscar didn't say anything. He was rapt.

"Some new game? I think two kids at the student center were playing it."

He made a vague nodding motion, before saying, "Silly…" Then he paused for a long time.

I almost said something, but he finished with "…Squirrels."

I had already guessed that was probably its name, of course. Maybe it was something along the lines of *Angry Birds*? Or perhaps it was providing a more immersive experience, like *Pokemon Go*?

Then, I noticed a plastic Poland Springs bottle filled with a richly yellow liquid on the coffee table.

"Is that piss?" I asked.

Oscar didn't say anything. He continued playing the game.

"Dude—that's not piss, is it?" I asked again.

He said, "Couldn't…" and paused again for as long as he had the first time. "…Stop."

Sighing, I climbed the steps to my room, brushed my teeth, and went to bed. As I tried to fall asleep, that "Silly squirrels / Pickin' up acorns!" refrain kept running through my head, infesting the uncomfortable space between waking and dreaming with its disquieting monotony.

When I came down the next morning, I saw that Oscar had passed out on the futon, his head pitched back and his mouth wide open. A thin river of drool issued hence. The pee bottle was still there. And, the phone, seated on the coffee table, now, without warning, played the same hypnotic snippet—

> *"Silly squirrels*
> *Pickin' up acorns!*

> *"Silly squirrels*
> *Pickin' up acorns!"*

15. "They Talk of Days for Which They Sit and Wait"

First thing, I had to meet with Professor Wilkes at 8 a.m. Getting up that early felt like a gross violation, but I managed to get to his office on time.

Wilkes was short with a beard and a ponytail, and his wet eyes occasionally had a reddish, somewhat stoned look. He was middle-aged, stranded somewhere in the wastes between the Baby Boomers and Generation X. He wasn't a bad guy, really, but it was difficult to tell *why* he'd become a professor in the first place. As far as I could determine, his only qualification was that he *looked* like a professor—of the aging hippie variety. Yet the décor of his office testified to the area of his true interests.

A gigantic, autographed poster of Robert Plant—depicting the golden-maned singer screaming into a microphone—was pinned to the wall directly behind Wilkes' desk. Vinyl covers for every Led Zeppelin album hung on the wall to one side, while the opposing wall bore a mounted replica of Jimmy Page's Gibson EDS 1275, the double-necked six-string and twelve-string guitar that Page used to play "Stairway to Heaven" in concert.

Clearly, Wilkes wished he'd been a roadie for Led Zeppelin—and probably should've been one, if the universe actually took any interest in fulfilling our deepest yearnings. But, fate being what it is, Wilkes had somehow become an Associate Professor of Anthropology. (How many fuzzy dandelion seeds land on sidewalks and never get the chance to sprout?) As he discussed a topic that obviously bore no real interest for him, his eyes would rove over his memorabilia, and his mind, divorced from the words he was actually speaking, would clamber onto legendary stages and grasp The Hammer of the Gods once more…

After falling into academic anthropology for unknown reasons (maybe academia was a family thing?), he ended up studying the anthropology of Central Asia for even more obscure reasons—reasons perhaps mysterious to himself. The Zeppelin song "Kashmir" was one of his favorites, and, maybe, given Kashmir's location near Central Asia, the area had attracted him for that reason? In fact, now that I've proposed it, I feel like this theory is almost certainly the truth.

On the day in question, we were discussing a paper I was writing for his class. He wanted to check on the students individually, and make sure each one had settled on a functional paper topic… but I think he usually ended up talking about Zeppelin. He'd told us an anecdote about John Bonham's death—that Bonzo drank sixteen shots of whiskey early in the morning and said the word, "Breakfast," before collapsing and dying—at least three times since I'd first set foot in his class.

"—So, that's why 'Hats Off to Roy Harper' is called 'Hats Off to Roy Harper'…'" Wilkes said, finishing another Zep anecdote he'd been telling me. "And, oh—you're cool with your paper topic? It's working for you, right?"

"Yeah, I think it'll work."

"Good," he said. "Seriously, it's a good one—very mysterious, Kafiristan."

I was writing a paper on Kafiristan, a province of Afghanistan featured in Kipling's story "The Man Who Would Be King." It had long been rumored that the inhabitants of Kafiristan were actually descendants of Alexander the Great's conquering army who'd stayed behind in India. The inhabitants had resisted converting to Islam until very recently, having managed to adhere to their own polytheistic religious traditions for hundreds of years after Islam's arrival in Afghanistan.

"In fact," Wilkes said, "some local guy from a nursing home died and it turns out he had a bunch of books on Central Asia. I think there was some Kafiristan stuff in there too. The nursing home people couldn't find any relatives or next of kin or whatever, so they dropped them off with me. But, seriously, I sort of looked through them, and I'm not really all that interested. So if you want to take the books, dude—like, even just temporarily—you can take 'em with you. Seriously."

"Alright. Sure," I said. "Could be useful."

With a nod, Wilkes directed me to the box of books, sitting on a spare chair by the door. Even though he wasn't interested in his subject, he still went out of his way to help you. The fact that he wasn't that into it made the extra effort mean more. It was kind of heroic, even.

Wilkes popped a Tums in his mouth and chewed vigorously. "I'm getting lunch with Professor Canzoni, by the way. For real."

"Oh, yeah?"

"Yeah, man. He wanted to go to the Indian buffet down the street. Hence the Tums." He chortled to himself.

"Really? What's the, uh, purpose of the lunch?"

I was surprised a Nobel Laureate wanted to hang-out with a stoner.

"You know what? I don't really know. Big aura of, like, mystery around this dude and his whole shtick."

"Not everyday you get to grab lunch with a certified genius," I said.

"Yeah, Canzoni must feel flattered at the privilege." He chuckled at his little joke. I chuckled in response, granting him some fleeting companionship in his light mirth.

He continued, "But, yeah, I seriously don't know why… He said he had something to tell me that might be 'of interest to my research.' I think he said… Oh, yeah, he said it was something 'interdisciplinary' related to our two, uh, disciplines, I guess. Didn't expound beyond that."

"Physics and anthropology? How do those connect?

"I don't know—he's a mysterious guy, that's for sure."

"Cryptic…" I said. "I just wonder what military mind control technology—or *whatever* he's working on—has to do with Central Asian anthropology…"

"Well, you know, I think the Soviets did experiments like that. They had a facility in Tashkent, where they'd invite yogis and miracle workers from other religions to come and try to find out the scientific principles behind their abilities. At least, I think I vaguely remember Canzoni saying something about that the first time I met him—a faculty get-together, end of year thing. Like, I probably wasn't listening too intensely."

"Interesting. Was he there in Tashkent? How did he know about all this?"

"I don't know, man. Seriously—all this freaky shit… But, you know, it's like Zep said in 'Kashmir.' In the song, Plant talks about seeing some old wise men and he's like, 'They talk of days for which they sit and wait… All will be revealed.'"

"'All will be revealed…' When does that happen? Sounds like the Apocalypse."

"That's right. Seriously. The Apocalypse."

16. Lost in Space

I lugged the box of books back to my apartment, but didn't have time to look through them. My English course was at ten and I wanted to eat some breakfast first. After grabbing a bagel in the cafeteria, I made it to class on time, and submitted my short paper on Eliot's poem (it would receive the aforementioned, incredibly unfair B-). For the next two hours, Professor Moriarty droned on and on about Eliot's lack of feminist credentials or something—she said he was "hetero-normative." But later, she somewhat surprisingly claimed he was a closeted gay man. Hetero-normative or not, her comments didn't have much to do with Eliot's actual *poetry*. The line hovered in front of me on the page—"Except for the point, the still point, / There would be no dance, and there is only the dance"—seeming almost to pop up, to embolden its own letters, while something utterly strange, divorced and distant, rambled on behind it: education.

After shaking off Moriarty's pedantry like a wet dog, I was free—and hungry.

By myself, I sat down with a sandwich from the cafeteria's deli section. It had some sort of olive spread on it. I also bought a little plastic cup full of mandarin oranges. As I ate, I started reading The Wilbur Picayune, our student newspaper. Like all provincial campus dailies, it assigned inordinate importance to trivial local affairs. The flaws in the college's recycling policy might send a columnist into hysterics, or an editorial would rave about how the author had seen a white person wearing an American Indian headdress at a Halloween party or wearing a sombrero at a Cinco de Mayo fiesta. Writers took aggressive stands over not much—minor violations of good taste in our fringe of the cosmos.

But, occasionally, the news proved interesting, and amounted to more than recreational outrage or what some visiting banker had said at a public lecture or what construction project the Board of Trustees was debating. For instance, on the day in question, I read the front page's headline article about a student who had recently gone missing.

Iphigenia Woods disappeared from campus about two months ago, a couple weeks before Christmas Break, leaving behind a dustbin full of syringes and coke spoons. This seemed weird—why wouldn't you dispose of all this used drug paraphernalia, before running away? It was odd, yet addicts aren't necessarily known for being big on logic. At first, people whispered that she might've overdosed in a ditch somewhere or committed suicide, possibly flinging herself into the Connecticut River from the bridge by which you entered New Hamelin from Vermont. (A few students had actually done this over the past decade). But now, according to the article, the police had discovered that she'd bought a plane ticket to Amsterdam with a departure time scheduled on the last day anyone could remember seeing her, December 2nd. So, case… closed?

I remembered running into her occasionally during freshman year. Our freshman dorm was heavy on drug use, but that was mainly weed. However, a particularly noted preppy pusher—Rutger Weatherblow, formerly of Phillips Exeter Academy—operated an opium den of sorts out of his corner room, a popular gathering place for the hardcore drug enthusiasts, like Iphigenia. I heard that Rutger felt up and fingered the prone bodies of his heroin-dazed clientele, including Iphigenia, without obtaining their consent.

"Iffie"—as everyone called her—left a dreamy, not-quite-there impression. A trust-fund kid from New York City, she always seemed to be floating a centimeter or two above the ground. She also had a gift for whimsical non-sequiturs. People would be talking about Radiohead or Kanye or *Breaking Bad*, and she'd suddenly say, "I wish I could hibernate like a chinchilla." She was a space cadet for sure.

17. Benchwarmer

When I put aside the paper, I discovered that Peter Surface was about to sit in the chair facing me. As mentioned earlier, he was the fourth renter in our den of inequity and my closest friend on campus.

While Curtis was a rich kid—and not the driven, pressured kind of rich person, aspiring to more wealth, but the content, drifting, cheerfully ignorant kind of rich person—and Oscar was a rich foreigner and therefore basically akin to Curt, Peter and I came from similar backgrounds. Both our mothers were nurses; my dad was a high school English teacher and his dad ran a hardware store; he was from Ohio and I was from Pennsylvania, two states that vibe along similar lines—although Eastern Pennsylvania, where I'm from, is culturally closer to the Northeast than the Midwest, with the exception of a few attitudes and elements. It's a little warmer than New England, emotionally speaking, and not so reserved.

We both liked old music like The Rolling Stones, Marvin Gaye, and Bob Dylan and relatively newer music like The White Stripes, Vampire Weekend, and Fleet Foxes. But, recently, despite many shared eye-rolls we'd enjoyed at the expense of our wealthier classmates during freshman year, he'd become enthusiastic about joining a frat. Although we weren't lacking in friendship, we still felt like outsiders, and the impulse to "belong" was clearly pretty powerful. I can't say that I've ever been much of a joiner, but I understood the pull.

Pete was a benchwarmer on the basketball team. He was tall, 6'6", but he tended to walk and run hunched forward, his posture bent except when he was standing still or sitting. Looking at him, you'd have thought he'd do better with the ladies than he actually did. Given his height and at least technical status as a jock, he *should* have, obviously—with the addition of a few social graces. But, when I first met him, those graces were precisely what he lacked.

In social situations, he was a very awkward conversationalist, a master of the not-so-pregnant pause, though one-on-one he was much more talkative. Now, conversational skills didn't particularly matter at Wilbur, since most socializing took place in dank, noisy frat basements, where carrying on a real conversation was impossible in the first place. Yet Peter's total lack of confidence around girls, his fundamental insecurity, wounded him even there. He would've needed just enough confidence to stand around at a party and receive attention from interested female callers, while responding with cut-and-dried normalcy. Strangely, he didn't have the ability to do this—he missed this rudimentary dash of poise. In short, he was afraid. (I've heard some theoreticians claim that all men are, in essence, scared little boys, though scared of *what*, I'm not sure. My ignorance on this question testifies either to my own lack of self-awareness, or a flaw in the claim. However, Peter would be a decently portioned slice of evidence in its favor, I need to say.)

Yet, things started to change once he began hanging out at one particular frat. He'd struck up a friendship with its president, Alex Calhoun, who was the starting point guard and captain of the basketball team. Alex invited him to different parties and private events, trying to entice him into pledging. I'm not sure this would've worked if it hadn't been for the fact that Calhoun, by example or advice, showed him how to get laid. That, after all, is the *point* of the Greek system.

So, on one level, Peter felt obliged to pledge. He also sensed that his budding relationship with Sheila Tomlinson, a girl introduced to him at a party at the aforementioned frat, could be credited to Alex. These sunny prospects of unbound sexual activity, now opening before him, were so various and new that Peter felt he owed Alex a seemingly infinite debt. At a deep level, I think he respected Alex the way Kamikaze pilots respected the Japanese Emperor—though respect is too weak a word. (Perhaps "love" would not be an overstatement?) Additionally, Pete had solidly practical reasons for wanting to pledge, believing that a frat would continue to provide him with the platform of security he needed to walk out and simply *be* there.

The fraternity Peter wanted to join was usually referred to as "Beta" (I will omit the other two Greek letters comprising its name). Whereas other frats had a broad type associated with them—say, squash players, or Asian students, or Lord of the Rings aficionados, or aspiring DJs—Beta had none. Its type was the anti-type, the "normal person." That was supposedly the type, anyway... Someone with an intense need to be perceived as "normal" is probably anything but normal, of course.

Beta was really a hodge-podge, in the last analysis, though all of its members were reaching for a common goal. Again, you might call it "normalcy," but that seems somehow inadequate. The brothers didn't want to stand out, but, nevertheless, they did stand out, because of their unclassifiable nature. Wherever everyone else was on the spectrum, they were in the absolute middle—and clinging desperately to it.

18. Faux Raybans

"You look hung-over," I said.

"You could tell by the shades," Peter responded. "The shades are my first line of defense. That, and coffee." He tapped the place where the sunglasses' frame intersected his left temple, then took a swig from the large Starbucks sitting in front of him.

"It was more the pale sallow sickly look that tipped me off…" I paused, noting his eyewear. "Are those real Raybans, by the way? Not that I, uh, care about brands."

"Uh…No. Not actually."

"Where were you drinking on a Tuesday night?"

"Well, Mom—I was with the Fellowship of Christian Athletes discussing theology over a calm pint."

"Really though."

"Pledge event. Beta."

"Weird time to schedule it."

"Tuesday? I guess… Maybe they want to find out who's really hardcore? They invited the top fifteen people they want to pledge, and I was on the list, apparently."

He sounded overly proud of this.

"What was the purpose of the event?"

"To play pong and get fucked up."

"Any girls around?"

"No. Wasn't that kind of event."

"Ah. This was more a male-bonding, camaraderie kind of thing?"

"Sure. You could call it that."

"The character building workshop."

"Yeah, whatever. There was free pizza too."

"Did a Turkish bath happen to be involved?"

"What?"

"Forget it. Half-conceived joke. Were you allowed to bring anyone with you?"

"They didn't say not to."

"Well, you should've called me, dude. You should've called me when you heard about the pizza. I would've gone. The pizza part was enticing."

"I thought you said frats represented everything you despised, and that you'd rather have a mariachi band blaring in your face at full volume for an hour while you tried to eat than join a frat?"

"That was rhetorical excess. And it doesn't mean I want to starve."

I hadn't told Pete I was reconsidering pledging.

"You said you weren't going to pretend a bunch of fucknuts were your brothers when you already have a real brother and that was more than enough."

"Well, Rob lives out in Oregon now, and we hardly see him anymore, so there's kind of a slight vacancy in the brother department."

"So… You're gonna do it, then? You'll rush Beta?"

"Well, let's put it this way. The next time there's free pizza, just let me know. Maybe I'll tag along."

"The next event like that is rush, and it's coming up. Thursday. Remember it."

"Maybe... Maybe."

"You know," said Pete, "You should really talk to Alex—"

19. Unripe Bananas

Someone interrupted him.

"Mind if I join you?" said the intruder.

It was Elmer Wiley, a kid who'd lived on the same floor of our dorm freshman year.

"Sure," I said.

When Elmer sat down, I noticed Pete's manner shift. He was less gregarious, less open. He grew real cool and sealed off all of a sudden—in retrospect, a bad indication of what this frat stuff was already doing to him.

Elmer looked like he'd just woken to the sound of someone screaming a few inches from his face. Hair eternally uncombed, he had the unpleasant propensity to grow a neckbeard and neglect grooming. At that moment, the neckbeard wasn't overly visible, but sometimes… Also, he always seemed to be wearing the same t-shirt depicting the cover of Pink Floyd's *Dark Side of the Moon*—a prism splitting white light into color. Occasionally, he wore a fedora, a choice that had become reviled as a dorky affectation throughout much of the wider culture.

But he was a nice guy, continually hungry for intelligent conversation.

Elmer blinked at Pete, whose body language suggested not revulsion but indifference, as if no one had joined us. Again, this attitude—evidently new in him—made me feel uneasy about frat life when I reflected on it later.

"You should really talk to Alex about it," Peter repeated, as if to highlight the fact that he wasn't going to alter what he was saying just because some dork had intruded on us.

Elmer continued to look confusedly at Pete, like, say, a platypus encountering a bald eagle. Then, he turned to me.

"You read the Eliot yet?"

"Yeah. I liked it. You?"

"It was interesting…" Elmer stared up at the ceiling for a brief moment, eyes fluttering. It was a kind of tic he had.

He looked back to Pete, and asked him, out of nowhere, "Do you like bananas?"

"What?" said Pete, who had probably heard the question clearly enough. Admittedly, it was an unexpected line of inquiry.

Elmer glanced at me, as if afraid he was committing some sort of faux pas. I didn't know how to respond to his expression, so I shrugged.

Transferring his attention to Pete, Elmer said, slowly, "Do. You. Like. Bananas?"

"Why?" said Pete. He seemed uneasy, as though worried he was being looped into a dirty middle-school joke, something that had been circulating but which he hadn't yet been privileged to learn. The nerd had got the jump on him, somehow, having mastered the obscenity first.

"Just answer the question," I said.

Pete scowled briefly. "Yeah," he said, with a blank look of menace. "Yeah, I like bananas."

Elmer removed a bunch of green bananas from his backpack.

"Here," he said. "I grew these. They're from the greenhouse. They're not quite ripe yet."

Pete stared at the bunch of bananas.

"Take one," said Elmer.

Pete took one.

"Peel it."

Pete peeled it, before staring helplessly and angrily at us both.

"Well—eat it," said Elmer.

Pete took extra-care in biting the banana, in order to avoid the appearance of giving it a blowjob—lest this become some sort of joke. But nothing in Elmer's manner indicated he was putting Pete on. Rather, he was gazing at him with intense interest, waiting to gauge his reaction.

Pete attacked it more with the side of his mouth, and chewed it meditatively before saying, "It tastes like there's cinnamon in it."

"Ha!" said Elmer, slapping his palm on the table. "That's exactly what it's supposed to taste like!"

Working with two other students under Professor Engelbert Weimar's supervision, Elmer had genetically engineered the bananas to have a cinnamon flavor. He told us this was going to win them a lot of fellowship money.

"I want one," I said.

He handed it to me. I ate it.

"They do taste like cinnamon," I said. It was true. "But they're not overloaded with it. You get a good balance."

"Thanks," said Elmer.

See? Even perfectly nice people like Elmer are in the business of perverting nature. It's a sign of the times.

"Things are going to be great in the future," said Elmer, preparing to draw a philosophical moral from the physical illustration provided by the bananas.

"Yeah," I said. Flatly. I had no such conviction.

"Yes. You'll be able to have bananas like this any time you want."

"Yay," said Pete, also flatly.

"—and," Elmer continued, "you'll be able to live in a virtual reality world like in *The Matrix*, and be Spiderman, or a medical doctor, or an Ottoman Sultan with a harem, or anyone else."

"What about God?" I said. "Could you be God?"

"Oh, for sure," Elmer said. "They're already designing that game."

"Hmm… I don't know whether I need less distractions in my life or more," I said.

"Yes, exactly!" said Elmer, not hearing me properly. "More distractions! That's what the future's going to be. Distractions! Better and better ones! You'll never need to be bored again because there'll be so many distractions, and you'll always have something *new*. We are riding out this great wave of novelty, leading us towards a moment of peak novelty—peak distraction."

At this point in the conversation, Elmer reached the peak of his own personal ecstasy—standing on a mental Mount Pisgah and savoring the not-so-distant prospect of the Promised Land, the streams of milk and honey a metaphor for one sweetly endless flow of distraction.

He kept going, winding down a bit: "You can immerse yourself, forget yourself. It'll be the truest religion, the purest escape from the self. It'll beat the hell out of receiving the Eucharist. Oh, uh sorry—" Elmer looked at Pete. "You're not a Catholic are you?"

Having attained his moment of vision, he began drifting back down to earth in a long wavering swoop.

"Nah," said Pete.

"Oh, okay. Good," said Elmer.

And then he got up and left.

It didn't occur to him that *I* might be a Catholic. I mean, I was raised as one at any rate. But he assumed that anyone he got along with would probably share all the same opinions as him. Despite this nerdy failure of empathy, he still wasn't such a bad guy. He'd at least managed to become interested in something.

"Thank God…" said Pete, watching Elmer leave. "What a fuckin' dingus! I mean, I want to have virtual reality sex with a harem as much as the next guy, but I'm not creaming my jeans dreaming about the future. He should try getting some actual pussy sometime."

I didn't agree with Elmer's vision of the future—it seemed like a perfect crystallization of error—but Pete's jockish, anti-reflective dismissal was just as irritating. I wasn't objecting to Elmer's nerdiness or probable virginity, and this vulgar bullying side of Pete was a troubling new development. Hard to take.

What bothered me about Elmer's vision was his disinterest in the Spirit of the Earth, in the fact that the living present might have some consolations of its own. He was wagering his savings on a future Utopia, and history had already proved that was a terrible bet. He thought our tools could save us, without considering the problem of the self that would wield those tools. You could eat a genetically engineered banana, and still go home and murder your spouse.

To my mind, anyway, the future is something that will never really exist. It seemed eminently unwise to let its eternal ghost—never fully manifest, never what was promised—haunt the back-corridors of one's skull until death. Perhaps those African tribes who imagine that we travel through time by facing the past, and moving backwards into the future, have the right idea.

20. Things That Slaves Can Do

I had another class at two (Ancient Greek Philosophy), which ran until four. After it let out, I went to the library and pretended to work while actually frittering my life away. Through the fog of memory, I recall a Youtube video with a cat picking its own nose. Also, I read an article about how female lab rats stay depressed longer than male lab rats for some unknown reason. Sickened by my own fecklessness, I decided the only remedy—aside from actually doing work—would be to go to the movies. Being a Wilbur Film Society member, I got into the college theater with a 50% discount.

The movie playing that night was *Mulholland Drive*, part of a David Lynch retrospective the film society was featuring. I'd already seen it but enjoyed trying to figure out more of the puzzle… It's certainly a movie that doesn't discourage re-watching. I understood that Naomi Watts was in hell (or perhaps a sort of purgatory or temporary hell), which was like a tape loop playing over and over again, leading from innocence to corruption, depravity, and death. The loop would keep repeating, unless something—some sublime feat of detection or act of mercy—could blow the mystery wide open. The entity creating the infernal

43

vision was, after all, just some feral creature behind a dumpster. How difficult of an opponent could that be, really?

After a solitary dinner at the cafeteria, I went back to the apartment, where Oscar and Curtis were smoking pot on the futon while watching *Koyaanisqatsi*. The hypnotic Phillip Glass soundtrack repeated itself with the insistence of a mantra—illustrating how life looked when it was out of balance—and the whites of Oscar and Curtis's eyes had turned red and extra-moist. They were eating a bowl of popcorn mixed with M&Ms, which Curtis kept hogging, provoking Oscar to elbow him—trying to get Curtis to sit the bowl between them instead of on the arm of the futon farthest from Oscar.

Ignoring my entry, they continued a stoned conversation.

Curtis was asking, "So, slavery is still legal in the Dominican Republic, right?"

"What?" said Oscar.

"You're still allowed to have slaves there, right?"

"No—what a racist-ass question! I mean, my grandmother doesn't pay her maid, but that's just because they know each other so well..."

"Man, I wish I had some slaves," said Curtis. "I mean, not black people— the slaves could be of any race. I think you could do some cool things with white slaves and Asian slaves too. Like, what *couldn't* you do with slaves? You could build a pyramid, take over Poland..."

I climbed the stairs to my room, where I unloaded my backpack and plugged in my laptop. I did assigned readings until midnight, but didn't manage to check what was in the cardboard box Wilkes had given me. Caught up in the usual tedium, I avoided catching onto the Quest, which even then, was preparing itself… The spiral winding down and down and down, as I slept-walked on the staircase, oblivious.

Finishing my work, I watched *Buffy the Vampire Slayer* on Netflix until two in the morning. (Okay, maybe three). Once I'd brushed my teeth and undressed, I moved to connect my phone to its recharger cord on my nightstand, and noticed there was a voice message on it. I'd missed it when I turned off my phone at the movies.

It was from Wilkes:

"Uh, hey—tried calling, and, uh, my texts aren't sending for some reason. Like, maybe I exceeded my monthly limit or something? Not sure… Anyway… Damn, dude, I hate leaving these kind of messages on answering machines. I always pause in the middle and I'm like 'What am I even…?' And then it's like, '*Doy*, that's why I was calling.' You know? Anyway… You still got that cardboard box with all those books I left you with? Well, there's one in there, one specific one, that I, uh, kind of need back. It's sort of urgent. But, uh, I don't know exactly what book it is. Yeah, that's the thing… So could you bring in the whole box? That would be awesome. I know how heavy it is, but it would seriously be a huge favor. You'd be doing me a solid. So, maybe eight in the morning tomorrow would work for you? I'll be here. Alright. Cool. I'll see you then, Simon. Keep it real—be a rock, but don't roll." (That last sentence paraphrased Zep lyrics).

Irritated, I set my alarm for 7:30. I can't believe that seemed so early to me at the time. The crosses we bear…

21. Buying a Bag of Ruffles

I woke to the radio alarm blaring "California Dreamin'." Rolling over, I rubbed the crusties out of my eyes and stared at the ceiling. I've never been a morning person.

Figuring I could shower after I returned from dragging the books over to Wilkes' office, I dressed and combed my hair with my fingers (for some reason, I had never bothered to buy an actual comb). I fished a granola bar from the lower drawer of my desk, and tried to eat it while simultaneously carrying the box full of books, which required both arms.

This was not easy: I had to balance the bar on top of the books, elevate the box to my face, grab the bar with my teeth, and crunch off a bite. Having limited success with this method, I paused outside and sat the books down. It was no longer cloudy or snowing—perfect uninterrupted blue. Aside from some professors driving their Priuses into campus, and a few other adults heading to real jobs, New Hamelin was empty. No one on campus seemed to wake until 8:30 or 9, at the earliest.

The quality of stillness in winter is always remarkable. It's both the season's best attribute and its most unnerving: it can feel refreshing or like death. On the day in question, I thought it felt refreshing.

After I'd finished the granola bar, I reassumed my burden and continued walking, whistling "California Dreamin'" as I went. A crow perched on The Pyramid as I passed and swiveled its head quizzically before taking off.

It was a ten-minute walk to Wilkes' office, located in the ancient red brick social sciences building. By the time I got there, my back was aching—the books were heavier than one might've expected. Plus, there was a three-story climb to

Wilkes' office. Mentally, at this point, I was cursing him—just a bit of recreational scorn for the incompetent old hippie.

To make matters worse, when I arrived at Wilkes' office, he wasn't at his desk. I figured he'd gone to the bathroom or something and that I'd just leave the books on the floor inside. But I considered that he really only wanted one specific text he was looking for, if he could even identify it, and thought I'd wait for him. I sat on a bench outside his office for about ten minutes, and then left the box alone while I walked down to the basement of the building to see what was in the vending machine. It was a terrible choice for breakfast, but I bought a bag of Ruffles, which I managed to finish by the time I returned to Wilkes' office. Fragments of chips fell on the front of my shirt, but I brushed them off, devouring with barbaric intensity.

He still wasn't back, so I decided to ditch the books and call him later about picking up whatever volumes I might need on another day. But as I bent to sit the books on the thinly carpeted floor, I heard a slow, creaking noise behind me. I dropped the box from the height of only a few inches, and turned around. There was no one in the hall outside the office, but I noticed that the door to the closet—a small-ish space typically used to store excess staples and paper and other supplies—was slightly ajar. Nothing unusual about that. Yet I stood staring at this slight dark crevice until I heard another extended creak, obviously coming from inside.

I took a step towards it, and relaxed. What did I think was going to happen? After a few more quick steps, I placed my hand on the knob to pull it open… And in that very instant, I heard the creaking noise again, except this time it was followed by a loud snap. Immediately thereafter, Wilkes tumbled out of the closet and fell on top of me.

Yelling with surprise, I shoved him off, rolling him sideways onto his back. I stood up with an irrational thought—*Wilkes was waiting to ambush me...sexually!*—running through my mind. But, standing over his motionless body, I realized that something wasn't right (in addition to the clear non-rightness of Wilkes tumbling out of the closet in the first place, I mean). His eyes were open, blankly glassing the ceiling, and his jaw hung slack. A leather belt was tied around his neck. Additionally, his pants had been pulled down around his ankles and his penis was sticking out of the fly of his boxer shorts.

Wilkes was dead. Despite his sordid position and terrified bulging eyes, he lay in a state of stillness at one with the early winter morning.

"Professor Wilkes!" I exclaimed to my deceased non-auditor. I contemplated administering CPR but realized that I had no idea how to do it properly and didn't want to shatter his ribcage and open myself to a lawsuit. So, I called 911 on my cell phone.

22. Wiener Roulette

Twenty minutes later, the cops had thrown a foil space blanket over my shoulders as I sat on the bench outside the office. I guess they always kept one handy in case they ever ran into anyone who was in shock—which, ostensibly, I was... Though I wasn't really. I mean, I might've cried a little bit at first. But I wasn't crying with those huge, childlike gulping sobs, except for, perhaps, very early on. What can I say? I was surprised, caught off guard.

I imagine if I was in the middle of a war, I probably wouldn't have reacted that way to seeing a dead body. It was just that it came out of nowhere.

Sitting in the hall, I could hear one of the cops inside the office saying, "Another choke and croak. Coroner's gonna rule this as 'death by misadventure,' easy." They had already put a line of yellow tape across the hallway, which they kept ducking under. This proved difficult for some of the overweight cops, as it was set fairly low and they were already out of breath from climbing the stairs.

Finally, the officer who seemed to be highest ranking tore the tape off entirely, and stuffed it in a nearby wastebasket. He sat down next to me on the bench, where I was still positioned with the rather small space blanket wrapped around me.

"Take it from us, kid. If you're gonna flog the bishop, stick with the basics. Don't get more exotic than hand lotion and tissues. All this kinky S&M Marilyn Manson who's-your-daddy freak-session shit… Believe me, the kind of stuff I've seen in this town—vacuum cleaners, water-intake valves in pools, pieces of dry spaghetti shattering inside urethras. It's enough to seriously make you consider becoming one of them, uh, Jehovah's Mormons or whatever. The wiener plays its own kind of Russian Roulette, that's for sure. Round these parts, autoerotic asphyxiation is just par for the course."

"I'll keep that in mind," I said.

"It's a lesson we all gotta learn. Takes time though. Oh, does it take time… I mean, don't get me wrong. I'm not a Puritan. My wife and I, we're not strangers to adventurousness. We've been known to pop *Caligula* in the ol' DVD player from time to time an' just kind of follow along... But you gotta know where the edge is. I mean, they really oughta distribute everyone some kind of pamphlet on these sort of things. Draw a red line. Know what I mean?"

"…Yeah," I said.

"I'm Lieutenant Sheerhan, by the way."

"It's nice meeting you," I said. "I mean, not under these circumstances exactly, but, uh…"

"Yeah. Tragic," he said. "I take it you knew the jag-off—I mean, the deceased?"

"Well, he was my professor. He was a nice guy," I said, before adding somewhat irrelevantly, "He really loved Led Zeppelin."

"Zeppelin, huh? I've always been more partial to that, uh, chick with the really peaceful vibes. You know? What's-her-name? Oh, yeah—Enya."

"Ah," I said.

"Well, uh, we clearly already know how this all went down. Autoerotic asphyxiation. Open and shut case. But, I guess, technically, I gotta ask you some questions." Sheerhan took a notepad out of his breast pocket. "You know anyone who wanted to kill this guy and then make it look like he died tugging himself off?"

"No."

"Did you kill him?"

"No!" I said. "God, no…"

"Don't worry, kid. Just had to make sure. I got a kind of mental lie detector and I can already surmise you're not the murdering type. You work a long time as a cop, it's like—you start to get lots of gut feelings and hunches. It's a cliché but it's true."

"You've dealt with murder cases before, then?"

"Oh, well, uh—yeah. Like, one. I mean, I was on desk duty, but I did some paper work on it. Confused grandma murdered her husband with a knitting needle. Very sad."

"Oh," I said.

"Though I guess technically that was manslaughter. Or was it just an accident? Anyway, anything else you think we should know? Like, anything suspicious?"

"Not really… I mean, he wanted me to return these books he'd given me, which was kind of unusual, since he normally seemed pretty detached from his subject and didn't really explain why he needed them."

"Professors, right? Which ones *aren't* unusual?"

"Also, he got lunch with Professor Canzoni the other day."

"Who?"

"The famous scientist?"

"Oh. Yeah. Him. That guy… Famous… Well, lunch isn't a crime or nothing."

"I know, I just… I thought maybe he wanted the book for some specific reason, like Canzoni had told him about it or, uh…"

"Okay, kid. I'll keep it in mind." He got up. "Nice talking to you. I mean, like you said, not 'nice' under the circumstances, but you know. I think we all know what happened here… So, you can go to class or go to the infirmary and get some kind of counseling or whatever they have for people who find dead bodies nowadays."

I stood up to leave, but before I did, I turned to Sheerhan.

"You think I can take the books with me?"

I was going to try to figure out what book Wilkes was looking for.

He blinked twice before answering, "Sure. Don't see why not."

"Cool… and, uh, do I keep the space blanket, or do I—"

"Oh, no. Sorry. We need that back."

On my way out, I noticed that a cop sitting in the police cruiser was playing *Silly Squirrels* on his phone—identifiable, yet again, from the theme music. It seemed like it was on its way to becoming a craze, or already was one.

23. Wheels in Wheels

Wilkes' death provided a reason—some might say an excuse—for sitting around with a blanket over my shoulders and watching more *Buffy the Vampire Slayer* on Netflix for the rest of the day, though I did manage to read a few chapters of John Irving's *A Prayer for Owen Meany* (for personal enjoyment, not for class). Technically, I had two classes scheduled for the day, but it would've felt weird to just shrug off the whole event as if nothing had happened. You're *supposed* to skip class when you have an unexpected encounter with a corpse, right? To be honest, I *did* feel a little traumatized.

If Wilkes had simply been sitting at his desk, dead from a heart attack, maybe it wouldn't have felt so jarring. As it was, with the stated cause of death being autoerotic asphyxiation and the sight of Wilkes' exposed penis flopping out of his underwear after his corpse fell on me... It seemed like a decent excuse to take a personal day. I mean, have you ever had the same experience? Probably not, right? (If you have—get in touch, and we can bond over it).

But it wasn't just the weirdness of what happened that put me in a funk. I already had the sensation that there was something sinister going on. I'm naturally a little paranoid by disposition, and I'd immediately entertained the thought that Wilkes' meeting with Canzoni, his request for the books he'd lent me, and his untimely demise were all interrelated. I found that I wasn't able to dismiss this thought either.

Finally, I pulled myself away from the computer, and decided to investigate the pile of books—first, looking for anything highlighted, dog-eared, or underlined. This was surprisingly difficult—the books were almost as good as new and appeared to have been read perhaps one time each.

The titles were certainly all related to Central Asia: *Return of a King* by William Dalrymple, *Kipling and Kafiristan* by Adelaide Wright, *Kafiristan Diary* by Ephraim Calder, the *Baburnama* (the diary of the Mogul Emperor Babur—not to be confused with Babar the Elephant), *The Road to Oxiana* by Robert Byron. But I couldn't come up with a hypothesis linking any of these volumes to a potential reason Canzoni might've had for meeting with Wilkes. There simply wasn't enough information. If there were any vital clues hidden in these obscure volumes, I didn't seem to have any choice but to read through them myself with absolutely no idea what I was looking for.

This was irritating. I like to assume there's always a way into any mystery. With enough creative speculation, you could get a rough idea of the larger picture from just a few puzzle pieces. But in this case, I had maybe two pieces.

As far as I was aware, there wasn't anything I could contribute to the investigation. Wilkes probably *had* died in that sad, small, sordid way—"death by misadventure." Sheesh… I returned to my computer, and watched Buffy hammer home a few more wooden stakes.

Yet, "wheels were in motion"—wheels within wheels within wheels within wheels…

24. Wilbur, Past and Present

A missionary named Isaiah Wilbur founded Wilbur College in the early 18th Century. His stated mission was to educate the Native American population of northern New England into becoming model American citizens and Christians. At that time, the white population was under the impression that Native Americans were literally in league with the devil. "Pagan" and "Satanist" were nearly interchangeable terms.

Thus, Wilbur believed he was venturing into the very heart of darkness, carrying the light of Christ into the depths of hell. In the course of his proselytizing, he managed to enroll around twenty Abenaki Indians in the college, which he considered a respectable number—twenty souls rescued from the everlasting flames. However, after a young Indian tried to murder him with a blunt club, smashing him on the head several times, Wilbur changed.

He claimed that he had been newly awakened to the nature of the Deity, and began to engage in Native American practices himself, while continuing to act as a Christian minister. The small congregation of teachers' families he had brought with him rebelled when Wilbur began instituting sacred dances borrowed from the Indians in Church, and incorporating prayers that acknowledged Native American gods as tutelary, secondary spirits attending upon the Christian God, which Wilbur had come to view as being identical with the Indians' Great Spirit. He was officially excommunicated from his Calvinist Church, living out the rest of his days with an Indian bride and the children he had with her. Despite the familial disgrace, his son, Willard Wilbur (Isaiah liked alliteration: he also had a daughter named Willa Wilbur and another son named Winslow Wilbur), was able to wrest control of the college's presidency, assuming his father's mission.

Willard quickly grew bored with this ostensibly civilizing project and rapidly transformed Wilbur into an institution for the education of the White Anglo-Saxon Protestant gentry. It became an elite liberal arts college, comparable to other New England schools like Williams, Amherst, Middlebury, and Bowdoin. The town that sprang up around it, New Hamelin, mainly existed to support the college, though it also provided seasonal lodging for leaf-peepers from New York and skiers who came for the nearby slopes.

Yet, domesticated as the campus became, its little trough was still surrounded by the New Hampshire woods, luxuriating in the same loveliness, darkness, and depth that moved Robert Frost in his day. The general "vibe" of Wilbur—if you will accept the out-dated hippie-ish vocabulary—contrasted with those ancient forests, lacking their peculiar gnome-ish quality. There was something contemplative about them—places to stand on granite and come to a reckoning. You could see why the atmosphere of northern New England, the land not quite tutored to civilization, called to the souls of so many great writers, from Hawthorne and Melville in the Berkshires, to Thoreau and Emerson in their excursions toward Monadnock and Katahdin, to Dickinson cloistered in Amherst, and to Salinger hunkered down in Cornish.

During the time in question—my tenure as a student—Wilbur was noted for its large frat system; roughly 70% of campus ended up going Greek. However, if you remained part of the recalcitrant 30% who didn't join, you still had lots of fun alternatives—for instance, you could take DVDs out of the library and watch them alone in your room.

This is what I was doing the day after I found Wilkes' corpse. The lights were out, it was around 7 p.m., and I was huddled over my computer, watching *Being There*, the Peter Sellers movie.

If my description of my life as a college student doesn't teem with adventure and moments of vibrant socialization, that's because—at the time in question—it didn't. I had friends, and I was involved in a few extracurricular activities (*The Muted Trumpet*, our campus literary magazine; Taekwondo; Fencing Club; The Wilbur Film Society; and—for some reason—the Huckleberry Picking Club). But I wasn't attending many *Gatsby*-style parties or going on lots of dates. Why? Well, it's not a failure I was intentionally *planning*. It just worked out that way.

At any rate, I was getting a little tired of this isolated, sexless and loveless existence, and while joining a frat didn't necessarily seem like a solution, it didn't seem like it could make things any worse.

Something else was bothering me. After finding Wilkes' corpse, I felt somehow cheated of a resolution. I wanted to know how he really died and what was up with Canzoni—there needed to be something to follow on the heels of the discovery, but there wasn't. It was irritatingly truncated—like the opening sentences I was always jotting down in my pocket notebook and never developing into full-length stories. If I hadn't been in this state of mind, I probably wouldn't have agreed to do what I did next.

25. Plucked from Despondency

There was a knock on my door.

"Come in," I said.

Peter entered.

"Jesus, Simon—you're in here with the lights out?"

"Yeah. I like it that way."

"What? Why? Did finding that dead guy get to you?"

"A little bit. It certainly hasn't elevated my mood."

"Turn a light on though—like, winter's not depressing enough as it is. People who are bingeing on heroin and shit like that, they always want to sit in dark rooms." He clicked the light on.

I shrugged.

"Anyway," he said, "frat rush is in an hour…"

"Yeah?"

" So…?"

"So what?"

"You made up your mind yet?"

"I like this movie I'm watching."

"What is it?"

"*Being There*."

"You've seen that before."

"Yeah. I know."

"Well… Why not 'be there' in reality? You're kind of like that gardener dude, anyway."

"Very funny."

"Seriously—put yourself out there."

"I don't know, man. I'm not sure I'm in the mood. Going to some sausage fest rush event with a bunch of dudes all giving you strong, manly handshakes and that kind of thing…"

"They're going to have free pizza."

I stopped cold.

"Yeah?"

"Yeah."

"Well… I *am* hungry… And free pizza is free pizza … But—"

"It's not like you're writing some kind of pact in your own blood. You don't even know if they'll select you. Maybe you'll get ding-ed." Getting "ding-ed" meant getting rejected as a pledge. "Just come for the food. Really…"

I paused, and bounced slightly back in my chair, summoning the will to stand up. "Fine," I said.

If it hadn't been for the promise of free pizza, I probably would never have gone with Pete. Consequently, I wouldn't have eventually discovered the truth about Professor Wilkes' death. Sometimes fate swings on a single, creaking hinge.

26. Non-Culinary Uses of Zucchini

After I put on a blazer and tie, Pete and I walked into campus together, chatting about what to expect. Frat row was roughly half a mile away.

"If I get in, I'm not going to get hazed, am I?" I asked.

"Well… Not any severe hazing. Just a lot of forced drinking I bet."

"Nothing involving the asshole, right?"

"What? Dude…"

"That's what I've heard—I mean, not about Beta but… They try to do weird hazing things at some of the other places. You know that squash player, Cowley Stinson?"

"Yeah?"

"He said the guys at Alpha stuck a zucchini in Milton Chavingham's ass. He'd drawn a short straw or something."

"They just want to create an aura of mystery."

"Well, that's some aura… How would that make anyone want to join? 'Oh, I'm just curious whether they'll sodomize me with a vegetable or not.'"

"Relax—no one's getting sodomized."

"If I thought you had any basis for saying that, only then would it be reassuring."

Obviously, the notion of pledging still irked me, didn't mesh with my sense of self. I figured I really *was* just going for the food.

As we approached Beta—a brick and stone building, three stories high—I noticed a BMW in a nearby parking lot with two bumper stickers: "Ski Killington!" and "No Justice, No Peace." It mixed privilege and radical social conscience in a way I found amusing—pure Wilbur College.

27. The Moose Casts a Cold Eye

Inside, the first thing I saw was a moose.

The moose looked out, surveying the high-ceilinged living room with jaded eyes, a cigarette drooping from its lower lip. To be perfectly accurate, it was really only the moose's *head* that was doing the surveying—the rest of the moose having been skinned and deposited somewhere in the Ontario woods forty years ago. Yet the complete character of a complete moose nevertheless seemed to be present in the room. It had grown accustomed to odd and even indefensible behavior during the course of its two score years affixed to the same oaken plaque, hanging above the big TV set (which got bigger every half-decade, when a new TV would be purchased). Its stuffed snout had snuffled noiselessly over too much depravity, its ears had heard too many boisterously profane shouts and the whispers of countless drunken seductions.

Overloaded, its fuzz-filled skull no longer sizzled with negative judgments on human nature (not that it had ever been capable of any, in the first place). It had run through the count years ago. Now, sitting in the moose's eye sockets, black marbles absorbed the arrival and departure of generations of fraternity brothers with utter disregard, unable to transmit any signals to the non-existent brain lying behind them—signals of longing, one would suppose, for the cold Northern marsh in which the former moose had made his home.

The moose presided over a large number of couches and a few arm chairs, most of them suffering from severely popped springs—twisted hunks of metal covered by a thin, conspicuously frayed layer of fabric, with rusting steel points often jutting through grotesquely. Fraternity brothers and prospective pledges were standing around the room or sitting on these broken down chairs, chatting each other up. But, in the center of the room, a number of pizza boxes sat on a large circular table—and there were plenty of slices left.

I went to town, trying to scarf down as much pizza as I could while simultaneously appearing nonchalant. I just wanted to get dinner, and get the hell out...

28. Sales Pitch

"Hey—are you Simon?"

I turned towards the voice with my mouth full, and found myself facing a tall, athletic guy with blazingly white teeth.

"Yesh," I said. I held up a finger to indicate I would require a moment to chew.

"Awesome. It's great that you're here—Pete really was hoping you'd rush Beta. He mentioned you to me."

60

The guy said this in a genuinely guileless way, as though he actually thought that it was great I was there. Quite a simulation.

"I'm Alex. I'm actually the President here."

"Cool," I said, warily. This was Pete's point guard friend.

"I know what you're thinking—a dude like you. I mean, tell me if I'm reading you wrong, but you strike me more as the introverted, writery-type—but you're also someone who needs socialization—just enough to sustain you. Like, some sort of intellectual community. Am I right?"

"Uh, well… Not exactly… I mean…" I paused.

This felt weird—snap judgments on my personality, probably based on something Pete had told him. But he'd captured my interest, if only through the suspicious nature of his eagerly projected charisma. I wasn't used to having my character read on short notice. It felt like something a cult leader might do. Yet, it was also kind of amusing.

"Okay, fine, I'll admit it," I said. "That sounds kind of like me."

"Good. I'm glad my pitch is working… How resistant are you to the idea of joining a frat? Strongly? Slightly?"

"I'm…somewhat resistant."

"Because you think it's all about acting like a dipshit."

"I mean, not necessarily," I said, defensively. "It just doesn't fit my—my self-image… I guess. I'm sort of an introvert... like you said."

"But what *is* your image of a fraternity? It's probably been culled from *Animal House*, *Old School*—TV and movies. Right?"

"Sure… It probably was culled from those things. No denying that."

"It's not always like that, though. I mean, it *is* like that in a lot of places. But Beta's different. It's not about pigging out or acting like a bunch of drunken assholes—it's more a way of fulfilling aspirations through fellowship."

Alex seemed *on*. I was impressed and a little intimidated by his energy. He was really focusing on me, making a lot of eye contact; it was unusual, like confronting an enthusiastic, chipper missionary who'd just knocked on your door. I didn't really *like* it, but I felt interested enough—from a writer's perspective—to continue chatting. You want to make a general survey of the humors that animate people.

29. A Thought Leader

He continued: "Just consider our most well-known alumni ... How many of those guys are really like Bluto Blutarsky? You know the two partners who founded Zin, the tech company—Timothy Fassbinder and Colby Stern? They were brothers here at Beta. I mean, at this very chapter."

"Yeah," I said. "I heard that."

Of course I'd heard it! They were two of the biggest technology leaders in Silicon Valley.

Alex explained that he had interned for Zin last summer, thanks to Beta's connections. He described the company's campus in extensive detail: a quasi-pastoral locale, with wide lawns crisscrossed by cement walkways where workers glided past on Segways, chattering away on Bluetooth headsets or gazing into Google Glass. Alex said that Zin always had a keg of organic craft beer available on the office floor, during work hours, and you could actually drink it as you worked. But the current CEO, the aforementioned Beta brother named Stern, had recently gone on a big health food kick and replaced all the sodas in the vending machines with pomegranate and carrot juices. That was the only negative Alex could think to mention, he added hastily.

"With all the experience I got during my summer there, I think I can probably land a job—consulting, coordinating systems, that kind of thing… What about you?"

"Me?"

"Yeah. What are your aspirations?"

I had to think about this. My aspirations didn't seem to involve anything particularly concrete in the external world. I liked writing, though I hadn't managed to write an actual work of fiction—like a short story or, God help me, a novel— nothing cohesive, or developed; just fragments, just beginnings. And I read a lot… But, as far as concrete career goals go (if they go anywhere), I'd been toying with the idea of becoming an English teacher. I didn't know if that qualified as an "aspiration" in Alex's eyes.

"I guess I want to teach English."

"Ah. As a Professor or in high school?"

"I think high school, actually. It was always my favorite class…"

"So, in a sense, you want to be a kind of 'thought leader?'"

"What?"

"Like, a 'thought leader'—dudes who give TED Talks and shit like that. Someone who's living the life of the mind and seeing how current trends will develop. Envisioning the future."

"I mean, I guess on one level you could sort of say that."

"Good. That's perfect. We want to create a future generation of thought leaders here—at Beta. Perfect. There's a place for you here, Simon."

30. The Beta Mold

The brothers seemed fairly diverse. They all had dumb nicknames, some of which seemed racially insensitive. "Turdburger" was a member of the crew team who had a single black uni-brow, like a long wooly caterpillar; "Jackie Chan" was a short, neatly dressed, gay Asian; "Merkin" was a scruffy looking guy who seemed to always be wearing the same Metallica t-shirt every time I'd seen him; "Louie Louie" smoked clove cigarettes and wore pajama bottoms along with a blue blazer, Oxford Shirt, and tie—he wore his pajama pants even to class. Alex's frat nickname was "Kaiser."

"A little ragged, I know," said Alex. "But we're fitting them into the Beta mold, gradually instilling the poise and bonhomie for which the Beta Man is renowned nationwide."

Despite the general friendliness pervading rush, feigned or not, there was one obvious downside to the frat: Beta's physical space was a dump. Although I didn't see anyone eating fistfuls of whey protein concentrate or jerking off to weird porn in the living room (something Oscar was doing once when I arrived at the house at midday; the video involved a watermelon and a seven foot tall woman), the Feng Shui situation wasn't much of an improvement. But, at the time, I hadn't seen overmuch of the squalor—I hadn't yet seen a brother chug ten beers before gagging himself in order to throw up in a trashcan. This being the case, I figured—why not? You can always run away from your problems.

(The reader will shortly see how my problems continued to hound me, nearly unto death).

I chatted with the other brothers—had about ten different conversations, all fairly short and each a replication of the last. It felt like I was speed-dating the entire house. I didn't get a great sense of who anyone really *was*—they all zoomed past me in a blur of back-slapping sociability, surrounded by the kind of social laughter and social charm that reveal absolutely nothing…

And, of course, I kept thinking about Wilkes the entire time. I felt somehow guilty to be participating in this ostensibly carefree social event so shortly after uncovering a violent death (even if it did turn out to be self-inflicted).

After rush was over, and I was walking back to the house alone (I don't know where Peter went), I decided to do something I'd been putting off: call my parents and tell them about discovering Wilkes' dead body. I might've done this earlier, but wasn't in the mood, for whatever reason.

31. Checking in with Mom and Dad

My mother's voice fell to a dreadful whisper. "You're saying he choked himself to death…" Her voice grew even more dramatic, as though she were pronouncing the final words of an evil incantation. "…While he was *masturbating*?"

"Yep," I said. "That's what the cops are saying, anyway."

"Whoa!" said my Dad, whom I hadn't realized was on the line. "I guess what the nuns told me in school was right. It *can* kill you. Or did they just say it would drive you blind?" He chortled inappropriately, before adding, "But, I know it's, uh, very sad and serious."

Being a master of the non sequitur, my mother suddenly asked me—"Are your hands dry?" Last winter, I'd complained about the dry skin peeling off my hands.

"A little," I said. I was irritated that *this* was the matter disquieting her, not the revelation about Wilkes' death.

"You should really buy some skin-repairing hand lotion—if you haven't already."

"Yeah. I'll get on it."

"Actually, you know what? I can buy you the lotion and Fed Ex it to you."

"*No*," I said. "I can buy my own hand lotion—obviously. "

"How are the new gloves we got you for Christmas? I hope you're wearing them. They're L.L. Bean and they're supposed to be 'Arctic Expedition Quality.'"

"No, I just walk around with my bare hands held out in front of me, exposed to the elements, getting frostbite and letting my fingers fall off."

"Well," said my mother, possibly hurt but certainly bringing her considerable acting skills to bear (she'd played a flying monkey in *The Wiz* in high school), "I guess you don't really *need* a mother to tell you these things. I guess I'm getting obsolete. You can fend for yourself now, right?" This was delivered in a tone of deadpan sincerity, as if her words weren't meant to be sarcastic.

"I'm *wearing* the damn gloves."

(To be strictly accurate, I wasn't wearing my right hand glove because I was holding the phone.)

"Good!" she said. "How are your classes?"

"Well, the one the aforementioned *dead* guy was teaching got canceled— naturally—so, I don't know what kind of grades we're going to receive or anything. But the other ones are okay. Well, actually, they suck. I mean, school is still school. Same old shit, different day."

As much fun as college is supposed to be—and occasionally is—the *school* part of school is always still… school. And I'll take "no school" over "school" any time.

"Have you declared a major yet?" she asked. "When do they have you do that, anyway?"

"In the spring… If it ever gets here."

32. Stabbed in the Sternum

The next day, I still felt optimistic about fraternity life. Riding high on this newfound sense of belonging—which, embarrassingly, felt pretty okay—I decided to figure out what was up with Canzoni and Wilkes. Naturally, I didn't want to confront Canzoni directly, but it occurred to me that Emma was in love with his class and that she might've spoken to him in office hours and got a better sense of the man.

I thought about shooting her an email. I was hesitant to approach her that way, though, since I'd previously asked a girl named Myrna Hoak to get lunch last year, via email. "You want to grab lunch some time?" I'd written. She wrote back, "Nice email. Now, try growing some balls and getting my number first or asking me in person. Dickhead."

I may be paraphrasing…

At any rate, it gave me the impression that email was a lame way of asking someone out, and I'd insisted on doing it face-to-face or by calling, since then. I mean, I wasn't actually asking Emma *out*; I wanted to question her about Canzoni. But the human heart is complicated and can entertain multiple motives at once: trying to solve a murder, trying to seduce a co-ed.

Momentarily putting the question of Emma aside, I decided that I'd start by doing some research. I would learn all I could about Canzoni and about Wilkes—I'd consider all angles, dig into their back-stories. And I'd commence reading the books Wilkes had given me, searching for some kind of clue. If I took it too seriously, the task seemed daunting—there was so much information to process, all while trying to attend class and function as a rough draft of a normal young adult male. But if I took it lightly yet slowly, and paced myself… Well, maybe nothing would happen. And yet… It requires an act of faith to imagine that, when you gaze at the chaotic muddle—at the discontinuous sequence of facts that we call life—some pattern, some order will manifest itself. I had that faith.

On one level, the idea that Wilkes had died from autoerotic asphyxiation seemed more than plausible. It was tabloid stuff—dark and gross, assuming merely superficial interest when set in print and extracted from its greater, more disturbing import. Plus, Wilkes *looked* like the kind of guy who might die that way. It's the type of icky truth we expect to leak out of a closed closet. Yet, the idea that he had been *murdered*, while in violation of Occam's Razor ("the simplest explanation is usually the most correct"), had a novelistic dimension to it. If this were true, it would affect all the facts around it—it would organize them into a narrative. The books sitting in my room would be potential clues, and old magazine articles on Carlo Canzoni would be a source of key context. Seen in a fresh light, tiny fragments, formerly bearing no relation to one another, would re-align. My daily life would become a wilderness of symbolism—to be investigated with the careful, persistent application of my attention. I could stop merely shuffling through it.

These were some of the thoughts swirling through my head as I drowsed through my classes, before meeting up with the fencing club in the gymnasium.

The basketball courts were located centrally, and, as I entered, the squeak of sneakers and brief grunts and shouts played acoustically around me. A hallway led towards the swimming pool, and a dim echo issued from it, like the blood rush sounds within a shell.

The fencing strip was laid out with red tape, off to the side of the basketball courts. I'd convinced Pete to join the club with me—initially, I'd wanted to join the Kendo club, but he said he wouldn't do it, because dressing up in that kind of uniform "wasn't [his] kind of thing." He was a little too cool, sometimes, as you've no doubt already gathered, and the malady's severity had deepened. In retrospect, this seems like another ominous sign, evidence of fatal insecurity and what I believe psychiatrists call "a damaged core sense of self."

We were facing off against each other.

I parried Pete's thrust, and he withdrew. Suddenly he yelled, "Look out—a dead guy's penis!"

Sad to say it, but I was actually disconcerted by this. He lunged again and scored a point, hitting me directly on the sternum and winning the match.

"That's *not* funny!" I shouted.

For some reason, the impress of the point of the foil lingered in the center of my chest for another two hours. It was irritating. I don't know why.

33. Entombed

As we were coming out of the gym, we were kidnapped.

A black van pulled up, and two balaclava wearing men leaped out of the back, tackling us.

"Ooh, we got ourselves a hoss!" said the one sitting on top of me. "I can make you squeal like a piggy!" He laughed.

At first, I thought these two dudes, busily stuffing us into the back of a black van and then hog-tying us, were the same people who had assassinated Wilkes. I was ready to attempt resistance, preparing my thumbs to gouge out an eye or two. But, absorbing context clues—like the fact that Pete seemed to be taking this rather pacifically—I realized that we'd both been accepted as pledges at Beta.

The van careened through campus, almost hitting two kids who were on their smart-phones at a crosswalk (maybe they were playing *Silly Squirrels*?) before screeching into Beta's parking lot.

Our two assailants—soon revealed as Merkin and Turdburger—dumped us on the floor of Beta's basement, next to other hog-tied pledges. The floor was sticky with stale-beer.

The other brothers entered and untied us. Now, it was time to perform the accepted motions: go through the initial fraternity rites, subject ourselves to the various humiliations reserved for new brothers, merge and become one collective organism, a kind of Portuguese Man o' War.

This ceremony was to occur in the tomb room, a high-ceilinged concrete cavern located off the main basement and accessed by a door that usually remained locked. A bare marble altar sat in the center, and the walls were lined with cold stone benches. Whereas the main basement repulsed with its proliferation of grimy detail—dozens of old empty beer cans tossed in the corners, cinderblock walls scrawled with jovially obscene graffiti, the floors coated with dried spillings—the tomb room's vacuity was unnerving.

At the very heart of the building was something utterly empty, and its altar was the altar of no received tradition of wisdom. The walls were bare, the floor was surprisingly clean; the room was used primarily for these initiatory rites (though occasionally, on big party nights, it was opened to accommodate the crowds). Only at the edges where the benches met the wall could you detect particulate matter—a fine silvery dust that came off on your finger when you traced it.

That's where I was sitting on my first official night as a Beta pledge. As I waited, somewhat nervous, I traced the edge and examined the dust. In the hot lights running across the ceiling, it glittered a little. But it was truly nothing.

I looked around at the other pledges, sizing them up. They were all familiar figures. There was Greg Ramirez, overweight and very pale, yet also Mexican. There was Sebastian Rauner-Weed, who wore a perpetual half-smile— I don't know whether this was meant to connote inner cool, a sense of detached and half-bemused superiority, or what. It may have been mere defensive or evasive action, meant to keep the spirit locked away safely somewhere down in the hold (to give it the most charitable possible reading). But it still made me uneasy and I didn't trust it. And then there was Duncan Connor, who had red hair and persistently fidgeting fingers—or, at least, they were fidgeting while we stood in the tomb room. They tapped manically along the side of his pant leg, and fingered the shapes of his keys and wallet through the fabric. They suddenly darted towards the pocket containing his cell-phone and then refrained. A few other pledges sat further down the bench—I didn't give them much of a look-over.

The winter pledge class wasn't particularly big, because the winter pledge class never is. Most students pledged in the fall. These were campus dregs.

To my eyes, the thin, ragged line in which I found myself seemed a chance assortment. Yet, underneath the superficial differences, in substance, they were comprised of the same human putty—riddled with insecurities, desperate to belong. These chumps were ready and willing, waiting to be aggressively molded by the fingers of fraternal authority, until they perfectly fit the "Beta Mold"—whatever *that* was! As I stood there, of course, I felt like an absolute idiot, though I guess "dolt" would somehow be the most apt word choice.

34. Amish

Alex, wearing a red hooded robe, entered, followed by the other frat officers in train. There was an inverted Catholic atmosphere to the proceedings—like a Black Mass parody. We had to sit and stand and kneel. We had to ritualistically chug beers. We had to be paddled on the ass with a wooden paddle, perforated with holes so it whipped through the air with ease… I don't want to lead you through the whole routine, which you've probably seen depicted in movies and TV shows before. It was intense, yet it had all the static atmosphere of a simulation, of roles enacted.

Eventually, we pledges were left to each chug ten (light) beers. I sipped at my first can of Keystone Light, growing increasingly doubtful about the whole business. This wasn't alleviating anything.

Concurrently, the senior brothers debated what our frat nicknames should be. Acres of solemn thought had been reserved for the free range of this issue.

After dispensing with Pete—who received the nickname "Schwartz"—they came around to the subject of my own nickname.

"What about 'Rhymin' Simon'?"

"What??? Does he rhyme things?"

"Occasionally," I said, breaking in. "I've been experimenting with writing poetry on and off for a number of—"

"Shut the fuck up!" said Alex. "You turds stay out of the process, entirely. In fact, get in the other room."

We left the tomb room, and went into the main basement, where we could still hear the entire discussion.

"What about 'Pubes'?"

"You mean—just 'Pubes'?"

"Yeah. Why not? He has dark brown hair, and it's kind of curly. Pubes."

"Hmmm…" Alex was thinking.

Someone else piped up. "What about Mr. Pubes?"

"Mr. Pubes… I like that even better."

My heart was racing with fear. I didn't want to be Mr. Pubes.

"Mr. Pubes… Mr. Pubes…" Alex paused for a long time, before definitively saying, "Nah."

He explained his line of reasoning. "We already called Murphy 'Merkin' when he pledged in the fall. I don't want to have more than one pube-themed nickname. It could get confusing."

The rest of the room murmured their assent.

"What about Jew Fro?"

"Is Simon Jewish? Plus he doesn't really have a 'fro, at all. His hair's short."

"No," said Alex. "We said we were probably gonna call that other kid, 'Jew Fro,' remember? The actually Jewy one… Plus, it gets confusing when you start going ethnic all the time."

"What about 'Black Rose'?"

"What? No. What the fuck does that even mean?"

"What about 'Amish'?"

"He doesn't have a neckbeard like that though."

"Yeah, but he's from Pennsylvania…"

"Hmmm…" Alex considered. "Alright—Amish works."

I felt relieved.

Thereafter they discussed whether they should name an Asian pledge Jet-Li or Bruce Lee, considering that Jackie Chan was already taken. ("General Tso" was also suggested, though rejected since a past brother had borne that title.)

Jet-Li won.

35. My Most Prized Possession

When released, I came home drunk to discover that Oscar and Curtis were both sitting on the futon, fiddling with their phones. The tell-tale theme song started up— *Silly Squirrels* again.

"Hey," I said, "What's the deal with this game? Like, what's so special about some squirrels, like, picking up acorns? Here—let me look at it…"

I pawed at Oscar's phone. He tugged it away and stared at me with a look of pure savagery. He actually bared his teeth, *snarling*.

"Curt," I said, obviously intoxicated, "Let me take a look at it. Hit pause or something. I want to get in on this *craze*."

"No," he said, listlessly, still focused entirely on the game.

"What? There's no pause button? You can't take a second to let me see the damn *craze*?"

"No," he said.

"Alright," I said. "Alright. Jesus. Alright—fine by me. Guess I won't get in on the *craze*. Guess it's just another *craze* I'll miss out on. Never get in on the crazes. Nope. Never. Not me… Behind the curve."

After I got to my room, I fished through the bottom drawer under my desk until I found "my most prized possession"—at least, you can call it that if you want, though I'm not sure how highly I prize any of my possessions. I thought I'd sell it in later years if I ever needed the cash.

It was a baseball signed by David Ortiz. I got it when he came to a kids' baseball camp I attended in elementary school. I held it and turned it over in my hand, feeling the seams. Something about this grounded me, established a sense of continuity with that earlier, better time. Then, when I felt calm and almost sober, I put it back in the drawer.

I slept a little better than I had the night before. .

36. Relentless Tedium and "Beaver Hunts"

People romanticize fraternity life—or rather, they curiously mingle romanticism with scatological interest and disgust. Consider all the frat comedies, from *Animal House* to *Old School*—the experience is always portrayed as being both rancid and idyllic. My own (brief) experience was totally different: in two words, relentless tedium.

I constantly stood outside myself, critically, mocking everything I was doing—and everything everyone else was doing. The feeling of drunkenness remains fresh if endured once or twice a week, but no more than that. And we pledges were drunk all the time. Drunk with the other brothers on a Tuesday or a Wednesday, I felt a sober revulsion constant within my own delirium. At the end of the night, I would look in the mirror and hate the scruffy, feral creature staring back at me with the beer-puffy face of a low-rent Mr. Hyde. In the midst of the constant partying, my mouth laughed—but no other part of me.

It wasn't Sodom, and it wasn't Gomorrah. It wasn't anarchy either. It was a loose arrangement, not very compelling—the silent deterioration of an old order into a mild, blandly decadent new one. I suppose it wasn't anything really. It was a celebration of the lowest common denominator. And it was, with a sigh, just what you were expecting.

My schoolwork suffered perceptibly during my brief sojourn in Frat Land. I'd only skipped class when I was sick once or twice, but I ditched *most* of my courses during the first awful spasms of pledge term—the only spasms that I, fortunately, would suffer. No one, as far as I know, had to put anything up his butt, but there was forced drinking every day. Occasionally, Alex would lean towards me after some particularly demeaning command ("you're cleaning out the puke barrel") and wink, letting me know it was all, essentially, an act. He even said once, "This is just pledge term shit."

I was consuming about 10 or 11 beers a day on average by virtual requirement, and began to look bloated and bleary-eyed within the initial week. Disconnected from that thin, luminescent sliver of self, always glowing within one's forehead, I felt hypnotized… I have never had a party boy's constitution.

As for hazing, we had to eat worms—fat night crawlers purchased alive from a bait shop. We were blindfolded and laid, one at a time, in a coffin before a bucket of maggots was poured onto us (that was probably the worst thing that happened). We were abandoned in the middle of nowhere and forced to hitchhike back home. A lonely and excessively talkative trucker picked up Pete and me. He kept looking out the window for attractive female drivers—or, actually, *any* female drivers.

Whenever he saw a woman, even if she was driving a mini-van full of kids, he would pick up his C.B. radio and say, "Beaver hunt in progress on Route

__ near Exit __." When we were getting close to New Hamelin, he wanted us to keep going with him to a strip club, which was a half hour farther down the road. He was insistent: "You gotta see this place. There's a girl who pours beer"—he paused for effect—"out of her ass!" We firmly declined, and he finally relented and dropped us off.

Parties happened in the disgusting basement, a concrete hole redolent of stale beer. It felt cramped, even without anyone in it, and it was usually packed to the gills with drunken idiots. The floor was always sticky with the spillage from the revelers' cups; the soles of your sneakers pulled off the floor with the sound of Velcro. I remember another brother telling me that he spent so much time drinking in the basement that when he stepped outside it felt weird when his feet *didn't* stick to the ground. I still find this statement extremely depressing.

One day, in unwitting imitation of a wager once made in 18th Century England, we bet on which raindrop would make it to the bottom of a window first. I lost fifty dollars.

Oh, and they seduced me into smoking hookah. I was under the impression that this was the healthfood version of smoking, but it's actually pretty terrible for you.

37. Character Typology

Still, within this external tedium, I managed to indulge my interior life—a source of secret excitement. Since privately deciding to investigate Wilkes' death—or, at least, developing my own speculations in a recreational manner (akin to so many hermetic conspiracy theorists, typing blog posts about the Grassy Knoll as they sit in their mothers' finished basements) a fantasy began to entertain itself, almost unbidden, in my mind. I had the idea that if I simply paid very close attention to my life, it would begin to manifest stories. These frat brothers around me weren't just privileged idiots, leading lives of quiet desperation. They were *characters*.

For instance, one of the brothers, a foreign exchange student, was a Senegalese Prince named Omar Seck (frat nickname: "Chumbawumba"). I have no idea how he wound up in Beta, and I can't recall ever seeing him participate in any of the routine debauchery. When approached, Omar was friendly, but he typically retained the posture of a detached observer. Despite being a senior member of the frat, he seemed to go largely unnoticed by the others—though not unnoticed in a hostile way. He was a secret stowaway in the ship. Because he was so *still*, so calm and collected, the average Beta bro couldn't *see* him—just as the visual acuity of the T. Rex is based on movement. He waited and watched; I imagined that he embodied the contemplative mindset I desired for myself. Perhaps he was already witnessing life as a story, rather than as a colossal muddle. He had attained that grade of perception.

Unfortunately, I was so swept along by the demeaning tasks and drunken delirium of pledge term that I didn't get to make much conversation with Omar.

Alex, too, could take on the dimensions of a character, though almost the polar opposite of the Senegalese Prince's type.

For one thing, you could tell Alex was someone who never second-guessed himself. I think he always thought his motives were pure, even when they obviously, explicitly were not. Or, more likely, he simply never thought about what his motives were.

In a sense, you could say that Alex "knew himself"—that is, he understood his *persona* in full. And since, by and large, that is what the world reckons by, you could say, in debauched English, that he had "self-knowledge."

But his *essence* remained unknown, both to himself and to everyone else. I won't go so far as to add "if he even *had* an essence to be known"; I think he did, but it was hibernating in some distant, internal cavern, which would've been extremely difficult—if not impossible—to access. It would've required a super-effort, of sorts.

Alex would sometimes play the charismatic figure he'd adopted the first night I met him—the smooth-talker, the worldly-wiseman. But, at other moments, he could embrace the role of comic pledge-master sadist, or of a sensitive soft-spoken young gentleman whom a certain kind of girl found intriguing, or of a student-athlete with surprisingly decent grades. Yet within all these guises, I did not know whether there was a "core sense of self." In Omar's stillness, I sensed this very "core sense of self," but none of the shifting miasmatic personas that Alex so habitually displayed.

I never managed to ascertain much about Alex's home life. If there was some dark nugget of childhood trauma, whereby Alex's more troubling tendencies might be explained, I couldn't recover it. The means of his evolution (devolution?) from mewling infant to fraternity house Pol Pot have been lost to history. As far as any family life goes, all I remember is Alex once saying, "Hurry up—I'm meeting my parents at the Kayak Club in fifteen minutes." (The Kayak Club was a fancy restaurant in New Hamelin, not anything involving traditional Inuit watercraft).

He had offered this comment about his parents whilst speaking to to a pledge—could it have been Jet Li?—who had been dressed in a tiara, assless chaps, and a hot pink brassiere. The pledge was in the process of force-chugging a half-gallon of clam juice, as punishment for some minor and possibly imaginary infraction, the nature of which I no longer recall. He kept pausing to gag audibly in a way that made me want to gag, audibly.

38. On the Periphery

In whining about fraternity life—a mode of existence that many budding men of leisure clearly find "fun"—I recognize that I run the risk of continuously bewailing my outcast state and making things sound worse than they really were. Yet, in truth, I staved off any potential depression, immersing myself in the search for clues about Wilkes and Canzoni. If I were only able to hover on the periphery and not pledge my actual *self* to Beta—well, fine, I'd hover on the periphery. But, internally, I'd be working on the mystery of Wilkes' death. I didn't make a wildly impressive amount of headway, gradually reading through the books Wilkes had left me with, reading old interviews with Canzoni in which he cryptically teased interviewers with details about his current projects. I wanted something to pop out at me. Not much did.

Part of the reason I joined Beta was because I thought that, if I wanted to be a writer, I mustn't refuse experiences. This was, in reality, a profoundly flawed notion. Some experiences are merely draining—they inspire nothing— and you can create more from pure imagination than people commonly realize. While "write what you know" is a noble piece of advice, justly repeated in all creative writing seminars from the dawn of time to the present, I wonder if the truly inspired moments in a literary work—the moments that *find us*, as Samuel Taylor Coleridge would have put it—really do emerge from nowhere, a sudden light flashing in the Deep. The writer is immersed intently in the project of writing what he or she "knows"—fulfilling that duty—when something suddenly enters the mind from outside the circumference of lived experience. Perhaps, it has no autobiographical referent, yet it is… *a new thing*. A good thing. The pieces of experience we *can't* have or have failed to have, come to possess, in our writing, the most vivid and truthful representation. That's what I think, anyway, if you're willing to excuse the digression.

The only reason I'm going on about this is to explain why I kept, and keep, a pocket notebook. I want to mark down what I'm really witnessing, but also that which I've never seen, heard, smelled, touched, or tasted, yet which somehow has entered my mind, has left an impression on me. I guess there are outer impressions and inner impressions—impressions left not by outside forces, but by mysterious internal visitants, strange animals coming to drink at an unusually quite and still pool (to rip a metaphor I heard once from a Buddhist teacher). At any rate, to record them requires a fisherman's patience, and some of the same submission to greater forces—to weather, to Fate.

As I grew occupied with the bizarre circumstances attending Wilkes' demise, I started to use the pocket notebook for another purpose. I know it's ridiculous to play private eye (the hobby of many manic people, investigating various conspiracy theories) but, nevertheless, I kept drawing up speculative scenarios in my little book, alternative theories of Wilkes' demise.

Obviously, after speaking to Officer Sheerhan, I had no confidence in local law enforcement whatsoever. So, even though I told myself I was doing this in a spirit of morbid curioisity, the idea of public service—of finding justice for poor Wilkes and catching a murderer—was never too far from my mind. But, at the time, if you'd asked me whether Wilkes had been murdered, I would've said, "No," while in the notebook, privately entertaining my suspicions. I jotted down stray details, which later turned out to have no relevance, culled from the Central

Asian books. I sensed the irrationality of my project, the way it was running strictly on intuition.

Also, I didn't like the uniquely *exposed* way in which he had perished. The idea that his (still hypothetical) murderer had arranged his corpse so that his penis would be dangling out upon discovery... Frankly, this enraged me. I didn't like the thought of being murdered myself, of course, but I strenuously objected to the additional indignity of being framed for autoerotic "death by misadventure." It made it worse, somehow—more unfair. Perhaps if I'd found Wilkes with his brains splattered over the wall and a pistol smoking at his feet, I would not have felt so moved to investigate...

39. Mr. T

While all this frat business was going on, I was still living at my old address. Only juniors and seniors were actually able to move into the frat. There wasn't enough space for anyone else. Back at the Barnum Street house, a dusty stasis had settled grimly into place. Curtis and Oscar stared at their phones while playing *Silly Squirrels*, urinated into bottles, and let drool seep down their chins. They seemed incapable of fending for themselves, infants abandoned on the rocks.

Then, suddenly, they would shift gears, becoming all activity. They would resume their Ben Franklin-esque postures as men of the world, as self-consciously ambitious Young Turks. I never observed the moment of transition happening, never saw when they finally put down their phones and got back to the business of living, but I thought it strange. When did they get their fill of the game? What shock was sufficient to rupture the spell, and affect a temporary yet effective cure on the zombies? Nothing I ever said to them while they were playing seemed to break through. They were completely locked in.

Somehow, at the same time, Curtis was taking a fraternity over. He had decided to winter-pledge a frat too, but instead of joining the frat with the other football players, he decided to pledge the nerdiest house on campus, Zeta (other letters redacted again). "They'll view me like a god—like a *giant among men*," he said.

Whereas Alpha was for WASP superheroes with ripplingly muscular jaws, and Beta catered to the nobody who wanted to be somebody (without also becoming painfully distinguished from the mass of fellow ostensible somebodies), Zeta was for lost causes. You could stand outside and hear the post-nasal drip and the low shush of collective mouth-breathing.

A crowd of young and eager disciples attended Curtis in the cafeteria, and hung on his words of pith and vital truth. He was like a less articulate version of your standard cult leader. I could easily imagine myself returning home and finding the bodies of dead Zeta pledges littering the hardwood, with an empty pitcher, formerly filled with poison Kool-Aid, sitting on the coffee table.

After the usual round of forced-drinking at Beta, I entered the house one night to find Curtis up, momentarily divorced from *Silly Squirrels*. Instead, he was picking his nose and sticking the boogers on a greasy paper plate than had been lying on the coffee table for a month.

"How's life at Zeta?" I asked.

"I'm like *Napoleon* to those sacks of puss," said Curtis. "I'm just a pledge but they already want me to be their president. Seriously. They nominated me."

"Wow."

"Yeah. They really don't have the first clue over there. But I'm nudging them along. You can't make any of these guys into George Clooney overnight— or, you can't make them into George Clooney, period. But you can do something with this human putty. Like, you can teach them to identify their female equivalents, and get them to spawn. It's very gnarly, real basic. But it's something, at least. I already tutored one kid into getting a handjob from some other computer nerd girl. I gave him a script, and he wrote notes on the back of his hand. The problem isn't so much the shitty social skills. The problem is will-power. None of these guys has will-power. They want to stay in their rooms and beat off to porn about British nannies getting banged by travelling gypsies. That kind of thing. You've got to push them out of their nest, you know? Like a mama bird. Just push them out. And they'll fly or they won't. But either way they'll thank you for it... They'll thank you for it. Also, just wanted to say, I looked at that T.S. Eliot book you left sitting on the coffee table."

"Yeah?"

"Yeah. It sucked dick."

Curtis explained that poetry was useless—actually, I think he said it was "faggy." In his eyes, only physically useful things were really useful. They were "real shit." If he'd read a poem instructing him on how to develop his lats, maybe he would've changed his mind. Curtis's intellect, while in some sense real, could not burden him, so narrowly was it channeled.

And me? Did I share similar prejudices, only in reverse? Did I think businessmen and bodybuilders were inherently anti-poetical? Of course not. In the eyes of a writer (even one who can only write bits and pieces like myself) a businessman is pure poetic material.

"I was looking at it," said Curtis, "reading about this J. Alfred Prufrock dude, who's apparently a bald guy or some shit."

"His hair is growing thin."

"Yeah. And I was like, 'What the fuck is this?' I don't view things that way."

"You don't want to disturb the universe? I thought you were all about that kind of disruption."

"Yeah. Disrupting it with my dick."

"How's the internship hunt going, anyway?"

"I'm up to my nuts in offers. I could intern at Seaworld, Microsoft, Chobani yogurt… But I think I'm gonna go with Zin."

"Yeah?" I was, of course, intrigued. "How did you finagle that?"

"Oh, you know, my dad is friends with some dude who knows some other dude. They all belonged to the same secret society at Yale. You know, the one where they have you jerk off in a coffin?"

"Skull and Bones?"

"If they make you lie in a coffin and jerk off, then that's the one."

"So… Zin. What do you like about it? How does it beat Seaworld?"

"The amenities. They have a masseuse you can visit any time during the workday when you're feeling stressed. I mean, they let you pet all the dolphins and whales you want at Seaworld…Which could be pretty relaxing too. But I thought the masseuse would be cooler. Maybe you'll get a happy ending…"

"Interns can use the masseuse?"

Disquiet and uncertainty passed over Curt's eyes.

"Yeah…" he said. "Yeah, I think so."

"That's cool."

"You looking for any internships?"

"No," I said. "Should I be?"

"Yeah, dude. Of course."

"What should I be interning for?"

"Something that gets you mad pussy."

I scrambled for a response. "Would interning at the Pringles company do that?"

"Pringles?"

"Yeah. Why not? Everybody loves Pringles."

"Nah, man. It's gotta be something with, you know, technology and finance and all that stuff."

"But I like Pringles better than technology and finance and all that stuff. Don't I want to meet a girl who shares my interests?"

"Yeah, but an interest in *chips*, dude? That's not really an interest. You have to be interested in, you know… you know… economics and synergizing and stuff like that."

I didn't try to explain that I hadn't made a serious suggestion. So I just asked, "What's synergizing?"

"I don't know, man. But I'm sure it gets you laid."

"Hmm."

"Business is tough right now, though. I'll give you that. You got to pick the right industries to intern for, cause they're all, uh, contracting. Like, it's cool to be an intern for Apple. But it wouldn't be cool to be an intern for, like, a Russian Church."

"Would it be cool to intern for *any*thing religious?"

"No, only if it was a company that made, like, customized meditation cushions that were designed to your own specifics with lasers. Too bad all these industries are contracting. Like religion. Too bad we didn't get a more traditional black man to be president when we needed one. Like Mr. T. He'd have sorted things out. Of course, the guys we have now are getting it together. Finally."

"What this about Mr. T?"

"You know. From that show in the '80s. 'I pity the fool.' The dude with the Mohawk. Black dude. He's black."

40. The Himmelman Valve

Curtis liked to play around at being a businessman. He would fiddle with spreadsheets on his computer, or rush about campus sipping a Starbucks. He liked the *idea* of being a businessman, of powering through the day before loosening his tie in the VIP lounge of a Manhattan strip club, better than he actually liked doing business. He didn't realize that movies like *The Wolf of Wall Street* were meant to be ironic (at least, theoretically ironic). He went all in on the image: the life of steel financial structures harboring a pure barbarism, glass skyscrapers soaked from the inside with Id.

Now, however, Curtis had a real business assignment. He was helping his father deal with the fall-out caused by the terminally faulty "Himmelman Valve," a product imperfectly manufactured by Curt's father's company. This widespread crisis began with the disastrous failure of a Slurpee machine at a 7/11 in Nebraska, before having a much broader destructive effect on an international scale.

Curt's father was the CEO and founder of an extremely large corporation that specialized in making valves—any kind of valve, to let anything out and keep anything in. There were artificial valves for hearts; valves for dispensing frozen yogurt; valves for injecting lubricating oil onto the innards of machinery. The valves came in all sizes and could (or, rather, could not) let blood flow through the heart or direct the course of water moving through the Hoover Dam. They were simultaneously all-purpose and totally defective.

Before becoming involved in the valve and seal business, Himmelman Sr. had, according to Curt, almost played in the NHL. I don't know the exact nature of this "almost," but it haunted Curt. He largely bought into the sports culture of his family (he was the second-best javelin thrower at Wilbur), while occasionally showing cryptic signs indicative of suppressed rebellion. Once, I returned to the apartment to find him wearing eye-shadow and listening to melancholic-romantic '80s New Wave music (The Cure, specifically). He looked up at me "like a guilty thing surprised." I simply stared back for a moment, blinking, not quite comprehending, and then went to my room. We never broached the subject, although I came close to bringing it up once or twice—in a spirit of helpfulness, of course. But I was unsure how to render that help articulately.

At any rate, the valves didn't work. They wouldn't let anything in *or* out. They merely clogged systems, remaining disruptive and anti-functional, until they burst, causing major leakage and total system failure. The valves were also made out of a special synthetic material, developed over many years in many laboratories, which turned out to be utterly fragile and susceptible to rapid corrosion. It would eventually shatter, permitting whatever fluid it had previously been channeling and restraining to come roaring through.

In this, one finds a parable. Like Emily Dickinson said, the human attention has its valves too, nationally congested as they may seem to be. They can shut like stone. They can crack in flood.

41. Scenarios

Scribbling in my notebook, I considered multiple possibilities.

"Wilkes having affair? Killed by jealous husband?" This seemed unlikely. Wilkes was in a happy if low-key relationship with a mousy entomologist, who, according to the police, was visiting her mother in Tampa when the murder occurred. At any rate, I had no reason to entertain such a conclusion.

"Wilkes killed by someone from a Zeppelin tribute band? Local music scene?" This theory *did* have slightly more evidence to back it up. Wilkes had been in a Zeppelin tribute band for a few years (he was the bassist, the John Paul Jones member) but told my class that he'd recently parted with the others over "creative differences." Considering that they only played covers, I have no idea what those "differences" might have been! Maybe they argued about whether the lead singer should stuff a cucumber in the front of his pants before concerts like the real Robert Plant? Who knows! At any rate, this theory seemed slightly more plausible, if still farfetched.

Had the murderer left Wilkes' naked corpse positioned in such a way that it indicated clues related to art history? Probably not.

Yet, the theories I mentioned were secondary or tertiary. The central theory—the "A" theory—had something to do with Canzoni, and likely with his government military connections. I imagined black ops swooping into Wilkes office, injecting him with an undetectable poison and then staging his autoerotic

89

demise. But why? I had absolutely no idea. There was insufficient evidence all around. Hence this wasn't even a "theory," since I didn't have any idea what it could be. It was more of a vague hypothesis, grafted onto the slightest circumstantial connection: the fact that he met with Canzoni for mysterious reasons one day, and showed up dead the following morning.

And then there was the one hint, the only piece of potential evidence— Wilkes' phone call, the request for the books he'd given me, which he'd made based on something Canzoni had presumably told him. But two professors grabbing a meal together was no big deal, after all… And what could Central Asian anthropology have to do with Canzoni's advanced topic physics and technological wonders? Something crucial was evidently hidden in the books Wilkes had given me. Why else would he ask for them back? And given his own lackadaisical attitude towards his subject, it must've been because Canzoni (or *someone*) had requested them. Or maybe something Canzoni had said reminded Wilkes of something else, and he realized he needed one of the books in order to… what? It was all too confusing, and I've never been a very logical, sequential kind of thinker. I proceed by intuitive leaps or by what Fortune reveals to me.

My scribbled observations on Wilkes and Canzoni mingled with my own attempts to write. I couldn't quell my passion for fragments, and my notebook became like an ashtray filled with the long stems of barely smoked cigarettes. Blaze once, puff, and discard... There's a release in paying close attention to something for a sustained period of time. You realize how un-free the tumult of your thoughts can be—a strangely deterministic chaos—and feel liberated into the clear apprehension of one thing, taking each moment at a time, keeping an even pace.

If I ever broke away from beginnings and followed through on a project, I supposed that I would write some kind of satire. I didn't sense the capacity within myself to create fully-fleshed or "deep" characters—at least, not yet. At the same time, a satire seemed irrelevant, given that the nature of my own reality required very little, indeed no exaggeration, to grant it the status of "satire." So maybe I would function merely as a reporter, a faint-hearted observer transcribing the harshly inked lines of Reality from a comfortable position on the sidelines. That seemed to suit my own personality well enough, and I didn't feel—at least, on the conscious level—impelled to become a protagonist in my own story. I would intrude with the occasional snarky aside, bitter reminiscence, or terse summing-up.

In my hunger for experiences (said hunger being my justification for joining a frat) I'd forgotten the words of Lao Tzu: "Without stepping out of my door, I may know the ways of heaven." Still, I don't particularly regret stepping out of my door, though it was not "the ways of heaven" that I learned. Rather, it was part of my inevitable development to be drawn first to that other realm, to stand in the midst of its furious downward turning gyre, and tell of what I saw there.

In stepping out of my door, I discovered a story—a true story. Yet, it seemed like it had been fermented within a sick and solitary mind, one that had never ventured outside its cavern, entertaining its fever dream in the dark interior of a sealed cask.

42. The Wilbur Bubble

Students at Wilbur lived in what was popularly called "The Wilbur Bubble." A place can be academically oriented, ostensibly cosmopolitan and connected with the problems of the wider world, and yet, outside the classroom, utterly provincial. "Kappas are such whores!"—I heard a member of Delta, a rival sorority, drunkenly shout this to her friend as I walked towards the cafeteria one day. It's a prime example of the kind of manufactured conversation topic (Greek Life stereotypes) that dominated discussion at Wilbur. The Greek system generated a lot of chatter, provoked numerous snarky judgments and alleged witticisms, but it didn't relate to anything outside itself. It was insular, a self-enclosed system.

Not to continue griping—I prefer to think of this as "analysis" rather than griping—but the same thing was true of the faculty. Their debates about the concerns of the age were frequently related to their own squabbles. They could conceive of the mind of a fellow elite liberal arts professor, but had no theory of mind they might apply to someone from, say, Nebraska or Ohio, or even rural New Hampshire. Thus, they assumed that the rest of America was primarily comprised of shirtless wild-eyed farmers in overalls, gibbering in tongues while attempting to exorcise the homosexual demons out of helpless youths.

Let's cite a relevant example of insular collegiate politics:

Wesley Cross was a white kid with dread locks who graduated from Choate before coming to Wilbur. He was very active in campus politics. One time, he'd stumbled drunkenly into the cafeteria bathroom while I was washing my hands. "Piece of advice…" he said, aiming for the urinal but splattering the floor. "Fuck a lot of bitches. Get a slice of that good Sicilian poon-tang—that's what the fuck I'm talkin' about."

The next week, I saw him spear-heading a Students for Feminism campaign. As I walked past the steps of the student center where he was standing, surrounded by a rapt crowd, I could hear him earnestly preaching, "Women aren't objects—they are our mothers, our sisters..."

I'd taken one class with Wesley, a mandatory "freshman seminar." These seminars were small classes, designed to facilitate close interaction with professors. There were about ten students in each seminar. I chose one on the works of Kafka, and for some reason, so did Wes. It would've been a decent class if he hadn't ceaselessly interrupted it with wild objections. He thought "A Hunger Artist" shouldn't be taught because it was an "advertisement for anorexia." During a discussion of Kafka's Zionism, and plans to emigrate to Israel, Wesley announced that, after the course had concluded, he would thereafter boycott Kafka in order to show solidarity with the sufferings of the Palestinians. He started wearing a *keffiyeh* to the seminar after that.

What became painfully obvious was that Wes's political objections were essentially a way of avoiding the reading while still participating in class. I doubt he cracked open *any* of Kafka's books throughout the duration of the course, but I imagine he passed since the professor praised him for his "social engagement." This exemplified his entire attitude: the frivolous application of serious charges, masking a fundamentally self-interested and hollow core.

Wes tried to drain the charm out of life whenever he possibly could. For instance, Wilbur used to have a Christmas display every year, with a big tree at the center of the Green. It was complemented by a giant menorah for Chanukah and a Kwanzaa thing (I can't remember what represented Kwanzaa) outside the student center. But, last year, Wes protested the display. He staged a hunger strike that lasted from after lunch on December 3rd to before dinner on the same day. He objected to the menorah, claiming it was "Pro-Zionist"—which, of course, seems like a fairly anti-Semitic equivalence, since any Jewish observance would then be politically objectionable. But Wes never considered these things. He also said the Christmas tree was objectionable because of "The Crusades."

Everyone seemed to be ignoring him and the issue felt destined to evaporate into the ether. Unfortunately, members of Alpha (allegedly, but everyone knew it really happened) filled Christmas stockings with stones, disguised themselves in bearded Santa costumes, and ambushed Wes as he was leaving the student center late one night. They beat him senseless, all while singing "Rudolph the Red Nosed Reindeer."

From his hospital bed, Wes raged online, claiming that he was urinating blood. He posted a picture of a plastic cup full of red liquid to prove it.

Thanks to this shocking display of violence, refreshing as it may have seemed to many, the administration actually *did* abolish the Christmas display. The tree, the menorah, and the Kwanzaa thingy were all carted away. The only public indication that the holidays were upon us was a banner hanging over the cafeteria, reading "Happy Winter!"

As leader of a cadre of activists, Wes proposed having a camera system installed on campus, which could be used to monitor "micro-aggressions" and punish students accordingly. Wes had taken measures to ensure his own eventual appointment as head student monitor, if the proposal could gain any traction. Since hysterical people tend to pursue positions of power, the student assembly granted this measure a hair-raising degree of support. It passed and was awaiting confirmation by the administration and the board of trustees. The College President, Brian Mackenzie (known affectionately as "Mac") would not give a clear answer on what he would do with the proposal. He would only say things like, "I recognize this is very serious and demands the most profound consideration from myself and the board." He wanted to stall and avoid action until students forgot about it—not a bad plan, in my view, though not as courageous as openly denouncing the proposal and vetoing it would've been.

It seemed to me that Wes and his followers had constructed a belief in their own suffering, which had made them oblivious to actual suffering.

43. Undercooked Rice

When I walked up the steps of the cafeteria and entered the foyer, I discovered that Wes and his contingent of social justice activists were protesting the (allegedly) undercooked rice in the cafeteria's sushi, which they claimed was an act of cultural aggression against Japanese people—a failure of respect. I can't imagine what the blue-collar Latino immigrants who worked in the cafeteria, preparing the food, must have thought of this.

Wes's protest was blocking the main entrance. I tried to get around the blockade, but a white girl with hipster glasses (no lenses, again) stepped in front of me and said, "Don't support the oppressor!"

"I'm just trying to eat," I said. "I'm starving. Seriously."

"Too bad!" she said. "Get food in town."

"I don't have any spare cash."

"Well…Too bad!"

I sighed, angrily. I walked around the outside of the cafeteria to the wheelchair entrance. There were a few protesters there, too, but they seemed a little less committed, and let me in.

After I paid for my meal—just penne pasta with marinara sauce and a small salad, nothing too expensive—I went to sit down, and noticed that Emma Kaufman was eating alone. There weren't too many people in the cafeteria. I guess they'd been deterred by the protest. Swallowing the lump in my throat, I walked up to her.

"Mind if I join you?"

"Not at all," she said, more warmly than I expected.

You could tell that Emma played on the field hockey team. She was broad-shouldered and her eyes were generously spaced and blue. It was an open and guileless look, without any secret self-interested agenda, and, after the psychic turbulence of the first week of pledge term, I found her presence oddly soothing. I imagined how I must've looked in her eyes, given all the alcoholic punishment I'd been taking: ghoulish.

We decided to talk about the same bullshit the campus was always talking about.

"You joining a sorority?" I asked. This was a dumb question, because most people pledged in the fall. I was universalizing my own oddly patterned decision-making.

"Nah. I mean, I went out for the first night of rush, but—eh—it wasn't really my thing. You?"

"'Am I pledging a sorority?' Hmm... You think I should?"

I was awkwardly trying to be cute.

Graciously, she played along, saying, "Yeah."

"I want to pledge the one with the girls who bake cookies all the time. What's it—the Delta Delta somethings?"

"Something like that. I'm not current on all the gimmicks and stereotypes associated with the different Greek houses. I've honestly been a little detached from that whole scene. But I'm aware there's a cookie baking one."

"Well, whatever they are, they baked these really dope pecan cookies with the powdered sugar on them. Those were the best... Uh, I *am* actually pledging a fraternity though. Now, I mean. I'm winter pledging."

"Ah. Where at?"

"Beta."

"Cool," she said, without much conviction but still trying to be polite.

"I mean... It's weird," I said, feeling suddenly impelled to differentiate myself from the mass of saps. "I don't really think of myself as a frat boy at all—I can't. I'm an observer. It's like I'm a conscientious objector or something. You know? I don't want to be a stereotypical 'bro' and be thought of that way... But here I am."

"You don't sound too enthusiastic."

"Yeah. I don't know..."

"Beta seems normal though."

"It's alright... I guess that's its reputation: 'alright.' There's nothing to overrate or underrate, and I wasn't expecting much. But still... I feel a little terrible. It's not good for your liver."

"You do look pretty ill."

"Well, I've been force-chugging Keystone Light for the last ten days, so... Tends to have an effect."

"Sorry."

"No, don't be. I'm the idiot who got myself into this mess."

"But you can just run away from it if you want to, right?"

"I don't know, really—to be honest. I think they torture you and, quote unquote, 'burn your bowels' if you try to leave."

"'Burn your bowels?' How?"

"I don't know. It was in an oath we swore."

"I mean, you didn't sign up to be a *slave*. They can't *force* you to remain a pledge against your will, right? Can't you just say, 'I quit,' and walk out?"

"I guess. But if that's the case, why doesn't everyone do it? Plus, I don't want to alienate all these people I've gotten to know."

"Maybe everyone asks themselves why everyone *else* isn't walking out, so that's why they stay in. It's group psychology."

"Probably… That's probably right… Though the real reason is that people actually enjoy this crap. Anyway, I don't want to keep yammering on about all this stuff that *I'm* doing. Anything interesting going on in your world?"

44. Yogis and Fakirs

"Yes," said Emma. "I'm applying to study abroad in India next year."

"See? That's actually something interesting. That's *worth* talking talking about."

"Professor Canzoni recommended me for this program: you go over to India and collaborate with scientists studying the physical and intellectual potential of human beings. Like, have you ever heard—this is true—about this Finnish guy who can sit in the snow in sub-zero temperatures without freezing to death? He can actually control his own body temperature—which, you know, is supposed to be an involuntary function. And this isn't a weird pseudoscientific thing either. He's been through lots of tests—at Harvard, Yale. We haven't got him here yet, but I wrote him an invite."

"That's interesting…"

"You sound skeptical?"

"No… Not skeptical. I mean if Harvard and Yale have proved it and everything." I suppose I *was* a little skeptical—but in a curious way.

"Anyeay, we're meeting up with a group of yogis and fakirs who've decided to submit themselves to these tests. We're talking about really hardcore ascetics, people who claim they have the same powers of self-control as the Finnish guy, and then some. The only difference is, the Finn's never developed his ability. He just happened to have it, accidentally, it seems. These yogis and fakirs claim to have developed their powers consciously. They've cultivated this inward attention and self-control to the point where they can slow their own heart rates to an extremely slow pace or even *stop* their hearts at will… I'm not saying that I believe all this, by the way. What's interesting to me isn't so much the ostensibly exotic nature of these things. It's the power of attention developed to do it. I mean, what *is* that?"

I didn't know the answer, so I responded with another question: "What's the difference between a yogi and a fakir? I thought they were both dudes who laid on beds of nails and walked on coals and things like that?"

"Not really," she said, her brow furrowing. "There *is* that side to it. Actually, the lying on nails and walking coals stuff is pretty common, but those are usually tricks. I'm interested in abilities people have arrived at through intense meditation. But to get back to the difference: a yogi is, typically speaking, Hindu, and a fakir is Muslim, a Sufi—which is a mystical Muslim. But they both practice techniques that are supposed to elevate themselves towards, well— towards the awareness of God. On the journey towards that big final Union, there are these powers and attributes that are supposed to come along with it. Those aren't supposed to be of interest in and of themselves, however. Many yogis consider them to just be distractions. These powers can sound fairly plausible, like those I described—slowing your heart-rate through your own concentration or reducing your rate of breathing to a very low level or going without eating for long periods of time. But they can also be a bit...weirder."

Something sounded familiar to me about this, but I couldn't recall precisely what...

"What's a bit weirder?"

"Oh, you know—transforming into animal bodies, learning knowledge of the future, being able to teleport or bi-locate."

"Bi-locate?"

"Yeah. That's being in two places at the same time."

"And Canzoni's into all this stuff? Isn't he supposed to be a scientist?"

"Well, yes. I mean, the idea is to learn more about the interconnection between the body and the mind. It's not meant to be some sort of New Age touchy-feely thing. But perhaps we'll be able to learn more about ourselves...or about the Self. "

45. Man of Peace

What Emma was saying was vastly interesting, and there was something strangely familiar about it. For some reason, it got me thinking of Wilkes' death again—there was a detail that seemed connected to Wilkes or Canzoni but I couldn't quite place what it was... Rather than concluding this train of thought, I suddenly blurted out, "Has Canzoni ever acted weird around you in any way?"

Emma paused. "Weird? Well, he's generally very weird, though I mean that in the best sense."

"I know... But, like, does he ever do anything *specifically* weird?"

"Well, he'll occasionally get lost in thought, and his eyes will drift up to the ceiling before he snaps back to the lecture. That kind of thing—typical absent-minded professor stuff. Why do you want to know?"

"Just curious," I said. I could tell all this from looking at Canzoni, but there was a bit more I'd observed. He certainly had the classic absent-minded professor look with his baldpate and tufts of gray hair nestled behind his ears. He possessed an endearingly ruffled appearance. You could see the man lost in worlds of thought as he walked around campus, eyes half-opened to this universe, half to another.

However, the few times I'd seen him, I thought I'd noticed something else creep into his eyes: a sly knowingness. "Yes," it seemed to say, "I'm aware precisely of how I appear to you. And who is to say that I am not in *control* of my own absent-mindedness, like a curtain I raise and lower? Maybe, suddenly, when you think I'm at my most oblivious and ridiculous, I'll turn the full spotlight of my awareness on *you*—and you'll see what powers of attention I really have." He clearly did have "great powers of attention," like one of Emma's yogis and fakirs, but he wisely kept them to himself, like rare jewels, to take out and reflect the light during lonely and private hours.

I asked, "Do you get any sense of, like, the projects he's working on for the government? Any truth to those weird rumors?"

"Not really. But—" Emma stopped short. She smiled.

"Yeah?"

"Well, he did say something about apps."

"Like spring rolls?"

"What? No. *Apps*—like for your phone."

"Oh, yeah. I was thinking of the other kind of app. You know—appetizers." When I'm talking to a pretty girl, even under casual circumstances, vast regions of my brain tend to shut down. I'm sure the neuroscientists have studied this.

"I got that," said Emma. "Anyway, Canzoni said something like, 'Smartphone applications are the final frontier of social control.'"

"Oh, really?"

"Yeah. Then he said, 'Why waste time exerting control over people, when you can get them to submit voluntarily by making them love the means by which they're controlled?'"

"Jesus, that's interesting… Very *Brave New World.*"

"He was saying this like it's a bad thing, though. Like, he wasn't saying, 'Oh, what a clever new way for me to dominate the world!' or anything like that."

"Ah. So, you think he's got good intentions?"

"Definitely."

"He's got a positive vibe?"

"I mean—yeah. I think so, anyway."

"You don't think he's up to anything?"

"What would he be up to?"

"Well, you must have heard about what happened with all those people who started laughing hysterically after hearing some sort of weird noise—and the townies who sneaked over the fence to try to find out what was going on with Canzoni's metal tower, and then all got amnesia?"

"…I see your point."

"You don't have any insight into that?"

I was worried I might be getting a bit contentious.

"Look. I can tell you this: he's not a bad guy. His whole thing is trying to develop non-lethal technology. It's what he's famous for. He hates war."

"Yeah, but 'Sometimes Satan comes as a Man of Peace.'"

"What?"

"Bob Dylan said that. It's from this '80s Dylan album—*Infidels*. It's very underrated. It's got 'Jokerman' on it. You know, the one where he sings, 'Freedom—just around the corner for you / But with truth so far off, what good will it do?'"

"I've never been a fan."

"You've never been a fan? We're talking about the *greatest* songwriter of all time."

"Uh, what about Joni Mitchell? Paul Simon? Leonard Cohen?"

"They're great, but none of them are as prolific and inventive as Dylan."

I couldn't *believe* she wasn't a Dylan fan.

"I feel like we're getting side-tracked here," said Emma.

"The point is—*I* think Canzoni's up to something."

"He's a sweet man."

"You're not…"

"What?"

"You're not—involved with him?"

"What? Don't be ridiculous. *Seriously*, Simon."

Gauging the sincerity of Emma's anger, I realized that I'd stepped in it. She obviously wasn't having an affair with Canzoni. I didn't meant to piss her off, and recognized that I was sort of being an asshole. On the other hand, I like it when girls sternly use my first name. It's better to provoke some kind of reaction than *no* reaction. That's passion. That's connection.

"Sorry," I said. "It's just that I suspect the guy. I really do. I've got this hunch about him."

"Why? I mean, aside from the mass hypnosis stuff you mentioned."

"Well, isn't that a good enough reason? Toying with people's brains?"

"Those were just *experiments*. He probably went a little too far and realizes it. He's a sensitive soul."

"Look," I said, lowering my voice, and glancing—somewhat theatrically, I'm afraid—to either side of me. "You know Professor Wilkes? The guy who was found dead?"

"Yeah. The masturbator."

"No. He didn't die from autoerotic asphyxiation—or, maybe he did. That's the official story, anyway. But I—" I lowered my voice even more. "I'm the student who found his body. And I can tell you there's something weird going on there. He had lunch with Canzoni the day before he died."

"So? That's pretty circumstantial, Simon."

There it was—my sternly pronounced first name again. We were really connecting.

"Yeah, but Canzoni told him something or asked him about something, and then Wilkes tried to get back some books he'd lent me. I was returning them when I found his dead body."

"So… Canzoni killed him—before he could get the books back? And why hasn't he killed you, or just asked you for the books, or stolen them or something? And what makes these books so important?"

"I don't know what makes them so important. A bunch of them are just normal library books. And I'm not saying he *killed* Wilkes. I just think he knows something. Plus, no one ever said that Wilkes told him anything about *me* having the books. So, he doesn't know I have them."

"What are these books about, anyway?"

"Central Asian anthropology, mostly focusing on Kafiristan."

"Why would Canzoni care about those?"

"That's what I'm trying to find out."

"Good luck with that."

"Thanks—but I thought you might be able to help me."

"How?" She posed this question rather aggressively. Were we still connecting?

I sighed. "Well, you've obviously talked with the guy. If you could insert some subtle hints into your conversation, something to tease out information about, you know—"

"Murdering Professor Wilkes."

"Right."

Emma paused, before saying, surprisingly, "Okay."

"Really?" I asked.

"No. Of course not."

"Oh."

"I have to get going. I have an aquatic scuba hockey class at seven."

"That sounds made-up."

"It is. But I'm finished eating."

I realized I hadn't touched my food.

"You don't want any desert?"

"No. I mean—sorry, Simon. But I'm not sure whether I should be fostering any paranoid delusions." She seemed offended. I probably shouldn't have suggested she was having an affair with the guy.

"Fair enough…" I said.

Emma got up and walked away. I commenced miserably to eat my cold pasta, which I'd barely touched until then.

46. The Good Fight

When I was finished, I started to leave. But, as I entered the cafeteria's foyer, a developing scene detained me. Mac, the previously mentioned College President, was having an awkward showdown with Wes and his protesters, who had just started chanting "No justice, no peace! No justice, no peace!"

When the chant died down, Mac broke in—"Look, I just wanna say one thing."

The protesters started to jeer, but Wes gestured for them to quiet down, saying, "Let's give the oppressor a chance to bury himself."

"Look here, guys," said Mac. "I'm gonna look into the rice situation. Seriously. But, uh, can't we stop blocking the cafeteria entrance? Maybe protest more from the side?"

"Shut the fuck up!" a girl yelled.

"Yo, old man," yelled Wes, "You know how a Japanese person feels when they buy sushi with rice that hasn't been properly cooked? That has been *under*cooked, in fact? They feel shitty! Alright? It's like you're not respecting their culture, like you're gonna stuff them into internment camps all over again!"

A course of righteous "Yeahs!" followed this exclamation.

Through the entryway to the cafeteria, I could see a Guatemalan immigrant, manning one of the cash registers, who blinked with confusion or incredulity at what Wes was saying.

"Okay. I take your point," said Mackenzie. "Is anyone here a Japanese-American or a Japanese exchange student?"

No one raised a hand. An uncomfortable pause ensued.

"Uh," said Mackenzie. "So you're protesting more on their behalf I guess?"

There was another lengthy pause, while Wes came up with an explanation.

"Yes," he said. "We're lending our voices to the voiceless."

"Well, okay… Keep fighting the, um, good fight."

Mackenzie walked away, looking as rumpled and dazed as ever.

47. Dr. Warningbone

Despite Wes's attempts to provoke hysteria, most of the students liked Mac—especially in comparison to Dr. Alfred Warningbone, the last college president, who'd left office in the middle of my freshman year.

Warningbone was an economics professor before becoming Prez, and reassumed his old position after a no-confidence vote from the Board of Trustees. He had crafted an evil scheme to transform Wilbur from the small, charming, student-centric liberal arts college it had always been into a research-focused behemoth. For example, Warningbone was the man who'd approved the giant, slug-shaped library extension, made of twisted metal and warped glass, which appeared to be parasitically devouring the old, original, brick library.

His face was expressionless, frozen, with a neat shell of whitish-gray hair clamped down over his skull. His glasses had a habit of catching the light and blanking out his stare (which, itself, was blank enough—menacingly so). Whenever he was speaking in his customarily steely tones (always on the verge of breaking out in wrath, reminiscent of Dick Cheney) he would pause and abruptly take an odd, nervous gulp.

Leaving Mackenzie and the protesters behind, I stopped in the bathroom in the cafeteria to urinate and could hear someone talking to himself, like a maniacal villain, in one of the stalls. After a moment, I realized it was Warningbone.

"Rip their fucking guts out—castrate those shits. What do these little shits even know? Harvard is beating the bejesus out of us, and these dumb fucks can't even realize it! I keep telling them—'We need more military contracts!' ...I'd skullfuck those turds to death..."

He was talking about the Board of Trustees.

Warningbone continued: "Every other major university is getting government grants out their ass and we're sticking our dick in the goddamn light-socket. And they voted down my elimination of the humanities departments. And what's this studio art shit? When I sit down to take a dump, I can look at the picture of Marilyn Monroe's titties hanging in my shitter, and that's all the 'art' I need. Rembrandt, Mozart, Shakespeare—piss on 'em all! I hope Wes and his band of no-dick degenerates can at least throw a wrench in that whole business, sick as they are. It'd be a pretty big coup, after the signage thing."

Warningbone wasn't president anymore, but he still sought influence. He'd managed to get himself appointed head of the school's Committee on Design, and changed all the fonts on campus signage. Now, all the signs were printed with sharp, angular letters; no sentiment, no ornament, just the sheer label. It was a font that made it clear that facts are facts.

"Alright, see you later," Warningbone concluded. "Love you too, Mom."

He hadn't been talking to himself after all. He'd just been updating his—likely extremely aged—mother about his schemes and dreams.

48. Free Trial

A few days later, on the weekend, I was hanging out in Beta, enduring the mandated time killing and the faux-jovial backslaps. We played pong all night, and it was surprising to see how many guys ignored the girls who were with them just to assume mastery over each other at this dumb game. The dangling carrot of status—you can hitch it to anything.

The Wilbur version of pong is played on a table with ping-pong paddles. If anyone hits a ball into the row of cups in front of you, you need to drink it. The ball bounces all over the room, landing on various surfaces, some of them coated with the accumulated grime of sneakers, some formerly the sites of intense vomiting. Yet, when the ball landed in one of your cups, you would merely pluck it out, and chug the whole beer. Everyone did this. No one, in my hearing, ever raised the logical sanitary objections. I suppose, in a way, this is a significantly lesser version of the mind-set that allows a true believer to drink water from the Ganges, despite the river's immense concentration of fecal matter. But, in that case, the believer has the legitimate excuse of a cleansing Faith—one that can purify and heal. In our case, we had only the flimsy excuse of togetherness, of artificial "brotherhood."

Later, after this night of robust triviality—in which I participated, and got badly beat—had wound its way down to a sad drizzle of lingering sociability, Pete and I stood in the perpetually decimated basement and chatted.

"Sheila Tomlinson," said Pete. "Damn... Did you see how she reacted when I smashed that ball straight up Merkin's ass? She was impressed. Her breath was taken away."

I could not verify that this was so.

Pete took my silence for agreement, and proceeded: "She's got a belly button ring, though. Doesn't that mean she's high-maintenance?"

"Well, she let you bang her the first night, after you met her in this extremely unsanitary basement. She didn't necessarily demand much prior 'maintenance' then," I said. " I don't know. In what way would you need to maintain her?"

"Like, you know—with presents and stuff. Maybe that first fuck was just a trial run. Like, a free trial, to try it out? Like you get when you want to download Quicken Loans on your computer."

"Quicken Loans? Do they still have that?"

"Or whatever. But then, once you've gone through the free trial period, you need to start paying on a monthly plan. And there's a subscription sign-up fee and all these other hidden fees and new offers to take it up to the next level or to get her to do exotic sexual practices..."

"You're thinking about this in such an unpleasantly mercenary way," I said. The frat was warping his mind, I thought, turning everything into a business transaction—a power game of give-and-take. It was the old cliché, sacrificing your individual imperatives to buy into the general culture, to merge and belong. It was an oddly *collective* form of capitalism.

"Definitely," he said. "That's how people think here! That's how people think in the *world*—in real life. It's how you've got to think. Look around, dude."

He was right. That *was* how people thought there.

As the next few weeks wore through, and our nervous systems became increasingly frazzled and sensitive through overmuch drink and the frictions of communal life, Pete and Sheila's "relationship"—to call it that—became increasingly puzzling, indeed Byzantine, in its complexity.

He told me that they were, ostensibly, "not" in a relationship, and that they agreed that they could sleep with other people. What was the point of being in a Greek organization if not to exploit the potential for sexual adventure to the fullest—to tease oneself with variety and disguise the colorless substance of life in a marinade of diversely spiced distractions?

But they were still each other's "number one," and continued having sex more frequently than with any other partner. Despite all this sexual freedom, at the end of every Friday night, Pete would wind up either arguing with Sheila in person or pleading/yelling into his cell-phone.

For example, the following weekend, this happened:

"You cunt!" yelled Sheila, tripping backwards into a snowdrift outside Beta.

"Real smooth," said Pete. He guffawed evilly.

"You always do this," said Sheila.

"What?" said Pete.

"The same thing."

"Oh, yeah? What's that?"

Sheila's eyes narrowed to what are commonly called "cold slits."

"*You know*," she said.

"Yeah. I know," said Pete, rolling his eyes. "You know, I don't mean this in a sexist way, but you're acting crazy. Like a crazy goddamn bitch."

"I'll kill you," Sheila growled. "I'll slit your throat while you're sleeping. Or, better yet, I'll sneak into your room and slice your tiny, little, *miniature* penis off. And I'll just chuck it out into the woods somewhere, so you'll never be able to find it. And it'll rot, until some bear or—or a wolverine eats it. And you'll have to go join a monastery and leave the world in shame."

Then Sheila started weeping—weeping like a toothless grandmother who had lived to see all of her grandchildren buried in a mass grave. Pete pounded his chest once, partly with Tarzan-ian rage and partly as the theatrical gesture of a future martyr. Then, he turned around and walked away, as Sheila sobbed bitterly, and her hot tears melted tiny holes in the snow.

I was left standing alone.

I called after Pete, "I thought we were all going to get mozzarella sticks at Greaseballs?" Neither Pete nor Sheila responded. I went by myself.

But this relationship was okay—well within the realm of campus-defined normalcy. Checks and balances were in place. They had agreed not to get too emotionally involved.

49. Empty Calories

If you wanted to eat off campus in New Hamelin, there were restaurants representing each of the most popular ethnic cuisines—Italian, Chinese, Indian, and Mexican. There was even a Hungarian restaurant, owned and operated by an Indonesian named "Chuck" (which, I'm assuming, was an Anglicization).

But if you were inordinately drunk or high, there was Greaseballs, a popular haven for the trashed late-night crowd, who came to dip their fingers dumbly and eagerly into their cheese fries, possessed and insensible. The establishment offered all manner of fried foods: fried pickles, fried oreos, fried pizza, corn dogs, fried mac and cheese bites, fried butter (!), and even actual "greaseballs"—whatever those were. I never had one, but they appeared to be quite gristly. The establishment also offered non-fried pizza, though it wasn't particularly Italian—thinly ladled tomato sauce adorned a grease-drenched crust, which was then covered by a dense, cancerous clotting of cheese. (This is a fairly common variety of New England pizza).

Since the place stayed open so late, everyone went there or ordered delivery in the small hours. It was a busy place. Greaseballs even delivered breadsticks (paid for by the administration) to the frats on certain big party nights. This was part of a policy designed to load the stomachs of students with carbs, preventing any fatalities due to alcohol poisoning, slowing the booze's passage into the bloodstream. It seemed to be working: Wilbur hadn't had a fatal case of alcohol poisoning in roughly a decade.

Yet Greaseballs attracted only to repel. The Beta brothers and I would go there after, say, a Tuesday evening's spell of serious drinking, intending to slow the flow of excess alcohol into our livers by cramming our systems with grease and carbs. Yet, the sheer volume of lipids, when combined with a bed-spinning level of inebriation, had the tendency to make one vomit—which, on the other hand, had the benefit of making you absorb less of the victuals' empty calories. The body has its own wisdom and knows what to reject—with force. I threw up after eating there a good four or five times, which you think would be enough to prevent me from coming back. But the hive mind is not the same as the beleaguered individual intellect.

Greaseballs was owned and operated by a Wilbur graduate, Jason Ayles, who chattered away endlessly on a Blue-Tooth headset as he stalked around the premises. As a promotional gag, he'd sworn that he would offer free meals for life to anyone who managed to have a non-fatal heart attack while eating at his restaurant. The year previous, a woman actually *did* have a heartattack while eating in Greaseballs. Fortunately for Jason, she died.

Formerly, Greaseballs had been a "Mom and Pop" florist shop, owned and operated by a Serbian couple. But the husband was extradited to the Netherlands to face war crimes charges at The Hague, and Ayles bought the place from the man's distraught spouse. He refused to put a salad or any fresh vegetables on the menu. It was part of his branding strategy: conscious unhealthiness. One item listed on the menu was but a small tub of lukewarm lard served with breadsticks.

Jason had been profiled in a national business magazine and hailed as a masterful entrepreneur. It would be hard to deny he had some kind of rancid talent. He seemed oddly pleased with his capacity to deprave his diners. "Catering to the lowest common denominator!"—that was the restaurant's motto. Literally. He had a neon sign installed.

50. Monogamy

At any rate, to continue my meditation on Pete and Sheila's relationship: I was sitting alone in Greaseballs, drinking a glass of ginger ale. I'd arrived with the other brothers, but stayed behind after they left. In a pensive mood, I was pondering the sundry whys and wherefores that have baffled Western Civilization for millennia. Rupturing my train of thought, Sheila suddenly plopped down across from me.

"What's the fucking deal with your fucking friend?" she asked.

"Which friend?" Of course, I knew who she was talking about.

Sheila exhaled, theatrically demonstrating her exasperation. "*Peter.*"

"Ohhh, that friend," I said. "Why? What's wrong with Pete?"

"He's just *impossible*."

"Are you in love with him?" I knew this question was bound to provoke. Despite not being shy about discussing anonymous blowjobs in Sears dressing rooms or whatever, the modern college student still blushes at the name of love.

Sheila blushed—an angry blush.

"What kind of crazy, idiot question is that?"

"Sorry," I said, smiling—though perhaps I was, sad to say it, smirking rather than smiling. "What's he being so impossible about? Do you want to be in a committed monogamous relationship with him? Tell me. I love wounded romanticism. I can't get enough of it—I *don't* get enough of it. I put on 'There is a Light that Never Goes Out' by The Smiths and cry myself to sleep every night."

Per usual, I'd been drinking at Beta before I came to Greaseballs, and when I drink—especially if I've been drinking for awhile—I tend to get a little weird.

"No," she said. "*Monogamous… Jesus.*" She spit out both words with an equally contemptuous emphasis.

"Well then, what is it?"

"He's the one trying to make *me* stop sleeping with other people."

"Really? I heard that you were doing the same thing to *him.*"

She paused, flustered, before continuing. "He's a liar," she snarled. "That's another thing wrong with him."

"If you two weren't already getting a room, I'd say, 'Get a room'!"

"What's that supposed to mean?"

"Just that you're hooking up with each other, and trying not to get your emotions involved, but—somewhat paradoxically—this has proved to be the perfect device for torturing you emotionally. You both scream at each other, yet

115

still insist that you're having casual, emotionless sex. It's the funniest thing since *Ace Ventura: Pet Detective*."

I must make it clear that I presented this supposed gold standard for American Comedy with my tongue in my cheek.

I concluded, sagely, "Your bodies are getting a room, but it's really your *minds* that need to get a room. No... Your minds and your *hearts* need to get a room."

"No," said Sheila, brow furrowing. Her usually smooth forehead grew labyrinthine in its wrinkles. "You sound like a fuckin' Care Bear... What you're saying is so totally off the mark."

"Is it? What's the mark, then?"

"*Him*—his idiocy, his arrogance, his general attitude about everything."

I stroked my chin in a mock display of thoughtfulness.

"Well, if you feel that way about him, why are you still hooking up?"

She sighed another exasperated sigh. "The whole point is that we're keeping our emotions out of it."

"Well, if emotions have nothing to do with anything—do you want to have sex with me?"

"What? Ew. No."

"But, what if we kept our emotions out of it?"

"That'd be disgusting."

"Yeah, but disgust is an emotion. So, we'd keep that out of it."

I was joking—obviously. I mean, in my depressed and disordered state of mind, I probably would've had sex with her if she, for some sad reason, had said, "Yeah," but I didn't think that was very likely. This was a drunken rhetorical strategy.

I continued: "Look, my point is just this: neither of you *are* keeping your emotions out of it. You should be honest that you're crazy about each other and admit the fact that you're regularly fucking each other maybe indicates this. Then, after you've exposed your raw bleeding hearts to one another, you should go get drive-through married in Vegas or something." I acted like I was going to further expound on this, but realized that I had nothing more to say. So, as a substitute, I gestured philosophically with my glass of ginger ale.

Sheila didn't say anything. Instead, she emitted yet another angry sigh, got up, and huffed away.

I felt disappointed—just another personality to bounce off your own, same as with the Beta brothers. Despite my general distaste for Sheila, I thought I'd tried to be helpful. But I was too explicit. That's the problem. I'd laid their whole emotional dilemma out there, failing to follow old Emily D.'s advice, "Tell all the truth, but tell it slant / Success in circuit lies."

51. Exploits

Enough about the scxual and romantic entanglements of others—did I get laid at all while I was in Beta? That's a necessary question, and I don't pose it merely to boast or, conversely, to provide an excuse for hand wringing. If I left the question of my sex-life duly shrouded in mystery, you might be left with the impression that I was, and am, a ghostlike observer, present in the world but without much involvement.

Well, a gentleman never kisses and tells… But does that apply to handjobs? Or just kisses?

Admittedly, I've never been a ladies' man, a renowned amorist, or a rake—never developed a technique of seduction. In the parlance of our times, I have very little "game." I tend to take what you might call a Taoist approach, a path of mystical quiescence, whereby I... wait.

Surprisingly, this has not been entirely unsuccessful.

I could guide you through the sordid details of my low-life but... Alright. Fine. I guess I should, in brief, if just to prove to you that I have some sort of connection with visceral *life* and am not just a homeless wandering mind.

In my three weeks as a pledge at Beta, I did manage to finagle my way into a few situations involving female genitalia and/or breasts and/or lips.

I got to third base—define it as you will—with Marlene Scheiffer, a Neo-Pagan who convinced me to frolic with her, heathenishly. After, I let her tell my fortune with Tarot cards. Predictably, it was supposed to be a bad future. The "Hanged Man" came up at one point, and I forget what else. Some of the less propitious minor arcana, I believe.

I got to second base (which maybe isn't worth mentioning) with Annabel Hutch, a rugby player who playfully put me in a full nelson... which stopped seeming so playful after a longish minute.

Finally—to break the gentlemanly code regarding kisses—I sucked face with Shanay Daniels, a slam poetess; Lin Tan from the Christian A Capella group; Lindsay Barclay (heiress to a nut company, yet a hopeless *Star Trek*-loving nerd); and Natalie Cavallo, an aggressively quasi-Communist opinion columnist for the school paper. They all wandered through Beta at one point or another, and into my temporary clasp, as they searched for some perpetually elusive fulfillment. So, I kept pretty busy in my month of pledging, even if I didn't access the innermost sanctum with much frequency.

Only Scheiffer, the Neo-Pagan, responded to my follow-up texts—but just to invite me to participate in a bisexual orgy, to be held in a giant tent in the

Maine woods. I politely declined. I was mildly concerned that she would try to harvest my seed for ritual purposes. And, of course, I needed to remain faithful to the one feminine eidolon (Emma's) still glowing in my imagination.

52. Metamorphosis

As I went through this series of abortive yet still slightly sordid encounters—anything happening in a basement reeking with stale beer and sweat is bound to seem partially un-wholesome—Pete continued changing. His face acquired a florid coloring, a perpetual drunken flush. It made him look both mirthful and angry at once—which *did* seem to be his disposition. He plunged into outer merriment, while remaining inwardly irritable and uncertain. These were his two default states and he couldn't distinguish them plainly. He was self-divided. And, as none other than Abraham Lincoln has told us, a house divided cannot stand.

If he had seen what was coming, maybe he would have gotten the hell out of there and forestalled his fatal seduction? Well, who wouldn't have?

As it was, his transformation from gawky adolescent to brash frat man-child progressed unabated. From the caterpillar's cocoon, a butterfly of fully-achieved bro-hood would soon emerge. Pete took on the qualities of the world surrounding him—dipped himself in the vat and emerged stained with the appropriate colors.

See for yourself how he was acting. Previously, he'd been nervous around girls, but otherwise self-contained. He could also be ironic and self-deprecating in a pinch. After his initiation into the fraternal rites, however, he'd become callously successful with the ladies—chucking aside one warm body after another

119

(and, to be fair, many were glad to be so chucked)—while becoming frantically obsessed with the proverbial carrots dangled in front of the proverbial noses of all the aspiring hedge-fund managers and Silicon Valley tycoons in Beta, his own vacillating nostrils included.

He'd applied for an internship at a hedge-fund, one of those places with an unassuming name, which you could easily imagine plastered above some glass and steel cube in the middle of an office park: something like "Still River" or "Oakford." When the alcohol momentarily drained out of his bloodstream, a tide of anxiety would wash into his circulatory system, replacing it. This internship became a source of endless hand wringing.

"You don't understand," he told me. "I *need* to get this internship!"

"Why do you *need* to get it?" I asked, unable to suppress the cynicism in my tone of voice.

"Because if I don't get it—I'm fucked!"

"In what fashion?"

"What? What do you mean? In the ass! Not getting the internship, I'm squarely and truly fucked! That's what fucks me!"

"That's circular reasoning," I said, not entirely sure what I meant by that. "Plus, since when are you interested in all this international finance crap? I thought you wanted to be a psychiatrist."

"What?"

"A psychiatrist—didn't you want to be a psychiatrist?"

"Did I?"

"Yeah! You used to talk about it semi-frequently." I couldn't believe he didn't remember that he'd once wanted to be a psychiatrist. He had mentioned, in a rare moment of personal confidance, that his older brother once suffered a psychotic break: the police found him running naked through the aisles of Big Lots, hurling extra-large bundles of paper towels at passing customers. Consequently, by his own account, Pete always felt moved towards helping those similarly afflicted.

"I thought you wanted to heal people and help them work through their issues? Because isn't that what's really important? Directing your attention towards others or towards some ideal, and not just the acquisition of lucre?"

I realize I sounded "like an afterschool special" or like a particularly irksome friend's distressingly earnest Facebook post.

"Dude, that's the most dated neo-hippie shit I've ever heard."

"Yeah?"

"Yeah, man. That's not the way things work nowadays. The economy isn't built around those principles. It's built around... around other principles."

"What other principles?"

"Rational self-interest."

"Who's ever rational about their own interests? Were Hitler or Osama Bin Laden *rationally* self-interested?"

"Here we go. Right into the Nazi and Al Qaeda comparisons. Typical Simon Senlin move."

That was another negative feature of Pete's personality since joining Beta: he'd started referring to things I said or did as "typical Simon Senlin move[s]." What an asshole!

"Anyway," I said, "I'm not saying people shouldn't pursue business careers. I'm saying that you shouldn't pursue a business career just to buy into the ethos of this frat house. If being a psychiatrist is something you wanted to do in your natural state, in a vacuum... I'd suggest following up on it. That way you know you're"—I nearly choked on the cliché—"following your heart, and"—in a last ditch attempt to reach him, I pitched for crudity—"not just eating jelly out of society's asshole like a prison bitch."

"Society" here was really a substitute term for "Alex."

"Yeah, well…" Pete's voice trailed off… He inspected an ugly-looking piece of black gum, trodden into the floorboards of Beta's living room. Then, he re-emerged: "Really? A psychiatrist? Dude, are you sure I said that?"

"Positive."

But Pete never rediscovered his former psychiatric calling. He kept changing.

"You've changed, man," I'd say, in a joking, ironic tone, when I was actually dead serious.

At the same time—despite my constant drunkenness and alterations in habit, health, and mood—I found myself oddly impervious to real change. I'd cranked my way through the routine of becoming a frat boy, trudging across one circle of the Inferno after another, without ever feeling that I truly *was* a frat brother.

I've never felt particularly connected to any external markers of identity—never felt "Irish-American" or "Catholic," though I'm technically both of those things (if somewhat lapsed on the second count). I've always felt more like an invisible man—yet, one who, paradoxically, is walking around in a suit made of skin.

An odd spirit of detachment has pervaded my life and I'm continually relieved when I return to my room after being in company. I can savor my non-identity in peace, without being distracted by any of the pseudo-identities that time and chance attempt to foist upon us. During my time at Beta, I always felt relieved when I got back home—back to Barnum Street, and Oscar and Curtis's foul den. My attitude towards *that* place had, surprisingly, changed for the better. This was not something I had expected.

53. Alpha Males

Ultimately, Peter didn't get his internship at the hedge fund. Instead, he got an interview for something much more prestigious: an internship at Zin. This was thanks to Alex's divine intercession. Ambitious young people who wanted to change the world were supposed to want to scoot around Zin's San Jose campus on Segways, blathering jargon-saturated techno-speak into Blue-Tooth headsets (I think I mentioned this before). That was the way ambitious young people changed the world; it would eliminate AIDS in Africa.

One day, Alex tried to bestow the same opportunity on me, mustering all the regal solemnity of Zeus offering a poor mortal the chance to fling a lightning bolt. When I failed to go into cardiac arrest, or levitate a few inches off the floor, he was incredulous—and suspicious.

"You wouldn't be interested in an internship at Zin?"

"It's not a *moral* objection," I said. It wasn't. "I'm just not really into computer science and tech stuff. I don't have the right kind of mind for it."

Alex got impatient. If you didn't entertain the same inner vista—the world as viewed from a Zin campus Segway—you were clearly a bit off. He renewed his pitch with a few strong italics, introducing me to the way the real world worked:

"This isn't about *interests*. I'm talking about the *business* angle. Not the nerd shit. This is about *dominating* all those programmer bitches. Think about it. Imagine you're a hot bitch with huge tits working in San Jose. You see the same kind of socially malfunctioning dipshit all the time. Non-verbal. Aside from the really rich ones—the future Bill Gates guys—who are you going to go for? You'll self-select like everyone does and go for the businessmen, spurning the weak-jawed Nobel Prize winners. You want the Alpha males."

I considered mentioning the widely acknowledged fact that Beta was full of *Beta* males, and the happy coincidence of the fraternity's name with that fact. But I didn't know how Alex would receive this information. It seemed rather tactless to state something obvious, so, instead, I said, "But I don't want to work with money *or* computers. I want to be a teacher or—" I hesitated and stammered, "—uh uh uh, a writer…"

Alex looked at me as though I had just said that my life's ambition was to artificially inseminate zoo animals for a living.

"And besides," I added, "no one would mistake me for an Alpha male."

Alex's eyes were cool and skeptically narrow.

"You're right," he said.

54. A Dead Cat

I was forever hung-over in those days. Without a regular effusion of caffeine—the classic cyclic dependency, uppers chasing depressants—I would've been a walking corpse, chewing the ankles of my classmates. Hangovers were always more liable to make me feel depressed than give me a headache: I would feel hollow, a dry gourd with a few pebbles rattling around inside it. And when pure *Being* started to pour itself in at my toes again, gradually filling my mood back up to bright—I'd dash it all with another night, ten cans deep.

The unpleasantness of forced drinking aside, I've always felt a little gross after losing myself in masculine bonhomie, as if my solitude had been sullied. If I wanted to use it (my solitude) again, I'd need to stand alone in a Laundromat watching it rotate through the portal of a front-loading washing machine. If this sounds misanthropic, it isn't, but you're perfectly free to think of it that way. By contrast, if I were chatting with a few yogis at the top of the Himalayas, or chuckling with the Dalai Lama over a hot cup of Yak butter-tea, I'm sure my solitude would not seem quite so tarnished. Talking to senile old people or kids doesn't much brutalize the psyche either—nor does speaking to cultivated women of any age. The problem, of course, is with the animal instincts that overtake any group of young men or boys.

For instance, we were sitting around playing video games in Beta's living room, when Turdburger turned to me and said, "You know [name redacted]?"

"Yeah. I know [name redacted]. She was in my astronomy class. Nice girl, kind of quiet."

"She used to be the anal queen of her high school."

Most conversations at Beta wound down to such pithy summations of people, situations, states of being...

I couldn't stand them—those terse, destructive, hyper-masculine formulae. In high school, perhaps, the low-grade, child-like racism of a nickname like "Jew Fro" or "General Tso" might have struck most heterosexual male barbarians as sort of amusing. And I probably couldn't exclude myself from that estimate—I refuse to be anything but harshly honest and indeed Ibsenian in my relentless self-examination. But, when you are inundated with that kind of humor, when it becomes the medium in which you live, the tidal pool in which your particular tribe of urchins decides to spawn (or whatever it is that urchins do)—it gets old

125

real fast. Such an atmosphere smothers even the slightest gesture towards sensitivity or contemplation.

To repeat myself, I've always been turned off by this kind of casual, humorous brutality, and there's a particular moment I'd like to single out, a moment when that aversion became conscious, and I realized exactly why, after abandoning myself to the mob mind, I had such a terrible aftertaste in my mouth. It happened when I was in sixth grade…

To make a long story short, a few of my friends and I found the corpse of a cat in the community park, freshly dead. It wasn't a stray—actually, it looked to be one of Mrs. Pringle's cats, who were all named Chester. She was an old, presumably feeble-minded cat lady, and either couldn't come up with any other names, or thought she was always interacting with the same cat, as if all cats were one.

After prodding Chester's remains with a stick, one of my confreres, Ryan Dorp, snapped out a pocket knife and gradually sawed through the cat's neck. It wasn't as easy as he thought it would be, but the feline noggin eventually popped off. He was about to punt it into the woods—but, inspired, I picked up a nearby stick and suggested impaling the cat-head on it. We did. I walked around, holding this grizzly, barbarous totem, while we joked and whooped our way around the park—at one point, leaping out from the bushes, and frightening a group of preschool age day-care kids with it. Their hefty minders tried to catch us, but these ladies were thick of ankle, short of breath, and slow of foot. We escaped easily, exhilarated by our own dark daring, by our evasion of penalty.

Yet, I've never been able to avoid subjecting myself to internal penalties, regardless of whether the world has blessed or condemned my actions. Granted, the cat incident didn't involve any real violence against a living being—we could legitimately say, "No cats were harmed in the terrorizing of these pre-schoolers"—but when I got home later in the evening, I felt weird. It occurred to me that if I'd been walking around by myself in the park, I probably would *not* have removed a dead cat's head before ceremonially impaling it and menacing small children with it.

It was a mild *Lord of the Flies* moment, forcing me to realize how terribly a group dynamic can shift or obliterate one's sense of identity. Since that day, I'd always felt compelled to guard against this feeling, to cultivate instead a stable, persistent sense of identity, not subject to the variable winds.

55. Aggression

"Microaggressions" were rigorously prosecuted at Wilbur. Wes Cross once picketed the lacrosse team's practice because he claimed a WASPy lax-bro by the name of Ingram Cutter had made an insufficient amount of eye contact with a Lebanese exchange student after she had asked him what time it was. (The Lebanese exchange student wasn't herself participating in this protest. I'm not sure if anyone ever asked her what she thought about it). Wes and a few toadies later came under disciplinary sanction for pelting the lacrosse player with falafel as he walked back to his frat one November evening. It later emerged that Ingram Cutter's mother was Algerian, rather damaging Wes's claims, and lending a crudely racial cast to the falafel throwing.

Yet, strangely enough, this leftist persecution-complex ran parallel to an *actual* cult of fascistic aggression—"macroaggressions," I suppose one might say. Wes wasn't typically in the right circles to experience it, or gingerly avoided it… (Aside from the already discussed Christmas Tree assault, which resulted in Wes urinating blood).

For instance, Turdburger once attacked Merkin with a cricket bat (property of a Pakistani Beta brother) after Merkin insinuated that Turdburger had been sexually aroused by a shirtless Brad Pitt in *Thelma & Louise*. Merkin got a concussion and saw double for a few days, even though he and Turdburger patched things up over a bottle of Wild Turkey.

On another occasion, Turdburger and Jet Li kidnapped a brother from Zeta and water-boarded him before letting him go. I'm not entirely sure why—I think he beat them at pong. Plus, they said they wanted to know whether water-boarding was really as bad as the "leftist media" was making it out to be. The Zeta brother told them that it was by no means pleasant, but that he felt like he had a "whole new lease on life" when he realized they were going to let him go. He thanked them (perhaps suffering from an early-onset touch of Stockholm Syndrome).

Pete got into a fist-fight with a visiting student from Dartmouth, who had been pawing Sheila in a dank corner of the Beta basement. The bout ended with the Dartmouth student projectile-vomiting just as he was about to land a decisive left hook on Pete's jaw. Pete regained the advantage, beating him until both of his eyes swelled shut, and knocking out two of his teeth. Then, Pete and Alex tied him up in a chair and acted like they were going to dentally torture him with a fork. The next night, The Dartmouthian was back at our frat, in a more pacific mood, drinking heavily. I guess they'd earned each other's respect, come to an understanding.

At one point, Alex even attempted to organize a fight club, inspired by the movie (he probably hadn't read the book). It was part of his pitch to mold us from being humble Beta males into broad-jawed Grecian deities. Yet, we had to call it off when Jet Li smashed Jew Fro with a folding chair, causing blood to gush from a smile-shaped cut on his forehead and leaving him with a pretty serious concussion. Alex and Turdburger rolled him up in an old carpet (I don't know why—probably in imitation of a movie) and pushed him out of Alex's BMW, half-suffocated, in front of the hospital. Demonstrating his loyalty, Jew Fro told the rightfully suspicious hospital staff that he'd merely "slipped in the shower." They gave him ten stitches.

When Jew Fro was released, Alex took him to the same strip club to which the lonely trucker had offered to transport Peter and me. I heard that he lost his virginity in a lap dance stall, thanks to a giant tip Alex gave the stripper on Jew Fro's behalf.

By the way, I would call "Jew Fro" by his real name (nodding to the unpleasantness of these heavily ethnic nicknames) but I honestly don't remember what it was. Nor do I remember Jet Li's. Merkin's first name was Murphy and Turdburger's first name was Wilson, but I cannot recall either of their surnames. The ancients were right: there's something magical in a name. Being called "Wilson" is apt to make you act one way, while "Turdburger" makes you act another. Words of power, words of power...

At any rate, it's funny that Alex and Wes coexisted on the same campus. At the same time that Alex would be telling a joke about AIDS in Africa, Wes would be protesting culturally insensitive Halloween costumes—in February, long after the holiday had passed (he'd begun claiming Ninja and Samurai costumes were racist, presumably if worn by non-Asians). If they ever walked directly into each other, would they suddenly vanish in a blazing flash like anti-matter and matter mutually annihilating? At the same time, I more than once wondered whether they were twins, separated at birth. There was something complementary about them, radical difference and radical sameness at once—like Fascism and Communism.

They seemed to live parallel lives, never intersecting. Alex and company lived up to virtually every negative notion Wes's cohort held about them, while Wes flamboyantly embodied the contrasting caricature. It was, strangely enough, okay to be a cartoon; there was strength in numbers, strength in easily identifiable labels like "Frat Bro" or "Social Justice Activist." They *wanted* to be categorized.

The non-categorized person lived somewhere beyond definition, in the margins—past a curtain of snow at the edge of the world. Who were these people, like me, thrust into non-being? There was no way to say. But once you were there, and had bid farewell to fear and hope, it wasn't so bad. Surprisingly, it was like anything else. You adapted and it became normal.

Besides, you didn't really lack anything—least of all, definition. You stood out more starkly, sharp against the emptiness. Finally, freed from the collective static, you were simply the thing you'd always been, that bundle of contradictions we call the self. But, behind the contradictions, there was a deeper self, a hidden harmony.

56. The Pattern

Silly Squirrels was officially a craze. A decent number of people on campus seemed to be playing it. Everywhere, the theme song would carol out its manic tinny reverberation. Yet within it there seemed to be a finer tone, the insistence of a snake-charmer's flute.

Oddly enough, Beta seemed immune to the trend—which was inexplicable, given its reputation as a place full of people eager to belong. Equally strange, there was nothing about it on TV, in the newspaper, or even online. On the phone, I asked my parents if they'd heard of it, and they hadn't—though, of course, parental obliviousness regarding a current technological enthusiasm is practically *de rigueur*. However, everywhere else on campus—the library, the cafeteria, the gym, the occasional classroom, even in the stands at sporting events—the ear-wig theme song wriggled its way into your Eustachian tube.

It didn't appeal to me. If I'm going to play a video or computer game—as I rarely do—I generally like directing a military campaign, presiding over the rise and decline of civilizations, or solving a mystery. The rudimentary time-slaughterer was never really my bag. Yet, it became so ubiquitous, so universal, I grew curious. Interestingly enough, I never saw any commercials or advertisements for the game—unlike *Clash of Clans* or *Candy Crush Saga* or those other primitive-looking cellphone diversions. (I've never played any of those games, for the record).

Alright, I thought, looking for an excuse to procrastinate on a Tuesday night, as I sat alone in my room—*I'm going to figure out what's so addictive about this* Silly Squirrels *bullshit.*

I downloaded the game on my phone and opened it, listened to the theme music, and started to play…

At first, the experience was… completely normal. It involved squirrels trying to gather as many acorns as they could in order to store them for the winter. It wasn't particularly compelling, I thought. Its charm eluded me. Nonetheless, I kept playing, hoping that something would turn me on to the game's popularity, revealing the source of its enchantment—would push me into a fugue state, help me bliss out and pacify all the pesky thoughts quarrelling in my head.

As I played, I noticed something. There seemed to be an occasional blip on the screen, a flashing image lasting but a nano-second. It was so quick, you easily could've overlooked it. But the longer I played, I became convinced that it was there…some kind of pattern. Strangely, my desire to continue playing the game grew the longer I kept at it… and a vacant bliss really *did* enfold me. The experience had a unique quality, like being lulled by warm ocean waves—a pacific return to infancy. It cradled your attention, softly rocking it, gently channeling it downwards into the screen, the little glowing rectangle opening like an entry to another dimension, opening and opening and—

A tiny voice inside me started shouting, asserting itself. "This is stupid!" it said. It was a miniscule irritant, the mosquito of consciousness buzzing at the sill. I did my best to ignore it—what with the gentle rocking, the slow hypnotic syrup of the game, the freedom from thought… Outwardly, I must've looked possessed, wildly clicking with my thumbs… Inside, however, I felt numb— *comfortably* numb (in the words of Pink Floyd). Yet that irritating little voice kept pricking at me, until I fairly heard it screaming, "Stop!" It had taken on such a persistent tone; I wished I could bat it away, crush it, squash it entirely, and just continue to gather the falling acorns…. There were so many acorns! The acorns kept falling… There was always another acorn… and another… and another… and—

Stop!

The voice grew so loud and so sharp that it seemed almost audible to me, as though it were coming from outside my skull. I wrenched my head up, annoyed—and realized from my alarm clock that it was now 10:00 P.M. I'd been playing the game for *five hours*.

Shaking, I dropped the phone on my desk like it was a syringe brimming with an overdose of premium heroin, which I'd unwittingly been about to inject into my veins. A second after I detached, the game's eerie siren song kicked up—

"Silly Squirrels
Pickin' up acorns!"

Quickly, I grabbed my phone and exited out of the game. Then, I went into the application manager and deleted *Silly Squirrels*. Sitting back in my chair, still anxious, I felt suddenly sick—captured by a topsy-turvy stomachache mood, with gravity pulling me down and down, and a tractor beam yanking me up. The nausea made you confuse heaven and earth all at once. I grabbed my wastebasket, and—just in time—threw up.

Feeling utterly drained, like a parasite had been enjoying free reign in both my viscera and my cranium, I dragged myself to the bathroom, washed my mouth out, and brushed my teeth.

Then, as I curled up in the fetal position in bed, desperately seeking sleep, I saw something.

When I closed my eyes, a red outline appeared—like you see after looking at a bright light. But this was not an amorphous blob, fleeting in its impress and quick to dissolve. It was a steady shape, sharp and unusually clear: a system of interlocking triangles, all pointing downwards. It seemed symbolic, like a Buddhist mandala of sorts, the representation of something cosmic. I felt sure that this was the image, too quick for the naked eye, which had been flashing on the screen of my phone as I played the game.

Yet, unlike the sand mandalas that Buddhist monks had made and ceremonially destroyed at Wilbur last year, this design—this *pattern*—left one with a feeling of immense interior *dryness*. It was of a piece with my headache and my nausea: an empty, aching, hollowed-out feeling. Before it finally faded, and I was able to get to sleep, I thought, semi-coherently, *That's the thing that's doing it—the pattern of the nightmare*. (I was kind of echoing *Mullholland Drive*, which I'd recently seen).

And in my admittedly crotchety reflections, dissolving fast into sleep, I wondered: who could make it through the deep, dark woods of a classic fairytale guided only by the brief and hesitant taper of a flickering, modern attention span? There *must* be a trail of bread crumbs...

In the middle of the night, without realizing it, I slept-walked for the first and only time in my life, and urinated in my sock drawer. I guess it was an after-effect of the insidious mesmerism the game had attempted to exercise on my neurons. The next morning, I felt like I had the worst hangover of my life, worse than anything Beta could've ever thrown at me.

57. Coke and Tits

After dumping a bunch of socks in our basement washing machine, I read up on *Silly Squirrels*. I googled it. There wasn't even a Wikipedia article for it—odd, given that I'd seen it, or heard it, everywhere—nor was there much news coverage. Yet, buried on a video game blog authored by one Ernesto D'Angelo (a morbidly obese young man with a neck beard, going by his profile picture) there was this: "Played a new game all day after getting jacked on Code Red Mountain Dew. It's called *Silly Squirrels* and is *SO* intense. My friend at Zin, Dylan

Hooper, who developed it, was letting me try it out. It's really involving… even though it just involves squirrels…. Picking up acorns."

Then the post got weird, repeating the all-caps sentence "SILLY SQUIRRELS PICKING UP ACORNS" over and over again, maybe thirty or forty times.

I googled "Ernesto D'Angelo," and discovered an article from the *San Jose Gazette*, relating that a promising young software engineer of that name had suffered a major mental break early last year. He apparently smashed open the self-serve nut containers at the local Whole Foods and began hurling cashews and almonds at customers while bellowing incoherently.

The date of the *Gazette* article was but three days after Ernesto's blog post.

Next, I searched for "Dylan Hooper Zin." I found an Instagram account, in which a series of selfies depicted a young nerd with a bland face and a weak jaw, attired in Ralph Lauren Polo and Raybans (one photo zoomed in on the frame of the sun-glasses, so you could tell the brand), hanging out with a rotating selection of identical-looking hot girls, all of whom made pouty duck-faces with their collagen over-loaded lips. Bottles of Hennessy and Patron were captured mid-pour, while captions said things like "two hot persian twins jazmin and mahtab in my camarro… I love LA," "drinking cristal with porn star jenna biscayne! she has literally inflatable tits!!!" and "pre-gaming with disaronno on the rocks, pre-orgy."

In one picture, he was evidently trying to grow a goatee, but managed to look more like an egg with a bunch of pubes glued to it...

After the Instagram account, the next item Google returned was an article, dated from several months previous, relating the fact that Hooper had died of a cocaine overdose while partying aboard a rented yacht with a group of adult film stars on Christmas Day. It briefly mentioned that he was a programmer for Zin, while also noting that his alma mater was Wilbur College.

After that, there was nothing.

I took out my pocket notebook and scribbled furiously. Under the excitement caused by this new information, and the stimulus of a cup of coffee, my video-game induced hangover began to subside.

58. Playing it Cool

Later that day, whilst at Beta for pledge activities, I decided to mention *Silly Squirrels* to Alex, given his Zin connections. Maybe he'd know something.

"Have you heard about this phone game craze? It's called *Silly Squirrels*."

Alex bit his bottom lip and drew blood.

"Oh, yeah—a craze?" he said, nonchalantly. He took a tissue out of his pocket (also nonchalantly) and started to dab at his bleeding lip.

"Yeah. It's called *Silly Squirrels*. It's supposedly 'really addictive.' I tried it for the first time recently."

"Huh, interesting. Guess I'll have to try it." His voice was artificially even, the Kleenex saturated with gore.

"Yeah, I mean, I don't know what today's idiots' find 'addictive.' But I think it's unfair for companies to manipulate the human hunger for repetitive thought-numbing crap. That's just my personal opinion, though. And oh—" I added, pretending it was an afterthought, "I think Zin developed the game."

"Oh, really? You don't say…"

"You sure you never heard of it when you were there?"

"Nope. No, it was probably top secret or something."

"Makes sense… Personally, I swore off phone games a long time ago. "

"Yeah. I don't really… play that much."

"*Flappy Bird* disrupted my world for a little while. So I can relate."

It actually didn't, but whatever.

I continued: "And you definitely don't remember Zin working on it while you were there?"

"No… No, of course not!"

"Why, 'of course not'?"

We stared at each other. Alex squinted at me. I widened my eyes.

"Well," said Alex. "That stuff's always… totally secret, you know? When Steve Jobs came up with the iPod, he didn't blabber about it until it got out of the lab."

"Ah," I said. "Indeed, that makes total sense."

"Yes..."

"Total sense…"

Suddenly, Alex came to a realization. He said, "Aren't you supposed to be downstairs getting your ass paddled?"

59. Like a Letter from Keats

Back at the Barnum Street house, ass smarting, I decided to call Emma. I didn't have her number, but I assumed that in our modern, hyper-technological society, a simple pretext, by which one might finagle it, would not be too hard to generate.

I sent an email to her student address (student addresses are just the student's first name and last name followed by @wilbur.edu):

Hey Emma,

What's your cell number?

All the Best,

Simon

In about ten minutes, I got an email back:

Why do you need my cell number?

As this was not the response I was anticipating, I considered carefully. My next missive should not appear excessively alarming and deranged. It should be qualified, calmly reasoned, perhaps a little evasive, delicately winding its way towards—

I think I've uncovered a conspiracy of global proportions. There's this new game people are playing on their phones — maybe you've heard of it? It's called *Silly Squirrels*. Anyway, I think this game is part of a plot to hypnotize the minds of fragile youths, hatched by evil executives at the Zin Corporation. It looks like they've been killing anyone they suspect of ratting on them or knowing too much, like this coke-addled programmer named Dylan Hooper. (Google him if you don't believe me).

138

And, also — I bet Canzoni's involved. I know you love the guy, but he has to be. The dude's all about brainwashing and hypnosis… That's his jam. Maybe he helped design the game or something? And, besides, Wilkes just turns up dead at the same time that all this crazy shit is going down?

(I recognize it seems like I'm losing my marbles... I should probably put on a tin foil hat as I type this, ha ha).

Am I crazy? Probably. But you should try playing *Silly Squirrels* first, and see if you understand what I'm talking about. It's creepy — it's like mainlining heroin or something. Not that I've ever done that. (Or maybe you *shouldn't* try it. Only do it if you can pull yourself away from it… Maybe try setting a really loud alarm to try to break the spell?)

Anyway, I know this sounds like the moment in a movie where the main character finds someone to rave at, and then the confidant is all like, "That sounds implausible." But it actually is plausible!

Do you want to meet me for lunch?

All the Best,

Simon

See? If nothing else, I'm noted for maintaining the even keel, the direct prow. Reason flowed. It was like a letter from John Keats.

60. Further Confirmation

I didn't receive an immediate response, so I decided to head over to the student lounge and procrastinate. Someone had CNN on, and I noticed that there was "Breaking News." Of course, nowadays, there's always "Breaking News" on CNN and Fox, even if the news in question broke a day previously or had been expected and scheduled well in advance. It's a tactic used to prime the public's attention, no doubt, and Pavlov the citizenry into overreacting to everything. (Though I imagine in the long run it wears off, and you react to "Breaking News" the same way you react to a mundane local report on municipal government). It so happened that this news actually *was* "breaking," and it pertained indirectly to Wilbur College… and Beta.

"Timothy Fassbinder, co-founder of technology brain-trust Zin, was found dead in Mexico today," Wolf Blitzer said, staring at the camera with an intensity that could somehow be described as subdued. "Reportedly, his body had been dismembered and placed in several garbage bags, which were left on the side of a highway. The trash bags were sprinkled with marijuana and cocaine residue… After taking a leave of absence from Zin, Fassbinder had been traveling on his own, according to our sources, 'trying to find himself.' At present, the authorities have assumed that he accidentally strayed into cartel-controlled territory…"

A famous Beta alum—murdered by cartel killers!

On my phone, I quickly sent Emma another email.

Check out CNN's website. See? Not a crazy man. One of
the founders of Zin just got murdered. They're blaming
it on drug cartels, but it's probably related to this
squirrels thing.

Also, it would probably be a good idea to delete these
emails. I imagine they have eyes everywhere.

I slipped my phone in my pocket and whistled to myself. Despite all the untimely and unnatural death surrounding me, it felt like spring was in the air—a mystery was unfolding one blood-colored petal at a time. Outside, however, it was still ice-encrusted February, filthy piles of snow lining all the streets…

61. Feigned Surprise

That night, I still hadn't received any response from Emma. I had to report for pledge activities at Beta, and decided to use the opportunity to further needle Alex.

"Hey, dude—sorry about Fassbinder."

"What? What's all this?" said Alex. He jammed his smartphone into his pocket and whipped around to face me.

"I don't know if you got the news, but Timothy Fassbinder from Zin was found dead. Murdered."

"Oh, really?" Alex feigned surprise.

"Wasn't he a friend of yours?"

"Eh, we knew each other socially, but... Hell... That's pretty shocking. I mean, murdered... Whoa..."

"Yeah, it sounded pretty gnarly. Some Mexican drug cartel dismembered his corpse and packed it into a bunch of trash bags."

Alex's reaction was strangely low key, regretful but nonchalant: "Oh—dismembered, really? Wow, that's a shame. A damn shame."

"It's totally crazy," I said.

He stared at a spot somewhere over my head on the father wall of the living room. And, suddenly, it seemed as if his private train of thought—whatever it was—had switched rails. He was about to say something, but felt too nervous. He hesitated.

He would spill the beans on Zin, and then I would find out who killed Wilkes, and then Emma really *would* respond to my goddamn emails, and then—

"Wait," said Alex. "Aren't you supposed to be upstairs chugging clam juice?"

"Huh?" Whatever brief wavering impulse I thought I'd seen in Alex was now gone—if it had ever even been there.

"That's what the pledges are doing right now, right?"

"What? Upstairs? Really?" I played innocent.

"Get out of here, Amish."

62. An Ear Lobe

Round about midnight, a severed ear lobe was floating in a trash can full of brownish punch. Greg Ramirez (nicknamed "Chalupa") was sitting on the sticky wet floor, cupping the right side of his head with his hands and moaning. Blood ran down his arm in thin streams, branching into minute trickles.

An irate, drunken squash player from another frat had gotten into a fight with him over who was next in line to play pong. (Greg probably *had* tried to cut in front of him). So, the squash guy pulled a Tyson, bit off his ear lobe, and spit the tender chunk into a trash can, which we had been using as a punch bowl for a rancid concoction the senior brothers had made. Greg wailed at first, but now remained fairly quiet, letting out small pathetic moans at choked intervals.

"Quick! Get some ice!" Alex yelled.

Someone threw the earlobe into a Zip Loc bag with a few ice cubes, and pressed ice wrapped in a white towel against Kevin's ear. The towel turned surprisingly red.

Merkin and Turdburger, who had chased the Squash player, came in from outside, panting. Merkin said, "We kicked him in the nuts once, but he got away."

"Good," said Alex, who was holding the Zip Loc bag. "Now, let's see if we can get this fucker re-attached."

After we had taken Greg and his severed lobe to the Carlton County Hospital (New Hamelin is located in Carlton County), we came back to discover that the culprit had kept true to the cliché and returned to the scene of the crime. The squash player had left a single picture-perfect turd—certainly his own—on the "Welcome" doormat at the front of the house. (To make matters worse, Greg never got his ear lobe back. They couldn't re-attach it.)

A little later in the night, Turdburger tried to ride a unicycle on top of a pong table and almost broke his neck. He actually knocked himself unconscious,

143

briefly, and later discovered he had a concussion. (Concussions were plentiful at Beta).

We all laughed.

I needed to get out of there.

63. Robbed

Yet, the mystery was centered in Beta, despite the sordid atmosphere and the cultivated low-life of its privileged inhabitants. Alex was involved with Zin and was involving others with Zin. For Zin was the crux—the key to motive, the "shadowy organization behind it all."

At the same time, I was feeling run-down and wanted to leave Beta.

How to quit? Technically, anyone was allowed to de-pledge any frat. This was a Constitutional right—freedom of association. At the same time, the frats were known to perform unseemly acts on the persons of those who de-pledged. You will recall the rumored use of zucchinis, eggplants, and other oblong vegetables for sodomistic acts.

After the ear-lobe incident, I collapsed on one of the couches in Beta's living room and took out my pocket notebook.

I'd already started to suspect that Alex suspected me. I was going along with all the dumb rituals, while still cherishing my secret, private, inner life to an extent that he undoubtedly found treacherous. And it *was* treacherous. It was worth being a traitor. "My heart wasn't in it"—its beat wouldn't synchronize to the collective thrum.

I made a note: "Discern Alex's role at Zin, possible connections—steal his phone? Borrow his laptop for fake innocuous purpose and make quick search of files?"

I'd been living more and more in my pocket notebook. I was filling up one every week. When I wasn't doing Beta stuff, and felt like baldly neglecting my homework, I'd sit around campus in an alcoholic daze, jotting down descriptions of people, noting their vital humors. I was using the notebook for much more than just the Wilkes mystery…

But my writing habit got me into trouble.

I headed back down to the basement and soon grew bored. I'd had about enough of the endless games of pong, the persistent sense of gears un-meshing within my liver, and more than my fair share of bro-ing out. While everyone else was preoccupied with their cups, I'd slipped off to a corner and started jotting down another thought.

Alex caught me.

"What's this?" he said, ripping the pocket notebook out of my hands.

"It's nothing," I said. "It's private."

"A private nothing. Hmmm…"

Alex started looking through it, and reading out loud: "'like a band of angry leprechauns playing beer pong against each other' … 'a chunky guy in a *Game of Thrones* t-shirt with a cud-chewing face—bovine, meditative.' What the hell is this?"

"They're descriptions of things," I said. "Descriptions of things I want to use in stories. But it's private."

He pulled it away again, as I reached to reclaim it. *Please God, don't let him read the last thing I wrote…*

Alex put the notebook in his pocket.

"I'm keeping this," he said. "You'll get it back… When pledge term ends. You're not mentally *with* us because of things like this—living inside your head all the time. That's a problem."

Alex knew he was dicking me over and stealing valuable intel. But he didn't fathom my own extremism, didn't realize that confiscating my pocket notebook was like hacking off one of my limbs. I would've felt less affronted if he'd torn off my glasses, stomped on them, and spit in my face. I imagined Alex had other reasons—aside from petty cruelty—for stealing it. The forced innocence with which I'd asked him about Zin probably caught his notice.

At any rate, I had absolutely no intention of letting him get away with this. I wasn't going to wait until the end of pledge term to get my mind's own mirror back. At the first opportunity, I would sneak into Alex's room and see if I could find it.

64. Not Funny

It was 2 a.m. when I checked back into the Barnum Street house. Taking out my phone, I checked my email. There was a response from Emma.

With all the excitement of a sugar-addled five-year-old, tripping on Hawaiian Punch and Skittles while tearing open his Birthday presents, I clicked on it. It read:

```
Not funny, Simon.
```

What the hell? I sat down on my bed and treated my beer-marinated brain to a brief ponder. I reckoned that Emma might be a moron, or the victim of some sort of childhood brain trauma, which could occasionally impair her mental functioning from time to time.

Ultimately, however, it was clear that the fault lay not with Emma, nor with the stars, but within myself. I can be a ruthless self-critic, especially when my sexual future is at stake. I saw that I'd gone all out in penning those emails, had heedlessly dispensed with the rudiments of strategy; I'd wagered too much.

After another moment of contemplation, deep enough in thought to shame Spinoza, I realized my error: I'd forgotten old Emily D.'s advice to "Tell all the truth but tell it slant / Success in circuit lies…" To put it quite simply, I'd come on too strong, too direct. A gentleman ought to have a little circumspection, instead of careening directly towards the point. You have to play these games with girls. It's the way the world rotates.

So, instead of writing the harangue I'd initially considered, I wrote:

Ha ha ha. Sorry I freaked you out! Yeah, I decided I was wrong about the Canzoni thing — apologies for the sick and excessively complicated joke.

But, seriously, do you want to get lunch sometime? Or dinner? I really enjoyed talking to you that one time during astronomy class, though I'm afraid I poisoned our second extended chat with my murder theory. But I'm over that, now. Sorely misguided.

Anyway, let me know if you're free.

I went to bed.

65. Agendas

The next morning, I checked email as soon as I awoke. Emma's message simply said "Alright" and then gave me her number. She didn't say when she would be available.

I let out an excited "whoop" as I dashed down the hall, before careening into the bathroom and nearly slipping on the wet tiles. The shower filled with my baritone rendition of "Hey Jude," which extended the "Na na na na na na na na, na na na na, hey Jude" part, interminably.

I only had one class on Friday, thanks to Wilkes' demise—Professor Kelway's class on The Mughal Empire. I decided to wait until that was over to call Emma. You shouldn't rush these things, or seem overeager. The idea is to appear stoically indifferent to the goal you're actually trying to attain.

I could barely concentrate on Kelway's lecture, interesting though it was. He discussed how the Mogul Emperor Aurangzeb had ordered his brother and rival, Dara Shikoh, beheaded, before having his head sent to their father, Shah Jahan, who had already been imprisoned by Aurangzeb. From the bare outline I picked up, it seemed like a pefect parable of how the "children of darkness" are always "wiser in their generation than the children of light." You take a peaceful, tolerant Sufi mystic like Dara Shikoh, and—regardless of what happens in Eternity—he's bound to lose the worldly and temporal battle to his fundamentalist bully brother.

Afterwards, I paced around campus with Emma's number entered into my phone, thumb hesitating over the call button. I had to meditate a response, I had to… Actually, I was just going to do what I normally do. Wing it.

After four rings, Emma picked up.

"Yo, Em'" I said, sounding self-consciously informal. "What up?"

"Not too much," she said. "Just waiting for my roommate to stop tweaking on Adderall. She's doing all these manic fingerpaintings on the floor of our room. It's totally covered in fingerpaintings."

"Huh," I said. "That sounds intense. Listen. You want to get lunch sometime?"

"I guess," she said. "In the cafeteria or at a restaurant or—?"

"Wherever your heart desires."

"The cafeteria is fine with me."

"Yeah? You sure you don't want to explore exotic and fine cuisines from the four corners of the—"

"No. Cafeteria's fine."

"I would pay, of course—I mean, at a restaurant. I'm old-fashioned that way. I believe in chivalry, noblesse oblige, bushido. If it's at all vaguely chivalric—I'm there."

"Don't pay, Simon. No point in paying for a lunch between two frien—er, acquaintances."

"Sure. Yes. Indeed."

"Is there something particular you wanted to ask me about?"

"Oh, no. I have no agenda."

"Good."

"Is that good?"

"Sure. So many people have agendas."

"Everybody."

"Except for you."

"That's right. And you?"

"My agenda? I just like to watch the grass grow—to quote George Harrison."

"That's a good agenda."

"Yeah. Well, I'll see you—when?"

"Tomorrow, say, at noon?"

"Works for me."

"Alright. Cool."

"Take it easy."

"You too."

"Bye…"

66. Get Help

After a night of searing spiritual vacuity—at Beta, in the basement—I awoke grossly groggy. This abated miraculously as soon as I remembered my date with Emma. Granted, it was a rather low-key date, given the fact that it would be occurring in the cafeteria; a thrifty date since I wasn't paying for her; and an ambiguous date, given that it had never been established as a date. Yet, for all those qualifications and hesitations, it had attained the status of "date" in my mind, nonetheless. I'll take what I can get. If you can twist something to mean what you want it to mean, it means it. That's good sophistry for you—the most you can extract from a modern education, I'd say.

I twiddled my thumbs, fiddled with my phone, re-read sentences about the Mughal Emperors, and generally let my mind zoom around with its anticipations and inchoate yearnings.

Come noon, Emma and I were facing each other across a cafeteria table, eating sub sandwiches. I always take a bite right before someone asks me a question, and that's exactly what I proceeded to do.

"So, Simon—have you actually played this *Silly Squirrels* game you were raving about? Or, I guess, that you were jokingly raving about?"

I held up a single index finger to politely signal my need to finish chewing. As I transferred the food to my esophagus, I paused.

"Yes… It's not a very complex or, uh, enriching experience. It just involves these squirrels that pick up acorns. You know? Yet, there's something about it—"

The *Silly Squirrels* theme song broke out somewhere in the cafeteria.

"Ah. There it is," said Emma. "On cue."

We paused and listened. I resumed once it had died away.

"But there does seem to be something *odd* about it."

"Oh, yeah? In what way?"

"Well… You'll have to play it to find out. But don't get addicted."

"Did you find it addicting?"

"Oh, I might've, if I didn't tear myself away from it. The thing is—yes, that first email I sent you was a joke. Truly." I lied. "But I do think there's something unusual about it. As I was playing, an image seemed to briefly flash on the screen—this strange, triangular thingy. Like, a bunch of triangles all pointing in one direction. Maybe I'm just insane, but—"

Emma looked funny.

"What?" I said. "Have you seen this thing?"

"No. No… It's just."

"What?"

"Nothing. I was distracted by something else."

"Oh. Anyway… How's life?"

"Ah, well. It's life."

"So that means it's…good?"

"Sure. Normal. Can't complain. You?"

"Well, I'm still dealing with this frat business. I never should've joined. Now, the problem is finagling my way out of it."

"How are you going to do that?"

"Probably go out in a blaze of glory, both middle fingers in the air."

"So, it's not exactly an elevating experience."

"No. It's just like every negative stereotype you've ever seen in the movies. A bunch of guys all devolving into collective animalism every night— like *The Island of Dr. Moreau*, and, yes, I mean the crappy Val Kilmer movie version. And how are you finding being unaffiliated? Alright? I guess it's just neutral?"

"Neutral works. Neutrality's not so bad… by definition. Most of my friends did join—last term. So, I still see them. I also see a lot of movies. Plus, I'm on the field hockey team, so, when that's in session, you have some social life there, thank God."

"Anyway…" I said. I paused. I seemed to be drying up in conversation. I felt like we were rehashing ground we'd already covered on an earlier occasion. Yeah, frats suck, etc. etc.

It occurred to me that I had no real options. I was always going to do what I was going to do, and draw the conversation towards its inevitable and unpleasant conclusion. I have no aptitude for subtlety! I'm not socially intelligent, I can't read all these cues—especially not the kind women are always supposedly giving you or not giving you. So, I cut to the chase.

"Actually, Emma—I'm gonna come clean." I paused, not intending it to seem like a stage pause, dramatic for effect. But it did seem like one. "I didn't ask you here just to bitch about my frat. I have real issues. Actually—I think I might be totally losing it! You know that first email I sent you?"

"The unhinged rambling one?"

"Yes! The crazy rambling one! Do you know why I wrote that?"

"Well, I could only assume it was a perhaps not entirely well-thought-out joke that—"

"No! Wrong! I believe all that. It was one of the most sincere statements I've ever written in my life. What do you think of that? Huh?"

"I mean… You can get free counseling at the infirmary if you're having some sort of manic episode or a psychotic break—"

"But did I seem to be having a psychotic break until just now? Until I started raving?"

"Not really."

"Look, I'm not going to try to explain why I think there's an evil global conspiracy involving a smartphone game about squirrels. It's going to sound ridiculous—in fact, the more artfully I attempt to articulate it, the more insane it will sound. The best thing to do would be to just play the game. Play the game, and then put it right the hell down! You know the scene in *They Live* where the one dude tries to make the other dude wear the sunglasses which can allow him to see the true nature of the world they're in? But he won't, and they have this huge fight in an alley?"

"No. Never seen it. And, uh, I think I should maybe—"

"Well, that's what I'm trying to do! I'm trying to get you to put on the sunglasses, Emma. I'm trying to get you to see what's really there. Because 'what's really there' is bizarre and confusing and—I don't know what I'm doing! I'm scribbling notes all the time, constantly drunk or hungover or fried! I'm the last person anyone should trust to figure out anything. But something's going on here. I swear it. Please, Emma—"

By this time, she was standing up. "Get help, Simon," she said. "I mean that. Sincerely. Get help." She put a depressingly gentle hand on my shoulder for a moment, and left.

I slumped in my seat. I almost involuntarily let my head fall forward, where it would've crushed the remainder of my chips.

67. Dead Animals

Of course, I didn't get help. Why should I have? I know that I'm an eminently sane and reasonable man. Playing up my hysteria was tactical—misguided, yes; but deeply tactical nevertheless. I was trying to provoke sympathy or curiosity, and maybe get Emma to check out the game on that basis. Alas, I had gone full freak show…

I was anchorless, dock-less, probably boat-less too if we're going to pursue the analogy as far as we might. I was treading water, with no puff of smoke on the horizon, vicious seagulls flocking about me, and the sun beating down savagely. Damned or saved, I had nothing but my own strength to carry me. So, I would pick a random direction and swim…

The first thing was to retrieve my pocket notebook. Even if it was just filled with a bunch of frenzied bullshit—even if my suspicions of Zin ultimately proved unfounded—getting it back was a necessary re-assertion of my manhood.

That night, there was a party at Beta, and as a pledge, I was obligated to be in attendance. "We" (if I may gingerly annex the pronoun for a collective of which I was never a true member) were having a sorority over for cocktails. The Kappas were known for being stylish women, rather out of our league. They generally only slept with the captain of the squash team. They functioned as his harem or something. If he wasn't available, and they were pretty desperate, they had to content themselves with sailors and lacrosse players. Despite their advanced pedigrees, the Kappas evidently found the pleasures of squandering privilege—spending Daddy's money on cases of Keystone Light instead of on vintage pinot noir—irresistible.

Yet, as the booze infiltrated their systems, our grimy basement seemed less the squalid den that it truly was. Alex steered them into our world, chatting up each girl before passing her off to another Beta brother, refilling cups, shepherding the ladies to different pong tables where they might participate.

Shoving Sheila (herself a Kappa) to the side, if not exactly rejecting her, Pete was now abusing his newfound lanky charm, becoming a stickman of either the first or second tier. With a gaggle of girls gathered round him, he would identify the two by whom he was most aroused. After acting as though he was interested in what one was saying, he would strategically ignore her, transferring his attention to the other. Then, having suitably simulated rapt attention, he would switch back.

Occasionally, he would make a backhanded comment, like, "It's cool you've been going to the gym. It's the effort that counts." I think he'd borrowed this technique wholesale from a tawdry book aimed at aspiring pick-up artists... A lot of the guys at Beta seemed to use it—Alex, of course, being a master.

155

On the other hand, some took the route of intellectual sophistication. I could hear Greg Ramirez saying to a pair of girls, "The cool thing about the pledge term experience is that it's so—*Dionysian*." His Nietzschean terminology seemed to be distracting them from the place where his earlobe had been.

I, for one, while pining after Emma in the heart of my heart, was left talking to Joanna Hecht.

Hecht seemed to have entered Kappa by accident. I imagine they let her in because she was a legacy—maybe her mother was a member? Whatever the case, she had no interest in the usual run of Kappa obsessions (cocaine, squash players), but had her own staunchly independent take on things.

"I'm really into taxidermy," she said.

"Oh, yeah?" I said. I was interested, but wasn't sure what "really into" meant. It could mean that you were some sort of maestro of the art, or that you had tried to embalm your pet hamster when it died back in the fifth grade.

"Yeah," she said. "Here, check these out." She started flipping through pictures on her phone. "This is my most recent creation—a badger."

An authentically fierce-looking badger crouched in a snarling, defensive position.

"And here's an opossum… and a pot bellied pig I like to call 'Mr. Snuggles'… and a bald eagle… oh, and here's a Bengal Tiger that I did last summer after visiting—"

I stared in morbid fascination, trying to think of an appropriate comment. Finally, I said, "Uh, did you see our moose head upstairs? We have a moose smoking a cigarette. I think some ancient alum shot it. You know, Thurston Weathersby the Fifth or whatever..."

I was getting a little buzzed, and took another sip of my Ocean Spray Cranberry Juice and vodka.

"How did you get into taxidermy?" I asked. "That sounds like an art that gets handed down through families or something."

"No," she said. "I first saw all the dead animals at The Museum of Natural History as a kid when my nanny, Yarnique (she was Trinidadian) took me. That was when I knew I wanted to make some of those. There was just something about them—I liked the way they were so still, yet... *alive*. Almost like—like a witch had frozen them that way!"

She laughed, somewhat disturbingly. The verb "cackled" would not be radically inappropriate.

"Like in *The Chronicles of Narnia*," I said. "The Snow Queen. She froze all the animals."

"What?"

"Never mind." You can't expect anyone to grasp any references these days. "How do you get the animal corpses? Do you, like, poach—I mean, hunt them yourself, or—"

"Oh, my brothers are avid hunters. They've killed things everywhere in the globe. Do you remember when that pet lion was shot on that nature preserve in Zimbabwe and everyone made a big stink about it?"

"Yeah, I seem to recall—"

"Well, we paid some grizzled guy from Montana to take the blame, but that was Chase's doing. Ah, Chase... always provoking these little hic-cups. He's the middle child."

"Huh. Interesting..."

I was appalled, though Joanna seemed nice enough (I guess). Creepy, but not aggressively horrible. What I'm trying to say is, I can't really fault anyone who will willingly talk to me.

68. Cross the Streams

That being said, I wasn't going to try to get in her pants. I had work to do. After taking her upstairs to see the moose head—she deemed it sub-par work—I excused myself politely to attend to a brimming bladder.

In the upstairs bathroom, Turdburger and Merkin were peeing into the urinal at the same time. Turdburger's head wobbled around towards me when he heard the door open.

"Come piss in this urinal with us."

"Uh—no thanks, Turd. I'm just gonna use the stall."

Turdburger couldn't control his urine stream and talk at the same time. He started to piss on the wall and floor.

"Suit yourself." His drunk-bobbling head swiveled back to the front. The stream righted itself.

Now, Merkin turned his head and cocked an eyebrow at me.

"Come on—don't be a fag. Cross streams with us."

"Cross the streams, dude," Turdburger chimed.

"Yeah. Cross the streams."

Pause.

"I'm not going to do that," I said, evenly.

I entered one of the stalls.

As I was taking my own drunken piss, my eyes wandered over the wall, where the words "Ahriman Lives!" had been written in black Sharpie marker. Immediately, this struck me as bizarre.

Ahriman is the name of the evil god in Zoroastrianism, the religion of ancient Persia. In fact, a few Zoroastrians are still kicking around Iran and parts of India—and I'm sure a few have turned up in New York City and other cosmopolitan metropolises. The most famous modern Zoroastrian—if non-practicing—was Freddie Mercury from Queen. (Your pub trivia and Jeopardy skills have just improved, albeit incredibly slightly.)

In Zoroastrian cosmology, the world is a battleground between the all-good God, Ahura Mazda, and his eternal opponent, Ahriman or Angra Mainyu, the Negative Power. It seemed like an extremely arcane thing for a frat boy to graffiti on a bathroom stall, but became less mysterious when I considered that it might've been the name of a death metal band or something. Then again, you had to consider the fact that most Beta brothers were Dave Matthews fans, which was certainly at the opposite end of the musical spectrum from death metal... Then, I noticed something even more perplexing.

Crudely sketched below the "Ahriman Lives!" graffito were a series of interlocking, downward-pointing triangles. It looked like the bright, red-outlined shape that I'd seen when I closed my eyes after experiencing *Silly Squirrels'* hypnotic mind-suck. It wasn't quite the same, though. The design appeared as though a very drunk person had been attempting to draw an identical figure, but had botched it. I couldn't be sure of the coincidence, and, overall, it felt like a random doodle.

Before I could finish this train of thought, I was out of the bathroom and onto the next phase of my mission...

I walked back downstairs, trying to act casual. Realizing that I was loudly whistling the tune to Christina Aguilera's "Genie in a Bottle" in an overly obvious cartoon simulation of casualness, I ceased. Silent and stealthy as a lone puma, I descended to the ground floor and proceeded to the far rear of the house, past the staircase leading down to the basement. The Frat President's room—Alex's room—was located in this hidden rear nook. I knew all the brothers were still down below. I also knew that no one in Beta locked their rooms.

I knocked on his door just to be safe—and entered.

69. A Romantic Idyll

Alex's room was surprisingly messy, even disgusting: pizza boxes, a half-eaten bag of Ruffles, a used condom actually dangling out of an over-full wastebasket, a moldy odor, and a fat laundry bag spilling its sweaty contents across the floor like a vomiting slug mouth.

His desk presented, in fractal-like miniature, the same degree of disorder as the rest of the room. I gently moved aside a Styrofoam container holding a small lake of barbecue sauce, along with several take-out menus. There was a brochure for white water rafting, and a printed picture of an extremely fat woman attempting intercourse with an actual walrus (I hoped it was fake, as it very well might've been: the walrus looked pretty CGI). Finally, I found my pocket notebook, which I immediately stashed in my pocket.

Suddenly, I heard Alex's voice in the hallway. He was saying, "I can make an even bigger muscle with my ass!" In response, a girl laughed—a high whinny.

I ducked into Alex's closet, and just managed to close the door before he entered. I attempted to recede behind the shirts hanging from their hangers.

As Alex made out with this anonymous yet apparently equine woman, I began to feel that ambiguous sensation one gets when trying to keep still—was something crawling up the inside of my left pant leg or not? Enough light permeated from the bedroom that I could read the labels on two of the suits in the closet. They were expensive, Brooks Brothers.

But along with this status-clenching menswear there was a stuffiness that seemed to sap your vitality as you breathed. A dried puddle of an indeterminate liquid lay spread on the floor beside Alex's boots and several pairs of loafers, where it had hardened into a crust. Still sticky though—I delicately pried one of my feet from the surface, careful not to make a noise of Velcro-like separation (not that the sound would've carried into the next room, through all that slobbering face-sucking). I crouched awkwardly between the hanging shirts and suit-coats, as I couldn't feel the wall behind me.

Alex was saying something to the girl.

"Wait," she said. "Don't you have a condom?"

"What?" said Alex, mock appalled. "Where's your sense of adventure? Live on the edge a little!"

Nonetheless, I heard him get off the bed and start moving towards the closet. I continued to recede and recede some more. The closet was surprisingly deep.

I hunched down behind the furthest rack of clothes (there were three), half expecting to tip backwards into Narnia.

The door opened and Alex picked a pack of condoms out of a boot. Then, he paused, speaking to himself quietly—"Did I leave the butt-plug in here, or…?" He started to reach into the back of the closet.

"No," he said. "I sold that on E-Bay, like, a month ago!"

"What?" said the girl.

"Nothing…"

Alex and the girl proceeded to engage in minimal foreplay, before Alex crammed it in.

Trust me, I was trying to tune all this out. And I wasn't watching—you couldn't really see past the closet door. By no means out of the proverbial frying pan—or was it the fire?—yet nevertheless relieved, I leaned backwards.

Unexpectedly, I fell down a flight of stairs.

70. The Secret Passage

They were hard stone stairs, which didn't really make much noise when I fell, aside from a muffled, belly-deep "Oomph!" at the bottom. I lay where I landed, twisted sideways. There were about six or seven steps total.

After a moment of unreasoning panic, I lay in complete stillness. Had Alex heard anything?

I waited. Apparently not. It was a loud coupling. The light emitted from the bottom of the closet door—now above me—did not wax with an opening.

After attaining a relative degree of calm, I proceeded to ask myself the next logical question: "Why are there stone stairs in the back of Alex's closet, leading down to an extremely dark and evidently very long hallway?"

Gently, I picked myself up. Nothing seemed to be broken, though my coccyx felt a little sore. I rubbed my ass.

And then, I realized—it was the passage to The Pyramid.

It had always been rumored on campus that a secret tunnel ran from one of the fraternities to The Pyramid. The President of that fraternity was, allegedly, also the President of The Pyramid Club. Everyone assumed that the fraternity was Alpha, not Beta, considering how much closer Alpha was to the Pyramid, and its greater level of social prestige. Well, we were wrong…

Quietly, and assuming correctly that Alex was distracted by his love-making, I started to investigate.

I immediately freaked.

There was no light, and I had to swat at my face manically after something dangled down from the ceiling and brushed across it.

I moved back towards the thin sliver of light from the closet, where Alex could be heard plowing his conquest. It was very noisy—on his part, not hers.

He kept saying, "Who's the champ? Who's the champ? *Aw, yeah.* Who's the champ?"

Trapped between this sonic grotesquerie and the darkness behind me, I remained still, if not self-composed, waiting for a rotten corpse's hand to fall on my shoulder or neck…and clutch.

Fortunately, Alex's bout of intercourse didn't last very long. Soon, he was alone, and snoring. I climbed back up the short stairway, ever cautious, ever stealthy. I pushed open the closet door slowly—but it started to creak. Alex turned but did not toss. I urged the door to a state just this side of ajar. And it creaked some more. Alex both turned and tossed.

I could slip through.

Instead of tip-toeing and extending the process, I simply bolted. I don't think I slammed the door to the room behind me. In fact, I probably left it open. Alex didn't wake up—at least not while I was still in the room.

And that was, seemingly, that.

On my way back to Barnum Street, I felt elated. I had won a minor victory. Of course, Alex would wonder what had happened to the notebook—but perhaps he would put it down to his own carelessness, and assume it was lost somewhere in the soup of his own comprehensive sloppiness.

It barely compensated for striking out with Emma, but it was, at any rate, something.

71. Pyrite

Now seems as good a time as any to relate a story of seemingly little relevance. It's liable to feel like an awkward digression anywhere I insert it—though, like that bit about Black Northface Jackets, it will eventually attain relevance.

My grandfather had been a gold prospector. He was one of those old guys you rarely see anymore: an unkempt, funny old s.o.b., who sat around his dusty house wearing the same pair of long johns every day. He seemed to know everything, from Tibetan folk cures for minor illnesses to bird-calls that could make a sparrow land on his hand. He wasn't one of these grandpas you see nowadays, who are trying to recreate their youth at a Floridian retirement community and who simulate going to "the hop" before breaking a hip dancing to Bill Haley and the Comets. Oh, no. He knew his station in life; he'd been an ambitious young man and a householder already. Now, it was time for him to ladle out what he'd learned, become a boon to future generations. Experience and wisdom attended him palpably.

Yet he'd won this experience and wisdom through a decent amount of half-assed fumbling. After striking a failed claim in the Klondike, he went broke. His wife and his son (my father, aged seven) were left eating tinned salmon in a drafty cabin with only the caribou and the Kodiaks in the way of neighborly company. Fortunately, my grandfather found a new avenue for his ambition, one that did not require dragging his family to another distant frontier. He decided to try his hand at alchemy.

I may look like a fool, he thought. *But at least I'll confine my foolishness to the privacy of my own home.*

He'd stay up all night, tinkering in the basement with equipment and ingredients he'd ordered from around the world—from wherever alchemy was still practiced, I guess. The old man obtained powders and rare metals used by Taoist alchemists in China, and delved into tattered Medieval and Renaissance manuscripts, which he'd tracked down on weekend sojourns to rare-booksellers in New York City. He had to learn Latin.

Gramps would hobble about in the basement, wearing his long johns, pumping a bellows, delicately pouring volatile powders into even more volatile liquids, interspersing cat naps throughout the day. His quest was for that metal or solution which turns all other metals into gold, the fabled Philosopher's Stone.

One time, he managed to locate a particularly promising recipe. After mixing and boiling and reducing and distilling, he generated something that seemed to be real gold. He was overjoyed—for a moment. After further analysis, it turned out to be nothing more than pyrite. Fool's Gold.

That wasn't quite the last straw, and the obsession wore on a little longer. But it stopped within the next calendar year. He went into New York and scammed a few chumps into buying his alchemy gear, and bartered away all those leftover Taoist concoctions in Chinatown. Thereafter, he became a mailman in Carlin, Pennsylvania.

I think that's where he gained his wisdom—where the real alchemy happened and transfigured his inner world. He had a lot of time to ferment on those long walks, in between the moments when he found himself hopping backwards over fences to escape Rottweilers and German Shepherds.

If a meaning is to be assigned to this anecdote—and I suppose one will be—I think there's one potential hint: there are methods that manufacture a Self in the same way botched alchemy generates Fool's Gold. It gets crystallized all wrong. You have to scrape it out of the bottom of a burned beaker.

72. Emergency Meeting

The day after my stealth operation, Alex called an emergency meeting of all the frat brothers. I was worried it was going to involve my re-acquisition of the pocket notebook, but it began with Alex ranting about keeping the bathroom clean. This was a new topic with him.

"I appreciate the enthusiasm of graffiti artists, but whoever the *fuck* you are— you're not Banksy. I just had to paint over one of the walls of the stall upstairs. Seriously—*girls* use those bathrooms when they're here. They should be *nice, clean, well-lit* places."

Guys were snickering. They thought Alex was making some sort of deadpan joke.

"Do I look like I'm being satirical?" Alex asked, rhetorically. "Just keep the graffiti on the *basement's* walls. That's part of its vibe."

"Girls hang out in the basement too," said Turdburger—who, it occurred to me, based on the strained innocence of his tone, had probably written the offending graffito.

"Yeah, but the basement's *supposed* to be shitty. That's part of its charm."

I tried to imagine a less charming room than Beta's basement… It would have to be some sort of evil Nazi dentist's office.

Of course, I thought about the glyph, the pictogram, the pattern—whatever the hell it was—and immediately concluded that it had something to do with whatever was going on at Zin. My sense was gut-level, intuitive, but I entertained no doubts. Reason bore no strong claims on me…

73. Deceased Zoroastrians

I tried to find more info about this hypothetical Zin conspiracy. I googled things like "Zin Ahriman" or "Timothy Fassbinder Ahriman." Nothing came up. I had no idea if the glyph was connected to Ahriman or not.

Still, I couldn't connect Ahriman to anything else—couldn't locate any bands by that name. It didn't make sense. As far as I was aware, none of the members of Zin had any interest in comparative world religions, let alone ancient Persian religions with very few modern day adherents. The association of Ahriman and the pattern from *Silly Squirrels* was utterly baffling, and I was ready to dismiss it as a pure anomaly.

But there are channels of information other than those made acceptable by Google. For instance… books. I continued trawling through Wilkes' collection, and while I learned some interesting things about the history of Central Asia, I had no idea why anyone would've killed him over this stuff. I didn't even know the name of the man who owned the books originally—the dead guy from a local retirement home. Which local retirement home? There were a few listed online.

I called the nearest senior living center, located in New Hamelin proper. It was a place called The Desert Palm.

"Hello?" A squeaky adolescent boy's voice spoke. It didn't even say, "You've reached The Desert Palm," or just "Desert Palm."

I decided to cut right to the chase.

"Hi, I was wondering: did any Zoroastrians happen to pass away in your facilities recently?"

"What?"

"Zoroastrians. Followers of an ancient Persian religion?"

"What?"

"It's a kind of religion."

"Not that *I* know… but, I mean, I guess it's a possibility. We have some pretty old foreign guys here. Like, some dudes who wear turbans and all—like Talibans or whatever."

"They're probably Sikhs," I said.

"What?"

"Sikhs. It's a religion from India."

"What?"

"Never mind. Just—if you find out if a Zoroastrian guy happened to die there recently, would you call me back at this number?"

"Yeah. Sure."

He didn't sound like he would do it.

"Great," I said. "Thank you."

I decided I would call the other retirement homes later.

74. Judas

After finishing the call, I made a stop at the local grocery store and bought a baguette. I'd developed a craving for a giant sandwich on fresh bread.

168

As I stepped outside, my phone started buzzing. It was a text from Pete, reading, "Dude. Meet me at Beta. Got to show you this crazy thing. Will explain."

Pete hadn't really been interacting with me much recently, despite being in the same pledge class. So, I appreciated this. "Be right there," I wrote.

I walked into Beta's basement, literally whistling, and carrying the baguette under one arm.

All the brothers were standing there, lined up, staring at me. They weren't smiling. For a minute, all was quiet.

"Yeah?" I said. "You want something?"

From my right and left, Merkin and Turdburger grabbed me by the arms, and tossed my baguette onto the filthy floor.

Alex advanced towards me, picked up the baguette, and cracked it into two pieces over his right leg. He tossed the halves behind him.

"Pete…" I said, looking at him.

But Judas evaded eye contact. He inspected one of the far ceiling corners of the room.

"You're under arrest," Alex said.

"What?" I said.

"Uh, *arrest*—ever heard of it? It means taking a criminal into custody."

"What?"

"Uh, custody. You want me to define that too?"

"You have no authority to arrest me," I said. "Nor do you have the grounds."

"Oh, we have grounds," said Alex. "Believe me. We have grounds."

"Inform me of the grounds, then."

"I don't need to waste any more explanatory breath on you, you treasonous anal polyp."

"I kind of think you do. Ever heard of habeas corpus, Alex?"

"Yeah. I have. You want to know why you're under arrest?"

"Yes. Yes, I do. The charges?"

I thought I was remaining remarkably cool under the circumstances—"cool as a cucumber," as is said, particularly a cucumber that has been adequately subjected to modern techniques of refrigeration. (I imagine that a cucumber, sitting out in a field somewhere, gets kind of hot).

"The charges!" said Alex. "The charges are disloyalty, theft from a fellow brother, treason, sedition, giving aid and comfort to the enemy, lewd acts, sodomy, gross indecency, morally polluting the minds of youth—"

"That's what they charged Socrates with," I murmured, even though the whole idea of charges was a vicious joke.

"—and conduct unbefitting a bro. You are hereby dishonorably discharged, unmanned, disbarred, and *banished* from Beta. If you set foot on these premises again, your bowels will be ceremonially burned."

"And he didn't cross the streams with us!" said Turdburger.

"Don't forget about that!" said Merkin. "We told you about that."

"I dare you to burn my bowels," I said, regretting the remark as soon as it came out. "I'll bite. I'll use my nails," I continued, snarling. I also regretted these statements as soon as they emerged. *Dignity*, I reminded myself—*in all things with Dignity comport thyself.*

"Jew Fro—prepare the rite of dismissal."

"What?"

"Get a bucket."

"A bucket?" I said.

"Yes."

"What? What's going to be in this bucket?"

I was nervous.

"Wouldn't *you* like to know?"

"Something gross I'd imagine," I said.

"*Oh, yeah.* It's very unsavory."

"It's going to involve a foreign substance."

"Bingo. But you haven't quite aced the cognitive target."

"What? More clam juice? I can chug clam juice until the cows come
home—"

"No. Nothing will be chugged. You're gonna get doused, dude.
Immersed."

I considered that this wasn't so bad. I would rather be externally covered
in a substance than experience it violating the purity of my innards.

"We're going to dump a bucket of piss over your head."

"Oh," I said. "Gross."

Alex rubbed his hands together—and stopped, self-consciously realizing
the implicit villainy of the gesture. He thrust both hands into the pockets of his
jeans.

"Yeah. It *is* gross. But first—"

Alex leaped towards me and stuck his hand into my jeans' left pocket, and
removed it, triumphantly clutching my pocket notebook. He proceeded to
withdraw a cigarette lighter from his pants.

Soon, my little notebook was burning on the grime-coated and eternally
beer-sticky basement floor. The pages shriveled.

There was no point in struggling. Turdburger and Merkin were both ripped, their muscles inflated to comic dimensions thanks to a steady diet of the same whey protein shakes that Curtis had been abusing at the beginning of this narrative.

Since the brothers had been drinking, they had no problem evacuating their bladders on short notice. Pete contributed his fair share of urine. Indeed, I would say that he took a fairly long piss. *That* stung. The only person who I didn't see whizzing in the bucket was the Senegalese Prince, Omar Seck. It occurred to me that he would often vanish for days, and no one would question his absence. He'd mastered the art of not being noticed.

To make things worse, asparagus had been served in the cafeteria for dinner. The smell was very pungent.

What else is there to say? Poetry pales. This simple, unadorned, declarative sentence should do all the work it needs to do without much labor on my part:

They dumped a bucket of piss on me.

75. The Jacket

They were going to throw me out the basement exit, which led into a small parking lot behind the frat. I protested.

"I need my coat you idiots! If I get hypothermia or die, think about the lawsuits! Think about the, uh, the legal ramifications!" Honestly, if I had somehow frozen to death while wondering home covered in piss, I have no idea how anyone would've been able to prove that Beta was responsible. I mean, the soaked-in-pee detail would certainly suggest the involvement of a fraternity, but it could just as well have involved a group of fetishists or an unfortunate and very complicated accident near a malfunctioning urinal.

It happened that my brain was moving a little faster than the sodden brains that were about to chuck me out the door.

"He's right," said Alex. He sighed. "Let him go. Just get the fuck out of here, Simon. And, you know—*don't come back.*"

"Never return," the others echoed, in an eerie monotone.

"You're hereby banished—after you get your coat."

A minute later, I was upstairs fishing for my coat in a pile on one of the large leather couches. I couldn't find one with a Patagonia label. They were all black Northface jackets.

(I said this would become relevant).

"Found it yet?" said Alex.

"Give me a goddamn second here!"

Finally, reaching deep down, I found a jacket that had been crumpled and wedged between two couch cushions. I pulled it out. It was Patagonia brand.

I walked out the door. Apparently, they didn't feel like hurling me bodily anymore. The strong asparagus-piss odor must have deterred them.

Despite having made such a fuss about the jacket, I didn't put it on. I didn't want to get any pee on it and then need to wash it. Instead, I somewhat gingerly held it away from my body.

Freezing and drenched in rapidly crystallizing urine, I half-walked and half-jogged, trying not to slip on the icy sidewalks. Coming around the corner near the campus chapel, I ran into Sheila Tomlinson and her cousin, a prospective student she was showing around campus. I didn't want to be seen in this state, but the chapel had shielded them from view until they were right on top of me. We came to a halt, facing each other.

"Simon?"

"Hey, Sheila," I said, staring at my feet.

Her nose wrinkled. "You smell like *pee*."

She stated this with a pronounced note of utter and final contempt.

By contrast, her cousin asked with a voice full of sympathetic concern, "Did someone pee on you?"

"Yeah. Sort of," I said. "Don't go here."

They went on their way.

I continued my lonely passage, half-hoping I'd collapse and freeze to death. I tried running to warm up but didn't watch where I was going (being distracted by my ongoing humiliation) and slipped on a patch of black ice, careening directly into a snow bank. For a moment, I thought about just lying there... not intending to die, necessarily, but simply to relax and slowly drift away until... But my inner fire would not abate. I picked myself up.

During the course of my forlorn trudge, I'll admit that I wept a little—not loudly, though. Tears merely trickled, one at a time.

(You might be wondering why I didn't skip over the weeping bit here, or in the part after I found Wilkes' corpse. I recount it merely to demonstrate what an honest and reliable narrator I am. If I'm willing to confess my humiliations in full, you're hopefully that much more willing to buy the rest of my spiel.)

The campus felt paralytic, a single unbroken shell of ice and hard snow fitting tightly over everything.

In front of me, on the sidewalk, a crow was skittering along. One of its legs was injured and the ice and slush were preventing it from taking flight. It hopped and skipped in front of me, almost comradely, until it managed to take flight. It perched on a phone line and proceeded to survey the world with its cold crow eyes.

An exemplar. That was a good way to be. Stick to your line and survey the world with cold crow eyes and no one will dump pee on you, or fall dead and naked out of a closet and land on you…

I made it back to the Barnum Street house. Formerly, it had seemed like some dreary opium den, but now it felt like sanctuary, a warm church. The rest of campus was the desert region, an amoral wasteland where people dumped buckets of piss on certain condemned outcasts—innocent persons selected for this punishment according to obscure and Kafkaesque regulations and rites.

I sat the jacket (which was still clean, if rumpled from its time betwixt cushions) on my bed, and undressed. With a towel wrapped around my waist, I walked to the bathroom and turned on the shower, making sure it would be almost painfully hot. Since I was so cold, it felt only moderately warm. After my body temperature had normalized, I turned the temperature down a little, still keeping it pretty hot. I stayed in the shower for a long time.

When I got out, it felt like emerging from a baptismal font. The stench of the asparagus piss was gone. I'd entered the shower feeling defeated, depressed, just short of suicidal, but I stepped forth feeling spotless, fresh and newborn, washed in the blood of the Lamb.

I'd done a little reasoning while I was showering. Ultimately, what *was* my humiliation? It was a way of escaping a situation that was pretty unpleasant to begin with. Fortunately, it wasn't particularly public, aside from running into Sheila and her cousin, which—since I didn't gel with Sheila—didn't bother me. Overall, I think I'd experienced worse. One time, at a classmate's Bat Mitzvah, a

175

kid named Max Weber (the same name as the famous sociologist) snuck up behind me and yanked down my pants and underwear in front of everyone... But that's probably not as bad.

Technically, I suppose pee is rather a polluting substance—if someone covers you in his or her pee, you're meant to feel defiled. But, realistically, urine is sterile and it's not like I was going to catch a disease. I regretted the loss of the pocket notebook, but I didn't really need it to remember the facts about Wilkes and *Silly Squirrels* and Zin.

So, really, I'd just learned an important lesson: being in a frat wasn't my cup of tea.

After showering, I gathered my urine-soaked clothes and threw them in the washing machine in the basement. Back in my bedroom, I picked my jacket off the bed, intending to grab a pack of ginger mints I'd bought at the student convenience store earlier in the day. They weren't there. The only object in either of the pockets was a ticket stub for one of the movies shown by the film society during the David Lynch Retrospective—*Blue Velvet*.

I hadn't gone to see *Blue Velvet*.

Now, I was relatively sure that this wasn't my jacket. It didn't fit particularly well. It was way too small.

I checked the tag where I'd written my name with a Sharpie marker, and saw someone else's, neatly printed in pen: "Iphigenia Woods."

The jacket belonged to the missing girl.

76. Anomalous Phenomena

Exhaustion sloughed off. I'd been on the verge of emotional and mental defeat, but now I couldn't get to sleep. Instead, I did a little research on my computer.

The ticket stub for *Blue Velvet* was dated for a 7 p.m. show on December 2nd. After looking up local news articles and police reports on Iffie's disappearance, I saw that the last day she'd been spotted on campus was… December 2nd.

I decided I'd better contact Officer Sheerhan and tell him about the jacket and the ticket. Tempting as it was, I couldn't really justify keeping this information solely in the hands of an amateur, occasional sleuth.

I rolled around, got about two hours of sleep, and shot-up straight at 6 a.m. After phoning the police station, I asked them to transfer me to Sheerhan.

"Hey-ya. This is Sheerhan."

"Hello, Officer. This is Simon Senlin, the student who found Professor Wilkes' dead body."

"Oh, uh… You mean the dead guy who was whackin' it in the closet?"

"Yeah. Him."

"I remember that. It's not a thing you easily forget. How's it going? You havin' any of that what's-it-called? You know, the post-stress-traumatic thingy?"

"Nah, I'm fine."

"Good. Some people, you know, they make that much contact with a naked dead guy, they're gonna be a little freaked out. Curled up in a fetal position, y'know, rocking in a corner. I guess it's 'cause of all these trigger-warnings n' stuff, people can't take a little trouble and—y'know—reconcile all the contradictions in their minds."

"Yeah… Anyway, I just discovered something. You know that girl, Iphigenia Woods, the one who disappeared?"

"Yeah, she went to Amsterdam. Probably off wearing them wood shoes in some pot-smoking café or whatever the hell they do over there."

"I found her jacket. It was stuffed between two cushions of a couch in Beta, the fraternity. Her name's written on the tag. People do that in case their jackets get lost or stolen when they're drunk at parties. Anyway, here's the crazy thing: I found a ticket stub in the pocket for David Lynch's *Blue Velvet*—not that that's important—and it's dated from the day she disappeared, December 2nd. Anyway, the time on the movie stub is 7 p.m., and that's a two-hour movie. So, unless she left early, she probably wouldn't have been out of there until 9 p.m, which made me wonder: for what time did she buy the ticket for her Amsterdam flight? What was the time of departure?"

"I've got to look this up now?" An irritated, impatient tone entered into his voice for the first time.

"I mean, if you're not busy…"

He sighed. "Alright, alright. Fine."

I heard him mumbling in the background. "Fuckin' record-keeping… Where the shit…? Fuckin' file cabinet... Goddamn it!"

I heard a file cabinet drawer slam. Sheerhan picked up the phone again.

"Alright, let's see here… The plane left at… 8 p.m. from Logan."

"Eight!?" I said, not exactly containing my excitement. "See! She couldn't have made the flight! There's no way she could've gone to the movies, left, taken the two-hour bus trip to Boston and made that flight! "

"*Or* she might've not gone to the movie."

"But this is a ticket *stub*," I said. "It had already been split."

"Look," said Sheerhan, with a tone of vast weariness—an abyss carved deep by the geological eons. "Some friend of hers probably *borrowed* the jacket. Girls borrow each other's clothes all the time. We've been called to sororities lots of times to try to sort out these issues. You know: someone borrowed a girl's blouse and keeps not giving it back. Usually open and shut. We just storm in and steal the blouse back for the girl it belongs to. It's fun. Sometimes we load the guns with blanks so we can wave 'em around when we do it, squeeze out a few sparks... Point is, you always run into things like this on any case. They're called, uh, anomalous phenomena. You're never gonna get all the facts to fit your theory perfectly, and a bunch of things aren't gonna be explained. But most of the other facts *do* fit. You see? So you go with those and leave the one fact that doesn't fit lying around."

"Uhhh..." I said.

"So you get what I'm saying?"

"Yeah, but—" I paused. "Okay, one more question. Did Iphigenia report any crimes to the cops before she was killed? Did she ever get in touch with you guys, maybe, about a stolen credit card?"

I was thinking that someone had stolen her credit card, in order to buy the plane ticket and provide cover for—what? Murder?

"Nah," said Sheerhan. "Not that I recall, anyway. I mean, you take a girl who's all caught up with smack and that kind of thing—if they run into a problem, they're gonna stay as far away from the cops as they can. Probably get some dude with brass knuckles to sort shit out, if they can afford it."

I tried to think of any local dudes I knew who functioned as private bodyguards or enforcers, but came up totally empty.

"Alright," I said. "Is it okay if I keep you posted? Like if I find out she really *was* at Beta?"

"Sure. But remember what I said about anomalous phenomena. They're always turning up."

77. A Brief Encounter with Judas

I didn't believe that bullshit about anomalous phenomena for a second, plausible though it may have seemed to Sheerhan. Iffie *had* been wearing the jacket at Beta, and had missed her flight—not that she even knew the flight was scheduled. Something had happened to her at Beta. I pictured the dark, damp passage leading from Alex's closet to The Pyramid (well, *presumably* to The Pyramid), and imagined an unconscious girl being dragged down that crypt-like passage, her kidnappers and soon-to-be killers inhaling the ancient air, the particulate matter of death and decay. Would I put murder past Alex? I wouldn't put dumping a bucket of pee on someone's head past him, that's for sure.

For the rest of the day, I tried to figure out my next move. It seemed like there was so much information to process, and I felt anxious, unable to get it all into one place and see it plain. Too bad I wasn't an actual detective, with a billboard where I could tack up all the relevant details and draw connections like on TV.

I was still preoccupied with this when I walked into the cafeteria, and almost crashed directly into Pete. We stood completely still, staring at each other. His eyes were dead. There was no personal hate, just something collective and tribal—a wolf's aversion to a badger who has wandered onto its turf... He was holding a cafeteria tray with a rib-wich and a small carton of milk on it.

"Hey, Pete," I said. I sounded, understandably, bitter.

He didn't respond. He just turned his eyes to the floor.

"How's it hangin'? No hard feelings about dumping that bucket of *piss* on me. " I was kind of yelling and sensed people were probably staring. Things seemed to get quieter around us.

He still didn't look up, but he didn't make a move to get around me either.

"What? Are you *shunning* me?"

Still nothing.

"You know, when the Amish shun someone, at least it's over a matter of religious principle. You're shunning me over a *frat*. Over a fucking circle-jerk." (I hoped the people around us realized I wasn't speaking of a literal circle-jerk.)

Pete moved to the nearest table and grabbed a seat. He took a big bite out of his sandwich, chewing slowly and deliberately. I stood next to him.

"Look at me," I said. "Look at me you fucking Judas…You rat-fuckin' son of a bitch."

Nothing.

"I heard that Preet Bezawada fucked Sheila…"

This had become a widely repeated rumor in Beta. Preet was the captain of the squash team and President of Alpha.

Pete slammed a white-knuckled fist on the table, disturbing three clucking sorority girls seated nearby. But he still didn't look at me, and he kept chewing.

I decided, sadly, that I had no remaining option but to walk away.

Eating alone, I speared my mandarin orange segments with a vengeance, as though I were stabbing fish in a Polynesian lagoon, stranded and bent on survival at all hazards.

I was now officially to Beta what Trotsky had been to Stalinist Russia: the traitor-in-chief, the heresiarch. Yet I doubt many of the brothers knew *why* I had been so labeled. They weren't privy to Alex's secret connections with Zin, and they didn't know about the things that were in my pocket notebook. I wondered if they would throw darts at my picture—though I imagined that would be assigning myself a bit too much importance. Rather than demonizing me, I assumed Alex would wisely consign me to non-entity status. I simply wouldn't exist to them anymore, regardless of whether the other brothers knew what my supposed offense had actually been.

Despite having been so humiliated, drenched in urine, booted into the cold, ostracized by my former closest friend, I couldn't help feeling like a rebel, a dissident. I felt cool. I was in the metaphorical gulag now—a miniature Solzhenitsyn. A dollar-store Solzhenitsyn, if we're being honest...

Also, my liver was more than grateful for the expulsion. Even returning to the old Barnum Street house wasn't so bad. Pete, Curtis, and Oscar were hardly ever around, all occupied with their own fraternal dealings. In fact, I didn't see Pete at all. He was, it seemed clear, consciously avoiding me, hoping to spare himself a repeat of the unpleasantness in the cafeteria.

I would be able to get things a little cleaner—comparatively speaking— and enjoy the silence. Powers of attention, which had formerly dissolved whenever one tried to develop them within the confines of Beta, began to return: I kept reading Wilkes' books, underlining text and theorizing in the margins. Futile, but it killed time, and provided the illusion of progress.

I went to class, thought about Wilkes and Iphigenia and *Silly Squirrels* and Zin and lived outwardly the usual life, dressing and undressing, eating and sleeping. I kept my own counsel, didn't speak to anyone, didn't bother trying to contact Emma or Sheerhan.

A week after my expulsion, out of nowhere, I had a fine and obvious idea. I was surprised I hadn't thought of doing it before. I suppose I'd seemed all too suspended in space, without bearings, staring off precipices, watching pebbles fall from where my feet had scuffled for grip. Following the most tenuous connection—the coincidence of Ahriman and the symbol in Beta's bathroom—I decided to look up "Ahriman" in the indices of Wilkes' books.

There was nothing… until I came to the only book I hadn't read yet. It was entitled *A Journey through Kafiristan: The Diary of Ephraim Calder*. The back of the book informed me that Ephraim Calder was a British surveyor who'd traveled through Central Asia in the late 19th Century.

Turning to the pages about Ahriman, I immediately grew excited. Here was something: the first firm foot-hold in months.

Or, scratch that. It was insanity. Yet, it was an insanity that fit the situation: the evil smart-phone game, the murdered professor, the vanished girl, the secret society…

I've excerpted the relevant passages.

78. From *Journey through Kafiristan: The Diary of Ephraim Calder*
Feb. 3rd, 1897

I have lost my raisins. It's my fault, in part, though the damned coolies offered not a bit of remediating assistance. In a sudden panic, provoked by a rearing pony, they bucked the satchel of raisins right over the mountainside, into an abyssal gorge. In addition, two of the coolies slipped and went over themselves, leaving me with but three greasy and unreliable knaves to tote the remainder of my luggage, though this is in part a convenience—a blessing in disguise, perhaps—given that three is a much more manageable number than the previous, conspiratorial five. Yet, I note how these survivors stare at me with their customary Asiatic insolence, even when they know they stand under my observation. They seemed so cheerful when the journey began, though I did rather resent being surrounded by the constant, incomprehensible babble of heathens. I long to hear the Queen's English spoken once more, preferably by some young filly with a fine Kentish accent, as she tends to me beneath a poplar and we enjoy a picnic lunch of tongue sandwiches.

Perhaps, for posterity's sake, I should note the crucial nature of the raisins, so none mistake me and believe that I am assigning more than due importance to dried fruit. Not so! My temperament is more than normally reliant upon proper nutrition; without a constant, readily available source of sustenance, I grow first moody, then melancholic, and soon despairing—vicious, even, if some unlucky acquaintance impinges or seems to impinge upon me. In my former quarters in Trinity College, Cambridge, you will find a bullet hole in the lower corner of the wall (the wall with the window facing the quad), if it hasn't been repaired recently. I am ashamed to confess it, but this hole is the reminder of a blessedly unsuccessful suicide attempt, in which I would've fired a bullet through my right temple, were it not for the intervention of my roommate, Harry Dormer, currently a barrister in Edinburgh. The cause of this attempt was, I believe, a skipped breakfast followed by a skipped lunch.

I am in nearly such a state now! To make matters worse, I keep thinking of bangers and mash… Bangers and mash! How the saliva pools within my mouth!

Now, I realize that the map I have been attempting to chart is an utter catastrophe. I look at it, and I cannot make sense of it. What is this random collection of squiggles?! It is preposterous. I wish I had gone off the cliff with my raisins; I have no idea where I am, and we seem to have been trekking around the same mountain for days. I am quite certain the coolies are plotting to roll me over the edge in my sleep, and I bloody well wish they'd get around to it. We have nothing left to eat but little bits of dried horsemeat...

I should have listened to Mother and never left Kent. Surely there is some property one can still survey profitably there? Will consider, when I return.

Feb. 4th, 1897

I have been abandoned and will probably be dead soon. Which begs the question—for whom am I writing this? Evidently, for myself—or for none. I am merely marking the time. So be it, if it will keep my mind from wandering in its own infernal loops!

A cold grave or a warm grave: what's the damned difference? A corpse feels nothing.

The snow began with a few stray, innocent flakes. But soon it fell in piles, heaps upon heaps, blinding me. We had arrived on a plateau of sorts; at least, it was some kind of open space; for all I know, we might be in the bottom of a canyon! The path wound upwards and downwards before we reached this place... We strove in vain to find some sort of outcropping to shelter us, but remained wide open and exposed. The coolies began to speak their lingo with considerable animation—and, like that, they were gone. I would not let myself consider the sense of what they said, until it became obvious—*let us ditch this troublesome white burden!*

I have written this entry in a poorly improvised and collapsing tent, with the last of my oil burning in a lantern next to me. The snow piles up outside, and

I feel submerged, sinking. Soundlessly, the element that will kill me accumulates. It is frightening how casual the Deliverer can be in his approach…

Fearful tears stream down and freeze within my muttonchops.

March 3rd, 1897

You will, I am sure, note the delay since my last entry in this diary. I am now in Kabul, feasting upon a "sam-oh-sah"—a delicious, deep-fried pastry of sorts, stuffed with potatoes and peas. It is quite savory… But to get back to what is certainly most relevant and pressing to you, as a reader: the manner of my escape.

When I last wrote, I had been left for dead—quite rightly, as I now see it, from the coolies' perspective—after acting like a perfect horror and becoming caught in a sudden snowstorm. As drift heaped upon drift, I was sure that my flimsy tent would not be able to withstand the storm. I felt overwhelmed, despairing. Having no idea what to do, or how to repurpose myself, I piled every remaining piece of clothing upon my person and swooned into the fabric of the now nearly submerged tent, my mind grown a fatalistic blank. I was sure that I would never regain consciousness.

To my great surprise, I awoke.

I wiggled my toes, and found that two on the left foot were either numb or not there. But the rest of my body was flushed with blood—warm blood. I was amazed at my own presence, and stunned that heaven or hell or (if the Papists happen to have been surprisingly right on one count) purgatory could feel so corporeal. Wouldn't they give me all my toes back?

It was not dark, and I felt near a fire. Fire did not augur well for heaven, admittedly, but this was too pleasant and comforting a fire… hearth-like, in fact.

It was not burning me. This, I reasoned, could not be hell... or at least not the strictest hell of John Calvin's imaginings. This came, of course, as quite a relief.

Someone came near me, and threw more wood on the fire, causing it to spark up and illuminate the fullness of the cave in which I found myself.

It was a native. He was a kindly looking sort alright—with a big bushy beard and sharp eyes. He'd been up here in the mountains a long while by the looks of him. A sadhu, I reckoned, a kind of ascetic holy man of the Hindu variety. You find them all about in India, typically beggars smoking hashish from little pipes. Yet, this fellow transmitted none of that squalid feeling. He looked at me with a kind of sardonic patience.

Bloody hell, I thought. *I've died in a pagan land and wound up in one of their afterworlds; it is just my luck. I'll never see another Englishman again... or another Englishwoman, most importantly and consequentially. I shall be painting my face with ochre and eating lentil stew with my cupped fingers and...*

"Are you awake?"

The face was certainly native, but the voice spoke unaccented English. This was perplexing, if a relief. Since he wasn't speaking his own lingo this probably wasn't the native heaven. It was a bit more accommodating.

"Your eyes appear to be open and appear to be staring at me."

I continued to stare.

"Well," he said. "I don't ask much of company—or can't—and a mute Englishman is not the most terrible dinner companion. Preferable to an especially vocal Englishman, at any rate."

"What?" I said, suddenly put-off.

"Oh dear... I'm sorry to have offended you."

"I should say…"

"But I think that when one man saves another man's life, the saved ought to be grateful, though I can't say I would be particularly upset if you were to snub convention. I like to think I'm past all that sort of cheap emotional response. But if you want to make the requisite, token gesture—of course, I wouldn't object."

"You're saying you saved my life?"

"Yes."

"So I'm not dead?"

"No, you're not dead. Do the souls of dead men arrive in heaven with toes still missing from frost-bite? Isn't the after-life a bit less corporeal than that? Though I'm not sure precisely what Christian theology has been saying on these maters—not these days, anyway…"

"Well, I was wondering that bit about the toes myself…" I started to feel a tad mournful. I was glad to be restored to life, but it did occur to me that I would never get those toes back. One lives in such intimacy with one's body parts, toes included, it's rather like a death in the family even to have a pinky toe go… I won't say it's like losing a sibling, but at least like losing a cousin you liked fairly well.

"Oh, and thank you…" I said. "Thank you—very much!" I said this in a still bewildered voice, but wagged my head up and down for emphasis. He smiled, if ironically.

"I wonder," I said. "How you got me out from under all that snow… I think I was fairly buried and… My coolies—I mean, friends—had all buggered off. And the snow was blinding… How did you…?"

"Oh, you know—a touch of supernatural powers gained from prolonged meditation and yogic exercises. Though I suppose that's more ammunition for you lot—you can have your signs and wonders, and a nice exotic story for an

Imperial penny dreadful, but you won't cut to the chase. Excuse me. I mean, you won't recognize what's made this 'magic' possible."

I was beginning to get a bit confused. "Why? What *has* made this magic possible? Not that I admit you found me through magic. I've read Darwin and Huxley, you know. You'll find no more confirmed agnostic in Britain than myself."

"Then you'll understand. It's a matter of knowing, of seeing—of where you put your attention. I was brought to you through the power of sustained attention, of deeply cultivated awareness. That's how I found you."

"And why did you save me?"

"One likes to rack up a bit of good karma from time to time. Get in some points with the Big Man." He spoke pleasantly, but he was clearly making fun. The entirety of the conversation felt dream-like.

"How did you get up here?" I said. "I mean—what is all this?" The cave appeared to be sparsely furnished, primarily with rugs and a few cushions, but comfortable. Smoke from the fire flowed up through a natural chimney between the rocks. A tea kettle started whistling.

"Fancy a spot of chai?"

"Yes," I said. "Oh, yes… Delighted."

The native began to pour the tea. "You asked why I came up here. I suppose I was seeking some peace and quiet in which to do my work. One is so battered by distractions these days, though I imagine it's going to get quite worse… Oh, it will, in fact. A century from now they will be floating on a sea of distractions—a few pieces of driftwood, life-rafts, and broken oars, keeping them afloat. It will get much worse indeed." He served me the tea and paused to inspect his fingernails.

"And you?" he said. "What are you doing here?"

"I'm a surveyor. I was supposed to be making a map. But that's been shot through the arse, now. I have no idea where I am, I've been abandoned." I stared into the chai, indulging my self-pity. Pulling myself out of it, I remembered certain ancient proverbs about keeping one's upper-lip stiff. I asked him, "How did you come to speak such perfect English?"

"Well, I lived in England for many years. I studied law in London."

I was astonished. "Is that so?"

"Oh, yes. You've deigned to afford a few of us natives certain prized opportunities—to the more privileged sorts, anyway. But I grew incalculably tired with the Laws of Man. I've come up here for all the reasons you'd expect— to look into the heart of things. And I've got an assignment. The Order of Asha wants me to remain here."

"The Order of what?"

"Of Asha—oh, aren't you acquainted with the teachings of Zoroastrianism? This isn't precisely the same thing as Zoroastrianism—what we're doing—but I take it your not an Orientalist of William Jones' caliber?"

I recognized the name of the great scholar. "Well, I, I—I certainly make an effort, but when you get into the more obscure sorts of faiths, it's hard to keep it all straight—Jains and Sikhs and God-knows-what. No offense."

"None taken. At any rate, I am on assignment from the Order of Asha— an assignment loose and binding at the same time. I barely know the other members, though they're about—even in your country."

"And what does this Order do?"

"Oh, save the world and that sort of thing. We counteract the influence of the Negative Power, of Ahriman. Ahriman—it's the same name as the dark god

190

of Zoroastrianism—is, as we understand him or it, a force that's always trying to get the world to move about on a grid, so to speak. If he can't regiment it, he'd rather it didn't exist. He sows disorder by spreading his own kind of malign order. What he wants, really, is your attention. Oh, he'll further any old thing as long as it's debilitating and as long as it siphons attention down to him. There's a book you might be able to find in Britain on this subject. It's called *The God of Smoke and Mirrors,* authored by an anonymous Anglo-Indian penman in the early part of this century. You should give it a look. It has an image on the front of it—a pattern of triangles, all pointing upwards. That's the Order of Asha's symbol—though, if you turn it upside down, it becomes the Order of Ahriman's insignia. For he has his votaries too…"

None of this palaver made any sense to me, though I politely posed questions and the chai was good. The man was speaking in a wildly associative burble, though his words were not without a heathen charm. I recalled some spurious stuff I'd heard from a devotee of Madame Helena Blavatsky about her teachings, known as Theosophy. The Theosophical Society held that world events were being directed by a band of Mahatmas, spiritually advanced humans living high-up in the Himalayas. It occurred to me that this fellow, whatever else he might be, could have fancied himself a Mahatma and journeyed up here to the mountains in the hopes of meeting with his confreres.

"I say," I said. "Are you—or do you believe yourself to be—a Mahatma? One of that Blavatsky woman's secret masters?"

"Ah," he said. "I think it would be hardly worthy of a Mahatma to say that he—or she—was a Mahatma. After all, the term means 'great soul.' So, for either truth's sake or humility's sake or perhaps their mutual sakes, I say, 'No.'

I'm not a Mahatma. But I suppose you could call me a member of the Inner Circle."

"The inner circle of what?" This seemed like a natural rejoinder; I was a bit tired of all this elusiveness, the caesura he invariably left in every utterance.

"Of humanity," he said.

"Ah, so you're part of some sort of power-mad cabal up here in the Himalayas, stirring up the nations?"

"Far from it. We're merely preserving the soul, giving it a place to grow—a still space set aside for its inner regeneration. We wish for humanity to attain concentration, fullness of being, and we make every effort to support that goal. We know that it is easy to concentrate in the mountains, with so much ground under your feet. But down below, the floor and the minutes seem to slip out from under you. 'Build a hedge around the Torah,' that's what a great rabbi said. He didn't mean to prevent people from reading—he meant give wisdom a place where people can come to it, can have access. That is what the Order of Asha works towards—that is *asha*, you see: 'order that springs spontaneously from the soul,' not order which is imposed from without. In praxis, however, we in the Order of Asha are utterly decentralized. We hardly know who our brothers-in-arms and sisters-in-arms might be. Yet the fact that they are there, that they are laboring mightily, makes the task run so much more smoothly. Ah, it is heavy stuff—but it all feels so light!"

"And why do you tell me all this?"

"Why, I can tell you are a skeptic, and you would die a thousand deaths before you confessed all this to your peers. Plus, you don't even know where you are. This could be merely an incredibly vivid dream, or an advanced hallucination in the mind of a man, dying in the Kafiristani snows. You are harmless."

He was, of course, correct, but I was a bit taken aback. I like to think I am not quite so fang-less.

"Well," I said, "even if you are a very articulate madman, I suppose I owe you my life. Is there any thing I can do for you?"

"Certainly," he said. "I don't care if you tell anyone about this or not but you should write it down, privately. Make a record of it. Who knows? A century or more from now it might prove of scholarly interest. It might prove of use."

"I record everything in my diary," I said. "And something so sensational as this will unquestionably get a full-ish treatment."

"There you go. When you wake again from sleep—you're feeling tired aren't you?"

"Yes," I said. Suddenly, I was feeling *very* tired.

"When you wake again, you will be in your tent on a plateau cleared of snow. Your, ahem, 'coolies' will find you. You must do your best by them, and make up for your awful, boorish, classically dreadful Imperialist behavior."

"Yes," I said, helpless to lodge protest in favor of my case.

"Yet, you will know this was real, because I will leave you with a gold medallion, bearing the seal of the Order of Asha—the pattern with upward pointing triangles, a kind of 'yantra' as the Hindus style it. It will find its way into your assorted knick-knacks but you will remember it from time to time and it will inspire a certain worthiness in you, further an aspiration to train your attention. And you will remember everything I say to you. You may yet serve our purposes in some obscure way… And we will need every drop of aid we can get. The forces massed against the development of human attention are vast

193

indeed. Oh, there will be great dictators"—he mentioned two names, sounding something like "Het-ler" and "Sta-leen" (gibberish designed to impress, of course)—"and great systems of distraction. If we cannot preserve opportunities to cultivate the inner self, Ahriman we'll scatter the seeds of attention to the winds— sift them like wheat. He'll melt everything down to a great soup of dullness, a vast gray ocean where no necessary words—no wisdom—will sound through the general noise. There will be a grand dissolution... For all of this was once a black ocean, infinities of night with courageous sparks isled throughout. But soon, if Ahriman gets his way, the mountains will melt into the ocean, and the ocean— black ocean—falls into the Sleep of God. Planets fall into the sun, the sun falls into the stars, and the stars fall into the Sleep of God. Everything falls into God's Sleep. Everything. In the end, it always happens like this." He shrugged. "But for a little while longer, we can remain—awake!"

When I awoke, it was just as he had said. I made peace with the coolies, and we trekked onwards, reaching Kabul after an uneventful week—but a week marked by beauty, by the pure serenity of the Himalayas, and a feeling of heavenly lightness. I felt as though something had gone into me through the sadhu's eyes (mad or imaginary though he may have been) and that I had brought with me a little chip of his own tranquility in the form of that medallion, which I have before me now. I turn it in the light, and something about it makes the soul want to aspire ever upward, to dare again the viewless summit...

Needless to say, this is all a very advanced psychological trick, lingering effects of some Hindu's admittedly pleasant form of hypnosis... In any case, he's damn right about my keeping my mouth shut, for the present.

79. Initial Skepticism

This was a lot to process. My first reaction was skepticism.

What was this? Fiction? At first, I couldn't prove that it wasn't. The book wasn't available on Amazon—odd given the breadth of out-of-print titles typically available there. Also, the parts of the diary preceding and succeeding the section I've just excerpted were of virtually no interest; the later chapters are slightly more pacific in tone, but Ephraim Calder has mainly resumed the litany of complaint that carried him through the earlier pages, though with less contempt and humbuggery. Bewilderingly, beyond the last entry I excerpted, he doesn't reflect further on the miraculous event that befell him. Rather, he focuses a great deal on the untrustworthiness of his bowels under the influence of Central Asian cuisine.

If it *was* a genuine work of non-fiction from the 19th Century and not some utterly bizarre forgery, it indicated, for starters, that an old hermit in the mountainous wilds of Afghanistan had mystically foretold the rise of Hitler and Stalin—and not in a vague, Nostradamus-type way. He'd actually called them out by name.

A little more online research confirmed that the book was an actual journal: on Google Books, I found a reference to it from an early 20th Century bibliography of first-hand accounts of the British Empire in Cental Asia. I was surprised that no one had mentioned the document since, given the natural attraction it would have for cranks; it hadn't made its way onto any bogus, conspiratorial History Channel documentaries as of yet. With that Hitler and Stalin business, it seemed like it would be at the center of *someone*'s conspiracy theory.

More important than that odd detail—an "anomalous phenomenon" if ever there was one—was the greater outline it had charted for my developing conspiracy theory: to wit, Zin employees were worshipping the dark god of Zoroastrian myth, Ahriman, while attempting to brainwash the Wilbur student body into being Ahriman's puppets through the use of a ridiculous and childishly simple videogame, *Silly Squirrels*.

I had to admit this sounded implausible. Fortunately, I'd been left with more than loose ends.

I decided to head over to the library—immediately—and find the copy of the book the hermit had mentioned, the Order of Asha's *The God of Smoke and Mirrors*. Perhaps surprisingly, the online catalogue listed it, though it was marked as a damaged book, located in an annex full of books that were missing pages but couldn't be repaired. They weren't considered valuable enough to be classified as "rare," yet also couldn't be thrown away. They were available to the student body and the public without special permission.

It's strange how things can hide in plain sight. By making an ostensibly esoteric and hidden text into a public document, you somehow ensure that people ignore it.

80. Misfit Books

To access the section full of ravaged misfit books, you entered the old library (the pleasant-looking brick one) and climbed through the stacks until you crossed a bridge connecting you to the new library (the gigantic steel-and-glass larva that appeared to be parasitically devouring the older structure). You wound upwards further until, within the most secret innards of the creature, you found yourself in a silent and surprisingly ill-lit room. I think this was the most infrequently visited corner of the entire edifice.

My feet tapped softly on the floor, a metal grate that looked down to the story below. The stacks were dark until you walked into a specific row. Then, a low orange light would come on in that passage, activated by a sensor, and barely illuminate the titles located in that aisle. The design was part of some energy-conservation effort, and provided just enough light to force you to squint at everything. It also made the stacks more than a little creepy, isolating you in a small pocket of weak light while the rest of the floor remained dark.

I found the book without too much difficulty: a thin volume bound in that green buckram which provides new covers to ancient library books. When I opened to the frontispiece, it showed the same insignia I'd seen after playing *Silly Squirrels*, although it was now turned upside-down—or, rather, right-side up.

As I pulled it off the shelf, I realized that someone else was in the room with me. A light clicked on a few rows away. Technically, this shouldn't have been anything to worry about. But, after discovering Wilkes' corpse and the missing girl's jacket (not to forget my encounter with the pee bucket) I felt a deep, bone-level disquiet.

I listened to the intruder's feet enter the row next to mine and saw the aisle light turn on. A figure was moving back there, inspecting books on the shelf, searching…

"Is that you Simon?" said the figure. I started to sweat and clutched the book with a slight tremor in my hands. But the voice was familiar. It bore a British-accent with a foreign tone lightly underlying it.

"Yeah," I said. "It's me. Uh, I'm fine." It occurred to me that the figure had not actually asked how I was doing, but I continued, anyway—"You?"

"I'm well, thank you." There was a pause. "What are you looking for way up here in this dismal place?"

I finally realized who was talking to me: it was the Senegalese prince, Omar Seck, the Beta brother who never seemed to participate in the debauchery, the man who lived in the margins without really seeming marginal. To the contrary, his presence was always imposing. You sensed you were encountering a man with definite powers of mind—or, I suppose, taking a page from Ephraim Calder's hermit, an intense degree of attention. But I had no idea whether he used this resource for good or evil.

"Oh, I'm just browsing," I said. " I like to check out the damaged misfit books from time to time. It's interesting—fragments of things, torn out of context. Can we ever know what they really, uh, meant? It's an interesting question…"

I was going to keep talking out of my ass, but Omar posed another, uncomfortably direct question

"What's that book you have there?"

"Oh, this?"

"Yeah."

"Oh, it's nothing, really."

"Well, it's got to be *some*thing. Clearly, it has pages, with words on them."

He was normally so quiet and spoke so infrequently. I could only assume that this was not a chance encounter. He was trailing me, presumably on behalf of Beta... or the Order of Ahriman.

"Oh, I think it's something related to the occult," I said. I decided to dare him to reveal a bit more. Since I barely knew what I was getting into, it couldn't hurt to force him to say something. Or, perhaps it could hurt—if he suddenly shivved me.

"Ah," said Seck. "Are we talking about séances, Tarot cards, astral projection, how to make a golem? What kind of occultism?" There was something teasing in his tone, like he already knew what the book was and why I'd been looking for it.

Accordingly, I decided to vary my directness with indirection. Keep him on his toes.

"It's about all that stuff. I'm actually really interested in the occult. Oh yeah—the occult and I. We go way back. Tarot cards, telling fortunes with tea leaves—you wouldn't think it, but that's my thing. I love the occult—love it… What are you up here looking for?"

"A book."

There was a pause.

"What kind of book?" It was my turn to pull a tooth and force an answer.

There was another pause.

"Well," said Seck. "It's rather obscure. I'd doubt you'd ever heard of it. It's something called *The God of Smoke and Mirrors*. Very dubious stuff—I need it for a paper I'm working on in a religion class."

I was terrified. We were still conducting the entire conversation from opposite sides of the bookcase. I couldn't see him, but I sensed he was smirking. He knew I knew he was lying.

"Never heard of it," I said. "What's it about?"

"Oh," he said, continuing in a humorously faux-bored fashion, "just the end of the world, cosmic conflict between good and evil—things like that… Does the book you're holding have a title?"

"I'd imagine."

"Well, do you know what it is?"

"No," I said. "I like to know as little about a book as possible before I start it. I like the element of surprise."

"Sure. But this is the *title*, Simon."

"I know, I just—"

"Look, mate. You don't need to freak out. I know you've got *The God of Smoke and Mirrors*."

I took a breath. "Okay. How do you know that?"

"That's not important. What's important is that you hand over… Alright, I don't want to say 'hand over the book,' menacingly, like a villain from Indiana Jones. But, essentially—yes, that's what I am saying. I need the book… and not for a religion class."

"Why?" I said, "So you and the other assholes at Zin can keep indulging all this freaky occult shit you're up to and erasing all the traces? It's nerdy and pathetic. That's what it is."

"No. You don't understand. I can't explain, but… Listen to me. It's better that you don't get involved. And, again, I know I sound like some sort of villain cautioning a main character not to get involved. But, *really*—this is a delicate situation. You're throwing a wild card into the mix, and I can't let that happen. So, just hand over the book—"

I bolted. The door was directly in front of my aisle, and I had the element of surprise. To be honest, I'm not sure if Seck even chased after me; he might've just stood there and sighed a classic sigh of exasperation. But I was, at the time, pretty concerned he was going shoot me with a blow-gun (or some damn thing),

200

and leave *my* naked corpse framed for autoerotic asphyxiation, strung up somewhere on campus. I got the hell out of there.

81. Green Dildos

Feeling like Seck was right behind me—even though he wasn't—I ran cross the bridge and charged down the stairs, swinging around corners with aid from the railings, panting as I set foot at the bottom, back on the ground floor of the old library. I stood there quietly panting for a few minutes.

Then, I saw Seck emerge from the elevator nearby.

He didn't appear to be in pursuit mode, but he immediately noticed me and gestured, urging me into some sort of private conference. Seck seemed concerned, eager to talk, not bloodthirsty. But I figured it was all a ruse. Having recently been doused in urine after being baited by a friend and having read about the methods of assassins in the course of personal research (how they have no problem murdering someone in broad daylight while provoking minimal fuss) I continued my escape.

The elevator and the stairway both opened into an area with computers for searching the library catalogue, along with shelves of encyclopedias and other reference books. This area led directly into the central hallway, which ran from one end of the library to the next. Fortunately, protestors were crowding the hall, right in front of us.

Wesley Cross was leading them, agitating against the school's mascot, the Wilbur Viking. It was not a new theme with him; I recall him disrupting a football game with a bullhorn and throwing a bucket of red paint on the Viking mascot, saying it symbolized the blood of those murdered throughout the centuries by Vikings.

Yet, at present, he couldn't quite decide on the angle of his outrage.

He was shouting through a bullhorn, "Vikings used to pillage—and *rape*! Plus, no surprise—they're *white*! I'd expect no less from the Wilbur hegemony…"

Shortly, he switched to a different tactic: "And also, who are we to culturally appropriate the image of a Scandinavian person?"

Coherence was never a high priority with Wes, and he switched from one approach to the next, as though they were not contradictory.

Finally, bored with repeating the same things, he started raving about the negative comments on feminist Youtube videos: "You know what some oppressor called Lena Dunham on there? A 'fat bitch'! He's talking about the Susan B. Anthony of our era that way… Although she has her issues too… I mean, I'm not saying I'm a fan… In fact, she's highly problematic. But this is the level of discourse we're at… Pieces of white dog shit!" He couldn't help digressing.

At any rate, as Wes harangued, I attempted to evade Seck. I plunged directly into the throng, dexterously weaving between protesters. They had a uniformly sad and doughy look—like human putty, unformed, looking for a hand to gently prod them into shape. I guess Wes's hand was the hand they'd settled on.

I looked back over my shoulder to see if Seck was gaining on me— and, in the next moment, I inadvertently crashed through a large paper sign held by two protesters, emblazoned with the words, "Fuck Your White Tears!" It tore neatly into two halves, one reading, "Fuck Your" and the other, "White Tears!"

I knew my mistake was bound to be misinterpreted. I stared at the two protesters who were clutching these separate pieces of paper, and they stared back. They thought I was attacking them, and the pasty pair prepared to meekly withdraw, already cowering. But Wes saw what transpired. He was ready to give direction, re-channel the willpower that was leaking away from this unfocused protest.

"Get that white motherfucker!" He shouted. An accusing finger jabbed in my direction.

Weak hands pawed at me. Fingernails scratched my cheek. I struggled and threw random elbows in all directions. They backed away.

"Fuck off!" I shouted. "Fuck off! I'm just trying to get through the library."

"Yeah, that's what we're trying to *prevent* people from doing. *Doy*," said a girl with large super-corrective lenses in her black-framed literati glasses. "We're making a statement."

"I know," I said. "I'm not objecting, I'm just... I'm just trying to make my way in peace..."

By this time, the crowd had parted, and I managed to cut somewhat free of the protesters. I was about to breathe a sigh of relief, when Wes shouted, "Get him! Get that frat boy motherfucker!"

I was already a bit winded, but I made it to the end of the hall. The protesters (many of them disastrously out of shape) were not lagging but not exactly close either. I stopped at the point where the hall entered the library's lobby, where the school had installed a piece commissioned from the famous and controversial Chinese artist, Deng Xizing.

Wilbur had requested a piece symbolizing cultural unity—which is what they thought they were getting, until Deng revealed his project at the beginning of the school year: a wall, lushly spiked with hundreds of dildos of various sizes, all painted green. Xizing had entitled it *Modern Life Force Testament*. After some internal debate the administration decided to mount it—in a small recession in the wall at the point where I now stopped. It had also been placed behind a curtain. Tour guides were under strict instructions not to show the parents of prospective students the dildo wall.

Without considering that I was desecrating a work of art, I tore the curtain aside. The school cared so little about Deng's project, that they hadn't bothered to nail it into place or do much to otherwise secure it: I discovered that the dildos were all attached to a piece of green fabric that was itself stapled to a large wooden board. Grasping the end of this piece of fabric, I pulled.

Dildos rained down as I artfully dodged away. They fell on the floor, dividing the protesters—who were just catching up—from me, their quarry.

I laughed a heroic he-man's laugh, and ran for the exit. When I reached it, I paused and turned around. I saw that the protesters hadn't slowed down, and were attempting to run over the dildos at full speed. The first arrivals tripped, and those behind them piled-up.

It was glorious. There were screams, moans, sounds of nearly suffocated terror as the entire deranged mob ground to a halt. I stayed long enough to hear the confused librarian, seated at the front circulation desk say, "Shhhhh!" to Wes's defeated followers.

Strangely enough, although the whole incident was probably caught on security camera footage, I never received any summons from the administration for desecrating an art exhibit. They were glad to have it dispensed with, I guess. I imagined a custodian dolefully sweeping up the scattered dildos before chucking them in a trashcan. Or, perhaps, they were re-attached to the fabric and shipped into storage.

Occasionally, I would see Wes around campus, but he never brought this incident up and studiously avoided making eye contact with me.

82. Excerpt from *The God of Smoke and Mirrors*

Back on Barnum Street, I settled in with my new treasure, which, it occurred to me, I'd never officially checked out of the library. I'd stolen it, effectively; it was so old and disregarded that it was apparently incapable of setting the library's security gate off as I'd passed through it.

Inside, the title read *The God of Smoke and Mirrors: A Brief History of the Order of Ahriman*, and the author was identified as "Rustam Suhrawardi, Order of Asha." Pictured below was the pattern of upward-pointing triangles. The words "Donated to Evergreen Books" were stamped at the bottom of the page. (Evergreen Books was a local used-books store. Somehow, it had made its way from there to the Wilbur Library.)

There were only two pages inside the book, a preface. Everything else was missing, had been torn-out at some point.

Here's what it said:

No one knows who first told The Great Lie, but the words were certainly inspired by that spirit of all-ordering disorder, Ahriman (or as he is otherwise oft known, Angra Mainyu.) He masquerades as the Lord of Law and the Keeper of Truth, when he is but little more than a Builder of Grids. Since the whisperings of his malicious tongue first wafted into the hearts of men, the laws have been instruments of punishment and control, rather than harmony under truth.

In the Golden Age, when even the dust of the earth tasted sweet, Asha, the divine principle of spontaneous harmony, still prevailed, proportioning the limbs and sustaining the bones. But, with that creeping and persistent insidiousness for which Ahriman is noted, The Great Lie proliferated and created a dreary round of being, a pattern that locks up the divine imagination and suppresses The Spirit. We dwell today within that dull circle, in this IRON AGE, mistaking disorder for order, and cunning for creation. Our eyes have grown accustomed to his darkness.

We first note the organization dedicated to the propitiation of Ahriman (though called by many different names) in ancient Babylon, that city of confusion. There, the gods were considered as slave masters and humankind as slaves, existing but to provide their overlords with sacrifices, burnt meats, and goblets of blood. ("They even forget, all deities reside within the human breast" – to quote Blake). In all ages and in all countries, human sacrifice has been a specialty of the worshippers of Ahriman.

The Aztecs worshipped him under the name Tezcatlipoca, "The God of Smoke and Mirrors," propitiating him with human sacrifices. The druidic cult of the Wicker Man—in which captives were imprisoned and burned to death within a gigantic wicker statue—is also believed to have a covert relationship to the Order of Ahriman. As Asha remains pure under many guises, so The Great Lie of Ahriman can be spoken in many tongues.

The Order of Asha, like the Order of Ahriman, has its origins in obscurity, though we suspect that many key figures from history were members. Thomas Cranmere notes that among the artifacts listed in Shakespeare's will, he left to his daughter a single gold medallion, which, the will notes, is embossed with "a strange symbol" consisting of "many interlocked triangles, pointing upwards" and "an inscription writ in a foreign tongue." The description of this triangular symbol strongly suggests that Shakespeare had been initiated into the Order of Asha.

But this is a subject for scholarly research. The truth is that the Order of Asha usually remains secret even unto itself; it is spontaneous order, not orderly order, and can never be held to a fixed form. Quicksilver-like, it runs through the generations, remaining the same substance, but always changing—fluid and flashing brilliant.

Ahriman has no such constancy, but is at his best when a society grows floppy and dull. And the soil has already been prepared... In the midst of a dreary laxity—a state neither here nor there—he constructs his iron order. Indifference is his most precious ally in this effort. For the Order of Ahriman exists to no purpose other than possession and domination, these being enjoyed not to an end but for their own sake. He hates the defined character and loves the empty suit.

It is said that someday, when the wheel has ground round its axis so many times, bringing it farther and farther from the Light of Asha, that Ahriman will himself step down to earth. Then will the false order reign, and Asha's harmony—the spontaneous bloom, the shaft of sudden light breaking through a cloud, the water drops slowly building an icicle—will retire. Asha will no longer be audible to gross ears, but will remain ever-present, super-audible, hidden like the silence that always lives behind noise.

Ahriman will rule over all...

But will his reign be long?

83. Burdens of Proof

Of course, that's the way Zin would do it. If you wanted to get everything moving in the same course, you'd work through a screen. Needle right in through the eyes and ears. Get intimate. Make them hold it right up to their faces so The Thing could jumps out at them with its tiny invisible tentacles and piercers and pincers and starts getting in everywhere, planting depots in all the organs—up the nostrils, in the butt, in the chest cavity. The downward pointing signal, flashing everywhere. Zin and Ahriman would localize Central Planning in the brain and build a tough, unpickable knot of mastery there. That's where the chartered river would flow through its chartered course. (If you want to get Blakean, it's very Urizenic.)

It all made ridiculous and confusing sense. Ahriman liked making sense. You could imagine him—or it or whatever—as some aristocrat in a white powdered wig, offering toasts and seducing with eloquent words. Insinuating.

He must've had different incarnations in different ages: a reasonable white-wig-wearing Loyalist flattering mentally-tottering kings; later a Commissar turning hot lights on sweaty and pale intellectuals, hiding manuscripts in secret drawers; and now… a Silicon Valley billionaire who wears flip-flops to business meetings, casually plotting mind-control. It was the perfect disguise; the final form of disguise, really.

I was—to cite a cliché—"shocked but not surprised" to discover that an evil secret society following a dark god of deception was trying to take over the world. The fact that it was using a tech company to do this made a lot of sense too—that was probably the least disconcerting part of the revelation. I mean, *of course* that's what Ahriman would be up to in the 21st Century. What had previously been true in metaphor—the mechanization of the soul—was now established in fact. It was *literally* his plan. It's always interesting to see a good metaphor realize itself…

What to do about it though? I guess I was morally obliged to try to stop their evil plan… Yet I wasn't sure how to do that. Too many people seemed to be involved. You couldn't just call the cops and point to Alex and say, "Arrest this man!"

But hold on…

I was skeptical. Or felt like I should be skeptical, guarding against my own taste for fantasy and the irrational. Certain details seemed blatantly false.

For one thing, I looked up Shakespeare's will online and there was no mention of any such medallion in it (though he did leave his wife his "second best bed"). And this Order of Asha business sounded like an incredible mish-mash: Zoroastrianism, Shakespeare, Aztecs, and Druids, all rubbing elbows at some bizarrely multi-cultural, implausible interfaith buffet. To my eyes, this document felt like a weird forgery.

Scholars claimed the same about certain Rosicrucian documents that had surfaced in early modern Europe. These documents stated that the Roscrucian Brotherhood, an esoteric and mystical society, was about to reveal itself to the world. If it *had* been revealed, it was in a pretty low-key fashion, since the world didn't seem to take much notice. The Order of Asha was, if it existed in any form, flying low under the radar.

Perhaps this was an elaborate hoax. But how did Omar Seck know that I was looking for the book, anyway? And what about Ephraim Calder's diary? Was that a hoax, as well? Sure, it had been mentioned in that old bibliography— but maybe the pages I had read were a modern invention, the interpolation of an eccentric publisher, who for some inscrutable reason, was in on the hoax? But how could such an obscure and odd hoax, revealed to virtually no one, cause Wilkes' death or involve a famous scientist?

One could only venture a shaky hypothesis: Canzoni had lent his mind-control expertise to Zin to help craft their videogame. He and the Zin higher-ups were somehow entangled in this Order of Ahriman business. Wilkes had accidentally received books related to the matter of this conspiracy, and Zin eliminated him after they discovered this fact. If that was the case, Wilkes had died for nothing; he never would've read those books, and certainly never would've noted anything peculiar. If he accidentally found himself facing the relevant pages, I'm sure his eyes would've brushed swiftly over the bit about Hitler and Stalin without registering the anachronism. Poor Wilkes.

Of course, this was assuming that the Orders of Asha and Ahriman even existed in the first place. Perhaps all that existed were people who *thought* they were in these ancient mystical fraternities. It was not entirely implausible, and the notion reminded me of Jorge Luis Borges' great story, "Tlon, Uqbar, Orbis Tertius" about an imaginary country which, in a non-supernatural way, manages to assert itself into reality. Perhaps the Orders of Asha and Ahriman were a relatively modern invention, the creation of a bizarre conspiracy? I couldn't rule anything out.

If Alex hadn't painted over the wall in that Beta bathroom stall, perhaps I could've shown Emma the "Ahriman Lives!" graffiti, and let her read the pages from Calder and Suhrawardi. Could that have been convincing? I badly needed an ally, just one other person I could confide in…

I didn't have one. For the present, I had to play Rambo, and launch some reconnaissance on my own. I'd seized valuable documents, but I really needed human intelligence: I needed someone living, in the flesh, to back up my speculations—speculations that seemed to be drifting around me like flakes in a snow globe, the atmosphere of a private world and no other.

Which must be how crazy people feel.

84. The Polar Bear Plunge

The following weekend, Wilbur's Winter Festival began. Drunk alums crowded the campus—collapsing on broken-down couches in their old frats and sororities, groping and berating the freshmen, turning the snow yellow. I had no natural position from which to experience the event, no home base; I would have to endure it as an infiltrator, dancing round the periphery and looking for a point of entry or contact or *something*.

To be honest, I wasn't a fan of the Winter Festival, despite its status as the principal annual on-campus event. The previous year, I'd found it an unusually bleak celebration. There was too much drunkeness extended over too long a time. By the end of the culturally sanctioned bender, you felt hung-over, anxious, out-of-commission. A burnt-out case. The wintry gloom enhanced the sense of desperation. Everyone seemed to be indulging in forced merriment to stave off Seasonal Affective Disorder. There was nothing *relaxed* about the Winter Festival, and letting loose on this occasion paradoxically seemed to generate a lot of tension (sexual tension, social tension, what have you).

Friday afternoon, I went to the Polar Bear Plunge at Monomoy Pond near the New Hamelin country club, which always signified the opening of festivities. The students carried thermoses of hot chocolate and Irish coffee; I, myself, was drinking a particularly Gaelic cup of coffee, though my liver was still trembling in its recovery from pledge term. Pete, Alex, and a selection of other Beta bros were all preparing to take the plunge. They, of course, wouldn't acknowledge my presence, just as I pretended to ignore theirs while actually observing them. The Beta cohort shivered in their bathing suits, looking both hung-over and intense, beleaguered yet aggressive.

Every Greek organization sent some members to participate. First the Alpha brothers (largely lacrosse and squash players and sailors) immersed their Apollonian figures in the frigid waters, before a group of nervously giggling sorority girls from Delta took the plunge. They screamed as though they were being ax-murdered.

Next, the Beta bros readied themselves at the pond's icy edge. They dropped their robes and revealed Speedo-appareled crotches, provoking scattered wolf-whistles from interested female parties. They stretched, flexing their arms, shaking limbs loose, exhaling steam.

Yet, when they were about to dive in, something weird happened.

The *Silly Squirrels* theme music rang out from one of the spectator's phones. In retrospect, this was inevitably going to happen at some point during the proceedings, given the game's popularity, but the effect was profound: Pete, Alex, and the rest looked around, seemingly unmanned, vulnerable. They huddled uneasily like wildebeests exposed to the fanged uncertainties of the Savannah. The tinny tune seemed to be affecting them in an unusual way, one I hadn't noticed in anyone else before. Usually, it just Pavloved nearby addicts into reaching for their own phones...

Soon, the source of their discomfort became graphically apparent. *The theme song was giving them all boners*. I emitted a single, high-pitched "Ha!" when I finally realized how the Speedos were being distended. It was a "Ha!" of discovery, the revelation of another mysterious clue. Everyone else remained silent.

212

I turned to gauge the crowd's reaction, to see if they'd noticed. A few of the spectators seemed unpleasantly prompted themselves—possibly to arousal, though it was impossible to tell with all the winter wear piled on. Some started reaching for their phones, reminded of their own addiction. But, for the most part, the crowd didn't seem to notice what had happened—though a few faces were on the cusp of hilarity. Emma's, thirty feet away from me, was one. I was pleased to see that she still hadn't yielded to *Silly Squirrels*…

Once the theme song died down, the Beta Bros. regained their bearings. They exchanged glances before jumping in at once. But the customary cheering had grown subdued—a small portion of the crowd was now riveted to their phones, and the rest had been slightly discomfited by the generally odd vibes. I was looking across at Emma, wanting her to notice me, wanting to communicate via a pregnant glance: *Don't you see what's going on, yet?*

I don't think she realized I was there.

85. Master of Disguise

I decided to sneak into Beta during their Winter Festival party and get down to some amateur espionage, make a real *Harriet the Spy* move. I felt oddly giddy as I prepared, experiencing a childlike strain of excitement—like how I used to feel running around backyards with friends, squeaking code words into walkie talkies. Albeit, the fact that I was a college student made those feelings seem wholly ridiculous and marginally pathetic. Yet I indulged them.

Beta's Winter Festival Party (every frat threw one) was nonsensically themed "Halloween in February." It provided the perfect opportunity to infiltrate them, synchronous with my purposes.

213

Friday night, I stayed in—I didn't strain after merriment, and I had no place to go, anyway. After an electric session of brainstorming, I came up with the perfect idea for a costume. It was face and form concealing... (No, not a burqa. That would be "cultural appropriation" mixed with transvestitism, something to offend the Left and the Right). But I had to see if Costume Outlet, over in Grover's Falls, still had it in stock...

Saturday, I got up early to catch one of the public buses that ran at seemingly irregular intervals through New Hamelin. After an hour sitting next to an old hippie, who had some sort of medical condition that made his mouth hang wide-open, I disembarked outside the shopping center in Grover's Falls, which had a vaguely post-apocalyptic feel to it. The outer white shell of the building looked somewhat charred, and the stores all appeared to be closed, their interiors in shadow, even though some of them were open. A former supermarket was utterly vacated, the outline of the letters that used to form its sign still visible— light white against the wall's dirty white. Through the large front window, you could look at the empty aisles. It gave you the erroneous sense that there had been a vast looting spree after a catastrophe.

Just two doors down was Costume Outlet, which also looked especially desolate on this frigid day in late-mid February. This was comprehensible, given how out of season it was. "All Costumes on Sale!" said a paper banner, ravaged by muddy footprints and trampled into the sidewalk outside. To the store's left was a tanning salon called Mocha Oasis, and to the right a Chinese take-out place dubbed Fortunate Wok.

Inside Costume Outlet, only one clerk was on duty. She was clearly a local; almost all the girls at Wilbur had perfect teeth, straight and blindingly white, but her teeth looked more like mine. There were no major dental problems, nothing severely uncorrected, but her choppers were not utterly and expensively ideal. They weren't downright *British* either—simply standard lower-middle-class American. She smiled and waved to me when I walked in.

It was clearly not the time of year for costume purchases. As mentioned, the lights were barely on, probably to save power, and one had to squint at the lettering and illustrations on the boxes in order to identify what kind of costumes they contained. At first, I wandered into an aisle that seemed to be filled entirely with outfits for male strippers—cop, fireman, lumberjack, all erotically-tinged with break-away crotches and mid-riff displaying tops—before dodging over to the next aisle, which had a science fiction theme. That was what I was looking for. After a moment of further browsing, I found what I needed.

As I purchased my disguise, the clerk said, "Oh my Gawd, that is wicked cute!" She smiled again, and I smiled back with my own relatively imperfect set.

Excited, barely self-contained, I waited around another two hours for the bus to arrive. It kept no apparent timetable. In the meantime, I ate a spring roll outside Fortunate Wok—before rocketing back into Fortunate Wok to use the bathroom. I emerged just in time to skip onboard.

Back in my room I spread the costume on my bed and admired it with an idiot-grin I was having trouble suppressing. I would be an Ewok, as originally seen in *Star Wars: Return of the Jedi.* No one would suspect an Ewok of being a spy! Cuddly warrior teddy bears—so much cinematic treacle to the critics of the '80s, pure cocaine for child fans ever since. George Lucas knew what side his bread was buttered on.

They would be checking I.D. at the party, so I moved to Phase 2 of my master plan: stealing Oscar's ID. This was too easy. It had been sitting on the coffee table, along with about fifty other random objects, for more than a month.

I don't know how that guy managed to function without it: you needed it to eat in the café, go to the gym, get into parties, and enter sporting events, among other things. Yet, he never had it physically on his person. Unwittingly, he'd conspired with Providence or Asha or whatever was guiding me. Oscar's example just goes to show that if you really don't give a shit, most of the accustomed formalities slough off like snakeskin: he didn't care, and he still survived. (Of course, his rich sugar baron parents helped facilitate his survival.)

I spent the rest of the day feeling alternately amped and nervous, my mind drifting off to the same Kafiristani peaks Calder had once (allegedly) visited. As I enjoyed a solitary dinner, scarfing down two slices of vegetable pizza in the caf, I pondered. What would Beta do to me if I got caught? I'd already received the piss treatment, so they'd presumably need to do something more drastic, in order to enforce the logic of deterrence. Expulsion was attended by humiliation and contact with a defiling substance; in order to uphold my banishment, another element would need to be added. I guessed it would be intense physical pain, and not just a fist in the face. It would be… *a violation.*

The stakes were very high.

86. Night of the Ewok

Back at Barnum Street, I geared up, put on my "game face" before hiding that face behind a cute and fuzzy, yet impassive Ewok mask. On my way to Beta, I walked past a freshman dorm, an edifice dating from Warningbone's administration. It was a giant concrete cube with little slits for windows. It looked like a place for suffocating excess lab rats. Some architects seemed to enjoy sucking the charm out of life, though I have to admit that there's something a little awe-inspiring about large-scale concentrated charmlessness. I reflected

216

that it had a distinctly Ahrimanic feel. Ahriman probably showers his blessings on all lifeless, functionalist architects—like the firm who designed the metallic and glass library addition that appeared to be devouring the old library (as previously discussed).

My range of vision in the Ewok costume was not exceptional. There was no peripheral vision, just a tunnel straight-ahead through the Ewok's mouth hole (which was actually the eye-hole). I stumbled through a campus in the already weary throes of Winter Festival debauchery: bleary-eyed frat boys staggered across the green, pausing to throw snowballs at a group of sorority girls who were stalking along on high-heeled pumps. The girls screamed, tried to run, slipped, crashed. The frat boys lurched over to them and threw more snowballs at their splayed bodies.

Boy meets girl… That old story.

Finally, I reached Frat Row, strolling casually over to Beta—just any old Ewok out for a bit of a jaunt, looking for a sexy girl Ewok to have Ewok-style sex with and produce many Ewok babies, who would grow into intense and violent warriors, like their ancestors and their ancestors' ancestors.

At the door, Pete was checking I.D. cards. I waited in line behind two freshmen guys, who were dressed as Batman and Robin. The Robin one was hissing at the other, "I'm not your sidekick. Remember that."

"You're just scavenging in my wake, getting all the bitches I reject… You're definitely a sidekick."

"Dude, that is so not the case. I—"

Pete said, "I.D.s?"

They removed student I.D. cards from their actual functioning superhero belts, and Pete—after some stage-squinting and internal debate—let them in with a show of cool reluctance.

I pulled my I.D. out of a Marsupial-style pouch, with which the Ewok costume had been outfitted.

Pete looked at it. "Oscar, dude! I thought you were going to New York?"

I shook my head no. I'd been so out-of-the-loop, I had no idea Oscar was supposed to be off campus.

"You said you were going to get drinks with your former Salsa lessons teacher. You said you wanted to seduce her and shit, even though she's over forty."

I shook my head no.

"You can't talk in that thing?"

Yet again, I shook my head no, then tried for a dim, muffled Dominican accent, "It's hard to be understood."

"What?" said Pete. He paused... And said, finally, "Alright, cool. Have fun. There's some hot girls in there in really slutty costumes. Like, dressed as Disney Princesses where you can see through their tops and look at their tits. It's awesome."

I walked through the living room, heading straight for the basement. As I stepped carefully down the stairs, a wave of humid heat swept up and into me, permeating the Ewok costume. Beads of sweat broke out everywhere.

Making my way into the scene of the party proper, conditions grew rapidly nauseating inside the suit. I smelled fresh sweat, stale beer, and witnessed masks and pale and painted faces flickering in the strobe light. The ordinary lightbulbs had been replaced with black lights, making all the spilt substances on the floor eerily luminous—Pollock paintings and Rorschach diagrams

A few pong games were in progress, and the Beta brothers looked to be dominating. I noticed Alex at one, with the Kappa president next to him—he'd evidently roped her in after that post-cocktail freak-session, which I'd done my best not to observe.

He was dressed as a Tele-Tubby, the purple one with the purse (I think it's called Tinky-Winky?), while she was dressed as another, the yellow one. Whenever they scored a point, they would bounce their Tele-Tubby bellies together, just like on the show. They were evidently beating the crap out of a surly-looking Turdburger, who was dressed as a giant baby, sucking a pacifier.

Meanwhile, a section of the basement had been cleared off to dance. A white girl costumed as Princess Jasmine from *Aladdin* was grinding her ass up against a guy appareled as The Mighty Thor. Making my way over to the edge of the dance floor, I crashed into Clifford the Big Red Dog—neither of us had any peripheral vision—before Chewbacca tapped me on the shoulder, apparently thinking that it was worth noting that we were attired in costumes from the same franchise. Elmo from *Sesame Street*—a girl with no mask, but in a furry red onesie—was surreptitiously massaging the penis of Teddy Roosevelt through the fabric of his Rough Rider pantaloons.

The DJ, a bored-looking and indeterminately ethnic student (himself a recent Beta alum, I believe), was chain-smoking. There were a massive amount of butts already dead in the ashtray in front of him. Presently, an EDM re-mix of an old song was playing: "I Want to Be Adored" by The Stone Roses. The singer was saying—

I don't need to sell my soul—
He's already in me...

The atmosphere could send your mind bouncing like a pinball, careening off odd angles in its neon pattern. Everywhere, there were hunters, surreptitious agents of Ahriman. And the hunted? The quarry was not conscious of its position, and chewed on a limp leaf of kale, ensconced in that bliss so notably characteristic of ignorance.

I noticed that the Tomb Room was open. Sometimes, during parties, they let people hang out back there, smoke hookah, fondle each other. It was a little less loud than the main room, and you could have a conversation by raising your voice, as opposed to communicating entirely through screamed monosyllables.

I found a seat on one of the cement benches, beside a group of extremely drunk Kappas. I tried to sit back, observe. I wasn't entirely sure what I was looking for, but I felt that if the Beta brothers wanted to momentarily have a private exchange with each other, they'd retreat back here. Maybe I could get a sense of something.

However, as soon as the drunk sorority girls saw that I was dressed as an Ewok, they wouldn't leave me alone.

"Oh. My. God! Look at that bear!"

"Ohjesuschrist, that's so *cuuute*!"

"Here—take a selfie!"

One of them bent in, and hooked her arm around my neck. She made what is commonly known as a "duck face."

"Oh, wait, I didn't have night vision on!"

"Okay…"

She made the duck face again, while her friend re-snapped the picture.

"Let's see if the costume has a little bear penis!"

"Maybe it's a girl bear?"

"It's not a girl bear…"

I was briefly groped.

"There's no bear penis on the costume."

"There's something in there though…"

"Who's in there anyway? Who are you Mr. Bear Man?"

I was enjoying the attention well enough, but I couldn't be distracted from my mission for too long. I decided to show them Oscar's I.D. to cover my true identity. But, when I fished the card out of my kangaroo-like pouch, their reaction was different from what I'd anticipated.

One punched me directly in the face, slightly rattling my skull around inside the mask.

"This guy's a total perv," she said.

"Really?"

"Yeah. It's the guy who snuck into Kappa and stole all our panties. Stole them so he could *smell* them."

It's kind of funny that they were calling Oscar a perv when they were just attempting to grope my Ewok costume's imaginary penis.

"This is the guy?"

"Yeah—Oscar Olazabal."

"But now, like, look how encumbered he is—"

I attempted to interject: "There's been a misunderstanding—" But through the mask and the layers of noise from the main room, it was impossible to hear.

221

There certainly had been a misunderstanding too, and not just because I was in the Ewok costume and not Oscar. Oscar wasn't the guy who'd stolen the panties. It was a dude named Orlando Ortega. It had been all over the school paper. But they were too drunk or stupid to consider that there might be another Latino on campus possessing a first name and surname beginning with the letter "O." (If Wes had witnessed this, he would've immediately launched a "Rally Against Hate," lobbying for the expulsion of all the sorority girls).

They were rearing up to assault me, when their phones made a high-pitched noise—all at the same time. It even carried over the EDM music. Strangely enough, they paused. They seemed to forget their rage instantaneously, and started fishing out their phones. Pretty soon, all three of them were playing *Silly Squirrels*.

I observed them—mouths slightly open, eyes riveted—and had to marvel at their total transformation. Ahriman had unwittingly cut me, one of his enemies, a break.

There were voices at the door. Alex and Pete entered the tomb room.

As they moved towards the corner where I was sitting by the sorority girls, I decided to slump over and look like I had passed out, stretching lengthwise across the cold stone bench.

They stopped near us, conducting their conversation in a volume-adjusted whisper. Technically they were yelling, but, in the loud context of the room, it sounded akin to a stage whisper. I could just make out what they were saying.

"You think this is a good place to talk?" said Alex.

"Sure," said Pete. "Those girls are locked into *Silly Squirrels*, and that fuzzy dude looks asleep."

"Cool. Anyway, I just wanted to say that we fixed the boner issue."

"Thank God…"

"Zin was transmitting a faulty signal, and had to re-adjust it. They worked out the kinks."

"So we're not going to need to get our brain chips replaced?"

"No. The chips are fine. We won't need to bring the surgeon back up. They'll keep insulating us from the effects of *Silly Squirrels* for the rest of our lives, thank Ahriman."

I remembered how Beta was mainly impervious to the Silly Squirrels craze. Everyone except its members seemed to be addicted to it.

"Yeah, praise Ahriman," said Pete. "I feel like such a nerd saying that, but—"

"It is what it is. Part of the gratitude we owe." Alex shrugged. "I don't question it. And Ahriman seems to be upholding his side of the bargain."

"Man, he really is. I just got notified: I'm going through to the second round of interviewing for the Zin internship. I wanted to say thanks—to you *and* to Ahriman."

"Dude…" said Alex. He clasped Pete in a husky bear hug.

"I owe you one," said Pete, post-embrace.

"Thanks, man. I appreciate that. And so does Ahriman, though you know how he *really* likes to be thanked…"

"Yeah…"

There was a chilly pause.

"Anyway," said Alex, "you should go back out there and talk to that girl dressed as a slutty Little Mermaid. She was all over it."

"Yeah. I can be, like, her Gaston."

"Uh, that's *Beauty and the Beast*. And Gaston dies in the end."

"Really? I thought he was the hero."

"No, dude. That was the Beast."

"Oh, yeah."

They ambled back to the main basement. I felt like my curiosity had been satisfied. I was, indeed, a sane man who had sanely stumbled upon a bizarre occult conspiracy—or I was totally insane and the world was conforming to my hallucinations. Whatever the case, I'd found the confirmation I needed. Of course, I wished they'd said something about Wilkes, or Canzoni, or Iphigenia...

I walked upstairs to exit through the main living room. On the leather couches where I'd found Iffie's jacket, a group of partiers were entangled. Evidently, they were all high on MDMA. A girl dressed as Xena the Warrior Princess massaged the left earlobe of a boy attired as Kermit the Frog.

"Oh God..." she said. "Your earlobe feels so... significant. It's *soft*."

"Errrrmmm," said the boy, contentedly.

"I think... I think I *love* you."

She said this with wonder, surprised at her sudden realization.

I headed towards the door, but noticed that a coat rack had been installed in the entryway. And one coat was hanging on it—mine. The label was Patagonia.

Since I'd never actually gotten it back, I did the natural thing and took it off the hook. As soon as I removed it, someone tackled me from behind.

"I got him!" he said, proceeding to sit on me. It was Merkin.

I struggled, but the costume made struggle difficult. My furry Ewok legs kicked fatuously at the air. Maybe I should've just gone as the Phantom of the Opera—something a little more nimble...

I heard Merkin pull out a walkie-talkie and croak, "He came back. Yeah, the traitor... *That* traitor... Jesus, yes, *Simon*... Anyway, he was trying to sneak in here, dressed like a fuckin' Furby."

"I'm an Ewok!" I shouted. The mask muffled my voice. I don't think he ever knew what I was actually supposed to be.

87. Interrogation

Turdburger and Alex arrived. Together, they dragged me back to an unoccupied room, down the hall from Alex's. It was a storage closet containing cardboard boxes full of unused and forgotten items—Christmas lights, a set of the complete works of Charles Dickens, a broken plastic pink flamingo, a grandfather clock that appeared to have been punched directly in the face, and a non-functioning pinball machine.

After removing my mask, Merkin and Turdburger held me by the arms. Then, Alex punched me in the stomach, knocking all my wind free. It hurt.

"What the hell are you doing here?" he asked.

"I could ask you the same question." Always stall. Evade. Obfuscate.

"I read some of your little notebook, by the way," said Alex. "You're a fuckin' weirdo. Walking around, observing people, wrapped up in your own theories about life."

"And theories about your girlfriend's pussy," I wheezed.

Alex punched me again, harder. I was mildly worried I was going to crack a rib, but the terror (the deep-rooted fear of... *violation*...) was worse. How were they going to do it? Pool cue?

"Shut the fuck up," said Alex. "I suppose you know what's coming next... I wish I could say I didn't want to do this, that it was a duty rather than a pleasure, but I'm always glad when leisure and business intersect."

He picked up something that was sitting on the box behind him. What was it? An... *eggplant*?

It was an eggplant—with considerable diameter in addition to its formidable length.

"Get him out of the costume first."

Turdburger and Merkin tried to wrestle me out of the Ewok costume but it was harder than they expected. I wriggled. I bit. I spat. I just avoided getting my nuts smashed, receiving another brutal blow to the solar plexus instead.

They got the costume off and pinned me down.

"I can make you squeal like a piggy!!!" said Alex, quoting *Deliverance*. (They had ample occasion to quote that line at Beta and did so frequently). He proceeded to laugh in a fashion that I would not hesitate to describe as "maniacal."

It was all over. My underpants were down... the eggplant was descending.

The room filled up with smoke. At first, I thought it was a mental aberration—the brain reacting under stress, falling out of phase with reality. But everyone doubled up coughing, myself included. The air had turned highly acrid.

In the middle of our respective coughing fits, Merkin and Turdburger accidentally let go of me. I bolted for the door.

In another moment, I was racing down the hall, pulling up my furry pants, as the smoke detectors started to go off. It was an utterly piercing sound. You could feel it in your bones. I think it was probably designed that way so that even deaf people would realize it was going off.

Before I reached the front door, without slowing down, I swiped my jacket from where it was lying beneath the rack, and blazed out into the winter night. The pledge checking I.D.s clearly didn't who I was as I shot past him.

Outside, it was snowing. I was glad to have that jacket back.

88. The Classiest Party of the Year

I was convinced that, if Alex had managed to sodomize me with the eggplant, he would've strongly considered killing me afterwards—probably dragging me into the tunnel leading to The Pyramid and slitting my throat somewhere in its inner reaches. I would've received the Iphigenia Woods treatment. Post-morten, they'd find a ticket for a spring break flight to Cancun purchased in my name... Eventually, people would presume I'd been killed by a cartel after venturing out of the safe areas, just like Timothy Fassbinder. Maybe Alex and co. would even mince me into pieces and ship my remains down to Mexico, where they'd turn up in plastic trash bags...

And the smoke... What was that all about? It was an uncanny stroke of luck that the alarms should go off at just the right time.

I kept running, almost slipping on the ice. I'd been wearing jeans and a t-shirt under my Ewok costume, which is part of what made it so hot. Now, while not exactly warm, I was at least re-united with my jacket and not freezing to death.

I decided to run through a patch of woods that cut through campus. Instead of taking the most direct route to Barnum Street, I would come in around the back of the house. I didn't want to arrive home only to have Alex and his goons break in seconds later and slit my throat after stuffing a zucchini up my ass. I'd see if they were staking the place out first. If so, I'd find somewhere else to go. But, if I could sneak in before they got there, I wanted to preserve my laptop, the Calder book, and *The God of Smoke and Mirrors*.

It was a frigid trudge—full of frosty pine branches and wind whipping snow in my face—but I made it back to the house with relative ease. All the lights were off. No one seemed to be there.

Which is probably how it would look just before they ambushed me.

But I needed to preserve the Calder book, needed to save the evidence. I didn't know if Alex had read the entirety of my pocket notebook—if he had, he had ample reason to murder me. It recorded my suspicions about Wilkes' death and the lunch with Canzoni, but it also touched on Ahriman and the nature of Zin's conspiracy. For some reason, I didn't think he'd read much of the notebook beyond the initial few pages… Unless Omar Seck told him about how I was checking *The God of Smoke and Mirrors* out of the library. But I wasn't sure of Seck's motives, or whom he was working for...

I'd thought more about it, and Seck didn't seem to be involved in Zin or in the life of the frat. Intuitively, he didn't strike me as a member of the Order of Ahriman. Perhaps he was a member of a certain other organization—the one utterly opposed to Ahriman? But the idea seemed too fantastic…

I entered the house through the back door and crept upstairs to my room. Without turning on the light, I stowed my computer in my backpack, along with the books. I also put a hooded sweatshirt on under my jacket, and donned my black woolen winter hat and a pair of gloves. I ditched the Ewok pants.

Downstairs, the front door opened. They evidently didn't think I was home, because they weren't trying to be quiet. It was Pete and Alex, the latter of whom loudly announced, "When that butt-fuckin' son of a bitch gets back here, I'm gonna ram this eggplant so far up his ass…"

I gently pulled open my window and stepped out onto the roof overhanging the porch, backpack slung over my shoulder. The roof was covered in snow and, beneath that, ice. Not the firmest place from which to make a clean and noiseless escape.

I managed to close the window behind me, before getting down on all fours and crawling towards the edge of the roof. The snow prevented me from totally slipping, granting a little purchase. I made it to the edge and saw where snow had been piled up off to the side, at the end of our driveway. Making sure my computer was securely fastened to my back, I jumped—and nailed the landing, with only the slightest sound upon impact.

I had to figure out my next move… Not so easy, since I'd alienated nearly all of my former comrades, not to mention Emma. I remembered how, freshman year, I'd written a paper for Preet Bezawada—the President of Alpha, and one of Sheila's sexual conquests (as I'd mentioned to Pete, earlier). We'd both been in the same class, "American Literature 1900-1950," and even though I was but a lowly freshman and he a socially superior junior, he'd identified me as someone worth parasitically binding himself to.

Normally, I would've refused helping him on ethical grounds, but he offered to pay me a decent amount—one hundred bucks—to write his final paper on Edith Wharton's unpleasant and disturbing black mass of a novella, *Ethan Frome*. I received due compensation, and, after my work earned him an A- (he'd only asked for a B+ quality paper) Preet was effusive—"I owe you, man. You need a favor, you need anything, just let me know. I'll make it up to you."

229

Of course, those were standard phrases to express appreciation, not a guarantee of anything. But it couldn't hurt to see if he'd let me crash on a couch in Alpha.

It being the midst of the Winter Festival, Alpha was hosting its own annual debauch, a party advertised as "the classiest way to dumb down on campus." All the pledges had to dress up in tuxedos and serve guests caviar on silver platters and champagne from ice buckets—at the same time, they had to leave their flies open and hang their wieners out while they were doing it. Invariably, a surreptitiously-taken photo of a pledge's member made it onto the internet after this event, and ruined his life. Yet, the tradition continued, senselessly, like public executions by stoning in Middle Eastern countries.

Alpha, fortunately, was not on Frat Row (part of its separate and superior status), which meant that I felt no need to cut back through the frozen, lonely woods. I merely pulled myself out of the pile, brushed the snow off myself, and dashed three blocks towards campus, stopping on Alpha's front porch. Pete and Alex didn't follow—the lights were now off in the house as they settled in to wait for me.

Alpha seemed curiously subdued. Only a little noise was emanating from the basement, and Preet Bezawada was standing on the porch, supported by two crutches, checking I.D.s—though no one was there to have I.D. checked but me. (I'd picked up my actual I.D. before leaving the house. Oscar's had been left inside the Ewok costume's pouch).

"Hey Preet," I said.

"Yo, Simon—how's it going? Haven't seen you around for a while. I thought you'd joined our arch-rivals." He laughed, but it was edged with bitterness—not towards me, but towards Beta.

"Not anymore. I de-pledged."

"Oh, yeah?"

"They dumped a bucket of piss over my head... As punishment for betraying them or something."

"That's gnarly."

"For sure."

"You want to come inside?"

Usually Alpha was more exclusive and selective than all the other frats—not so inviting. But Preet's voice was unusually eager.

"Of course," I said. "You mind if I crash here? I'm kind of evading some people. It's a long story."

"No problem. I think there's a spare recliner in the living room—lots of alums passed out on the couches in the common room, though. They're all drinking themselves into comas—that's basically who's here. Seems like most of the sorority girls are hanging out at... other places."

"Like Beta?"

"Seems like it. For a bunch of status-less no-names—no offense—they seem to be doing pretty well for themselves. First they poached Kappa, and Alex got their president all up on his dick. Now, a few more sororities are hanging out there—Gamma and so on. We had a few Epsilons over tonight, but one got her lip stuck in her braces and started bleeding, so her friends had to call an ambulance. I think she might've been, like, a hemophiliac... Point is, things aren't the same. I can't keep up with the pace of the changes... It's like, we used to be on top of the world. Now, half of us are just addicted to games on our phones...

"We used to be golden he-men, Masters of the Universe. Tom Wolfe would've slobbered over the tiniest minutiae of our culture, our internal organization. We were a sociologist's or an anthropologist's field day—a case study in *dominance*. We were dripping in status, and every drop fell to the ground and magically became a lake of even more status. It was self-perpetuating, eternally renewing.

"But, now, we're receding, shriveling up. It's like this whole cycle of decline. I don't really get it, and I've never read Spengler or anything, but I guess we reached our apogee, and now it's the ebb tide. It really sucks to be the president who presides over that… I mean, I feel kind of responsible. It's like being George W. Bush, but I think I'm really more of a Gerald R. Ford type. I'm just kind of… there, you know? I'm supposed to be the doer of doers, but I've become a spectator—a spectator at a moment of decline that I am helpless to arrest. And I slipped off the balcony a week ago and broke my leg, which sucked too."

After this gush of uncharacteristic eloquence and self-revelation, Preet lapsed into silence. Clearly, these experiences had worn him haggard, hollowed out the area around his eyes, given him a gray ascetic cast. I could hardly believe that I would've applied the adjective "robust" to the same person a mere two months ago. But, physically and mentally defeated as he was, decline had certainly made him articulate. Back when I'd written that paper for him, he'd spoken in a telegraphic series of "dudes" and "bros" and "dude-bros" and endless repetitions of "like." Now, he was capable of delivering a fairly lucid and sober oration on the front porch of his frat at one in the morning, on a night when he would've normally been incoherently drunk, upbraiding pledges as their scared, shrinking penises attempted to retreat back into their open flies.

89. Tashkent

Upstairs, the bodies of alums littered the surfaces of broken couches and Barcaloungers, as was occurring in every frat on campus. (Recent alums frequently visited on big party weekends.) They were all sleeping; not one stirred or checked his email messages. It was like the Island of the Lotus Eaters.

Yet the quality of sleep varied greatly: some slept a deep infant sleep, mouths wide open, drool pooling on the already stained couch fabric, while others slumbered fitfully, moving about and causing springs to squeak. Some appeared to be having nightmares, and cried out. Others talked in their sleep, cryptically. Obtuse snatches of dream issued from their lips:

"The milk should be in the fridge... not out here... not out here..."

"I can only give you two of my fingers. I need to keep the other ones."

"The sign says... *No mayonnaise for sale!*"

I found the single remaining unoccupied armchair and, still keyed up and not particularly tired, took out my laptop and began to do some research. Not for class—no, I was still ignoring all that. The research related to what was now, quite obviously, the central and consuming matter.

The day before he died, Wilkes told me that the Soviet Union had conducted experiments on psychic phenomena in Tashkent, Uzbekistan—a fact he'd picked up from Canzoni. It seemed like an interesting detail, one that jumped out at me because it actually had something to do with Wilkes' subject and was not another morsel of Led Zeppelin trivia. When Emma mentioned her meditation research and her study of yogic superpowers to me over lunch, this is what I was trying and failing to remember. I decided to unearth some info about whatever had gone down at Tashkent.

There were a ton of conspiracy-oriented websites with ostensible information on the topic, though these tended to veer off into discussions of ancient aliens and the like. Eventually, I came across some more reliable data, an article written for a respectable weekly news magazine. It was entitled "Soviet Psychics Exposed" and was based on a KGB report that leaked in 2016. It dealt directly with the secret experiments in Tashkent, which occurred in the late '70s and early '80s.

According to this leaked report, one psychic the Soviets studied claimed to be able to shoot milk out of his nose—*without first drinking it*. He would simply stare at an un-opened carton of milk, concentrating deeply, doing a certain breathing technique. Then, the milk would come out of his nose, first drizzling in a thin stream and then spurting forth. The discharged milk would be collected and then measured against the milk missing from the carton. It apparently was the same amount. The Soviet researchers were convinced that this was a trick, however. The psychic seemed like an utter charlatan—he out-Rasputined Rasputin—and hadn't undergone any real occult training. But, whatever his secret was, they couldn't figure it out.

Another psychic could pop balloons with her mind. That was the only thing she could do, but they figured it might help them bring down high-altitude weather balloons—if they ever, for some reason, needed to. And a third psychic, who was actually a yogi from India, presented a classic example of inedia: he could survive without eating, losing no weight in the process. In order to see if he was for real, the scientists locked him in a small cell for a number of weeks, denying him all food and water. He survived, and emerged cheerful and content, having lost almost no weight—less than half a kilogram. Afterwards, he broke his fast with a Pepsi (a popular beverage in the USSR since the time of the

Kitchen Debates), which he said was refreshing but compared unfavorably with the *amrit*, the divine nectar, with which he was normally sustained through divine succor.

I thought it was funny that the Soviet Union had experimented with the supernatural, given its status as an officially atheistic state. I suppose there's a kind of logic to it: studying the supernatural can be a means of controlling it, or penning it in—putting it in its right place within a thoroughly rational and intellectually circumscribed cosmos. Maybe the Soviets were actually trying to devise a thoroughly materialistic explanation for telepathy and telekinesis and all the rest? I imagine Marxism doesn't rule out belief in telepathy as some hitherto unsuspected physical property of matter—little telepathic particles rocketing through the ether between attuned brains. (At the same time as the Tashkent study, the U.S. Government had run a similar program, peering into the dim regions of the psychically anomalous, trying to get psychics to describe the details of enemy airbases and WMD manufacturing sites and the rest. Results were mixed.)

The Soviets, after all, had a very typical reason for hooking up with psychics and wonderworkers and yogis in the first place. They wanted military applications. That was their primary motive. The Pentagon dabbled in psychic stuff for the same reason. Predictable. I thought about Canzoni's government grants, his hidden compound and mysterious metal tower out in the woods, the uncontrollable laughter of the vibration-possessed villagers...

The rabblement of miracle men and women whom the Soviets studied were more interesting than the standard faceless apparatchiks of Communist military might. Here's another example: there was a Lithuanian nun with stigmata who could remotely view objects that were thousands of miles away.

Unfortunately, her remote viewing capacity seemed perfectly tuned to only a few square miles outside Omaha. Soviet satellites confirmed her accuracy on this count, noting the presence of swimming pools and gas grills in the backyards of suburban Nebraskans at precisely the coordinates she'd indicated, but try as the nun might, she couldn't direct her powers towards any U.S. military installations. (Although, being a Catholic, it may be possible that she never intended to help the Godless Communists in their schemes.)

Finally, I found something that seemed potentially relevant to the matter at hand: the Soviets reported that "a lone surviving monk from a Central Asian monastery" had participated in their experiments. They were extremely impressed by him—in fact, they said that he was "almost certainly genuine." He appeared to possess all the standard psychic superpowers—and was able to move objects with his mind—along with a few more shocking varieties. The monk seemed to have total access to all information: he could read minds, he knew details about everyone's past and everything about the future. (According to the KGB documents, he told the researchers that Communism would "basically be over by 1990.")

Yet the monk disappeared. He was at the testing facility one day, and the next—vanished. The scientists found that, after having applied their testing apparatus to him, many of their instruments and computers no longer functioned. He more or less ruined every piece of equipment in the lab, which, in fact, helped bankrupt the project. The monk, they noted, left behind only a small golden medallion with "an unusual triangular design on it." Was it an emblem of the Order of Asha?

And had Canzoni been there? Is that how he'd become entangled in the cosmic drama, the war between Asha and Ahriman? According to his online biography, he hadn't immigrated to the United States until 1993. It was thus entirely possible he had worked for the Soviets in the 1970s and 1980s, when the Tashkent psychic studies were in full swing. After a little more sleuthing, I discovered that he had participated in "a scientific exchange mission" between Italy and the Eastern Bloc in the early eighties, though no details were available on the nature of this mission. Other than that, there was nothing. But "the absence of evidence is not the evidence of absence" (to quote someone in the process of justifying a bad idea). I felt positive that he had been in Tashkent. At any rate, the Order of Asha, represented by the lone monk, had crossed paths with these antique Communist experiments and scuttled them... Perhaps the Order of Ahriman had been involved in some way too. (Again, unless the revelations from these old reports were part of some Byzantine hoax).

At any rate, that was enough for the night. Fairly exhausted, I tried to assume a comfortable position in the armchair, which, despite a lever, lacked the ability to recline. I'm not sure I actually went to sleep, so much as floundered on the edge of slumber, lost in the slush of disjointed thought that separates dreaming from waking.

90. An Unexpected Reply

The sun and my aching neck woke me up. The terrible posture enforced by the chair had given me a cramp—vertebrae cracked as I swiveled my head. The Beta alums were still asleep, soundly and unsoundly. I grabbed my stuff, headed out, and managed to sleep for a couple hours on a couch in one of the dormitory common rooms (not an unusual thing to do). No one noticed or bothered me, as it was the early morning after Winter Festival's culmination.

When I woke up again, around 8 a.m., I headed outside. The campus was peaceful and appeared barely populated. I felt incredibly lonely, simultaneously burdened by all the information I was carrying and ruefully amused. Who had selected me to unravel this nonsense narrative, the drama of these ancient mystical fraternities warring with each other? No one. It wasn't my responsibility. I didn't have the proper resources, and I'd already come pretty close to ending up hideously violated and possibly even dead...

Such were my thoughts as I ate a bowl of oatmeal in the caf. I had reached the nadir of my self-pity and decided, automatically and without thinking, to check my email.

As it turned out, Emma had sent me a messsage. The subject line said, simply, "Silly Squirrels." The note read as follows:

Simon,

I played it... for five hours yesterday evening (missed the last night of Winter Festival in the process). We should talk about this in person. You might be crazy, but there's definitely something weird going on... or it's possible that I'm just as crazy as you. In either case, let's chat.

Let me know when you're free.

Best,

Emma

Of course, I wrote back immediately:

```
I'm free tonight — let's meet up at the college pub.
```

91. Santeria

The college pub was the perfect place to meet. Hardly anybody ever went there, since the frats all provided free booze and, unless you were over 21, you couldn't buy beer at the pub, just soda and mozzarella sticks.

First, I figured it was safe to head back to Barnum Street and check out what Pete and Alex had done to my room. I wasn't looking forward to this.

As I entered the house, I noticed Oscar sitting on the living room couch, fishing around on the coffee table—picking up various objects, randomly moving them to different locations. His brow was wrinkled like he was concentrating on some maneuver requiring fine motor skills.

He looked up and asked me, "Dude, have you seen my I.D. around?"

"Nope," I said.

He went back to fiddling with the objects on the coffee table.

From what I understood, Oscar's family ran a Dominican sugar cane plantation. They were incredibly wealthy. Yet, while Oscar certainly was a foreigner, he was also a stoner, and between the stoners of one nation and the stoners of another, there is really no great difference. I am sure that "The Stoner" is some sort of universal Jungian archetype.

Yet, I figured that he might have familiarity with forms of magical praxis less common in these frosty climes. I didn't know precisely what they did in his part of the Dominican Republic, but I guessed that Santeria might be prevalent there. Since it involved goat sacrifices and the like, I thought a first-hand account might provide some insight into the mindset behind the Order of Ahriman—though human sacrifice was supposedly more to Ahriman's taste.

"Hey, Oscar—you ever practice Santeria?"

"No, I don't practice Santeria—and I don't got no crystal ball either. What kind of racist-ass question is that? That's some fuckin' assumption, dude."

"Jesus, I didn't mean it that way. Relax."

"Yeah, well…

"You're telling me people don't practice Santeria in the D.R.?"

"Sure. Occasionally."

"And that involves animal sacrifices, right?"

"Goats n' chickens n' shit."

"You ever know that to work for anyone?

"Yeah, man. That's how I got into Wilbur. My grandmother sacrificed a chicken."

"I thought you said you never—"

"Well, that was my grandmother. Not me."

"So you're saying that it's purely instrumental? It's all about getting things?"

"For sure."

"So why don't business majors at Wilbur get in on that? Sacrifice a goat before hunting for internships..."

He shrugged. "I don't know. It'd probably work."

Upstairs, I discovered that my room had indeed been trashed, but nothing important seemed to be missing. I was half-expecting them to have taken a dump on the floor or something, but it looked like they mainly tore out drawers, chucked clothes and paper around.

One thing *was* missing though: the David Ortiz baseball, my most treasured possession. I felt like such an idiot for not grabbing it before I left.

92. Saint Simon

Despite these events of cosmic import, the drear business of school was still occurring. I couldn't wait until my meeting with Emma, but I had to sit through Moriarty's awful class first. My excitement disappeared as the boredom provoked by her droning pedantry washed over me. My eyelids fluttered involuntarily; I felt so tired, I could barely keep them open. I had to keep blinking erratically. You can exercise your will on an arm or a leg easier than on an unwilling eyelid.

At one point, I came to—as though I'd been sleeping (had I?)—and found a cool rivulet of drool extending from the right corner of my mouth down to my chin. I wiped it off with the back of my hand. School, and life, are comprised mainly of moments like these—the discovery of drool—and not the unraveling of diabolical conspiracies.

Yet, I was exhausted precisely through my efforts at uncovering such a conspiracy. Anxiety over my own potential insanity was also a little taxing.

After class let out, I checked my email inbox obsessively, hoping Emma would get back to me. This compulsion became increasingly neurotic… Then, I began screwing around on the internet, and before I knew it, I was watching a video of a dog who sounded like he was able to say, "Give me some peanuts."

To kill time, I went over to the religion section of the library, and browsed for anything Ahriman-related. During these solitary hours, I got side-tracked, and ended up reading an article about Saint Simon Stylites. It had absolutely nothing to do with Ahriman or Asha or any of it, but the image resonated: Saint Simon sat alone on a pillar and never came down. He lived his whole life up there. It seemed like a metaphor for my own condition—taking survey of the world from a high-held, singular space and not much liking what I saw.

93. Partners

Finally, Emma wrote me back, saying she'd meet me at nine.

That night, the campus felt snugly suffocated outside—insulated. If you thought about trying to hitchhike out of town, it felt like no cars would be able to stop for you. The sensation of being in that proverbial "Wilbur Bubble" could not have been more palpable.

A mood of anxiety and tension settled over all—and I don't think this was just a projection of my own nervous state. Something needed to give. The Apocalypse needed to happen, heads needed to roll, someone needed to win a hundred million dollar lottery ticket, the library needed to break into a spontaneous orgy. The center—wherever and whatever it was—could not hold.

The school's shitty stand-up comedy group was performing in the sparsely populated pub. The pub was rarely used for actual socializing (the frats siphoned all that away), and what you were left with was a bunch of sad, lonely misfits, drinking coffee and grumpily typing on their laptops, irritated at the unwanted amateur comedy suddenly assaulting them from the little stage set up in one corner of the premises.

Occasionally, mixed in with these studious types, would be a group of a few friends—chaste and sober, probably not drinking, probably from the chemical-free dorms—who got their jollies by assembling jigsaw puzzles and

242

other sedately innocent pastimes. They'd be working on one of the puzzles from the pub's game shelf, generally depicting a fuzzy white kitten playing with a ball of yarn (or something similar). There were board games available as well, like a chess set missing one of the white knights, where you had to use a red checker to replace it. Many of the puzzles were missing a few pieces besides.

Anyway, no one was going to overhear us, and, as I said before, it was a perfect place to meet with Emma. I got there a little early, and listened to the comedians tell their jokes—often ill-conceived or baffling, with a tendency to jump to a punch-line without really setting it up.

When Emma arrived, she immediately sat down and started talking: "It happened to me too. I puked and everything."

"Great!" I said, and smiled. I realized that this might not have been the most logical way to react, but I couldn't help it. It was a massive relief, finally being on the same page with someone else. "And did you see a symbol when you closed your eyes—like an imprint left by a bright light?"

"Yeah… Actually, I did. That happened to you too?"

"The triangles. All pointing down."

"Exactly. It was this fairly vivid geometric thing—this intricate design. It made you feel really strange… in a bad way. In a terrible way, in fact."

I pulled *The God of Smoke and Mirrors* out of my backpack as Emma continued: "It felt like my… *self* was quivering down at the bottom of my toes. Not like I was in control. It was like some force—some sort of bodysnatcher thing—was vying for possession of me."

"Now you sound as crazy as I did! No, crazier. I didn't say anything about bodysnatchers. You're adding a whole other layer of stuff."

"God, I know… We should be putting tinfoil hats on our heads."

243

"Or ringing up an exorcist."

She laughed, a bit coldly and ruefully.

"The symbol you saw… Did it look like this?"

I showed her the frontispiece to the book, held upside down in order to transform the symbol of the Order of Asha into the symbol of the Order of Ahriman.

"Yes," she said, almost instantly. "That's it. Definitely."

"I saw the same symbol carved on a bathroom stall at Beta."

"Like, from someone who saw it after playing the game?"

"I think it has more to do with Zin and the way Beta keeps getting internships there."

"Zin? The technology company?"

I had to explain everything from the very beginning: Wilkes' trove of books, my odyssey at Beta, playing *Silly Squirrels*, the mysterious deaths of Zin employees, getting expelled from Beta (indeed, I even mentioned the bucket of pee and thought she gave me a brief look of tender sympathy), finding Iphigenia's jacket, reading Calder's account and *The God of Smoke and Mirrors*, my reconnaissance mission as an Ewok, and my narrow escape from Pete and Alex and subsequent flight to Alpha.

When I finished, Emma sat back, marinating in this new information, absorbing it. After a longish minute, she spoke: "Fine. I'll buy it. It's nuts, but… I guess I'll just go with it. What's the motive though? How does Ahriman turn a profit out of this, so to speak?"

"I think Zin is attempting some sort of mass brainwashing. How it benefits them—I mean, I guess they're getting people to buy their products?"

"But *Silly Squirrels* is free… At any rate, it's something subliminal. Something tied up with the Ahriman image, those weird triangles. But why? What do they think Ahriman's getting out of it?"

"I don't know," I said. "Based on the things I've read, I think that it—whatever *it* is, this dark god or whatever—might just want their attention. Attention is its food and its currency. Also, as far as Iffie's disappearance goes—I think they sacrificed her to Ahriman. The same thing goes with Wilkes' death, though that might have just been because they thought he knew too much. Human sacrifice is something that *The God of Smoke and Mirrors* talks about, and I did a little research on it earlier today. It's an ancient idea really—strengthening your gods through blood offerings, with human blood being more potent than the other varieties. I mean, do you know anything about death cults? Do you have any insight into what these people might be after?"

"Well, uh, I've read *Helter Skelter*—and an article about that suicide cult, Heaven's Gate, whose members thought they would go to a spaceship behind comet Hale Bopp once they were dead."

"Okay. That might be useful."

Emma was quiet. Then, she said, "But isn't the simplest explanation usually the most correct? Isn't it easier to go with what the cops said and believe Wilkes autoerotically asphyxiated?"

"The key word there is 'usually.' What do you do when the explanation really is complicated? Aren't there complicated explanations for things, sometimes? Plus, who's to say what's simple and what isn't? At any rate, we know Iffie wasn't on that plane, and we know there's something sinister going on with *Silly Squirrels*. We have direct knowledge. That's the main thing… I think in some sense we've *seen* Ahriman, encountered the dark god himself through that game. So, I can't doubt the evidence of my own experience, presuming I'm sane. And you've corroborated it besides."

"Agreed. But how do we get started?"

"The cops aren't going to listen to me. That's for sure. I've talked to the lead detective, Officer Sheerhan, a couple of times. He's a totally well-intentioned moron. We need to get something air-tight—catch them in the act, getting ready to commit a sacrifice."

"And in order to do that, we need to start with first things," said Emma. "Think sequentially. We need to trace everything back to its origin. 'What's the root here? How do we get to the beginning?'"

Emma seemed so… competent. I guess "formidable" would be the ideal word. I could dream my own life away with relative ease, but she seemed capable of realizing things in the concrete world. That was part of the attraction—here was someone who had all her cards in order.

"I guess the earliest place to start is with Wilkes giving me the books."

"But where did the books come from?"

"Some dead guy at a retirement home—it might have been a place called The Desert Palm. It's the nearest anyway. I tried calling but they never got back to me… Wilkes didn't tell me the dead guy's name."

"Then that's where we'll look first. Maybe the dead guy was in the Order of Asha? Or the Order of Ahriman…"

"We don't need the dead man's name?"

"Why should we? We'll just show up, act like we're interested in scoping the place out for a grandparent. We'll simply ask the retirement home director if he remembers Wilkes taking the books… if it seems advisable. We'll figure out a way. There's always a way in."

"And, oh—I just remembered this." Taking out *The God of Smoke and Mirrors*, I showed her where the words "Donated to Evergreen Books" had been stamped. "We could go there, and see if they remember who donated it."

"Great. We'll hit that up first, then the nursing home."

"And, uh, this might be kind of a big request but I was wondering—could I sleep on your couch? I don't particularly want to go back to my place and get assassinated in my sleep or violated in some way. And I've made enemies of all my former friends, so…"

"Sure," she said.

Sure! Just one word! It was that easy. We were partners now. I'd be lying if I acted like I wasn't considering asking her this question from the very beginning, if things went well. I try to plan ahead.

Emma lived in an off campus apartment, a living situation akin to my own on Barnum Street, except she only had one roommate. This roommate rarely appeared, however, spending much time locked in her room while high on Adderall and engaged in various speed-freak art-projects…though, one night, I thought I heard the muffled *Silly Squirrels* theme playing behind the door to her room.

Outside, as we walked to Emma's place, the campus took on an eerie appearance. The full moon's beams ferried a malign magic down to earth. Wilbur College no longer looked like the quintessential New England campus—wide lawns, ancient brick—but like a distinctly modern puzzle. It was a digital enigma, a pattern requiring solution. There was something blue and computer-like in the coloration of the lights, something prompt and methodical in the movement of the wind.

94. The Donor

Sleeping on a lumpy futon in the living room of Emma's apartment seemed like a Parisian excursion. I was happy just to be there and finally got some high-quality sleep, relieved from the solitary burden of my own thoughts and a little less worried about being killed as I slumbered. Let Emma stay up and think things over for a change...

Sharing the same experience with *Silly Squirrels*—which, oddly enough, no one else seemed to have publicly mentioned having—had undoubtedly brought us closer. We were in the same tribe. But, if a make-out session was going to happen, it had been, for the present, postponed.

The next day, we had breakfast—I made pancakes for both of us—and walked over to Evergreen Books, right on New Hamelin's main drag. It had unusually poor lighting for a bookstore, a low yellow coloring cast over everything, though it was fairly clean. The store was perfumed by that lovely old book smell, along with a little incense burning at the checkout desk.

The bookstore's owner stared up at us through a pair of giant spectacles with bright orange frames. The whimsical color of the glasses offset the severity of her gaze. Silvery gray hair hung down to her shoulders, and she wore a vaguely Indian dress of flowing lime green fabric. Did I smell pot—or was the incense burning on her desk merely pot scented? That must've been it.

When she spoke, her voice was preternaturally calm, in a way that made me feel uneasy, as though I expected her medicinal-syrupy tones to suddenly crust over and harden into irrational anger. Her softness felt somehow forced.

"Can I help you?" she said.

"I was just wondering if you remembered something," I said. "It's kind of a longshot, but... We found this book, and I think someone donated it to your store—at least, it was stamped with an Evergreen Books logo. I thought maybe you remembered who might've dropped it off? I think they might be able to help us with a project we're working on"

"That would violate a privacy policy we have." She said this in the same extra-soft, sweet, and mild voice, increasing the sense of tension.

"Yeah, well—this is kind of a big deal," said Emma.

"Our privacy policy is *also* a big deal," said the lady, still disquietingly calm except for that emphasized *also*.

"Anyway, here's the book," I said, sitting *The God of Smoke and Mirrors* before her.

"Ohhhhh, *this*," she said. "I remember this…"

"Really?" I was excited.

"Yes… But I really shouldn't say… There's the *policy*."

"Who designed the policy?" asked Emma.

"I did," she said.

"Well, can't you change your own policy?"

"A policy means nothing if it can be changed at the whim of its creator…" She paused. "Okay—I'll tell you. But I'm not breaking the policy. The person who donated the book is dead and the policy only applies to living people. I just remembered… It was that young man who co–founded Zin. I think he's a Wilbur alum. You know—that sweet boy who was found cut up inside a trash bag?"

"Oh, God," I said. "That was Timothy Fassbinder." Things were making too much sense.

"He came in here and told me to donate this to the library, though not in his name. He said he didn't want to do it directly, but that it was crucial it be made quietly available to the public. And he paid me to do it. I won't say how much, but it was…more than was needed." She giggled. "It's such a shame though. I mean, getting cut to pieces and put in a trash bag—do you think they dismembered him after they killed him or that was *how* they killed him? Via dismemberment, I mean?"

"I would guess 'after' but I don't really know," I said. "If you dismember someone while they're still alive, I'm assuming they'd die pretty quickly—like before the dismembering process got too far along. Unless you started with the toes or fingers and hacked off little pieces. Then it could probably go on for a while."

"That is *so* true," she said.

Emma and I felt awkward coming in and asking all these questions and retrieving essential information without buying anything. So she purchased a copy of Salinger's *Nine Stories* (our taste in books was compatible) and I bought Aldous Huxley's *Brave New World*, which I'd been meaning to re-read. I imagined Ahriman would consider Huxley's dystopia a perfect model of organization.

95. The Desert Palm

Finished with Evergreen Books, we caught a local bus and took an hour-long journey to the retirement home. Earlier, we'd called ahead and told the receptionist that we were a brother and sister who were attending college in the area and whose parents had wanted us to scout out local retirement homes to find a potential place for our grandfather. She bought it, said it would be fine if we stopped by.

The Desert Palm Senior Living Center had Spanish architecture, which is highly unusual for New Hampshire. It had a certain decaying splendor, looked like the mansion in which a faded drama queen of a former age was busy guzzling gin and blistering her liver. Placed under a cold white sky and distant calcium sun, situated next to barren birches in which no birds sang, the building was both out of place and out of time. Its outline was bold and vivid, setting it jarringly forth.

As soon as we entered, we found ourselves in a sweltering, tropical climate. The air was humid, filled with the collective sweat of its residents. It felt like the interior of a forsaken greenhouse left to nurture slowly decaying life at the back of a ruined estate. (Alternately, you could say it was like being inside an armpit). Tiny Tim's bizarre novelty song, "Tiptoe through the Tulips" was playing from a nearby speaker as we stepped onto the mosaic tile in the lobby—too perfectly creepy an accompaniment. I wondered who was responsible for selecting the music, as a receptionist detached her eyes from a crossword puzzle and stared at us from under half-drooping lids.

"Yeah?" she said.

"Uh, we're here…" I paused. *Don't choke.* I've never been a good liar. "We're here checking out retirement homes for our grandfather."

A copper statue of a one-winged angel stared at us from above a tiny fountain, clattering off to our left, opposite the reception desk. The angel had holes for eyes. A small plastic fan sent gust after gust of stagnant air into the receptionist's mascara-caked face.

"Did you have an appointment?" she asked. Tonelessly. An ancient voice, something speaking out of a tomb.

"Yes," said Emma. "We're Rob and Anna Hogan."

251

"Brother and sister," I said, and looked at my feet. I'm really a terrible liar—dripping in tells. I'd make an awful poker player, sitting there bluffing, twitching, soaked through with sweat.

"You look a little young to be searching for a retirement home," said the receptionist. You would've expected her eyes to narrow, but instead, they flared. "Shouldn't your parents be doing this?"

"Gramps always wanted to retire to the mountains, back in New Hampshire where he grew up," said Emma. "We were both up here at college, and our parents wanted us to check this place out and report back. Then, when they visit later on, they'll bring Grandpa and check it out for themselves."

"Yeah, that's right. Our parents…" I stared harder at my feet.

"I see…" said the receptionist, in a completely empty and even tone of voice. She picked up a phone and pressed a button. "Barron? Barron? Yes, we have visitors. Oh, yes. Oh, yes, indeed. They are." She paused and looked us over again. "Oh, yes, definitely…"

We stood surveying the lobby, soaking in its bland and lifeless atmosphere—neutral linoleum and white walls—bleakly modern, aside from the fountain with its bizarre angel statue, which looked like part of a Venetian ruin. The Spanish-style architecture only applied to the building's exterior.

As the receptionist scribbled something in a ledger, I noticed that her pen had been severely damaged from chewing.

Barron Cabot, administrator of The Desert Palm, arrived with a brilliantly white sweater hung over his back, its arms loosely tied across his chest—perversely, considering the heat.

I shook his small, soft hand, which felt like the hand of someone running for office, a hand that had shaken many millions of hands in its day.

I said, "Hi, I'm S—uh… Rob." What an idiot! I almost used my real name. Emma gave me a brief and chastening look.

"And I'm Anna," said Emma, much more convincingly. "We called you earlier about checking this place out for our grandfather."

"And where is your grandfather?" asked Barron, pleasantly.

"He's back home in Nebraska," said Emma. She ladled out the same shtick we'd just given the receptionist.

"He's beset by various illnesses," I said. "And he's in a wheelchair."

"What a shame," said Barron. Despite working in a profession geared towards care giving and service, Barron looked like a preppy villain from an eighties movie. He had whitish blonde hair, super-Aryan.

"Let me show you around."

Fortunately, The Desert Palm was a lot cooler in the residential areas. It had to be. I assume all the old people would've died if their rooms were kept as hot as the lobby. Yet, the corridors of the place were painted a shade of yellow that could, if you were not already as senile and demented as you probably were, momentarily induce madness, provoke a sudden descent into a deeply convincing and vivid fantasia—anything to escape the sick shade of pale-puke yellow surrounding you at every turn. Barron described the facilities in an entirely fluid manner, never pausing, never hemming or hawing. He touted amenities, explained how much of the food served in the dining hall was "farm-to-table." But the place itself was eerie, and the residents we passed wore oddly expressionless faces, even though Emma did her best to smile at them.

At one point, Barron asked us, "So, you two are attending Wilbur, presumably?"

We said yes.

"Ah, I went there myself... This is sort of a new gig for me. I'm really more of a businessman. But I know something about managing systems—which has proved useful here. You aren't in any of the Greek houses by any chance? No? I was in Beta."

Entering the "Recreation Room," I saw something I hadn't expected to see. Old people, sitting at rows of card tables, some in rocking chairs... all hunched over iPads... all playing *Silly Squirrels*. The ever-familiar theme song blared at irregular intervals. Steely-eyed nurses, equipped with anesthetic smiles, were bent over the confused residents, setting up the game and explaining how to play.

"This is a new initiative," Barron explained. "A charitable—eh—donor bequeathed these iPads to us... And these nurses, too, actually. They're all trained in a special computer literacy program for the elderly—to help them enjoy the full benefits of the Internet. They can experience all the same *enhancements*, if you will, as the rest of us, even though they're aged and decrepit."

"So, you're training these old people to play *Silly Squirrels* on iPads?" I asked, despite the fact that he'd just explained all that.

"Yes."

"Why?" I said.

"Because," said Barron, patiently, "we feel they have the right to enjoy all the benefits of the Internet that the rest of society—"

"They look like they're being tortured."

They did. They seemed miserable. Unable to turn away from their iPads, and infected by the Ahrimanic magic, they compelled their aching finger joints to continue picking up digital acorns.

"Yeah," said Emma. "Don't old people, like, hate computers?"

"No. What?" said Barron. "Look at them. They're totally into it."

"That lady just threw up," I pointed out. A woman had just barfed into a small wastebasket, held out for her by one of the eerie nurses.

"She threw up with all the positive *excitement*. Some of our residents get a little over-stimulated from time to time."

Emma and I were, of course, horrified. We took a break for a dreary lunch, partaking of the bags of saltless pretzels being served in the cafeteria while abstaining from the curiously pale variety of meatloaf. Barron wandered off to chat with residents in a loudly insincere tone.

"The world is going insane," I said. "Everyone's losing their shit."

"I know. We need to ask one of these old fogies what's going on here."

At the same long table where we were sitting, an old lady was squinting through bifocals at a copy of *The New Yorker* while picking at her pretzels.

"Hi, ma'am," I said. "How are you doing?"

She looked us over. "Fair to middling," she said.

"We're checking out this place, seeing if it would be a good fit for our grandfather. Do you like it?"

"No. They're always messing with my margin. Trying to make me do things. 'Eat this.' 'Look at this.' 'Take this pill.' 'Play this fruity game.' Can't I just die in peace?"

"Anyway," said Emma. "We were wondering if you know a man who lived here who might have been from Central Asia. We think he died. He might've been a friend of our grandfather's from when he was younger. Our grandfather used to live up here."

"We have a Mexican lady and a guy from Somalia. But no one else."

"We're talking about a dead guy," I interjected. "Not someone currently alive. Anyone die around here lately?"

"People are dying all the time."

"Yes, but what about anyone more, you know, foreign?"

"Let me think…" She drifted off into a reverie. I thought she was starting to fall asleep or forget the question, when she suddenly said, "Mr. Singh. He was an old Indian feller. Wore one of those turban things. Yeah, he wasn't with us too long. He was here about a month or two, then he just croaked."

"Thanks," said Emma.

Barron came back to us and said, "Here. I'll show you the courtyard."

96. Going Round

As we walked down the hall to the courtyard, I asked Barron, "Was there someone named Mr. Singh who died here recently?"

"Oh, yes… Mr. Narasimha Singh. Did you know him?"

"He was a friend of our grandfather's. Who, of course, grew up around here…" I added this nervous and suspicious explanatory note, repeating something we'd already told him earlier. But Barron didn't seem too suspicious.

"That's interesting. Yes, he was a very old Sikh. A bookish kind of guy, but he had an extremely fierce look to him. Not unfriendly… Just this sort of intensity."

We reached the courtyard and looked around: there were a few Lays' Potato Chip bags caught in the hedges, torn open so that their silver-lined mouths gulped wind like fish out of water. As it was late February, the wind had arranged the snow in minor haphazard drifts which were now turning to dirty-icy clumps, and the stunted-looking trees and bushes were barren.

Only, at the absolute center of the courtyard where the sun beat down directly, there was a patch of grass growing in a perfect square. It looked artificial in its greenness, chemical. I couldn't determine if it was a sickly color, a false veneer of seeming growth, or (miraculously) completely vital. Someone seemed to have trimmed and raked and maintained it persistently up until the present moment. I couldn't tell how it remained free of snow… At first, I thought it might have been Astroturf, covering up a drain or hiding the concrete entrance to a septic tank, but when I stepped on it, it felt oddly real.

Near the central point of the square, an old pipe, somewhat rusted, stuck out of the ground, as if at attention. It may have originally been part of a water-pump that no longer existed, inherited from whatever ancient New England farm had once stood here, long since reduced to tinder. Or it might've still worked, still served a function. I never found out.

Three residents were walking counter-clockwise around this pipe, padding in their boots over the grass, eerie in its freshness. They were all dressed in winter-coats and pale robin's-egg-blue pajama bottoms. Emma and I stood and watched them as they went. They seemed to be entirely unaware of our presence for nearly five minutes, until all three stopped at once, as though they had telepathically communicated their plan to halt to one another instantaneously.

The patient nearest to Emma looked over at us. His eyes were wide-open, pale blue like his pajamas, and completely guileless. I held his gaze for a few seconds before the shrugged and said, in a perfectly sane and clear voice, "We like going round."

And so they resumed.

"Seen enough?" asked Barron.

97. Interlude

We left The Desert Palm with more questions than answers (to indulge a cliché).

Who was Narasimha Singh? Where had he come from? Why was he in possession of Ephraim Calder's diary, which I couldn't locate anywhere else, in any bookstore or library system?

And there was an equally important question: was Emma interested in me? She must have realized that *I* was interested in her. Right? Whatever the case, working with her was easy. It felt right. I experienced a calm, constant current of desire towards her, not brief spurts of squirt-gun lust. To paraphrase a Bob Dylan lyric, I could stay with her forever and never realize the time. Or perhaps Vampire Weekend's lyrics from "Hannah Hunt" were more appropriate—we were discovering that we had our own sense of time. It was not the same sense of time that governed the world of Zin and technocratic conspiracies… Not ticking clock sounds vanishing down rusty drainpipes. Considering the ocean of weirdness brimming around us, it's funny that we seemed so relaxed around each other. I felt more relaxed with her than I ever felt while enduring the experience of "brotherhood" at Beta (though perhaps that's a given). Our friendship (relationship?) provided a still point at the center of a wildly turning world.

We would've continued pursuing answers to these questions, but we were hijacked by mid-terms—two weeks of papers and exams. After that there was another two weeks of class before spring break, during which we failed to come up with a plan. We couldn't find anything about Singh and couldn't figure out how to penetrate Beta or Zin's inner circle. Also, Emma still wasn't willing to admit that Canzoni might be involved, and I didn't want to press the point, figuring we could fit him into place when the other pieces came together.

I was still sleeping on Emma's couch, primarily, though I spent a few semi-sleepless nights on Barnum Street, a chair shoved up against my door, an alarm system (empty tin cans on a string) attached to the window. Nothing happened. Alex had lost interest or assumed that I wasn't a threat and had been suitably cowed.

Emma and I spent more time together, ate lunch together, watched Netflix together, went to the film society together, played tennis together. We kissed one evening, after watching *Leaving Las Vegas* and agreeing that it was terrible— abject misery porn (though I have to admit that Nicholas Cage offered a surprisingly good performance, given his current reputation as a ham *par excellence*). The night before we left for spring break, I graduated from sleeping on her couch to sleeping in her bed.

Then, the whole time I was in Pennsylvania, lying around on my couch, reading texts about Zoroastrianism (or the Occult, or anything else that seemed relevant), I felt tense. It seemed like the Fates (or maybe Ahriman) were waiting for me to let my guard down, waiting until I didn't particularly feel like anything was going to happen. That's when something really *would* happen.

I talked to Emma over the phone every night, and we both felt the same way—sensing the impending confrontation with Ahriman while being incapable of preventing it, delaying it, or even comprehending what form it would take. It was frustrating.

When we finally got back to campus, it was spring. On the trees that lined the campus walkways, little pink and white buds were opening to taste the void.

The winter takes a long time to end in New Hampshire: piles of dirty snow lay heaped at the backs of parking lots, reminding you that the world is no longer fresh; dust and grime are universal presences.

The process of coming back to life feels as much like death as birth. Before Nature arrives at the pure consciousness of spring, it passes through a groggy period of uncertainty. All the snow has melted—and another two feet fall, before melting in a few days... But these hesitations and reversals finally deliver you into the lap of spring, surprised to be so young.

98. 4/20

Back in New Hamelin, on April 20th, Emma and I were walking into campus from her apartment. We stopped on the Green to part ways—she had a class, and I was going to eat something in the caf and read the paper.

"It's funny, Emma... It's a sunny day, the best weather we've had in months. The birds are back. My allergies haven't kicked in yet. But...

"It's like there's no time at all, and time is moving too fast."

"Yeah. It's just like that."

I smiled at her, and was (as I continually am) surprised when she smiled back at me—guileless. Nothing missing in this picture.

There was an event every year on 4/20; students and wandering neo-hippies from out-of-town would gather on the Green to smoke pot en masse. The cops, for some reason, would back off and let this happen. Maybe it was good for the local economy, since the wandering hippies would pop into local restaurants in search of kale smoothies... You could actually see the smoke hovering above the crowd, like a morning mist. There was, I suppose, an obvious symbolism to it all—lost in the haze.

This year, when the date came around, nothing seemed to be happening. At first, I was pleasantly surprised by the lack of sinister hippies lining the quad, filling balloons with nitrous oxide and blasting Phish and The Dead through their speakers. Apparently, the festival had been canceled... or something...

The whole campus seemed depopulated.

In the cafeteria, however, there were quite a number of people—which relieved me. I bought an apple and a bagel, and sat down, munching and reading a copy of the free *New York Times* (copies of the Times and the Boston Globe were provided gratis by the school in two big bins near the cash register). On the front page, there was a headline: *Zin Merger Creates Silicon Valley Super-Conglomerate.*

Zin wasn't doing too bad for itself, apparently. By gobbling up tons of smaller and medium-sized companies, they'd managed to create a technology and software empire just slightly larger than Apple's...

At one point in my reading, I looked up. It occurred to me that I hadn't heard any of the other breakfasters say anything—the ambient murmur of conversation was missing. About thirty or forty other students were in the cafeteria and they were all bent over at their seats, gazing at their cellphones without exception.

Suddenly, from one of the phones, I heard that well-worn soundtrack:

"Silly Squirrels
Pickin' up acorns!"

Immediately, every phone in the building responded with the song. A single manic blare rose and died—chaos announcing its order.

Yet everyone seemed calm, concentrated, contented. Their brows weren't even furrowed as they stared at the screen. Instead, their faces bore the imprint of a cud-chewing, bovine passivity.

Then, all at once, a high-pitched sonic bleat emanated from all the cellphones simultaneously. The spell was broken… The students put away their phones, picked up their books and backpacks and walked out of the cafeteria, some of them chatting. It looked totally normal.

A partially chewed piece of bagel fell out of my open mouth. In a minute, I was the only person left.

I jogged back to the cash registers and asked the two Guatemalans workers, "Did you see that?"

"Oh, yes," said one. "It is very… peculiar."

"What do you think is going on?"

The other shrugged and said, "I have found, on the whole, that I prefer not to understand too much."

Leaving the cafeteria, I decided not to panic. Maybe I'd simply witnessed a very odd coincidence—although it was obvious I hadn't. While I'd previously described the game as a "craze," I really meant that, in any crowded location, three or four students might be playing the game. Not literally all of them.

I continued to class.

Seated at my desk, I watched Professor Moriarty give us her classic stare of hostile nullity. She looked like she was in the mood to crush some serious testes.

But, again, thirty phones rang synchronously, all playing the *Silly Squirrels* theme. Without altering her dauntingly empty expression, Moriarty reached into her pocket and took out her own phone. All the students did the same. Pretty soon, the *Silly Squirrels* theme was caroling out, over and over and over… ringing in the reign of Ahriman.

I picked up my books and ran.

99. Ahriman Enthroned

I saw the truth: Ahriman was not enthroned on a literal *seat*, but in the human skull. His downward pointing symbol was glowing there, evilly, in all its rigid abstraction. The world would "run like clockwork" but you'd still be able to take ecstasy at a rave or watch *Naked and Afraid* on the Discovery Channel. Your freedom was assured, within definite limits. You just had to give the dark god your due—a significant chunk of your attention every day.

Ahriman's clockwork could incorporate all the seeming irrationalities of life—it would let the human race seem to stumble onwards, while actually controlling it from within. It would allow fratboys and sorority girls to haze and get black-out drunk, but, in their hearts and brains, Ahriman's machinery would keep on ticking. All the normal human moments, divorced from the phone addiction, would feel like the usual roughness in the world's texture, wrinkles in time and space—perfectly natural. Nothing wrong with this picture. But seen from a god's eye-view, aerially, at a height suitable to observe Nazca line drawings, you would notice how smooth and sleek the field of action really was. Ahriman's design would rule over all.

Yes, the world would be flat again—and that seemed like a liberating dream to the brain trust at Zin. Not flat, of course, in terms of an *even* or *fair* playing field, but two-dimensional, in that nothing could come looming up at you from the third dimension, or (God forbid!) the fourth. Everything would take place in mental limitations established by Ahriman. You could cruise up and down that flat earth with your hood down and your hair blowing back—no limit, save the dimensional limit of your flat cosmos itself.

The actual nature and purpose of the design still remained somewhat unclear. It seemed odd that Ahriman and Zin would simply distract people with their phones until… what? The economy collapsed? The world ended? Who would be left to feed Ahriman with attention?

Since people were able to stop playing when cued by that loud electrical bleat I'd heard in the cafeteria, it seemed like the program was functioning in such a way that they would still be able to go about their day. Ahriman could distract them at will during any vacant moment, but would permit them to fulfill the necessities of life. (This explained why Curtis and Oscar had been able to both pursue their ambitions and be addicted to the game at the same time. Their phones would bleat, at some point, freeing them temporarily from their addiction, and permitting them to satisfy their worldly ambitions.) They'd remain in motion, but during every period of stillness, Ahriman would intrude. You'd have action instead of stillness, fingers twitching on the screen of your phone, shoveling acorns into the hole of modern meaninglessness.

As I left the English department building, I checked my own phone. There was a text from Emma: "It's happening," she wrote. She told me to meet her at the student center.

On my way over, I looked in the main study hall adjoining the library. Everything appeared typical—whispers, giggles, and the delicate clicking of laptop keys.

Soon, the theme song kicked off on one phone, before spreading to the others. Enraptured silence ensued, ruptured from time to time by the eternal

theme's repetition. In this eerie interval, time moved both too fast and too slow…
A reeling nightmare.

At the student center, Emma and I found a table in the corner.
Fortunately, no one was around.

"Emma… This whole thing is seriously *fucked*."

"I know. Looks like Ahriman finally made his move. Unless this is some
sort of initial testing phase."

"What should we do?"

"Jesus, I don't know. Call the cops?"

"Sure. We'll walk in and Sheerhan will be like, 'Give me a second, guys.
Just got to pick up these acorns.'"

"Not everyone's doing it. All the students are completely brainwashed,
but I saw a janitor who seemed kind of perplexed."

"The Guatemalan guys who work in the caf were looking on a little
baffled too… Also… I didn't want to bring this up before, because you love the
guy, but… you're personal friends with the mind-control specialist."

"Canzoni—"

"You don't think this has something to do with him? When does he have
his office hours? Maybe we could confront him…"

"I mean we're in the middle of social breakdown here, so I think he might
not be at his office hours, regardless… But I also got an email saying his office
hours were canceled today." She volunteered that last piece of info very
reluctantly. Still protective.

"Interesting," I said. "He's changing his schedule, whereas everyone else
seems to be *on* schedule. Moriarty still turned up for her class, and she's as
brainwashed as the rest. There were people in the caf at breakfast time, and in the

library... If you didn't know the game was dominating their attention, it would seem basically normal. But Canzoni's doing things differently, and it just goes to show that he knows something's up. Emma, what if he really *is* involved with this *Silly Squirrels* plot and with Ahriman and everything? He's not going to be one of these wacked-out zombies, presumably. He's going to be on top of things—unless he's playing the game himself, dipping into his own stash, so to speak. I mean, what's the deal with this dude?"

"Well, I think—"

"I mean, I thought he wanted to end war, but now he's murdering people and sacrificing girls and—"

"Jesus, hold on a second—"

"Sorry," I said. "But you can't still believe he's innocent?"

"I do."

"Why?"

"I'm not saying he hasn't gotten tangled up in this somehow... He's got to be on the right side, though. He's one of the good guys. He volunteers at an animal shelter."

"Hitler liked animals."

It's true. Nazi propaganda depicted the Fuhrer as an animal lover.

"No," said Emma. "Hitler *claimed* to like animals."

100. No Presence

We were still arguing about Canzoni when we walked outside and bumped into Sheila Tomlinson. Sheila seemed less harried than usual, but distant, as if wrapped in the gauzy padding of a drug stupor. Given the events of the day, I figured drugs weren't the real culprit...

"Hey, Sheila. How are things?" I asked.

"Oh, they're great. So great. Yah." Sheila delivered this in an utterly light and insincere tone of voice.

We stood and talked with her for a little while. She continued babbling about some sort of charitable undertaking her sorority was engaged in. It all seemed fairly normal… But there was something profoundly unsettling about our conversation.

Emma saw Sheila, I saw Sheila, but Sheila somehow talked to us without really acknowledging that we were there. It was like communicating with a hologram, floating in and out of phase. Her thoughts weren't just preoccupied with sundry topics—she wasn't *present*. She was speaking in such a way as to deflate the possibility of an actual conversation. Emma remained calm and still and friendly, looking out from her still center on the scrambled moving flotsam of Sheila's mind.

"…And then, we baked *sooo* many cookies," Sheila was saying. "It was, like, the cutest AIDS fundraiser ever."

It wasn't like when Pete was ignoring Elmer, being coolly contemptuous. Sheila was very talkative—gassing on about her sorority's plans to throw a party where all the girls were going to dress up like sexy Easter Bunnies. Yet, in nothing she said was there any *contact*. She might've been delivering this very enthusiastic monologue to an answering machine. Words bubbled out at a point in mid-air before dissipating back into the ether.

The monologue was cut-short when Sheila's cellphone abruptly squealed with the notes of—you guessed it. She took the phone out, left us without a word of farewell, and sat on the nearest bench, playing *Silly Squirrels*.

By this point, all the potheads *were* smoking pot on the Green, phones pocketed, lost in a different kind of mental fog. Or was it the same kind of fog? Evidently, the Order of Ahriman wasn't going to deny anyone their vices. The hippies could still smoke weed. Why wouldn't they? If you're going to control people, you might as well make them enjoy it.

I remembered Joanna Hecht and her taxidermy hobby… All those animals frozen in place, as if by magic…

"What do you think about this, Emma? Why are the mind-control people letting everyone do what they normally do—smoking, studying, eating—instead of transforming them into straight-laced, efficient worker drones?"

Emma shrugged and said, "I guess if Ahriman can get your attention, he doesn't need to care about anything else."

I had a sudden apprehension—all that attention flowing downward and outward through the simmering blue radiance of the mesmeric screen. In the Halls of Ahriman, on whatever warped metaphysical plane, I pictured the dark god's slaves stacking up particles of human attention, just like the Silly Squirrels pickin' up acorns, pickin' up acorns, pickin' up acorns…

"They're harvesting our attention for fuel," I said. "Or maybe for food. Like, attention *tastes good* to Ahriman…"

"You want to see what Mac thinks about this?"

Visiting the College President didn't seem like an entirely mad next step.

"If he can still think. Sure."

"I mean, we should at least make a token gesture towards contacting an authority figure…"

"Probably a good idea. Then, if we have to take matters into our own hands, but completely fuck up in the end, we'll know it was our only option. We tried to pass the buck."

101. Nazi Measuring Stick

We ran back across the Green, tore through the antique wooden double doors of the Administration Building, upon which two carved dolphins kissed, took the marble staircase two steps at a time, and arrived panting outside the President's office on the third and highest floor. We knocked and entered without waiting for an acknowledgment.

"President Mackenzie—"

Mac held up his right index finger, signaling for us to give him a second— as he gazed down at his phone, evidently preoccupied.

He continued staring at his phone.

Suddenly, he exclaimed, "Ah, goddamn it!"

The all-too-familiar theme song started up—"Silly squirrels / Pickin' up acorns!"

"Just let me get to the next level," Mac muttered, without looking up. "Son of a bitchin' acorns... Damn acorns..."

In horror, Emma and I backed slowly out of the room.

"Do you think this is happening everywhere?"

"Maybe," Emma said. "Have you watched any TV today?"

In the student lounge, the couches were filled with people playing *Silly Squirrels*. Sportscenter was on, and the announcers were not (at least, not in that instant) on their phones. Note that the compulsion to play the game seemed to correlate with when people had free time, Moriarty's class excepted (though that wasn't much of a learning experience in the first place). We found the remote, and changed the channel to CNN. No one seemed to mind.

CNN was on a commercial, but when it came back, there was a split second in which a loud beep rang out, and the daytime anchor looked up, before stashing something under her desk. It seemed clear that she'd been playing the game during the break…

Of course, the news wasn't covering any of this mass-mind-control business.

"I know another authority figure we can talk to," I said. "If the bad guys are the only ones who haven't been brainwashed—aside from us, weirdly—then he might be conscious, might know something."

In a few minutes, we arrived at Professor Warningbone's office. It was extremely clean. The file cabinets seemed to twinkle. The room's sole decoration was a framed steel ruler (for measuring things) with a plaque under it.

"Professor Warningbone?" I said, rapping gently on the inside of his door, which had been propped open with a wastebasket. I could see Warningbone at his desk, typing on the computer. He seemed like the kind of guy who would typically leave his door closed. Maybe he was intentionally leaving an opening? Perhaps he wanted someone to yank him out of the situation in which he had become mired?

"*Yes?*" Warningbone's response was abrupt. It sounded like a pained, angry yelp extracted via thumbscrew. He looked up.

"Could we talk to you?" Emma asked.

"Does it *look* like you can talk to me?"

"I guess?" I said.

"No. It. Does. *Not*." Warningbone stared down at his desk and pretended to be busy. He began shuffling papers, reigning his angry bluster into the world's twitchiest poker face.

"It's your office hours." Emma pointed this out, gently. It *was* his office hours—we'd checked. She strained to sound amiable; it was hard to be gentle around Warningbone. It would've seemed more natural to hold any conversation with him by grabbing his lapels and screaming directly into his face.

"My office hours have been canceled," he said.

"Look," I said. "We know about Zin."

"What?" said Warningbone. He remained staring down at his desk, but he'd stopped shuffling papers. His frozen face and body seemed to be vibrating, seething under the surface—all that cold blood suddenly draining into his toes

"We know," said Emma.

"About Zin," I said—just to be clear.

"What," said Warningbone, speaking slowly and quaveringly, "in the world is a *Zin*?"

"You know," I said, "It's a computer company, like Apple or Google or—"

"That plaque on your wall," said Emma. "It says it was presented by the Zin Corporation to Alfred Warningbone, in recognition of his distinguished contributions."

I stared at the plaque and realized it was embossed with the Ahrimanic symbol, the downward pointing triangles. According to its inscription, the ruler had apparently been used during the invention of the V2 rocket—which was, of course, a Nazi project. It was bizarre that Warningbone would hang this in his office openly (though I imagine no one came to his office hours). Perhaps it was another indication that he wanted to be caught…

"That," he said, his voice still constricted, "is just some junk that came in the mail."

"Things are getting crazy out there, Professor," said Emma. "There's some kind of mind control experiment going on."

"That's insane."

"And we think Zin's involved," I said.

"And…" Emma hesitated… "And Ahriman."

At this, Warningbone finally jumped. "I… I … don't know—"

"*Jesus*," I said. "Tell us the truth. We're not going to just walk back outside into the apocalypse because of your totally unconvincing bullshit act."

"Yeah, dude," Emma added.

We advanced into the room and stood directly in front of his desk. I was thinking of knocking all the papers off, but this seemed a little too dramatic, like I would've been imitating the movies. Instead, we both simply glared at him.

"They… They… They made me put a chip in my skull," said Warningbone. It seemed like he had a fever and it was breaking: sweat started pouring off his face, a big drip hanging from the end of his nose. "It prevents me from getting addicted to this *Silly Squirrels* thing. If I try to play it, I just feel a little queasy. It doesn't permanently alter the rhythm of my brain like it does for most people. Plus, the chip would let me get into their club in New York, where they take their hookers and snort their blow. Not that I go in for that… But, for business purposes, I need to show up from time to time."

"And, just to be clear," I said, "the 'they' you're referring to is comprised of Zin and the Order of Ahriman and all that shit, right?"

"Yeah," he said.

Warningbone explained how they roped him in, promising to transform Wilbur into a sleek, modern research university, with a low-priority on teaching and a strong emphasis on developing new military technologies. He couldn't resist. It apparently didn't occur to him that converting everyone into phone-addicted zombies wasn't exactly the most enticing prospect. You want a *little* fight in the people you're trying to subject. Otherwise, you'd be living in a lifeless void.

As Warningbone talked, his formerly frozen and rigid façade leaked away. What was left was something soft, unformed, and indefinite, a personality that had never really become anything, had remained in potential. It was desperate, scared, wild-eyed—with nothing to hold onto, floating free in space for the first time. He blubbered and blabbed, the poor guy.

He told us that Zin was setting up a system that would channel and direct the internal rhythms and desires of everyone on the planet. The *Silly Squirrels* game would subliminally implant the Ahrimanic pattern—the multi-triangular design—in the psyche of the player. This pattern was, in fact, *alive*. As I'd suspected, *Silly Squirrels* was meant to eat up every spare moment of the day—moments that could otherwise be used for reflection, for developing one's interior self. Under the guise of harmless distraction, the gamer would wind up performing the devotion of Ahriman.

"It's totally unscientific," said Warningbone. "So I'm not saying I believe it. But that's what's supposed to be happening out there."

Grafted deep in the minds of his unwitting devotees, Ahriman could detect when their brainwaves were falling into potentially contemplative states, and redirect them for his own purposes. Whenever anyone had a decent amount of

273

spare time, Ahriman would activate the *Silly Squirrels* signal in their devices, forcing them to take out their phones and play. Of course, I assumed that Canzoni had helped them set this system up…

"Was Canzoni involved in this?" I asked.

"Who?" said Warningbone.

"The Nobel Laureate, the professor!"

"Oh, him." Warningbone shrugged. "It's possible. I don't know everyone they contract with."

"More importantly," asked Emma (who shot me a dirty look), "do you know if there's any way we can stop this thing?"

Wearily, Warningbone shrugged again. "I don't think so."

"What? Why not?" I asked. "We can't blow up Zin headquarters or smash some server or something?"

"It's not that simple," said Warningbone. "I'm not privy to all the details, but the idea is that Ahriman is actually *living* inside people now. It's like demonic possession. The phone game sustains him—without people regularly staring at that pattern in the game, he would quickly lose power over them. It's food for him. Refreshment. The only way to stop it would be to destroy every cell phone in America."

"Do you think there's any way of doing that?"

"Well…" said Warningbone. "Technically, yes. But…"

"He's thinking about an EMP," said Emma. "An electro-magnetic pulse. An EMP could definitely take it out by frying every electronic device in the country."

"Cool," I said. "Let's do that."

"But the cure could be worse than the disease. Hundreds of thousands—no, *millions* of people might die. Maybe more. It would cause mass social chaos, the possible destruction of American Civilization."

"Oh," I said, disappointed. I was more than sick of hearing the *Silly Squirrels* theme song and almost made the old crack about needing to break a few eggs to make an omelet. But I figured it would probably come off as insensitive.

"What about a hacker?" This was Emma's bright idea. "Don't we know any hackers who could delete the game or send a virus out or something?"

"They've got pretty good anti-virus software protecting their program," said Warningbone.

"Eh," said Emma. "The best hackers can always find a way in. Plus, I think it makes more sense to try to come up with a virus that could bring down *Silly Squirrels* instead of—you know—immediately leaping to the conclusion that we should nuke America."

We fell into thought.

"A kid from my highschool is in prison for pirating fetish porn videos," I said. "He developed some method for stealing videos off pay-sites all at once, en masse. Actually, he was pirating fetish porn videos *about* pirates. That was the fetish, apparently... But, uh, aside from him—no. I don't know anyone. We weren't really close friends, by the way."

"I see," said Emma.

"You know anything else?" I asked Warningbone.

"No..." said Warningbone. He obviously knew something.

"What is it?"

"I don't want Ahriman to kill me. I don't want to die."

"I thought you said you weren't sure if you believed in him?"

"I'm hedging my bets."

"But you've told us so much already. Ahriman has plenty of reasons to kill you!"

Warningbone appeared disconcerted. "Fine… They're going to sacrifice someone to Ahriman to thank him this evening. It's a formality, but he demands it."

Emma and I exchanged looks.

"Who're they going to sacrifice?"

"Ah, just some nerd."

"So maybe we should go to this Officer Sheerhan?" asked Emma.

"If you insist…" I said. "I mean, I have no expectations for this guy. None."

102. Another Authority Figure

I definitely had *not* misplaced my skepticism. When we got to the New Hamelin police station (just off campus on Main Street—most local crime occurred on Wilbur's campus, after all), the two cops behind the front desk were playing *Silly Squirrels*.

"You mind if we go back and see Sheerhan?"

"Enh," they said.

So, we walked through the station—it wasn't very big, just a few poorly ventilated rooms with cheap acoustical tile on the ceilings, slim light-restricting windows, and fluorescent tubes glowing along the tops of the halls. It was dispiriting enough to make any drunken fratboy confess to whatever he'd been apprehended him for doing.

We found Sheerhan's office, but the door was locked. I thought I could see a human shadow behind its blurred glass window, seated at a desk.

"No worries, Emma."

I went back to the front. "Hey guys… I need the key to Sheerhan's office."

"Unh. Munnh," they said.

I took a set of keys that was sitting on the desk and started trying each one. Finally, the last one—isn't that always the way?—worked.

Inside, Sheerhan was bent over his phone, eyes red-rimmed and wild; a mess. A water bottle full of urine was seated on his desk. He looked like he was suffering from malnutrition, had a yellowish waxy look to him.

"Officer Sheerhan?" I said. He didn't respond.

"See, Emma? It's pointless."

"Just gotta pick up these acorns," said Sheerhan, manically moving his thumbs over the screen. "Yep, one more acorn… But there's another… There's always another acorn! *Silly squirrels pickin' up acorns! Silly squirrels pickin' up acorns!*"

He laughed like a madman, eyes still fixed on the screen.

"We should probably take his gun," I said.

"What? Do you really think—?"

"Yeah. I do think. Hey, Sheerhan—I'm going to take your gun out of your holster."

"Unh. Yeh. Get it outta here…"

I plucked the handgun—a 9 millimeter Glock 22—right out, checked to see if it was loaded. It was.

"We're packing heat now. Let's go stop this sacrifice … Take the pins out of the voodoo doll—metaphorically speaking."

103. A Keepsake Recovered

We left the police station, the gun stashed awkwardly in the coat of my jacket's pocket. I probably should've taken the holster too…

I thought it was funny, this world we'd created. We became united through invisible waves and electrical currents—the web seemed tight. But everything was diffuse and far away. You had to squint to pick any figures out of the glare and haze. Technically pushed together, we were fragmenting until each individual, each human consciousness, was left alone, occupying an empty circle of space, filling it up with scattered thoughts, none cohering, just shaking little flakes of thought on the absence. But you never seemed to season the tasteless fundamental substance quite adequately…

Silly Squirrels was merely the final logical manifestation of this. Everyone was playing it, so it appeared to be an evil movement towards mass-unification… which it was. But, under the surface, it was also cutting everything up. It broke up the day into discrete chunks, with no relation to each other. The stream of consciousness could not persist uninterrupted. Attention could not be sustained.

I told Emma: "I know where we can go to crack this open. Stop the sacrifice. It's gonna be risky, but it doesn't look like we have any choice."

"Where?"

"The belly of the beast—The Pyramid. I'll bet you anything that Alex is the head of The Pyramid Society too, and that's where they sacrificed Iphigenia Woods. It's where they'll kill this new kid too."

"Makes sense. But we don't know how to get in."

"Actually, I do."

"What? How?"

"There's a tunnel in Alex's closet."

"Really? Why didn't you mention that before?"

"I don't know. I found out because I was hiding in his closet while he had sex with the president of Kappa."

"Uh…"

"I mean, uh, I wasn't trying to spy on them… I was, uh, trying to get this notebook back, and uh—"

"Okay. It's fine. How are we gonna play this?"

"Walk up to Beta, pull the gun, tie up the dude who lets us in."

"What if there's more than one?"

"I don't think too many bros will be around at this time of day, anyway."

In a few minutes, we were standing on the front porch. I tried the doorknob and it appeared to be open. Frats generally didn't lock their front doors in the daytime.

I kind of wanted to pull the gun on someone—scare them in revenge for the pee bucket thing. There are few occasions in life in which one can pull a gun on someone in broad daylight on a college campus and still feel in the right. It was a unique opportunity and, for psychological reasons, I wanted to take advantage of it.

"Be casual. Cool," said Emma. "Just walk in."

I felt a little tense, and said, sarcastically, "You think that's a good idea? Really? I was planning on having *no* cool."

We walked inside. No one on the first floor; people mainly studied or watched TV in the upstairs common room. From the basement, we could hear the delicate echo of a single ping-pong ball, bouncing. Two hardcore frat boy alcoholics must have been down there, engaged in a mid-day bout of pong.

"We just walk down this hallway," I whispered. "Alex's room is in the back."

We were halfway down the hall when a toilet flushed in the bathroom next to Alex's den, and the door opened. It was Jew Fro. I guess he wasn't going to wash his hands, so brief was the moment betwixt flushing and opening. Maybe he washed and then flushed? I don't know. This question was never resolved.

I pulled my gun—slowly, nearly fumbling. He just stared, didn't make any move to interfere, was still processing.

"Alright, dude," I said, with the gun finally pointed at him. "You're coming with us."

"I—"

"Do you know where there's any rope we can tie you up with?"

Emma added, "We'll untie you later. Don't worry."

"I—"

"Actually, do you want us to leave you some snacks? Like granola bars? Are there any of those around?"

"But if he's tied up, how's he going to eat the granola bars?"

"I—" said Jew Fro.

"He'll just bend over with his mouth and bite them. We'll leave them unwrapped."

We guided Jew Fro into Alex's room.

"No rope in here," said Emma.

"You figure with his sexual proclivities, there's gotta be handcuffs or something…"

"You guys aren't gonna kill me, right?"

"Dude. Of course not. Also, do you know what's going on with Zin and *Silly Squirrels* and all that?"

"What? No."

He seemed to be telling the truth.

I had an idea.

"Yo, Emma—I know how we can keep him preoccupied. Jew Fro—do you have a cell phone?"

"Yeah."

"Give it to me."

He handed over his phone. I checked to see if *Silly Squirrels* was on it: it was.

"Here, just sit on Alex's bed and play this."

"Okay…"

In a moment, he was rapt. Fortunately, Jew Fro was not in the inner circle of Zin-connected Beta brothers. They hadn't installed the insulating microchip in his brain and he was still susceptible to the game's hypnotic effect.

"Using the enemies tools against him," I said.

"It's very Sun-Tzu."

"The passage is in the closet… Watch for that first step."

We were already on the first step down, when I remembered something. "Just a second Emma. I have to retrieve a keepsake."

I backtracked into Alex's room. My Ortiz baseball was sitting on his desk.

104. Pre-Sacrifice Preparations

Long stretches of the tunnel felt ancient, as though they pre-dated the college itself and had been created through the wrigglings of some prehistoric worm. Rotten-looking yet apparently sturdy boards held up the walls, like in a mine. The air tasted of dusty dead things, the essence of long-decaying mummies (which, given that the passage led to The Pyramid, seemed appropriate if unpleasant). Ventilation down there wasn't so great, but you could stand up straight and just barely manage to walk side by side.

We lit our way with our cellphones; both had a flashlight app feature. It provided yet another instance of turning the enemy's tools against him (or against *it*—I'm still not sure of the precise ontological nature of Ahriman). Behind us, we noticed that smaller passages were branching off from the main route we were on. The mouths of these sub-tunnels were shrouded in cobwebs, and the atmosphere behind them seemed even danker. Perhaps if you walked too far down one of those, you'd expire like a canary in a coalmine, victim of a sudden influx of bad air, low oxygen.

We walked for what must have been a mile before we saw light up ahead and heard voices, which, in the bad acoustics of the tunnel, became a murmuring indistinguishable mush. We turned off our flashlights and tried to be extra quiet. The effort made me uniquely conscious of my own breathing and my heartbeats—they seemed awfully loud.

We carefully climbed a few stone steps, leading up to the mouth of the tunnel, and peeked over the threshold. There was a fairly large, though not Olympic-sized swimming pool.

"So the rumors are true…" said Emma. (She was referring to the rumor that there was a large swimming pool located beneath The Pyramid, explaining the organization's supposedly high water bill).

The pool was surrounded by unadorned stone walls, while low orange electric light—apparently intended to simulate torchlight—revealed the scene. A large collection of pipes, running from floor to ceiling along a protruding concrete wall, prevented us from seeing around the corner to our right, where voices, two of them, were speaking. We could hear them clearly now, as they vibrated through the open echoing space:

"So, dude—we place the skull on the altar?"

"Yeah."

"The middle of the altar?"

"Yeah. Sure. I don't think it matters." This voice sounded like Alex. Pete's was the other.

"I'm just thinking aesthetically here."

"Put it in the middle, put it wherever."

"And the triangle symbol thingy?"

"We're gonna hang that down so it drapes behind the altar and we can all look at it. It's supposed to make Ahriman present in the room when the sacrifice happens… or whatever."

"Uh… is that gonna be, like, manageable?"

"I brought some clothespins."

"Thank Christ—or, I mean, uh, thank Ahriman. Ha."

"That's it. See? You're getting the hang of it."

"Good. I just didn't want to go back through the passage just for some fuckin' clothespins."

"Well, you won't. They're here."

"…This is gonna work, right?"

"Dude—how can you even ask me that? You've seen his works manifested. I mean, *I* got the internship, right? You heard about that."

"Yeah, but—"

"I had to go through a lot of work to get that internship. And that was the first time—it wasn't easy."

"The first sacrifice, you mean?"

"*Doy*! Yes, the sacrifice! All that shit! I had to buy goddamn chloroform off the fuckin' blackmarket. Which was expensive. Then I had to drive down to Boston, navigate its confusing-ass streets, find a homeless person, sneak up when no one was looking… It wasn't easy!"

"Do you think Iphigenia worked as well as the hobo?"

"*Better*. Turdburger and Merkin both got internships. The hobo was just a hobo, but she was a beautiful young college co-ed. I think that makes a difference—in Ahriman's eyes. It's gotta be worth something."

"But wouldn't it have been better if she was a virgin?"

"What? Why?"

"Isn't that in movies and everything? Like, don't you typically sacrifice a virgin to a volcano or Satan or whatever?"

"No one at Zin mentioned anything about virgins. They said a *life* is what Ahriman wants—a token of respect to get your foot in the door."

"Okay. I'm just nervous they'll reject my application. The second interview went well, but, I mean, my GPA sucks, and it's been going down during pledge term in a big way, and—"

"*You're committing a human sacrifice.* Doesn't that mean anything to you? How do you not get that that's so much more important than grades? Plus, look at what's going on out there! Ahriman's running shit now. So, don't worry, Pete. You'll get your internship."

"Well, alright… Personally, I'm just glad they fixed the boner issue. I was getting hard-ons every minute of the day, every time that theme song came on. I was worried, you know? Like, it was violating all those warnings on the Cialis commercials. Contact a doctor after four hours or three hours. I even came in my pants one time."

"Oh, dude. Me too. Don't even—"

"Yeah. It was gnarly. I was showing a prospective student the gym when it happened."

"Ugh. I was wishing my grandma a happy birthday on the phone. She'd just turned ninety."

They both laughed. Echoing around the pool, it sounded particularly ghoulish.

"Why are we letting Curtis perform the invocation?" Pete was asking. "I mean, I was just thinking it might work better for me, at least, if I did it myself, even if we're all supposed to be in on it together…"

"Because Curtis has billed serious hours for us—for Zin. He got everyone at Zeta addicted to *Silly Squirrels*. That was crucial. That was how we got a hook in the nerds, and they're definite vectors for spreading these things."

I was not at all surprised to hear that Curtis was working for Zin. Typical.

"Ah," said Pete.

"Besides. You're gonna get to drive a knife in. Curtis is just doing the ritual prayer part."

"Yeah. The thing is, I think I'd rather do that part, and not do the knife part, if that's okay…"

"Dude. Don't puss out right now. You've put in so much work."

"I know…"

Suddenly, Emma and I heard footsteps behind us in the tunnel. They weren't extremely close, but they weren't distant either.

"*Quick,*" I whispered.

We crawled forward and hid between the pipes and the concrete wall. I drew the gun.

Now, Peter and Alex were talking about Zin, about all the perks and prestige.

"They throw these parties with hookers and blow. It's just like *The Wolf of Wall Street.*"

"They let you go to those as an intern?"

"Yeah, dude. And it's good blow, too. It's, like, organic. And every year, they go on a big trip to Thailand and do all the gnarliest shit."

"I literally can't wait…"

105. The Invocation

Finally, four people stepped out of the tunnel. Peering through the slim spaces between the pipes, I could see Merkin, Curtis, and… Wes. I almost laughed out loud. The fourth person—apparently male—was not entirely visible, standing on the other side of Wes. I couldn't tell who he was.

Wesley Cross and Alexander Calhoun were both members of the Order of Ahriman, both playing the same game from different sides of the board… They seemed such contrary personalities, yet it occurred to me that the primary principle in both of their cases was identical: power. I'd heard rumors that Wes was planning on applying to work at a hedge fund…

In the Kafka class we'd taken together, he'd made some brief, artificially bitter allusions to a future career at one, anyway. "You know," he said, "I'll probably stop this protest thing when I sell out and become a corporate whore… Like, I'm being ironic?" One of his comrades in the class angrily pointed out that the preferred nomenclature was no longer "whore" but "sex worker." Wes said he was re-appropriating the terminology to use against oppressors.

At any rate, I was mildly surprised to discover that this "sell-out" business wasn't just a joke—it was the truest thing about Wes. He wanted to be where the center of power was, in the same way that Alex and Peter wanted their pre-packaged corporate hedonism experience. He and Alex were the same: a truly dark mirror.

The four new entrants turned the corner and fell out of our range of vision. I motioned to Emma, and we duck-walked behind the pipes until we could almost peer around the corner. But we weren't courageous enough to actually *look*; the tops of our heads would be totally visible.

"Hey, guys." This was the unknown fourth arrival speaking.

I recognized his voice instantly—concentrated in the nose, kind of goofy sounding. It was Elmer's.

He was in the Order of Ahriman?

Elmer continued, "It's really cool you guys are, you know, letting me join The Pyramid. I feel honored—and I'm not just saying that. This is exciting. It's—it's *awesome*, really."

"Well, we're glad to have you," said Alex. "To get things started, we're going to need you to lie down on this altar here. Actually, we tie you down."

"Oh, uh—"

"I mean, we all did it. It's not really hazing. More a kind of initiatory thing. You know… Just a formality."

Oh. Elmer was the sacrifice. That made much more sense.

Fortunately, I had a gun… My hand was sweating onto the grip. It felt clammy, charged with nervous electricity. I knew that, at some point, I was going to need to bust out of my hiding place and try to hold off five guys. For the time being, I decided to wait.

"…You got the ball gag?" Alex was asking.

"Yeah," said Turdburger.

"Great," said Alex.

"Ball gag?" asked Elmer.

"Again, just a formality... So, let's get that ball gag in… Blindfold on… Ear-canceling headphones… Perfect! Then just guide him over, lay him down… Bind the hands… The feet too… Can you hear anything Elmer?"

Elmer was silent.

"Perfect! Curtis, you want to get started with the invocation?"

"Sure." Curtis cleared his throat, and recited, apparently reading from a sheet of paper:

Ahriman, today we come

To consecrate this dead stone

With living blood,

To warm you and slake your thirst

For the souls of men.

Here, humbly, we beseech you

With this offering:

Let his blood run over the coldness

Of your dead stone,

Your ancient altar:

Blood for power

We beseech you

Blood for power

We beseech you.

Praise Ahriman!

And everyone else responded, "Praise Ahriman!"

106. Knives Out

There was total silence, followed by a reverential murmur.

"That was perfect," said Alex. "Let's get in position."

"Emma…" I whispered, handing her the Ortiz baseball. "Take this. I'm going to bust this thing up."

"Simon…"

"There's no other option… Also… I love you."

It was the right moment.

"…I love you too."

We kissed. Before I came out from behind the pipes, we gave each other a long look—freighted with romantic meaning, of course.

I knew enough to make sure the safety was off, but I'd never actually fired a real gun before in my life (only a pellet gun). I imagined I might be a terrible shot… And I only had six rounds… I should've scrounged around for more ammo in the station. That was one bullet for each bad guy, plus one extra. And, ultimately, I didn't want to kill anyone in the first place.

Hand and gun shaking, I came out from the space between the pipes and the wall.

Alex was saying, "We have to call on Ahriman to enjoy the pleasure of the sacrifice, just like we did when we strangled Wilkes and butchered Iffie."

They were all standing around the altar over Elmer, who remained placid and unsuspecting. I saw the gleaming steel of knives held at their sides.

"Stop…" I said. For some reason, this came out hoarse—barely vocalized.

They raised the knives.

"Stop!" I yelled.

They all turned around.

I pointed the gun at one, then another, before settling on Alex. They stared at me, expressions ranging from irritated (Wes) to empty and emotionless (Pete).

"Put the fucking knives down!"

They didn't move.

"I said put the knives down!"

"There's six of us, and one of you," said Alex.

"True. But there's only one gun, and I have it."

They did nothing—just stood there with their knives fixed, waiting for Alex to make the first move. Elmer continued to lay there like a can of Spam, a tin of meat waiting to be horribly popped.

"You don't have the balls," said Alex.

My hands were shaking—I couldn't quite keep the gun fixed on Alex's chest. But, to dispel any notion that I was too much of a wuss to shoot someone, I decided to blast Alex right in the kneecap.

I aimed and tried to steady my hand, recalling advice I'd heard once in a movie: *aim small, miss small*. I focused on the precise bump of Alex's patella—and squezzed the trigger.

The shot echoed loudly in the enclosed chamber.

Part of Wes's left hand—the hand that had been holding the knife—blew off, fingers mangled. A few drops of blood spattered the faces of his fellow conspirators. The knife clattered to the ground.

It took a moment before a loud keening cry went up, like that of a little kid, seated in a sandbox, who's just had his eye sprayed with sediment.

While Wes howled, the other guys remained standing around Elmer, knives still raised. As for Elmer himself, he remained perfectly still. Yep, he was definitely wearing some high quality noise-cancelling headphones…

"There's more where that came from..." I said. Then, trying to sound tough, I added, "…Motherfuckers."

Alex remained immovable. In fact, he was grinning, albeit tightly. The others looked a bit more uncertain, but they still didn't lower their knives. Before they could rush me—which they were about to do—I decided to take another shot.

I repeated the aiming process, focusing on Alex's knee again.

This time, Merkin's leg buckled under him. *His* kneecap exploded. Merkin's wounded warrior-cry was married to the still ongoing, banshee-like lamentations of Wes:

"Ah fuck, man! Ah fuck!"

Was I using the wrong eye to aim or something?

"Put down your fucking knives!" I yelled. "Seriously, guys—I can do this all night."

"Have faith in Ahriman," said Alex to his increasingly anxious comrades. "This will work out." Although their knives were still ready for action, I sensed that they weren't going to stab Elmer until they'd dealt with me.

I moved the gun so I was targeting Pete.

"Pete!" I said. "You get that you're about to commit a murder—right? That you're about to plunge a knife into some kid's chest? You see how fucked up that is? Right???"

Pete said nothing. His expression didn't change even slightly.

"Pete, I was listening before—I heard you saying you'd rather invoke Ahriman than stab Elmer, right? You know what they did to Iphigenia! You must have some kind of conscience, you need to—"

Someone tackled me from behind. I squeezed the trigger reflexively and a shot ricocheted off the ceiling. Everyone ducked.

The guy who tackled me turned out to be Turdburger, joining the party late. He was reaching for my gun, which was still in my right hand. I couldn't aim it at him, he had my arm pinned tightly, and, because of his superior strength, he was bound to get it… But I flicked it away with my wrist. The gun spun across the floor where it fell into the pool. This wasn't going to prevent them from shooting me, obviously. Death by knife, unpleasantly, seemed to be in the cards…

The deranged crew leapt down from the altar, ready to slaughter me. Wes, however, was left behind, still crying. His shrieks swirled around the interior of the chamber.

Turdburger got me in a full nelson and pulled me upright, facing the rest of them.

Why hadn't Emma called out when she saw Turdburger emerge from the tunnel? Had she saved herself? I didn't want to call her name, of course, given that she'd likely end up skewered as well.

"Pete…" I said. It was hopeless. I was speaking the name of a conscienceless killer.

They advanced with identical blood-hungry expressions, eyes like something factory produced—plastic, rubber.

"Pete…" I said. "You don't want to do this."

Pete didn't even pause. He buried the knife directly in my sternum, in the same place he'd stabbed me whilst fencing so many times previous. Then, he couldn't pull it out. He tugged at the knife, while I struggled to get free.

Next, Turdburger stabbed me in the back. I think he was trying to sever my spinal cord, but he buried the blade in my scapula instead. Simultaneously, Alex shivved me right in the ribs. Fortunately, I think my continued squirming kept them from finding the vital organs they were intending to hit.

As they tore at me, a kind of hunger seemed to be satisfying itself; there was something ravenous in the act. *Ahriman's hunger*…

Merkin, hopping forward wildly despite his injury, stabbed me in the gut, which seemed the most serious; yet it was the only wound I didn't really feel at first—coldness rather than pain, slipping in through muscle and blood and fat, the sense of something alien intruding. As Pete continued to pull at the knife stuck in my breastbone, the handle snapped off, leaving the blade lodged in place. Curtis was about to slash my throat—and then I'd certainly be dead.

Where *was* Emma? Why weren't they stabbing *her* to death too?

In answer to this question, an extremely powerful jet of water knocked us all across the room, roaring from seemingly all directions. I fell on my back, spinning in a circle on the floor under its compulsion.

Above the din, Alex could just be heard, screaming, "Wha' the fuh?"

107. Escape

Rolling over, I spat out water and realized that I was in a lot of pain. I'd always thought being stabbed with a knife would be a terrible sensation, and—in truth—it wasn't so great. Not as bad as being torn apart by dogs, probably, but I wouldn't say it was better than I expected. In fact, it was exactly like I'd always imagined, really; I've imagined dying in any number of ways, at one time or another.

The water was still blasting forth, more powerful than a firehose, sending the cultists flying violently. Everyone was disoriented.

Then, Emma was pulling me up from the floor. "The tunnel..." she said.

Tugging me in the right direction, I stumbled towards the entrance and down the stairs. With no cellphone light to guide us, it got pretty dark pretty quickly.

"Simon, I'm sorry... I didn't see Turdburger come in..." she said, keeping her voice soft. "I was busy. I noticed a significant-looking leak in the main pipe running along the farther wall, and I was trying to judge where to hit it with your Ortiz ball. I thought if I could somehow bust the pipe open, it looked like it might gush out and knock them all over. Which it did... But I lost the ball, for the record. I had to throw it. It was lucky."

"Ugh..." I said. I meant to say, "Good job." I remembered she'd told me that she'd pitched softball in high school.

"I saw the word 'Himmelman' printed on the big metal circular thing, right where the water was leaking out, and I thought—isn't that that defective valve that they were recalling? So, I threw the baseball up at it, as hard as I could—they were about to cut your throat. And, thank God—it worked!"

"Yurgh…" I said. I meant to say "That was lucky," but it came out "Yurgh…"

"We need to get you to a doctor…

Emma had saved me. She'd found the flawed valve within that concrete heart and smashed it open. The Himmelman valve, manufactured by Curtis father, saved us by breaking, by failing.

As we went deeper into the tunnel, we could hear footsteps behind us, running, coming closer. We tried to speed up, but I was only able to do a lame little jog. I wasn't in good shape… I was covered in blood.

Wet footsteps echoed—were they coming our way now, from The Pyramid? It was impossible to tell if they were headed towards us or away from us, before us or behind us. It was isolated, un-localized pitter-pattering in the middle of sheer dark. I thought Alex might've phoned some of the other Beta brothers to head us off from the other end of the tunnel, in which case we were truly screwed.

I was getting weaker and weaker, but Emma felt almost supernaturally strong as she supported me. Faint and light-headed, I could see no light anywhere.

"I have an idea," said Emma. "It might kill us, but it's an idea…"

We detoured into one of those sub-tunnels we'd passed on our way to The Pyramid—the unused routes branching off to God knows where.

Things touched our faces, crawled over our necks. There was a rancid odor—decay birthing gross and obscene forms of life down there. Roots struck out from the walls and dangled from the ceiling—the forest must have been above us. It felt like we were journeying through the intestines of a gigantic dead animal.

Finally, the air got cool and blew against us. We couldn't see light until we stumbled through a net of roots, which brushed our faces with dirt.

When we stepped out, we could see the stars.

108. Foaming at the Mouth

We felt grateful, conscious of air and earth—not exactly home free but close. Yet, I was still bleeding, feeling faint. Little piles of unmelted snow were sitting in the shadows of big pine trees. I had reached a point in which the effort I was making to escape ceased to pain me, but only because I felt totally lightheaded and numb.

"Wait," said Emma… She looked around, noticed something. "I know where we are. Go this way…"

She dragged me onwards, as I disassociated from the situation and watched my adrenalin-saturated body stumble through the woods and leak blood. Then, I sat down—involuntarily. Emma looked almost panicked for a moment, before she said, "Stay right here. Just sit still… I'll be right back." She tore off.

I breathed heavily, looking up through the tree branches, praying for life. I don't know how long I was lying there—when you're conscious of death, time does strange things. Every second was sharp and whole.

My eyes had closed when I heard feet scuffling around nearby. They grew closer, right next to me. I looked at the person standing over me, expecting to see Emma.

It was Alex. His cool, empty look had been replaced with raw animal rage.

I moved my lips but couldn't say whatever I was trying to say. I wanted to mutter something cold to him, something stoic and spiteful, but I was losing too much blood.

Alex bent down and began strangling me with the concentrated attention of someone attempting to squeeze the last useable bit of toothpaste out of the tube. I felt his fingers on my throat, and tried to resist, tried to move my arms. I had been clinging to consciousness in the first place, and could now feel it abandoning me entirely. Dreamlike thoughts and images rolled through my mind—squirrels picking up acorns, bees gathering honey, preparing for a winter that would not end...

But instead of falling more deeply away, I came back to consciousness. Alex's fingers had slackened around my neck. An un-focused image resolved itself, and I could see his face. Alex looked like he was foaming at the mouth....

Then, I realized Alex actually *was* foaming at the mouth, quite literally. So was I, oddly enough. I tried to put my hand to my face, but my hand was flailing around, as was the rest of my body.

Alex fell to the ground, while I rolled around in the dirt. We both seemed to be undergoing convulsions. Oddly enough, my mind remained completely lucid, but my body was completely out of control.

I became aware of a strange tone vibrating around me and *in* me— something like Tibetan throat-singing.

Soon, I lost consciousness entirely.

109. Sanctuary

I woke up on a foldout couch in a cluttered room. I tried to sit up and discovered that I couldn't. As soon as I made the effort, I faded away again, went back to sleep...

A little later, I came to with greater awareness. An I.V. was running into my arm, and a heart-monitoring machine was attached to my chest. My wounds, it became clear, had all been stitched up. The effort to raise my torso was still difficult, but I could turn my head well enough to gain a view of things.

The room's clutter had a certain order to it. On the shelves and piled on tables, books were arranged alphabetically by author before falling into an entirely different arrangement, based on the publication date or the color of the book's binding or some personal meaning known only to the arranger. It was order, yet spontaneous order. On the wall, there was a large poster of the human inner ear in very developed detail, a Tibetan mandala, a large Catholic crucifix, prints of William Blake's paintings of Nebuchadnezzar and Newton—and a print of a design that I first mistook for the Ahrimanic symbol. But I realized that all the triangles were pointing *up* not down.

It was the Order of Asha's emblem.

So, while puzzled, I felt I'd fallen into the right hands.

I noticed that some of my favorite books were on the shelves, and considered that their owner might be something of a kindred spirit. There was *Franny and Zooey*, *Siddhartha*, *Walden*, and the collected poetry of T.S. Eliot, Emily Dickinson, and W.B. Yeats. In addition to these, there were numerous books in Italian…

I took a fairly educated guess as to where I was and felt a bit sheepish.

My suspicions soon proved correct. In a few minutes, Carlo Canzoni entered the room.

When he saw that I was awake, he said, "*Simon, Simon, behold: Satan hath desired to have you that he may sift you as wheat.*" He paused and repeated the end of the sentence, "'*sift you as wheat*'… and how is it that we are like grains of wheat? Because we are meant to grow, I suppose? Yes. But if the growth is stunted and arrested—what then? How many grains are scattered, fall on stones or in the cracks of sidewalks, never to mature into anything…never to develop into…*consciousness*! That's the big word isn't it? Arrested attention. Stunted attention. Never growing. Scattered. *Dispersed*. That's the crisis we're seeing with the squirrels, on the TV, and whenever one has to go out and buy bread and milk. Not a crisis of conscience, but a crisis of consciousness. And there's probably a crisis of conscience wrapped up in that too, somehow."

What a nut! Who talks in that kind of free-form monologue? But I felt immediately comforted. And, again, sheepish for having suspected him.

"I think I owe you an apology," I said. "…And my thanks. You saved me life…"

"Oh—by no means, Simon! You don't owe me an apology. Emma told me the whole thing, with Wilkes' murder and so on. Your suspicions were quite understandable. No need to explain yourself."

He was certainly a friendly man, I thought. Jolly, even.

"The brothers at Beta killed him," I said. "They were gloating over it, how they strangled him, how they asked Ahriman to savor his pain…"

"Yes. I've received some intel from a friend of mine, another agent of Asha—because I *am* a member of the Order of Asha, just to make that clear…

299

Anyway, I believe the Beta Brothers lured Wilkes into their secret lair with the promise of great pot. Then, they killed him, and strategically arranged his body in his office... I warned him after our lunch: go straight home, send the books to me... You see, I wasn't sure which one I needed or what the title was. I merely knew that Mr. Singh had instructed one book to be sent to me and the others to Wilkes. Yet, there was something of a mix-up—perhaps an intentional mix-up by the retirement home's administrators."

"Yes, the guy who runs The Desert Palm—he's a former Beta brother."

"Indeed. But I don't believe he's in the inner circle. I think he just relayed information—telling them Singh had left his books to Wilkes—without knowing its significance. Somehow, the higher ups at Zin were aware that Singh was one of Asha's agents."

Someone else entered the room. I was expecting Emma, but a masculine voice said, "Is it alright if I join this chat?"

It was Omar Seck. This was not entirely surprising. He must've been Canzoni's source on how Wilkes had been murdered, for starters. His behavior made a lot of sense.

"And you were in Asha too..." I said.

"Yes," said Seck. "I'd been trying to bust open this bloody Zin conspiracy practically since it began. I knew they were going to sacrifice someone, I'd figured that they were behind Wilkes' death... But I didn't know what you knew: the location of the passage to The Pyramid. Alex only let his closest confederates know about that."

"It was in the back of Alex's closet," I said.

"Really? God, I'd assumed you had to press some sort of brick in the tomb room in a certain fashion, and a hidden door would swing open or something." He punctuated this with a short, bitter laugh.

"Yeah... That's what I'd have thought too."

"Also, I saved you with a smoke bomb when they were about to violate you with that eggplant. You know, when you were dressed up as a teddy bear?"

"I was an Ewok... But thank you! I really owe you one."

I really *did* owe him one.

"Anyway," said Canzoni. "I'm glad we are on the same page. I wish I could've performed espionage of my own, but I've been busy trying to figure out how to disarm and defeat Zin. It's been difficult..."

"But, wait—" I said. "What happened to Alex? I mean, how did you save me? And where's Emma?"

"Alex got away. You passed out because you'd lost so much blood and were half-strangled. This actually insulated you from the full effect of the vibration."

"You mean the throat-singing noise I'd heard?"

"Exactly. I can broadcast various sonic patterns on the giant metal tower I've constructed on my property. That particular vibratory frequency is intended to induce a state of amnesia and prompt you to wander back on the route from whence you came. You know the rumor about the townies who sneaked onto my property and then walked back into town with no memory of where they had been? That's completely true. I used the same frequency on them as on you and Alex... So, we can assume Alex wandered back into the tunnel... I don't think anyone else had come with him, but if they had, they would've done the same.

Fortunately, Emma saw my transmission tower and she knew my house was somewhere nearby. She got here just in time."

"I owe you my life," I said, quite sincerely.

"Ahhh," said Canzoni, who gestured with his hand dismissively. "Emma's really the one who saved you."

As if on cue, there was a knock on the door, which did not wait for a response. Emma entered the room, ran over, and embraced me.

"Don't squeeze him too hard!" said Canzoni, laughing. "He's still healing."

I felt only slight pain when I hugged her. It barely registered.

"Thanks," I whispered.

110. Answers

As I ate breakfast—a bagel with butter and jam, some canned peaches, and a glass of orange juice—the three others sat around my bed and talked. I joined in from time to time.

Emma was asking Canzoni, "Why did you invent this amnesiac tower in the first place?"

"It's a by-product of my research. I'm interested in first principles—the subtle vibrations which give rise to everything, Primordial Light and Sound. Pythagoras called this 'The Music of the Spheres.' It's at the intersection of physics, aesthetics, philosophy... I know you already know all this Emma. This is for Simon's benefit. Anyway, the more I delved into the matter— fundamentally elusive as the subtlest vibrations are—I discovered unexpected applications: I could generate sounds that could alter mood. And not alter mood the way ordinary music does, which depends on how you're feeling that day, what frame of mind you're in. I could change mood in a way that was *exact*. Exposed to these vibrations, you inevitably would become happy or, with a change in frequency, sad. Naturally, I was aware that the power to change the very rhythms of the mind without the subject's volition was too vast for any government or private citizen to possess, myself included...

"But, you know, I'd already developed the technology, and I needed a grant. So, I demonstrated a few tricks to the government—not my best tricks, but impressive enough. I told them I'd let them have it once I perfected the technology, but planned on 'running into complications' somewhere down the line... Also, as far as the rumors go, like the thing that happened to the townspeople in Lake Panoosacut Village, where they all started laughing for no reason: the *military* tested my machine. Or, to be honest, they pressured me into testing. It wasn't my idea. They'd been pestering me, constantly peering over my shoulder and harassing me, harassing me day and night, threatening to take away my grant money. So, I had to show them something to get them off my back... I can only follow the path of *wonder* I tell them—I can't be worrying *constantly* about every damn potential application of my technology. It wasn't the best, but I went along with it...

"All the while, I was actually trying to get the jump on Ahriman. I knew that members of his Order were trying to figure out how to enslave the human race and provide their god with new devotees and fresh sacrifices. Once I learned that Zin had become the new headquarters for Ahriman in North America, I attempted to develop a system that could halt them. Unfortunately, they progressed more rapidly in their designs than I'd anticipated... But I've been developing a method of defeating them and disrupting the *Silly Squirrels* game. It will still take a few weeks to be perfected—there are still some kinks to work out.

At any rate, it's a special sonic pattern. My tower will send out a signal, which will disrupt the malign Ahrimanic frequencies that are being broadcast from all the cellphone towers in America. I wish things were moving faster, but I have to make sure I get everything right. I don't want to inadvertently destroy every electronic device in America—like with an EMP."

"But how did you—both of you—get involved with the Order of Asha in the first place?" I asked. "And what *is* the Order of Asha, exactly? I mean, who's in it? If you're allowed to say…"

"I'm from Senegal, as you know," said Omar. "And there's a very mystical form of Islam there with spiritual leaders called marabouts. My grandfather happened to be one of these marabouts—and before I left for college, he gave me a small golden medallion, embossed with the Order of Asha's symbol. He told me, 'Only concentrate on this design when it's rightside up!' explaining a bit about Ahriman and the downward symbol. He told me to consider myself an initiate of Asha, and to await further instructions… That was all.

"And I did receive further instructions, usually in the form of printed letters that would arrive in the mail, and simply say something like 'Join Beta Fraternity,' or 'Report what you learn about Ahriman to Carlo Canzoni'—which is how we met and became friends, Professor Canzoni and I. The Order of Asha only dishes out one or two sentences at a time, brief imperatives. It almost felt like a joke. Yet… I had to listen. Sometimes, I think a little more *detail* in these letters might've been useful. Perhaps I'd have been able to crack the case quicker, discover the passage to the Pyramid… Oh, and I figured out that you'd accessed *The God of Smoke and Mirrors* entry in the library catalogue thanks to a bit of computer hacking—I set up an alarm that would alert me if anyone searched for the entry…in case you were wondering how I found you. You were the first person who ever looked that book up."

"As for myself," said Canzoni, "I worked in the Soviet Union in the late seventies and early eighties. I wasn't a believer in International Communism—in fact, I started passing information to the Italian government—but it was a high-paying job and I felt I needed the money to continue funding my own experiments."

"Wilkes actually told me that you'd mentioned the U.S.S.R.'s psychic experiments at Tashkent to him."

"Yes. It's true. I was in Tashkent—that's in Uzbekistan—working with the Reds—but as a spy for the West. I had to fabricate many Communist credentials and associations. It was very time consuming. I'd worked my way into the heart of their psychic operations—but then, I had an encounter with a remarkable man. I can't say much more about him, except that he astonished all of us scientists, shattered the underlying presumptions of our work most joyfully, and finally gave me the same sort of medallion that Omar's grandfather gave to him. That's how I became a spy for the Order of Asha."

I jumped in: "I seem to remember, Emma, that when I described the Ahrimanic design to you for the first time—the pattern I'd seen while playing *Silly Squirrels*—you paused like it sounded familiar. Is that because you'd seen one of these medallions?"

"Yes," she said. "I was at the Professor's office hours and I noticed something sitting on his desk. It was a medallion with the Order of Asha's symbol engraved on it. I didn't get a very good look at it, and I thought you were totally deluded, so I assumed that it was just a vague, coincidental similarity."

Canzoni interrupted. "But back to what I was saying... You see, the Soviet system was an invention of Ahriman, one of his greatest performances—perhaps until now, with the advent of Zin and this *Silly Squirrels* business. In the '40s and '50s, agents working for Stalin annihilated centers of the Order of Asha in Uzbekistan and Turkmenistan. Yes, the Order does have centers—still—though we can hardly know where they are. For safety's sake, it often operates within the monasteries and temples of other esoteric organizations—among Buddhists, Sufis, Jewish Kabbalists, or Christian Gnostics. It grafts itself onto them quite naturally. The marabouts to whom Omar's grandfather belongs are another great example.

"When I was spying on them, the Soviets were nominally conducting psychic research, but the goal of the Ahrimanic cult members in their midst was really to take the attention of yogis, fakirs, Buddhist monks, and other remarkable men and women, and re-appropriate that attention for Ahrimanic purposes— technological and military ends, leading towards the destruction of free societies. The monk from the Order of Asha whom I had the pleasure of meeting had been sent to disrupt that plan—which he did.

"Stalin and Hitler, by the way, were both worshippers of Ahriman, and the closest thing we've yet seen to his living incarnations, aside from the *Silly Squirrels* game itself. Also, Mao's followers destroyed monasteries committed to Asha in Tibet, during the Cultural Revolution. So, we live precariously, in the margins, and are always on the verge of disappearing! But we don't, because we avoid overt organizational structure and draw our strength from individuals. We 'go where the wind listeth,' I suppose you might say..."

Canzoni continued: "In the past, Ahriman controlled kings and ruled Empires. He always installed a sacrificial cult, because his goal was to appease his hunger, to be *fed*. And, more than the sacrifices—which are just a means, a formality to demonstrate devotion—he feeds on human attention. He is the cosmic parasite. This system he erected with the game, with Zin, *Silly Squirrels*—it is essentially a *drain*, down which the human attention span is free to rush. On the other hand, The Order of Asha—a natural home for saints, artists, and poets—has been constructing a means by which attention can be channeled upwards and inwards, into the regions of pure Spirit. In a sense, it is fair to say that, in the same way that Ahriman is building his own body in the form of this inferenal system, the Order of Asha is building new bodies for God on earth—in a higher poetic sense. It's giving people the means to see through their situations, concentrate their attention, and connect with the transcendent."

We paused for a moment to absorb this, stew in the meaning.

I broke the silence.

"Emma," I said, "there's one thing I don't get. *We've* played the game. We made our minds vulnerable to the power of Ahriman's symbol. But we didn't get addicted. We had the willpower to turn the thing off."

"Yeah. It's funny…"

Canzoni spoke up, asking, "Have either of you ever had a period of reflective solitude, in which, perhaps, you read many books, considering them deeply and planting their meanings within yourselves?"

"Hmmm…" I said. "I think so. My summer vacations are still kind of empty, and I read a lot generally."

"My whole *life* has been like that," said Emma.

"Hence your insusceptibility," Canzoni concluded. "Ahriman cannot easily shatter the already crystallized attention. He can only work with *fragments*."

"Fragments…" I murmured to myself. I recalled how my consciousness malfunctioned in the house I shared with Pete and Oscar and Curtis, and the way it bounced aimlessly from one object to another during my succession of spiritual belly flops at Beta. I was a bundle of fragments too—of loose, flimsy, un-integrated elements. But I remembered playing *Silly Squirrels*, and how I suddenly *yanked* my attention away, like there was something inside me that wanted to resist this fragmentation, that had developed just enough to put in a single moment of major effort.

I have to admit that I felt a little self-satisfied.

"Here," said Canzoni. "I want to show you a quote from a man named Anthony Bloom."

"Was he in the Order of Asha?" asked Emma.

"Oh, I have no idea. We usually don't know who the other members are, beyond our own chapter. At any rate, Bloom—an Eastern Orthodox Archbishop—wrote this: 'If you watch your life carefully you will discover quite soon that we hardly ever live from within outwards; instead we respond to incitement, to excitement. In other words, we live by reflection, by reaction... We are completely empty, we do not act from within ourselves but accept as our life a life which is actually fed in from the outside; we are used to things happening which compel us to do other things. How seldom can we live simply by means of the depth and the richness we assume that there is within ourselves.'

"So," Canzoni continued, "that's what *you've* done. For at least a moment or two, you lived from the inside. You may have blundered into it, not understood it, but whatever little bit of attention you managed to center within yourself—it *did* something. It insulated you from the influence of Ahriman. This is a rare thing. Perhaps he could've broken through with more exposure—but he didn't. Attention is the outward expression of the soul. *That* is why Ahriman tries to steal it, stifle it. He knows that if people could collect their attention for a few moments too many, they might get wise to his tricks. They might develop a longing for *Home*."

111. Flipping a Pancake

We stayed with Canzoni and Omar for the next week. It briefly occurred to me that class was still continuing and that I was probably going to fail most of my courses—an utterly absurd thought. Yes, the world of grade point averages and final papers was still operating, but it had been utterly assimilated into the New Order.

When we occasionally turned on the TV to check the world situation, we noticed that commercials for *Silly Squirrels* were running during every break on every channel, flashing the Ahrimanic symbol. Yet, to all appearances, dystopia had not dawned. Things were eerily the same. But, at the corners of the presentation, you sensed who was in control. There was a slightly dazed look in everyone's eyes. Attention, the outward expression of the soul, was being channeled down odd drainpipes and aqueducts.

I was able to get out of bed on the third day and started to improve. Canzoni, being a Da Vinci-esque polymath, was as good a physician as any and was well supplied with medical instruments and equipment. When you're caught between so many conflicting powers, performing tremendously sensitive research, it's not utterly mad to embrace the habits of a survivalist.

Emma and I shot hoops at the basket which hung over Canzoni's garage (mainly playing H.O.R.S.E., at which I'll admit she occasionally beat me), chatted with Omar and Canzoni about science and philosophy, played Scrabble with

Omar (who had a tendency to crush us, despite being a non-native English speaker; I suspect his British boarding school education gave him an edge), and simmered in anxiety while scheming how to best defeat Ahriman. As mentioned, Canzoni wanted to generate a new vibration, which would disrupt all the Ahrimanic waves in all the cell phone towers in America—without otherwise impacting service. Evidently, he was working on the computers in his office—which determined the frequencies issued by his transmission tower—trying to discover the answer. This was easier said than done. His previous attempts had been stymied: Ahriman had managed to arm himself with great scientists and devious computer programmers. It was hard for the altruistic individual to suffer and serve when facing such a vast, self-interested collective.

Canzoni's house and the surrounding woods normally would've been peaceful, easing one into the contemplative life. The pressure of external events, however, made it impossible to relax. We all sensed something was coming.

The following week, on a Wednesday, Canzoni was making pancakes for breakfast. A dewy silence clung around the house, and the sun was barely up. There was something both dreamy and clear-eyed about the day—soberly intoxicated. As he flipped the flapjacks, he was telling us a funny story about a scientist he worked with in Russia who had attempted to learn the language of bears. The experiment didn't work very well, resulting in a vodka-saturated near mauling.

"Now watch this," said Canzoni. I am going to flip this pancake into the air—precisely ten times. It will land exactly in the middle of the pan on the uncooked side. See if you can count."

He flipped the pancake and it somersaulted over and over—yes, precisely ten times—before landing on its uncooked side.

"You see?" he said.

We applauded, and he made a little bow.

As soon as he straightened up, something smashed through the kitchen window above the stove. Canzoni made a choking sound. Blood started to gush out of the side of his neck. Yet he remained standing.

Horror seized us and we stood up from our chairs. More glass fell from the shattered window, and we realize bullets were flying through the window and the kitchen wall, evidently fired from silenced weapons. We all hit the ground, and Canzoni fell too, still making an awful choking noise. He seemed to have been hit again, through the chest and the shoulder.

Crouching, I ran as best I could to the front door and turned, slid, and chained the three additional security locks into place. I took a quick peek through the window on the top of the door, and saw Alex, Pete, Turdburger, and Curtis all carrying high-powered rifles and running up from the side of the house. As fast as I could, I turned and chained the door's three locks, and then pushed an armchair in front of the door. I ran back to the kitchen just as their footsteps reached the front porch, and fussilade blew in the windows. They tried the door and then attempted to blow the locks off with their guns.

I was in shock. How had they circumvented the security system? Canzoni's property was wired to alert him when anyone unexpected entered.

Emma and Omar were on the floor near Canzoni. Emma was sobbing, trying to stanch the blood gushing from his neck with a previously pale yellow kitchen rag, now incarnadine. It had been the nearest thing handy.

But Canzoni was dead.

Unfortunately, there was no time to mourn.

"Are there any guns around?" I yelled.

Canzoni couldn't answer and neither Emma nor Omar knew.

Omar got up and joined me. We grabbed kitchen knives and moved into the passage leading into the livingroom, hoping we'd be able to get the jump on Alex and the others when they got through. They were already firing their guns at the locks.

"Do you know how to throw a knife?" asked Omar.

"Yeah," I said. I actually *had* thrown a knife at an old dead tree in my backyard in Pennsylvania a few times... But I'd never actually got the knife to stick in the tree...

"Good," he said.

"Emma," called Omar. "Go into Canzoni's office. It should be open, but if not, the pin code is 8341."

"Alright," Emma snuffled. She abandoned her mentor's body, and ran down the hallway.

"We'll throw our knives when they get through the door and then run after her," Seck said. "Just to slow them down."

"Let's slow them down a little more, first... Alex!" I called out.

They continued their attempts to break the door down. The rifles actually hadn't made much of an impact. They were now using an ax that Canzoni kept outside and normally used to chop firewood.

I yelled again, "Alex! Pete!"

The ax stopped.

"Listen for a fucking second," I said. "You guys should just go home. The whole inside of this house is booby-trapped."

There was a short pause.

"You wouldn't tell us that if the house was really booby-trapped," said Alex.

Good point.

"Well," I said, "don't say I didn't warn you. Right now, Canzoni's got his finger on the button. That whole front porch is going to blow in a second or two."

"Fuck you, Simon," said Alex. "We know the old fucker's dead. Turdburger's an expert marksman, dude."

"He was just wounded," I said.

"You know what?" said Alex. "You're a real piece of shit. It would've been so easy to just go with the flow, get an internship, be rich, be happy. You had to fuck it all up."

"Yep," I said. "That's exactly right." Then I whispered to Omar, "This is slowing them down, right?"

"I think so…" he said.

"So, Alex, you're not at all worried about the consequences of siding with a dark god?" I called. "You're not a little concerned that evil is, like, *not* going to actually win out in the end? And you, Pete, and you, Curtis: you're not a little worried that the human-sacrifice god might sort of be an asshole? That you're becoming murderers for a really stupid reason? None of this is resonating?"

There was silence.

As though reading off an inspirational refrigerator magnet, Alex said: "There is no good and no evil. There is only one side to any issue, and that's who has the most power. That's why Wes—social justice warrior Wes—is on our side. He gets it. He knows it's all about power. He wanted to be empowered, and, well—we're empowering him."

"That's beautiful!" I said (sarcastically, of course). "Really! That's unimpeachable logic!"

With that, Alex splintered the door open with the ax. It swung wide. In the same instant, Omar and I flung our knives. Both buried themselves in the same place in Curtis's collarbone. Curtis screamed—about as loud as Wes did when I wounded his hand.

The other three were momentarily distracted by Curtis's cry. Before they could raise their guns, Omar and I turned. We ran down the hallway to Canzoni's office (which none of us except Omar had previously been permitted to enter). Just as we leapt inside, bullets hit the wall at the end of the hall. Omar locked the door behind us.

Canzoni's office was neatly kept, but spare. It had none of the organized clutter of his library. One wall was lined with computer monitors and consoles, electrical equipment, and a long panel of controls, all of which operated the transmission tower. It was the largest room in the house by far.

We could hear Alex and the others rapidly approaching down the hall. Omar rushed over to the control panel, where Emma was already sitting—her face pained and anxious. He pressed a button. Apparently, this was an attempt to activate the same throat-singing, amnesiac vibration that had earlier deterred Alex. (We would be insulated from its effects within Canzoni's office.) We listened and heard the odd hum surrounding us outside… But the intruders' footsteps reached the door.

"Damn it!" said Omar. "Zin must've upgraded their microchip implants to shield them from the effects of the vibration. That's probably why they didn't trip the security system when they entered the Professor's property."

"So what do we do?" I asked.

We could hear Alex hammering on the door with his ax. It hadn't cracked yet, but it wasn't so strongly reinforced that they couldn't break through it.

Muffled but still distinct, Alex cried, "I'm gonna skull-fuck you to death! All three of you!"

Someone fired a rifle at the door, which caused a dent, but didn't break through. The bullet apparently ricocheted back into the hall, provoking noises of consternation.

"I don't see what choice we have," said Omar. "The Professor was almost finished crafting the vibration that would disrupt Ahriman's signal. We can try it. I know the activation code… If that works, maybe it'll affect their microchips and disrupt their shielding effect—provided they're tuned to Ahrimanic frequencies. I can activate it—now. Immediately. I just don't know if there will be any kinks… "

"Let's do it," I said.

"Yeah," said Emma.

Omar removed a key from his pocket and inserted it into a lock on the control panel. He turned it, popping open a small metal door next to the lock, which contained a keyboard. Next, he entered some numbers and letters, before finally pressing a large black rubber button situated above the keys. Outside, Alex continued to rave, "You ball-lickin' dick-suck faggots! We're gonna rape your dead bodies! We're gonna—"

We waited for a moment. The moment lasted just long enough for us to feel hope leaking away… Emma and Omar both looked pretty desperate and I imagine I looked the same.

Then came a noise—an immense sucking-sound, like all the air being vacuumed out of the world at once… And there was silence.

In the hall, no one stirred.

We waited… Still, there was nothing.

Cautiously, we stepped to the door. On the other side, we felt no sense of movement. Either they had suddenly decided to fake us out by being totally quiet, or the transmission had affected them in some way… Maybe it had killed them? Perhaps that was one of the "kinks" Canzoni was worried about? I wondered if we hadn't accidentally set off an EMP or murdered everyone in America… Hopefully, these kinks in the vibration weren't quite so dire.

I opened the door.

Alex, Pete, Curtis, and Turdburger were sprawled on the floor. At first, I thought they really *were* dead. They looked like pieces of defunct machinery that had been forcefully decommissioned.

Then, they started to re-boot. Eyes fluttered open. Mouths yawned. Fingers grasped awkwardly at the air.

Concerned that they were about to spring back to life, we picked up their rifles and ax.

But they couldn't stand up. Instead, they rolled from side to side, helplessly. First, Turdburger began to cry, weeping in the exact manner of a hungry infant—or, in his case, an infant with a dirty diper. The shit smell hit us at that moment; they had all evidently voided their bowels.

While Pete and Curtis began wailing like Turdburger—red, meaty frat boy faces howling simultaneously—Alex placidly blew a spit-bubble.

"Oh, God…" said Emma. "We fried their brains."

"Did we fry *everyone's* brains?" I asked.

"I hope not!" said Omar.

We exchanged solemn stares. Alex's spit-bubble popped.

I looked at Pete for a moment. He continued crying and attempting to turn over on his side. He rolled unhappily back and forth, side to side.

After stepping over their incontinent bodies and walking into the living room, we gathered around Canzoni's corpse in the kitchen. Despite the violent nature of his death, the Professor looked calm and peaceful—almost as though he were aware that his invention had saved the world without causing any fatalities.

Nature seemed as close and benign as it had in the moments before he was murdered. The sun had fully risen. We could hear birds chirping and, a little way off, the river running.

112. Epilogue

Fortunately, we *hadn't* fried their brains. We'd instigated a more interesting and poetically just effect, as it turned out…

It took us a few weeks to figure out what happened. When we left Canzoni's house and walked into New Hamelin, we discovered that everyone in the town was alive and that their brains were fully functioning—no one was playing *Silly Squirrels*. At worst, they seemed pleasantly bewildered.

We were relieved.

Alex, Pete, Wes, and their fellow chip-implanted confederates at Beta and Zin hadn't suffered permanent brain damage due to Canzoni's transmission. They'd undergone a fate that was, in some ways, more disturbing: their identities had been completely wiped out.

When Canzoni's transmission blocked the Ahrimanic frequences—which were being broadcast from every cellphone tower in America—it caused the microchip implants to malfunction. I think this may have been a "kink" in the vibration, but it ended up serving justice. Everyone who'd sold out to Ahriman, who'd joined the conspiracy, suffered the same final end—their brains were completely reset, as though they'd become infants again. Every memory they'd ever developed, every skill they'd learned and mastered, vanished in an instant. They had to start over from square one. It was—finally—game over for *Silly Squirrels* and all of its votaries. There were no more acorns to pick up. The squirrels had cashed out.

All the people who suffered this fate—from the CEO of Zin, Colby Stern, to Pete and Alex—were gradually collected and institutionalized at a special center. (The conspiracy even included a few congress people). Since the microchips had totally combusted, the immediate cause of their catastrophic identity loss was unclear to the investigating doctors. It's still considered an unsolved medical mystery.

Professor Warningbone, however, had avoided this fate—luckily, he'd dug his own chip out of the side of his head with a screwdriver a few days before the vibration scrambled the chips. Consequently, he'd been hospitalized and put on a medical leave from the college due to mental instability—but he'd managed to avoid any serious brain damage.

All these identity-less cases began the process of learning how to be human over again—progressing through playing with blocks, learning their ABCs, reading Dr. Seuss books, and the like. I actually saw Alex on a *60 Minutes* feature on the phenomenon, cheerfully burbling while a nurse fed him a spoonful of baby food, saying, "Open wide for the choo-choo!"

In an odd way, it reminded me of my grandfather's experiments with alchemy. In trying to forge themselves in the "Beta Mold"—to become alpha dog frat bros—Pete and the rest managed to turn themselves into the human equivalent of Fool's Gold. Ahriman had crystallized within them false and ultimately worthless selves. They had to be melted down, to abandon their identities in total—start anew. Try to become gold again.

Recently, Emma asked me a question.

She said, "Do you think this is fair? I mean, Alex and Turdburger and Colby Stern—those guys were *murderers*. They killed Iphigenia and Canzoni and Wilkes and a homeless man. I'm not saying I believe in the death penalty, but shouldn't they be in, like, *prison* for life or something?"

"But they *were* punished," I said. "In fact, they were punished so severely—and justly—that they don't exist anymore. Those identities—'Alex,' 'Turdburger'—disintegrated. I mean, they were absolutely *annihilated*. It's the ultimate punishment, in a way. All that remains is their underlying consciousness, the soul that always existed behind those identities—suppressed by evil impulses and made totally voiceless. Now, it has a chance to try again, to do a little better this time and learn how to put its attention in the right place. When you think about it, what could be more just than that?"

She thought about it and agreed with me. Isn't agreement pleasant?

Elmer survived. He remained prone on the altar in the chamber beneath The Pyramid for an hour—he was merely spritzed by the water from the pipe Emma broke—until he realized something was wrong. Removing his noise-cancelling headphones and blindfold, he wandered down the tunnel—fortunately avoiding an encounter with any of Ahriman's toadies. He simply walked out of Beta's front door, and, immediately, booked a bus ticket back to his home in Jersey. He sat in his room and played *Silly Squirrels* for a couple of weeks before the game was finally and fatally scrambled. Emma and I got a Christmas Card from him last year—he has no idea that we saved his life.

You will recall that my frat nickname was "Amish." Funnily enough, I'm now living a quasi-Amish existence—though I do most of my writing on a laptop. Emma and I are growing organic vegetables on a farm in Vermont. Her great aunt died recently, and she inherited the place—providentially, at about the time when we were ready to check out of Wilbur College for a while. So, against strenuous parental objections, we moved there. It's hard work, but more engaging than sitting in Professor Moriarty's awful lectures (*her* identity wasn't wiped—she's still teaching at Wilbur).

Lately, we've been debating selling the farm and resuming our education, but, for the present, we're enjoying this back-to-Nature trip so much that we might delay college for another year. I've managed to read more than I did in school, finally making my way through *Moby Dick* and *The Brothers Karamazov,* and I've started getting a decent amount of exercise. More importantly, I've been writing a little in the evenings, besides—finally putting the fragments into order.

Yes, the story is semi-autobiographical. And yes, it focuses on a rather tumultuous period in my collegiate education.

Also, we recently received two gold medallions in the mail, along with a note telling us to "await further instructions." They have a familiar, interlocking triangular pattern engraved on them. I'm slightly apprehensive, but intrigued. As Ahriman rebounds from his most recent defeat, I think the Order of Asha wants to make sure that things don't get out of control this time around.

Overall, society has been adapting wonderfully to the destruction of *Silly Squirrels.* After the game was fried—and all the conspirators who developed it were incapacitated—the former addicts (meaning the vast majority of people in the United States) gained a positive aversion to their cellphones, largely eschewing unnecessary apps. It's surprising how content and tranquil many people seem to be now. Sheila Tomlinson, for instance, was on a mindfulness and meditation kick the last time I saw her at Wilbur.

I wonder if Canzoni had put some *good* vibrations in, when he programmed that final transmission? As far as I could tell, it didn't just counteract Ahriman—it made us all a bit more relaxed, gentle with others and with ourselves.

This period of relative peace might not last, but I hope it persists for a little longer, at least. The effect might sound modest, but it was actually profound: we had suddenly been jolted out of a long, anxious train of thought—had been shaken out of our collective stupor. We were surprised to see the world around us, the faces of people, the simple elements of nature. For a moment, in between the end of our trance and the re-adjustment to computerized routine, everything seemed super-charged with color and feeling.

The sky and earth had been startled awake.

Made in the USA
Monee, IL
11 November 2020